*Terri —
Hope you
enjoy!
Nell*

The Bone Trail
A Novel
By Nell Walton

This is a work of fiction. While, as in all fiction, the literary
perceptions and insights are based on experience, all names,
characters, places, and incidents are either products of the author's
imagination or are used fictitiously. No reference to any real
person is intended or should be inferred.

Dear Readers:

Currently, the Bureau of Land Management's oversight of the Free-Roaming Wild Horse and Burro Program is extremely controversial, and, according to many experts, is in desperate need of an overhaul.

There are many fine people across the United States that are extremely dedicated to preserving our Wild Horses and Burros, which are one of the last remaining symbols of the American West. These people include some Bureau of Land Management staff, Madeleine Pickens and the Mustang Monument Sanctuary, the Mustang Heritage Foundation, the Carr Ranch, Grass Roots Horse, American Wild Horse Preservation, Respect 4 Horses, The Cloud Foundation, American Herds, the Equine Welfare Alliance, the Habitat for Horses Advisory Council and many others. But, it is a complicated issue, and needs input from all sides in order to come up with a realistic, workable solution to preserve our Wild Horse and Burro herds.

The Burns Amendment which was passed by Congress in 2004, (with little debate or input from the American public) states that wild horses older than 10 or that have failed to be adopted after being offered three times can be sold at livestock auctions without limitations on the number of horses purchased or the intentions of the buyer. This opens the door for our Wild Horses to be sold to slaughter buyers.

The assault on our public rangelands by mining and energy companies and other special interests is rarely reported in the mainstream media, but it is something that every American should be concerned about.

Hopefully, this book will help raise awareness of these issues in the minds of the American public.

To my brothers and sisters in Indian Country, you have my enduring respect and admiration. For all of you that took the time to educate me on Reservation life, I thank you from the bottom of my heart.

Hoka Hey!

Nell Walton

First off I would like to thank my beloved <u>duibichi'</u> husband for the support he gives me in all of my endeavors.

Also many thanks to my beta readers and my Internet friends, without you I couldn't have made this book happen. Included in this are: Denise Ingeman, Mikey Porter, Aubern Mason, R.T. Fitch, Marcy Sims, JJ Virgin, and my good friend and 'twin,' Betsy Mercer.

And for all the wild horse advocates, thank you from the bottom of my heart for the work you do to save our Wild Horses and Burros.

And a very special thanks to advocates Laura Leigh and Leslie Peeples.

Part I
The Gather

Chapter 1

On the afternoon of the last day of Lindy Abraham's life, she stood leaning against an old Jeep Cherokee, once red, now faded to kind of a dusky umber, tapping her heel impatiently against a tire. She waited in the Nevada desert in the middle of June; it was hot, and her peach colored cotton tank top stuck unpleasantly in the hollow between her narrow shoulders. She reached into the Jeep and dug around in her cluttered purse until she found a pack of cigarettes and a lighter. Pulling a cigarette free, she lit it, took a drag and exhaled a puff of smoke that hung in front of her face like a shroud. *It is at least 109F*, she thought, and while her long dead mother used to say of the heat in Georgia, 'Well, it ain't the heat so much as the humidity,' Lindy knew that this desert heat today was just plain HOT. She felt like a cornmealed fish that had just hit the grease at a summer fish fry.

The dry air had long lost the slightly herbal, earthy scent that comes with the desert morning. The flat plain, dotted here and there with low sagebrush, could be breathtaking at dawn, but now, at noon, it looked like the devil's own playground. The mountains in the distance were now barely discernable through the heat shimmer coming off the dirty, salt colored sand.

The air conditioner in the Jeep had long since gone to the great A.C. cabin in the sky, so there was no relief to be gained by sitting in the idling vehicle. Lindy glanced into its interior. Julia Evans, her plump, cherub-faced friend, was still crouching miserably in the passenger's seat with the door open, trying to convince herself that the small scrap of shade from the Jeep's roof was actually helping to keep her a little cooler. Julia was very fair-skinned and pretty, with blue eyes and dark hair, and the sun was no friend to her. She had pulled her boots off in an attempt to cool off and rubbed the instep of each foot periodically with an ever-shrinking piece of ice from the cooler. Lindy's, skinny, brittle frame, with its sun damaged skin, slightly crooked teeth, shoulder length blond hair and muddy brown eyes was a stark contrast. At first glance, Lindy struck people as very grim looking, but when she smiled (which was rare these days) her face completely changed and showed a bright gentleness that was startling.

"Jesus," Lindy said. "How LONG have we been waiting?"

"About five minutes longer than the last time you asked me," Julia said tiredly.

"Well, how LONG is that?" Lindy asked.

"Nearly two hours now...and I wish you wouldn't smoke. It only makes things hotter."

Lindy sighed and shook her head. Julia could really come up with some ridiculous statements sometimes. Anyways, whose fault was it that they were now sitting here, in the Nevada desert, in the middle of June, frying like fish?

*

Two years prior, Lindy had been a senior editor for a national equestrian magazine. She loved her small horse farm outside of Spokane with its medium-sized boarding stable and indoor riding area. Marsha Tiranowski, a riding instructor and her barn manager, ran the boarding operation and gave riding lessons to a substantial number of clients. It was wonderful to have someone as competent as Marsha running the business side of the farm. Lindy was well aware of her own limitations when it came to managing the day-to-day operations of the boarding operation. She was not a people person and boarders had left in droves when she attempted to run things herself. She wasn't even riding much anymore. Her Thoroughbred gelding Rocket was more than 25 years old and was becoming a bit decrepit. When her old friend, Marsha, approached her with a proposition to take over the riding and boarding operation, Lindy happily accepted.

She found herself with more and more time on her hands. Her husband had left her a few years earlier and moved in with his secretary. Her two sons, both grown, had busy lives of their own and lived on the East Coast. They kept in touch on Facebook and saw each other occasionally at Thanksgiving and Christmas but that was about it. Not wanting to let loneliness rule her life, Lindy threw herself into her work more and more until it practically became an obsession.

One day, while reviewing her daily lead list for the magazine, she found a story about a group of twelve mustangs that had been rescued from a horse slaughter facility in Canada. Mustangs, more appropriately named wild horses, were a protected species under the Wild Free-Roaming Horse and Burro Act, passed by the United States Congress in 1971. To Lindy, like many Americans, they were as much a symbol of America as the Bald Eagle, and she treasured the idea of them running free as one of the last living symbols of the American West. Congress charged the Bureau of Land Management (BLM), a division of the Department of Interior, with the management, safety and protection of the wild horse and burro herds. So, there was a big question as to how these horses had wound up in a Canadian slaughterhouse without the BLM knowing. Lindy, sensing a story, had called the group that had rescued the horses to get more information. She talked to Marsha Owen, the Executive Director of the Wild Horse Protection League.

"It was one of the BLM's long term holding contractors. Apparently he slipped these out the back door when no one was looking. Not that the BLM looks too hard mind you. These twelve are probably only the tip of the iceberg unfortunately," Owen said bitterly.

Owen went onto explain that in both government and privately contracted facilities throughout the country, tens of thousands of wild horses were warehoused after being rounded up and removed from public rangelands.

"But I thought that they had to remove them for their own protection," Lindy asked, "to keep them from starving due to overpopulation."

Owen snorted.

"They've done a good job at convincing the American public that's the case, but believe me, it's FAR from the truth," she replied. "We have had experts review their environmental impact statements they put out prior to the roundups. They are a joke. We have also had range scientists do field evaluations. Most of the time they find no evidence to support the BLM's arguments for overpopulation. Only in rare cases. The horses are just in the way, Lindy. The BLM puts mining and ranching interests before everything and I do mean EVERYTHING."

"But this is outrageous," Lindy said angrily, "They belong to the American people! They are supposed to be protected!"

Owen sighed heavily.

"Look Lindy, there are rumors that wild horses are being quietly shipped off to Canada and Mexico to be slaughtered and butchered all the time. The meat is then shipped over the Europe and Asia where people pay a premium for it. Now, I'm not saying ALL the contractors involved in the Wild Horse and Burro program participate in such an atrocity, I know some contractors that are very good and honest. But, some are unethical and just want to make a quick buck. On the front end they get the per diem payment for horses in their care, and on the back end they slip them out the door to the slaughter pipeline. The BLM just doesn't monitor its program effectively."

"But what about the adoptions, and those famous horse shows, the Extreme Mustang Makeovers?" Lindy asked.

"The Mustang Heritage Foundation is doing a great job with the Extreme Mustang Makeovers, it has helped the BLM's adoption program immensely. But, that is only a drop in the bucket in comparison to the number of wild horses that are in long-term holding, or the ones they are constantly pulling off the range. The BLM doesn't even let the public view them, so we can only rely on their own reports as to how many they actually have in these holding facilities. We do know one thing for sure, more are now warehoused than running free."

Once Lindy finished her conversation with Marsha Owen, she started doing her own research into the wild horse issue. The lack of transparency and accountability in the BLM's management of the wild horses, as well as the American public's willingness to buy into the public relations farce the BLM put out, was appalling. Speaking with the various wild horse advocacy groups and researching in more depth only increased her outrage. She vowed to become a full-blown wild horse preservation activist.

Her magazine had previously carried stories that were light and neutral, so as not to offend advertisers. Now, the magazine's managing editor became weary of Lindy's strident arguments for running copy on the plight of the American Wild Horse. One day, after a heated argument with her boss, Lindy found herself being escorted out of the building by security – any personal items from her desk would be shipped to her in a box, she was told.

As soon as she arrived home, she called Harlan Finney, President of the Wild Horse Squad, the largest Wild Horse advocacy group in the country.

"Harlan, it's Lindy. I want a job."

Finney was delighted to take her on. Lindy's editorial experience was one thing his group was sadly lacking.

One of Lindy's jobs at the WHS was to attend BLM roundups as a 'humane observer' and report on them afterwards. She also took video and pictures of the conditions of the wild horses both before and after they were rounded up. The BLM's contractors used helicopters to chase the wild horses, sometimes for miles, and there were always a significant number of injuries as well as some deaths.

However, as time passed, and she attended more and more of the 'gathers' as they were called, the BLM became extremely defensive in regards to Lindy's take on their activities. She found her roundup access was becoming more and more limited. Very often, armed BLM personnel, whose main job seemed to be to make sure she saw nothing but the dust raised by the horses as they were driven into traps, accompanied her constantly to make sure she didn't stray into restricted areas.

Things had elevated to a crisis level when Lindy gave a heart wrenching report on video that went viral on the Internet. In the video, she was squatting on the outside of a BLM trap - inside the trap a young foal lay just within arm's reach, unmoving.

"This poor baby ran his feet off trying to keep up with his mother. That helicopter chased them at least for 10 miles over rough ground," she said into the camera, tears flowing down her cheeks. She held up one of the foal's delicate, bloody hooves to the camera.

"We have asked them to send the vet, but no one has come. We asked an hour ago."

Then her plea was interrupted.

"Get your hands out of there!" came a harsh voice, and the video shut off. BLM security had discovered them and made them quit filming.

A vet had finally arrived, but he came too late for the injured foal. It died as Lindy and Julia (who was the videographer) stood weeping outside the trap.

*

On this particular trip, however, Lindy and Julia had made a mad dash to northern Nevada just the day before. The WHS had gotten a call from a Sierra Club group on an outing in the area; they had been turned back at a BLM roadblock set up on one of the main roads running through public land, about 50 miles south of the Idaho/Nevada state line. One of the BLM officers had happened to let slip that there was an unscheduled emergency wild horse gather, and that the area was closed for public safety. This was very unusual, because the BLM had made no public announcement of this event, as was required by federal regulations.

Lindy had called Sam Conner, the BLM security manager in the area, and he had agreed to meet her at the intersection of Bureau of Indian Affairs Road 19 and Shelley Road at 2 p.m., to escort her to the roundup for the purposes of humane observation. However, it was now nearly 4 p.m., and Conner had not shown up, nor had he returned phone calls from either Julia or Harlan Finney.

Julia had agreed to ride shotgun with Lindy, at Harlan's request. This 'secret' roundup had infuriated Lindy and Harlan was worried that she would become reckless and do something rash and stupid. Lindy, while a superb writer, was becoming something of a loose cannon. Julia, on the other hand, had always kept a very cool head when dealing with the BLM. She was also an excellent videographer, and had done some good undercover work recently using only her Smartphone. She had even brought a large professional video camera along. It was stored in a case in the back seat of the Jeep.

Lindy paced back and forth on the dusty white hardpan that passed for a road in this part of the world. She raised her head quickly as she heard a noise in the distance. Someone was coming. It was the first vehicle they had seen during their two-hour wait.

"Get the big camera out, Julia. We need to get some good video of this asshole making his excuses for WHY he left us sitting here waiting for two hours, frying like fish!"

"Do we even know that's him?" Julia asked, calmly pulling on her socks and hiking boots and ignoring Lindy's order. Lindy often became bossy when she was upset. If you did what she said, she just got bossier.

"Well, just who exactly the fuck else could it be?" Lindy snapped. "We have been sitting here for two solid fucking hours, and this is the first fucking car we have seen. So I think it is pretty good fucking guess that it is that fucking fuck from the BLM!"

"Lindy!" Julia said, chuckling. "Kudos to you for creative use of a four letter word…"

"Oh, shut the fuck up. I don't even think it is the BLM," Lindy said.

Julia got out of the Jeep and walked over to stand beside Lindy, who was shading her eyes with her hand and watching the dust cloud heading steadily towards them. As the vehicle burst through the heat shimmer, they saw to their great disappointment that it was a very old, very rusty green Ford F-150 pickup truck, not one of the new white Ford Explorers generally used by BLM staff in Nevada. Lindy waved at the truck and it slowed down and stopped.

Two middle aged Hispanics, obviously workers from one of the local cattle ranches, peered out at her.

"*Holas, senoras!*" the man in the passenger seat asked politely. "Everything okay?"

"We're looking for a horse roundup," Lindy said. "*Rodean los Caballos, entende Senor?*"

"Oh sure," the driver responded, in good English. "We saw a helicopter up by the big mine...about 50 miles that way...straight up 19." He pointed up towards the mountains.

"Great, just great!" Lindy said loudly. Then, seeing the alarm in the men's faces she said, "I'm sorry. Thank you so much. *Gracias.*"

"Are you sure you are all right? We can take you to Antelope Valley. You have a phone? Not much coverage out here."

"No. No, we're fine. *Gracias, Senores, muchos gracias.*"

The two men looked at each other uncertainly, then the driver shrugged and they pulled slowly away. Lindy stared after them, taking time to light another cigarette. She was practically trembling with outrage.

" I knew it, I KNEW it, I knew Conner was just FUCKING with us..."

"Ok, Lindy, OK," Julia said, trying to placate her. "It's not like this is the first time they have pulled this shit. Honestly, I think this one's a wash. I mean what else can we do? Let's just head back to the hotel and COOL OFF for God's sake."

Lindy turned, looking at her coldly.

"I can't believe you just want to give up after we have come all this way. What about those horses, Julia, you just want to give up on them? God knows what they're doing to them."

Julia sighed heavily. "Again, I ask you, what else can we do?"

Lindy turned and began looking up the road toward the mountains. Julia could almost feel Lindy digging her heels in.

"Call Harlan and tell him we are going to look around some more. Julia, there is something bad happening here; I can feel it in my gut. I won't be able to live with myself unless I at least make an effort to find out what it is."

Julia stared out into the desert for a moment, biting her lower lip. She shook her head. "That's restricted property up there you know, around that mine. Even though it's technically public land, it's still restricted. Conner warned you earlier about tooling around in the area unescorted. They are blasting up there, you know. That's what he said. It could be dangerous."

"Oh, and I am just SO scared," Lindy said bitterly. "They always have some reason to keep us from seeing what they are doing. Always 'for your own safety.' It's a crock of shit and you know it."

Julia looked at her and shook her head again. "You know there's a good chance we might get locked up this time. Conner warned you; he said he'd have no choice but to arrest us if he caught us in a restricted area. And you know he's a big enough asshole to do it too. He'd probably arrest us just on general principles, if we even got near one."

"Yeah, he's a Grade A prick all right," Lindy said. She pulled out a cigarette and smoked for a moment. Then she turned to Julia and smiled. "Well, at least they have air conditioning in the jails here in Nevada…"

Julia sighed and rolled her eyes. "Harlan won't like it at all you know. He'll pitch a fit, and look, it's past 4 now, so there's a good chance we will be banging around up there after dark in Old Yeller, or Old Browner, or whatever it is you are calling this bag of bolts these days."

"Harlan's always pitching a fit – that man needs to learn to relax...and THE JEEP," Lindy responded pointedly, "has had an engine replacement and is well up to the task…"

Julia looked at her friend with a rueful smile. There would be no reasoning with Lindy at this point, as she knew from experience. "All right, all right. You drive, I'll call Harlan."

"Yes!! I knew you would see reason. *Vamos la, chica*!" Lindy said, grinning broadly and sliding into the driver's seat.

*

Three hours later, at the third roadblock they had run across since they had headed up towards the mine, Lindy threw the Jeep into park and stepped out of the car. They had long ago left the BIA 19 roadway, making their way up several roads utilized by the local ranchers. Several times they had glimpsed two different helicopters off in the distance, confirming what the men in the truck had reported.

This roadblock was different than the others. Those had been just stock gates or rubble piled up to block the road, with fencing or some other sort of barrier on either side. This one had a lightweight orange-striped barrier that simply said 'Road Closed.' Two security vehicles from St. Martjin Mining were parked just behind the barrier. Two men stood leaning against their brand new pearl colored SUV, with two more sitting inside their own idling vehicle. They were clearly enjoying the air conditioning, even though the desert was cooling quickly with the setting sun. One man slowly stepped away from the car and walked towards the gate. He was tall and thin, in his mid-40s, weathered, and slightly balding. He moved confidently and lithely; his walk had a sinuous quality to it that was vaguely disturbing. He stepped around the barrier and stood a few feet away, watching them.

Even though Lindy's anger and frustration was practically volcanic, the way he stared at her gave her an icy chill. She felt her hot words stick in her throat, and she inadvertently stepped back from the gate.

"We need to pass here," she said finally, when the man remained silent.

The man gazed at her evenly. "Are we lost, madam?" he asked. He had a slight smile on his face and seemed amused.

"No, WE are not lost," Lindy said, rallying, determined to get past the little sliver of icy fear that had lodged itself her belly. "How about you? Are you lost?"

The man looked down at the ground and shook his head. "No, not in the least. We are just working this evening, that's all. They're blasting tonight, and they sent us over here to this area to make sure no one... stumbled in on something that might inadvertently cause them harm." He cocked his head at her for a moment, birdlike, and watched her.

"This is public land, we have a right to travel here, and as far as I know you have no right to block this roadway," Lindy said angrily.

The man rocked back on his heels, and looked at her coldly. Lindy noticed that his eyes were like icy black stones in a winter creek, and she shivered, even though it was still very hot.

She started to speak, but then Julia quickly came to stand by her side.

"Sir?" she said. "We were supposed to meet Sam Conner from the BLM – we had heard they were having a wild horse roundup here. We saw the helicopters, the ones they use to roundup the horses. Do you know Mr. Conner?"

"No," he said.

Lindy rolled her eyes. She knew full well that Conner and other BLM staff worked closely with mine employees on various issues, including the approval of road and land closures.

The man was watching them both easily, with a cool smile on his face, but Lindy felt a bone deep chill and she noticed that Julia was even paler than normal. Lindy took a couple of steps back toward the Jeep and reached into her purse for a cigarette.

"STOP! And get your hands away from that car!"

Lindy had not even seen the man and the other guards reach for their guns, but they all had them in hand; three were pointed at Lindy, and one was pointed at Julia. Lindy quickly put her hands up in the air, one clutching a pack of cigarettes.

"Oh, what a joke on us," the tall man said with good humor, putting his gun back in the holster. "Gentlemen, we can relax. The lady desperado just needs a cigarette."

He quickly walked past Julia to stand beside Lindy. He plucked the cigarettes from her hand, took one out of the pack and handed it to her, then shook one out for himself.

"Do you mind, Ma'am? I'm just a bit nervous and could use one myself."

Lindy shook her head quickly. The man smiled and pulled a lighter from his pocket, lit his cigarette, and held the lighter out for Lindy to light her own. To her disgust, she had a hard time because her hand was shaking so badly. The man grasped her hand and steadied it for her, while he held up the lighter and lit the end of the cigarette. Lindy stared at him, wide-eyed. He began slowly caressing the back of her hand with his thumb while he stared at her evenly, a slight smile on his face. He took a deep drag off his own, and politely turned his head and exhaled with enjoyment. He then squeezed her hand until she winced, then let her go.

"I quit a couple of years ago, but every now and then I just feel the need to calm my nerves. I guess it must help you that way too?"

His tone was conversational, gentle almost, but Lindy had to struggle to keep from scrambling back into the Jeep and hightailing it out of there. She took a drag, her eyes never leaving the man, and he sighed. She fought the urge to wipe her hand on her jeans.

"Look, ladies. I promise you, there is nothing up here that you would be interested in, and whoever this fellow is that missed your appointment is not here, nor has he been here. As I said, we don't even know the man. If you turn around now, and head back to Elko, you will get there just before they roll up the streets and you can get yourself a nice supper, a hot bath, and a good night's sleep. Then you can go looking for him tomorrow. But take my word on it, tonight is not the night for you to be up around this mine. You need to think about your own safety," he said, smiling at Lindy.

Lindy nodded and motioned for Julia to get back into the Jeep. The man smiled again and nodded, like a father pleased with errant children who have learned the better part of obedience. After Lindy slid into the driver's seat and started to turn the key in the ignition, the man stepped quickly to her window, reached in, took her hand again, and pressed the cigarettes gently into her palm.

"You know, these things will kill you one day," he said quietly, placing a hand on Lindy's shoulder in a strangely intimate gesture.

His breath felt like silent death on Lindy's face.

"Could we have your name, sir?" Julia asked in a small voice.

"Why, of course, my dear. I'm Victor Shelton, Chief Security Officer here at St. Martjin Mining. Good night, ladies, and please be careful driving back to Elko."

Lindy put a shaking hand on the gearshift, put the Jeep into reverse, and headed back down the dusty side road, back the way they had come.

*

About 20 minutes later Lindy pulled over to the side. Her hands were shaking so badly that she was having a hard time driving, and she had a burning urge to pee. Julia had been silent since they had left the roadblock, but when Lindy stopped the Jeep she turned and looked at her.

16

"Are you crazy? He's probably following us back there somewhere," Julia said.

"I don't think so," Lindy said. "I've been watching. And Julia, I just have to stop for a minute. I am shaking so bad I can hardly drive."

"OK. OK, but that man was the scariest son of a bitch I ever met in my life."

"God, yes," Lindy said, reaching back to the cooler to pull out a bottle of water. She undid the cap, but didn't take a drink.

"You know, he was slick though. Even if we had recorded what he said, he would have sounded very professional and polite, even when they pulled out their guns. He's clearly had a lot of experience scaring the shit out of people, and never having to deal with any blowback," Lindy said.

Lindy took a drink of water and looked out across the desert. Unconsciously, she scrubbed the back of her hand against her jeans. She then looked at her hand and scolded herself mentally. *There's no reason to be so upset. The man didn't hurt you.* In another setting she might have even been flattered by the attention. It had been so long since a man had touched her it was no surprise that it seemed alarming. Her mind was just playing tricks on her. *Making mountains out of molehills.*

It had become cool. She reached behind the seat for a long sleeved, battered chambray shirt and pulled it on. The sun, now a huge yellowish, smoky ball, was just beginning to drop down in the flat plain to the west.

For a moment, she reminisced about the scuba diving trips she and her ex-husband used to take together. *Back in the days when we still cared about each other*, she thought. She remembered sitting on the boat with a couple of beers at the end of the day, watching the sunset. Lindy had always heard that if you watched really closely, you could see a green flash when the sun dropped below the horizon. She had never seen it on all her many scuba trips, and she didn't see it now.

"Julia, I just have to go pee, I can't hold it, and I don't really care if that Shelton or whatever his name is comes after us with all the Orcs of Mordor, I still am going to have to pee." As she turned, she added, "And if he sees my bony backside squatted down behind a sage bush I guess that will be his just punishment."

Julia looked at her and laughed. "Well, proceed then, and damn that man and his minions."

Lindy stepped around the Jeep and made her way down the shallow embankment of the road and out into the desert. She walked slowly, checking for rattlesnakes. Dusk and dawn were their favorite hunting times, and although Lindy had no problem with snakes (rattlers generally were fair minded creatures that left you alone if you left them alone), she didn't like unnecessary confrontations with them. She found a likely bush and peed, then stood up.

She looked up and marveled a bit at the sky. The western horizon was a rimfire orange, fading to the palest of blues and then to a midnight blue further up. The apex was scattered with the bright jewels of stars, as well as several aircraft with white running lights; one flying rather low, others miles high. Lindy wondered briefly who the people were on those planes, where they were going and why. The pale half-moon was rising in the East. An old cowboy had told her once that this used to be called a Rustler's moon; just light enough to move stock, but dark enough not to get caught.

Lindy kicked the sand a bit at the memory and smiled. A strange noise suddenly startled her. It came from out in the desert.

"Jules – JULES! Did you hear that?" she called out back to the Jeep.

"Hear what?" Julia answered.

"I could have sworn I heard...I thought I heard a horse out here...I thought I heard one snort..."

"I didn't hear anything. Lindy, come on, this has been like the WORST fuckin' day EVAH – can we PLEASE just follow the advice of our new good friend at St. Martjin's and go back to Elko and TAKE A BATH?"

Reluctantly, Lindy started walking back to the Jeep, but she stopped once when thought she heard it again: the light, soft snort that a horse makes when he smells a familiar scent, one that he may not have smelled in a long time, and he takes a deep sniff of the air just to double check.

Twenty minutes or so later, as they were driving slowly down towards BIA 19, Julia yelled out, "STOP!"

Lindy slammed on the brakes.

"What? WHAT?" Lindy said, looking around wildly.

"My God, Lindy – LOOK!" Julia said, clutching at Lindy's arm.

Lindy leaned forward to look around Julia, and gasped.

Standing in the desert, about 30 feet away from the Jeep, stood a horse.

The horse looked back at them, relaxed, one rear foot resting on its toe like a prima ballerina. His coat had a silvery shimmer to it, and his mane and tail were long and the color of the moon. He gently tossed his proud head, and gave a low soft snort, then looked at them expectantly, blinking his large, dark eyes.

"Have you ever seen one do that before? Just stop like that?" Julia asked, her voice trembling with fear and wonder.

"No. Never," Lindy whispered.

"Maybe he's lost? He must be a ranch horse that is just lost or something."

"Sorry, Jules, but that is about the least lost looking animal I have ever seen. Think you can get a picture?"

"I can try."

Slowly, Julia reached into the glove box and pulled out her Smartphone. She tapped the screen to activate the camera, but when she held the camera up to take a picture, the horse suddenly reared slightly and galloped off a few steps.

"Lindy, I don't think he likes the camera."

"No, no, he doesn't. Let's get out."

Julia looked at her then slowly reached for the door handle and opened the door. Lindy stepped around the Jeep, slowly, consciously making herself relax her shoulders; her eyes slightly lowered to keep from frightening the strange horse. She fully expected him to dash off into the night, but instead he turned to face them and waited expectantly.

As she and Julia approached, the horse snorted softly and pawed at the sand a bit, as if irritated by their hesitancy. Lindy looked at his eyes and smiled, and it was almost as if he smiled back.

Lindy slowly walked up to the horse and stroked his neck. His coat was softer than the softest milk thistle seed, so soft her hand could barely even feel it. He tilted his head slightly away from her, so she could rub the big muscle that ran down the side of his neck. *He has an odd smell* she realized. It was not the pleasantly musky smell of a healthy horse. He smelled of wintergreen, orange blossom, almonds, chocolate, and every other good thing she had ever smelled in her life. Soon, Julia was standing beside her, scratching his withers. The horse arched his elegant neck and stretched in pleasure as she scratched him, pursing his long lips and nodding his head in ecstasy at each movement of her fingers. He was tall; Julia, who was just a little over five feet, had to reach up with her hand a bit to touch his withers.

"I don't think this guy is from one of the herds," Julia said quietly.

"I'm not even sure he is even from this Earth," Lindy responded fervently.

The horse shook his head and snorted again, as if laughing.

"Well, what are we going to do with him? Just leave him here?" Julia asked.

Lindy looked at her as if she were crazy. "What do you suggest? Loading him up and taking him back to the hotel? This horse obviously belongs to someone, and I am PRETTY sure he is smart enough to find his way back home."

The horse pawed the sand a bit again and looked at her.

"Look, baby boy," Lindy said quietly, still stroking this horse's strong neck, "we just got into some major trouble a little while ago, and it is in our best interest if we get the hell out of here in a hurry. Understand?"

The horse turned his head, staring off into the distance.

"Julia, call Harlan and let him know what we have found here."

"Problem there – I haven't been able to get a cell signal since we got off 19. I actually tried to call Harlan about 57 times since we left that roadblock, and about 900 times before that," Julia said sheepishly.

"Well, that's good thinking," Lindy said dreamily, still stroking the horse's neck.

"Lindy, we still don't know what we are going to DO with him," Julia said, poking her friend in the shoulder.

"I don't think we do anything with him, as he seems to be perfectly capable of taking care of himself. We can't do anything anyway, since we don't have a trailer or any other way to transport him," Lindy replied. "I agree with you that we need to get out of here. I never want to run across that Victor Shelton EVER again!"

She turned to the horse. "You just look after yourself, boy, and stay away from that mine," she said quietly to him.

Reluctantly, the two women turned away from the horse and started walking back to the Jeep. The horse wuffled softly, then trotted quickly in front of them, blocking them from the Jeep. He turned and looked at them.

Lindy laughed. "Talk about spoiled. We don't have anything to eat, fella, so let us be on our way. Maybe we'll see you again tomorrow."

She and Julia stepped around the horse and headed back to the Jeep again.

The horse neighed loudly. They turned and watched him gallop off a few strides into the desert, set his back feet and spin on his hindquarters; he then trotted back towards them, flagging his tail and stopping just a few feet away.

"Lindy, I know this sounds crazy as hell, but it looks like that horse wants us to follow him."

"Jesus," Lindy said with exasperation. "Could this day get ANY crazier?" She yelled,"Hey, Gorgeous! SHOO! We are not going out into the desert in the dark with you, and we don't have any hay in the back of our car, so, SHOO!"

The horse snorted and backed up a few steps at her shooing motions, shook his head and looked at them intently.

"OK, let's just get in the car and get out of here," Lindy said with reluctance in her voice.

Julia nodded and they walked quickly to the Jeep. They heard the horse snort again, and then listened to him trotting off into the distance.

"There, he gave up. Let's head back to the hotel. I'm worn out," Lindy said.

They both got into the Jeep. Lindy cranked it up and pulled off onto the road, which gleamed pearly in the moonlight.

"That was the most beautiful horse I have ever seen in my life, Lindy," Julia said quietly.

"I know, I know, and there was something really STRANGE about him, something...........SHIT!"

Lindy slammed on the brakes – the horse stood blocking the road, about 15 feet from the Jeep, watching them. His eyes glowed a greenish yellow in the headlights.

"Jesus Christ Bananas!" Julia said, softly. "OK, now what?"

"This is one stubborn animal," Lindy said. "We'll just ease up on him slow. He'll move out of the way for a CAR, for Pete's sake."

Lindy pressed the accelerator and the Jeep crept forward. She and Julia leaned over the dashboard, agog. The horse stood quite still.

"He's not moving, Lindy."

"I SEE that. Should we get out again?"

"I don't think so. I think that will just encourage him," Julia said.

Lindy moved her foot slightly off the accelerator as the Jeep rolled closer to the horse. He continued looking at them until the rusted bumper tapped his hock slightly. Lindy quickly slammed on the brake.

The horse shook his head again then rocked forward on his front end, and double barrel kicked the Jeep's bumper so hard that Lindy felt her teeth rattle. He then reared, raced up a little wash that was beside the road, stopped, and looked back at them.

"OK, what now?" Julia asked wide-eyed.

Lindy chewed the inside of her cheek.

"This is the craziest fucking thing I've ever seen in my life. "

"Uh-huh."

"I need a smoke."

Lindy could literally feel Julia rolling her eyes, but she ignored her. Quietly, she got a cigarette out of her purse and lit it, watching the horse. He trotted off into the desert, then trotted back and stopped, looking at them, like a dog asking for a walk. He shook his head again then looked off to the mountains.

Lindy took a deep drag on her cigarette, and then threw it into the roadway. It lay there, glowing slightly, the brown filter clear against the white powdery surface of the road.

"We are SO going to follow him!"

"Yes," Julia said a bit dreamily. She dug her fingers into the ripped seat upholstery of the Jeep, as Lindy turned up the little wash, following the silvery horse that glowed softly in the light of the Rustler's Moon.

*

Two hours later, a sparking new pearl white Lincoln Navigator driving slowly down the dusty road rolled to a stop. Victor Shelton stepped out of the SUV, reached down and picked up the cigarette butt. He looked at the clear tracks running off to the north across the desert.

"Some people just insist on learning everything the hard way," he said quietly to his driver, as he picked up his radio to call his team.

Chapter 2

Kate Wyndham usually slept better in a jungle tent than she did in some of the better hotels the Washington Gazette booked for her when she was on assignment. Lately, however, the four star hotel bookings had been few and far between. Kate was just grateful that she hadn't had to deal with the bedbug epidemic yet, as had some the other correspondents. Their descriptions of the nightmare of bites and itching sounded almost as bad as some of the chigger attacks she had dealt with as a child growing up in Kentucky.

Kate, stepping out of the tent, looked up to the emerald summit of one of the Virunga Volcanoes, where Dian Fossey had done her seminal work on mountain gorillas. The bush was relatively quiet tonight, and the smell of wood smoke clung to the air. She could hear the rest of the team talking and laughing quietly around the fire. Sleep had eluded her, as it had so many times lately. Chewing her lower lip, she reflected on her life. She was unhappy, and she had no clear reason to be.

She had a job at the Washington Gazette, one of the premier newspapers in the nation's Capitol as an environmental and nature correspondent. Her job gave her the opportunity to see and experience things that most people only saw on the PBS series *Nature*, or on some of the many live Internet video sites of animal sanctuaries that had appeared recently. Her significant other of 13 years was a successful Capitol Hill staffer; they were an up and coming power couple, something John Ridley talked about frequently with relish. She had a little country farmhouse she had bought less than a year ago. She had actually been able to scrape enough money together finally to buy acreage just outside of Annapolis, MD, and she had moved her horse, Manitou, into his new personal barn from the boarding stable where she had kept him for years. She was the envy of many of her friends because she had been able to accomplish this lofty goal, but Kate was thrifty, and when a farm came up for sale that was next door to one of her colleagues at the Gazette, she bought it– with little support or input from John.

When Manitou, whom she had always called Manny, had first arrived at the farm, he had somehow KNOWN that he was finally

HOME, and had taken to his new digs with equanimity. It helped that her neighbor, Maria Nuncio (who also worked at the Gazette and had tipped her off that the farm was coming up for sale), also had horses; Manny had others of his own kind to canoodle with over the fence. John seemed to enjoy what little time he managed to spend on the farm. Usually, he could only make it out on the occasional weekend. He was the Chief of Staff for the Senate Majority Whip, and routinely worked 14-16 hour days, and thrived on the pace. They also had the small row house on Capitol Hill, purchased just a few years after they moved to DC. John stayed there most of the time while Kate spent more and more time on the farm, as the Gazette was relatively lenient on letting the writing staff work from home. However, when John did come to the farm, he would say, as he sat on the small deck that overlooked the rolling Maryland hills that ran down to the Chesapeake Bay, "I'm glad we did this, such a great investment." And Kate would sigh. The farm had been purchased with her money.

When she and John had first moved to Washington from Ann Arbor all those years ago, John had begun to change. John's father, who had been a state senator for many years, had gotten John a job in Senator Bryce Dotson's office as an analyst. Over the years, John had demonstrated a political acumen that not even his father had suspected. The Senator had come to rely on him more and more, until he made John his Chief of Staff when he assumed the Majority Whip position in the Senate. John was completely dedicated to his job, and like most people who were totally plugged into the political side of the federal government, he enjoyed the complex (and often silly, Kate thought) Machiavellian machinations that were the stock in trade of Capitol Hill.

However, Kate had grown weary of living in a town where, when you were introduced to someone, the first question out of their mouths was 'And what do you do?' Your answer then determined where you were in the complicated Washington Food Chain, and you were either courted or politely (or not so politely) dismissed accordingly. Once, at one of the interminable Capitol Hill cocktail parties that John dragged her to, Kate had told people that she was a mailroom clerk at one of the least influential lobbying groups in the city. It amused her to see how quickly people discarded her after this revelation, like a used paper towel in the bathroom.

John had been furious with her afterwards, and they had had the worst fight in their 12 years together once they got home.

When Kate had first met John in Ann Arbor, he had been different. He was four years older than Kate, but she had met him when she was a freshman and he was a grad student at the University of Michigan. He had spent four years in the Peace Corps in Sierra Leone, helping to build schools and roads. Kate had never known a young man to be so balanced and focused. And kind. They had met at one of John's fraternity's numerous beer parties. Her roommate, who had a crush on one of John's fraternity brothers, had dragged Kate along to the party. Kate had stood in the corner nursing a beer; she was tall, gangly, red-headed; too conscious of her zits, skinny legs, and bony knees to talk to anyone. John had come up to her, smiled, and handed her another beer.

"You're the most interesting looking person in this room tonight..."

He was the first boy that had ever paid attention to her, and Kate was struck with something that she thought must be love. They had eventually become a couple.

Kate had always wanted to be a journalist; to her, it seemed like the purest sort of public service, and John had encouraged her to follow this dream. His father helped her get internships that had enabled her to achieve this goal, and she was grateful to him. Journalism school at University of Michigan was followed by a position at the Washington Gazette, one of the premier newspapers in the Unites States. She had ridden on the UM Equestrian Team all through college and when she moved to Washington, her horse came with her. She continued riding as much as she could, although overseas assignments (particularly in Africa) took up a lot of her time.

Besides, now Manny was older; at 24, he was slowing down. Arthritis and an old bone spur kept him out of the serious competitions. Kate was really fine with that, as she had less time to train anyway. Now, just spending time in the barn with him, brushing him, and doing the dozens of little chores it took to care for Manny in the manner to which he was accustomed, had become as rewarding as winning all the ribbons and trophies that were still packed away in boxes stored in the attic of the little farmhouse.

Kate shooed away a mosquito that was buzzing about her ear, and went back into the tent, zipped the door shut and settled down on her cot for sleep.

She tossed for a bit, thinking about Manny, and hoping that he was all right; the neighbor, Maria, was looking after him. She squirmed a bit more, then slipped off into a restless slumber.

Chapter 3

Lindy and Julia had long given up complaining about the jostling and even the banging of their heads on the roof of the Jeep as they followed the silvery horse up the wash that was not quite a road. The Jeep's interior fabric was beyond worn, with holes where the seat springs poked through in some places, making the trip all the more painful. They drove slowly. The horse kept his haunches just within the outer reach of the headlight beams, and if they had to stop to negotiate some tricky place in the creek bed, he waited, looking back at them, his eyes glowing an odd blue green in the headlights.

"I think this is the craziest thing I have ever done in my LIFE," Julia said, after hitting a particular bone-jarring bump.

"So, you want to turn back?"

"No, we've been at this nearly two hours now; might as well see it through. How are we on gas?"

"Well, with the five gallons we have in the spare tank in the back, I think we should have enough to get back to Elko," Lindy said.

"Somehow that statement does not inspire confidence," Julia responded, a bit sourly.

"We'll be fine as long as we don't go too much further. We haven't really come a long way since we left the road. It has just taken a lot of time, since we had to go so slowly. Old Silver there doesn't seem to realize that our four wheel drive is different from his."

Suddenly, the horse stopped and turned to face them, the headlights gleaming brightly on his silver coat. He tossed his head and pawed at the sandy, rocky gully that had been their road.

"What's he doing?" Lindy asked.

"He's stopped," Julia responded.

"What you think he wants us to do?"

"I think he wants us to get out."

"Well, that's a relief. Looks like we've driven into some kind of small canyon," Lindy said.

Lindy and Julia looked to each side of the wash. Striated walls rose into a soft arc just above their heads, but they could see that, where the horse was standing, this quickly rose higher and led into a steep canyon. Fortunately, the moon was riding high and it was at an angle that shone directly into the cleft, so they would be able to follow the horse on foot. Lindy grabbed a flashlight from behind the seat.

"Can that Smartphone do video in low light?" she asked.

"Yes, surprisingly well, in fact. But tonight is really pretty bright, considering. And remember, that horse didn't like the camera before."

"Well, he may just have to get over it. There is no way I am going to go back and try to tell this story to Harlan without some proof."

Lindy turned off the headlights and waited for her eyes to adjust. Julia was right. The moonlight reflected off the light gray walls of the canyon, and she could actually see the dry creek bed plainly running on before them.

"Let's go see what he wants us to see then," Lindy said. "Just to double check – are you getting a cell signal?"

"No – zero bars of course. Nada."

"Well – I don't think that is necessarily a bad thing (aside from us having no contact with the outside world, of course). I think they probably have cell service at that gold mine, so if we can't get a signal, that means we are far enough away that those security guys won't be around. I don't want to run into them again. I just wish WHS would invest in a satellite phone."

Julia nodded, then slowly opened the door of the Jeep and stepped out, as Lindy did the same. The silvery horse looked at them briefly, shook his head, and then took off at a trot up the canyon until he was out of sight.

"Hey! Wait a minute!" Lindy yelled. The two women began trying to trot after him. They quickly realized that a broken neck would soon be in the cards if they continued. Finally, they gave it up for a bad job and went back to a slow, careful walk.

"Well, it's not like he can go anywhere but forward," Julia said, panting.

"That's true, although something tells me that if there is someplace this horse wants to go, he will manage to get there…"

They walked on in silence for a bit, stepping carefully to keep from falling. They came to a perpendicular intersection where the creek bed they had followed ran into a larger canyon. There were stock panels blocking the left of the new canyon, so they turned to the right. That's where the strange horse had to have gone. They walked for a while longer until they began to hear noises up ahead.

Lindy stopped, listening intently. She could hear faint whinnies and an occasional banging noise.

"I think we've found our roundup," Lindy said fiercely. "Do you see our friend anywhere?"

"No, not for some time now."

"Get that video camera up and working," Lindy hissed.

Lindy held the flashlight for a few moments, to help Julia find the proper settings for the video camera on the Smartphone; then they walked with some trepidation towards the noise that was becoming clearer now, echoing off the canyon walls. They heard harsh snorting and an occasional weak sounding whinny, punctuated by deep groans. Lindy shone the flashlight in front of them and eventually they saw some rusted blue stock panels completely blocking the canyon. To their right, in what looked to be a large blind canyon, were closed stock gates. On the other side of these gates were what looked to be a hundred or more horses.

It was a horror.

They were sick, dying. Most were already down and some were staggering and falling to their knees. Two stood looking towards the canyon walls, moving their heads rhythmically in a circling motion. Several had fallen up against the stock panels, all dead. One had bloody froth still flowing from its nostrils and one of its legs was wrapped around the steel tube of the panel, as if even in its death throws it still was trying to escape. Foals and weanlings appeared to have been the first ones to go; their small bodies were scattered, sometimes under the bodies of adult horses that had simply fallen and crushed them. One staggering white mare kept nudging a dead weanling at her feet, until she too collapsed, thrashing her legs violently for a few moments. Then she lay there, motionless. The air was clotted with the smell of urine, blood, and horse feces.

Lindy stood in mute horror and held the flashlight up across the canyon. Most of the horses further in were already dead. Some had large bare patches of skin that looked like some kind of horrible leprosy; those that were alive were drooling uncontrollably, eyes cloudy with pain. Lindy heard Julia gag and vomit, and she felt the bile rising in her throat, but choked it down.

"Julia, get that camera going and get this on video," Lindy said. "I don't know what has happened here, but by God, someone is going to pay for this."

Julia nodded mutely and tapped the screen on the camera to start recording. The Smartphone cast an amazing amount of light over the grisly scene. Julia felt sick again, but dialed her mental focus down to just getting the documentation done – that was what was important, that was what mattered.

"Let's get on the other side of those panels," she said tightly. Slowly they climbed over, taking care to avoid stepping on the dead horses lying up against the steel bars.

As they walked through the charnel scene, Julia focused on filming what they saw. How she did it Lindy had no idea, for she had to fight back the urge to vomit with every step. They found some living horses, though even most of those were already down on the ground. Some of them continued to make weak attempts to stand. It was clear that most were more dead than alive. They paid little attention to the two humans as they walked past, and did not shy away from the camera light. They were scattered across the bottom of the canyon like some remnant of an ancient, hopeless, valiant cavalry charge, but there wasn't even the poor excuse of war for this nightmare.

What was the worst were the young ones, the babies, with their long elegant legs now sickeningly skewed, and their once innocent eyes emptied of life.

Although it seemed an eternity to Lindy, eventually they did reach the far end of the canyon, where it angled up steeply on all sides into the hills. No horse could escape this tomb. Lindy didn't see how they had ever gotten a helicopter down this narrow canyon, but when she shone her flashlight on the sandy ground she could see the tracks of ATVs. So, they had used the helicopters to move them into the canyon lands and had then used ATVs to drive them into this death trap.

What Lindy couldn't figure out was why the horses were dying; she didn't know if it was anthrax, or some other type of illness.

"Julia, what do you think happened here?" she asked quietly.

"Poison," Julia said bitterly. "It looks like they were all poisoned."

"Jesus," Lindy responded," Is this what it has come to?"

Julia just shook her head briefly and kept on filming.

"Where is our friend?" Julia asked, lowering the camera for a second.

"I don't know, I haven't seen him since he took off without us."

"Well, somehow, someway, that horse knew to lead us here. I am not even going to try to get my head around that just now. Let's just get as much of this as we can on video, get back to the Jeep, and get out of here," Lindy said.

"OK," Julia responded.

Slowly they made their way back through the dead and dying. For the first time in her life, Lindy wished she had a gun so she could end the misery of some of the ones still fighting for life. She realized that she was weeping as she walked, and could see the wetness shining on Julia's cheeks also.

Occasionally, Julia would stop for a moment and capture a particularly sad scene, but soon they had reached the far barrier where they had entered. Julia took a last video of the dead horses piled against stock panels, then they climbed over the panels, slowly, like old women, and made their way back to the Jeep.

"I wish we had gotten a picture of that silver horse," Julia said, as they approached the Jeep, both moving like sleepwalkers. "No one is going to believe how we found this…abomination."

"I'm not sure we could have, even if he had allowed it," Lindy said after a time. "I don't think that horse was of this world."

Julia looked at her oddly and shook her head, but didn't respond. Finally, they saw the Jeep up ahead, and, relieved, they slid into the battered seats. Lindy cranked the Jeep (secretly grateful that it started), then she threw the gearshift into reverse.

"I'll have to back out a ways, until I get to a point where I can turn around. The floor's too steep here," she said.

Julia just nodded in the dark, although she knew Lindy couldn't see her.

Lindy moved the Jeep backwards slowly, her right hand braced against the console and her head turned so she could see over her right shoulder. Suddenly, she slammed on the brakes and Julia looked up quickly, alarmed.

"Oh, shit," Lindy whispered.

The whole world suddenly went white, as a vehicle behind them flooded them with its high beams.

"Good evening, ladies," came a voice over a loudspeaker. "Could you please exit the vehicle, hands in the air…"

Both women complied, but just before putting her hands up in the air, Julia carefully slid the Smartphone into the wide tear in the Jeep's upholstery, making sure it was securely lodged between two springs.

*

Halfway across the world Kate was locked in a terrible dream – she was riding Manny over a cross-country jump course that seemed as if it was designed in hell. Jumps higher than her head were lined with briars as long as her thumb, and the ground seemed to be littered with bones, glowing white in the moonlight. They were riding at night, something she had never done before. They were running full out. Manny's neck was slick with white foamy sweat, and she could hear him breathing raggedly, but they had to run, run, run away, or it would get them – the nightmare thing that chased them inexorably through the dream. Manny started to take another of the thorny jumps and he went down in a crash, screamed in agony, then lay still and didn't move. Kate had been thrown clear as he fell and she rushed to him, calling his name over and over again, but Manny remained motionless. He lay there like some hell horse; teeth pulled back from his lips, his eyes open and wide. She rested her head against his neck and wept in horror and anguish as she realized that, in her fear, she had ridden him to death.

She became aware of sound; the soft sound of hoof beats coming towards her at a trot. She felt a soft nose nuzzling her. She looked up, and there, standing in the moonlight, was a silvery horse. In the way of dreams, he suddenly became clear and bright, and she stood up to stroke his neck. He lowered his nose to Manny for a moment, sniffed deeply, then nudged him. The silvery horse shook his head and looked at Kate, and in her dream, she felt a sense of peace and rightness settle over her. She sighed.

Suddenly, the horse threw his head up in the air and began neighing loudly, both in challenge and alarm. He trotted away from her and screamed again and again, louder and louder, to the point that Kate collapsed and threw her hands over her ears. She began screaming, "STOP! STOP! STOP!"

She sat up in bed, completely disoriented. The sleeping bag was drenched in sweat. Her satellite phone was ringing over and over again. She hesitated before answering, but then grimly reached for it and answered with a weak hello.

It was John. His voice was distant as if he were calling from another world. Kate shook her head, clearing the last remnants of the dream from her thoughts. John was talking, but what he was saying wasn't making any sense. Finally, she shook her head and spoke.

"What? John, I'm sorry but I was dead asleep. What's wrong?"

"I'm sorry, Katie baby, but we didn't have any choice. The vet said so."

"John, what are you saying?"

"Honey, Manny colicked tonight, badly. We had to put him down. We did everything we could. The vet said it was for the best. He's gone Katie. I am so sorry."

When the words finally sank in, Kate screamed so loudly it woke others in the camp; they came rushing to see what was wrong. Kate threw the satellite phone against the tent wall, then collapsed onto the cot with great wrenching sobs.

She knew that someway, somehow, she had ridden Manny to his death.

3 Months Later

Kate sat impatiently in David Meyers' office, tapping her toe nervously on the floor. She looked at the engagement ring on her finger, a half-carat solitaire diamond in a platinum setting. Her girlfriends in the office had cooed and exclaimed over it, but somehow, when she looked at it, she just felt bitter and numb.

When she had returned from Africa, the first thing she had done was go to Manny's grave on the farm. They had buried him far from the house, on a little rise that overlooked a creek running through a neighbor's property. She had sat there, in the hot June sun, completely lost. Manny had been so much a part of her for so long, she felt like she had lost a limb, or an eye, or a piece of her heart that was critical to keep life beating in her body. She pulled at the grass at the base of the newly piled dirt, remembering how she use to play a game with Manny, pulling grass and playing keep away with the clump of blades in her hand. She dropped the grass and walked away. Somehow, tears just wouldn't come and she felt her grief like a tight hard fist in her body.

John had been the most understanding and kind that he had ever been the entire time she had known him, and Maria Nuncio, who had fed Manny the night he died, seemed to be nearly as devastated as Kate. When Maria called, Kate told her woodenly that it wasn't her fault, and that she shouldn't worry about it. Then she cut off the conversation. When Kate did go into the newsroom, she avoided Maria. As time passed, she found going to the farm to be far too painful, so she spent more and more time in town, and found herself accompanying John frequently to parties and other events. Anything was better than sitting at home alone. Her editor had only sent her on a few easy assignments during this time. The piece she did on the Virunga Volcanoes turned out to be one of the best things she had ever done and she was able to coast on that success for a time. She still didn't know how she had managed it.

Several of her riding friends from her old barn called with condolences about Manny and offered her other mounts, but she refused them coldly. It just wasn't fitting for her to ride another horse after what she and Manny had had together. She was never going to touch another horse again. That would be her punishment. She should have been home, not in Africa. Manny would not have died if she had been home.

It had come as a complete surprise and shock when John had proposed.

He had taken her to dinner at a small, expensive restaurant near Capitol Hill; one of the restaurants that was very in with Hill staffers and members of Congress. It was Saturday, and the restaurant had been crowded. John had acted a bit nervous during the meal, but Kate hadn't paid much attention.

When they had finished, John had come over, knelt down beside her, then had taken her hand and pulled an engagement ring out of his pocket. Then he slid it on her finger.

"Kate, darling, will you marry me?"

Kate sat shocked for a moment, and the next thing she knew a flash blinded her – someone was taking pictures.

When her vision cleared, she saw that everyone in the restaurant was looking at her expectantly, and the smiling photographer was poised for another picture. She found herself nodding; John gave her a dramatic kiss, then the restaurant erupted in applause.

On Monday morning, the picture appeared in the Hill Newspaper 'Roll Call,' and also on the liberal blog 'Daily Kos.'

It didn't help that their friends and people she worked with went on and on about how romantic it was that John Ridley had done such a thing.

In her heart, Kate knew that the entire thing was done simply for effect, and that she had been skillfully manipulated.

So, now when she looked at the beautiful ring, she just felt resentment.

The slam of the office door jerked her from her reverie David Meyers walked in; a man who was about as far away as a person could get from the looks of the stereotypical big city newspaper editor. He favored Armani suits, weekly manicures, and $300 haircuts (which, considering the financial state of the Gazette, it was lucky that he had been born with money AND had married well). Meyers was in his late 60s, but was still fit and lean. He moved lithely behind his desk, sat down, and looked at her impishly behind his $1500 designer glasses. Kate stared back at him, unsmilingly. Although many people called David Meyers the Dragon of DC, Kate had always had a good relationship with him, dating back from the time that he had been the DC city desk editor and she was an intern.

"So, Kate, how is Soon To Be Married life treating you these days? Still grieving about Manny? I know how you loved that horse."

Kate knew Meyers well enough to sense the sincerity in what he was saying about Manny (he and his wife had both called right after Manny had died to express sympathies), but she also knew that he was trying to work out the best way to sell her on some scheme or idea of his that he KNEW she would not been too keen on. She frowned at him.

"Well, out with it. You and I both know you are up to something so let's just cut to the chase shall we?" she said.

Meyers looked abashed for a moment, then shook his head and smiled. He shuffled around for a few moments through the papers on his desk and tossed a manila folder at her across the wide, custom designed, walnut monstrosity. She caught it and looked at him suspiciously, then opened the folder.

In it were many email correspondences, as well as a letter sent by regular mail. There were also several pictures of two women; one appeared to be in her mid 40s, a very stiff, intense looking woman who looked like she spent a lot of time outside. Of the half dozens or so pictures of her, there was only one of her smiling, and that was when she was standing with a tall, handsome bay horse. He looked to be a Thoroughbred to Kate's practiced eye. The other woman was the polar opposite of the older woman, young, mid 20s at the most, a bit on the plump side, with dark hair, deep blue eyes and a milkmaid complexion. In every picture, this woman was smiling and happy, and there was one picture of her riding a nice looking palomino horse with a Western saddle. Kate pulled out the letter and saw the Wild Horse Squad logo on the stationary.

"What's this all about, David?"

Meyers sighed and looked at the ceiling.

"An old friend of mine, fraternity brother from Yale as a matter of fact, is on the board of directors of this organization. Charlie has been nagging me to death about these two women. Apparently they were out tooling around somewhere in Bumfuck, Nevada and managed to get themselves into a permanent state of missing, or worse."

"So why is he calling us? Don't they have cops out there?" Kate asked.

"Oh yes, the local FBI office has been working on it as well as the sheriff's office, and even the Nevada Highway Patrol, but these two gals have managed to vanish without a trace, and Charlie is in a state, to say the least."

"OOOOOO...kay, so I am missing something here. I am an environmental and nature reporter, not Sam Spade private eye...what has this got to do with me?" Kate asked.

Meyers gave her a long measuring look, then put his elbows on his desk and leaned forward.

"Kate, these women were wild horse advocates. They were out investigating a clandestine roundup and they vanished. Harlan Finney, the executive director of the Wild Horse Squad, had gotten several phone calls from them the afternoon before they disappeared. They were supposed to have met a representative from the Bureau of Land Management – they are the ones that were in charge of this roundup. But, the man got busy working on an emergency and never made the meeting. They vanished into thin air apparently – left no trace."

"I still don't get where I fit into this scenario."

"My GUT, Kate, my GUT," Meyers said gleefully. "Plus, you are the only one I have on the writing staff who knows anything about horses."

Kate groaned. Meyers' legendary GUT feelings (always put into capital letters in the minds of the staff) were infamous for being either brilliant or catastrophic. Meyers loved to throw good reporters into an unfamiliar area of expertise; he said it brought a freshness and insight that someone who worked 'the beat' was missing. Meyers' GUT had brought the Gazette four Pulitzer prizes, but had also managed to get one Gazette reporter locked up in a French jail for a week, and nearly ended in the divorce of one correspondent who had been asked to investigate a brothel in Reno. The man had taken the phrase 'deep background investigation' to a whole new level.

Kate looked at the two women in the photos, and felt an odd sense of kinship. As she glanced at the documents in the folder, her eyes caught sight of the terms 'dedicated horse lovers,' 'their families deserve an answer,' and 'fearless advocates.'

She threw the folder back on his desk.

"No, David," she said evenly, looking him straight in the eye. "I have no real skills as an investigative journalist, nor any interest for that matter. Plus, John and I are working on wedding plans. I know you are my boss, and you can fire me, or do other horrid things, but quite frankly, I don't give a shit anymore."

Meyers looked back at Kate, nodded, smiled, and held up his hands in placation.

"OK, OK, no need to be so HOSTILE, Katie, no need at all," he said, shaking his head. "What's gotten into you anyway? I didn't call you in for a fight."

He looked at her steadily for a moment, a slight grin on his face.

"Will you just do me ONE favor though, since I am in such a jam here with an old friend? Will you just take this file home and read through these emails and the letter? If you still feel the same in the morning, then I'll assign it to someone else. Gonzales might be good," he said musingly.

"Oh, PLEASE," Kate said without thinking. "Gonzales is a FILM CRITIC, for crying out loud."

She stopped herself, suddenly realizing she had had fallen for one of Meyers' little ruses, and not even such a sophisticated a ruse at that.

Meyers beamed at her beatifically.

"Just look at the letters and sleep on it, OK? That's all I ask. If you come in tomorrow and it's no go, that's fine. I'll assign it to someone else."

"Not Gonzales," he continued, grinning at her.

"Fine. One night though," she said.

*

Kate sat at the island in the kitchen with her laptop, while John flailed wildly at the gas stove, working on some new Thai dish. Kate had never been fond of cooking, and on John's rare nights at home, he enjoyed exploring 'new culinary territory,' as he called it. Some of his efforts were less disastrous than others and were actually quite good. Kate, who could only cook 'peasant dishes,' as John called them, was perfectly happy to let him fulfill his fantasy to be the world's top chef. She had gotten to be very skillful at spitting out the more putrid foods by distracting him with a request for a different type of wine.

Tonight though, she was oblivious to his racket as she did a Google search on the two missing women and found their blogs.

What she found on Lindy Abraham's blog shocked her. Kate had grown up in Berea, Kentucky, just south of Lexington, which was the Thoroughbred capitol of the world. While there were many instances of abuse of horses in Lexington (Kate had never been particularly fond of Thoroughbred racing), she found the photographs and videos on Lindy Abraham's Wild Horse Roundup blog beyond shocking.

Small foals separated from their mothers, burros run to exhaustion by helicopters and cowboys on horses, horses dead or severely injured from being run into unpadded steel traps, weanling horses being roped repeatedly and brutally dragged into a traps. Helicopters hovered over terrified horses, to the point they banged into them with landing gear; horses with tangled and broken legs in protective 'jute' fencing. The worst was a young foal that had actually been run to exhaustion in the stampede. He had collapsed and died in the stock pen, but no one even noticed until someone had pointed out that he was in distress. The wranglers, who stood by without flinching as one stallion bashed in his own brains on a stock panel in terror. It was just business as usual to them.

Kate had been to rodeos, and never liked them. It seemed to be a senseless waste of time – what was the POINT anyway of these men (mostly) going to such lengths to subjugate animals in such a violent fashion? She never forgot the first (and last) time she attended a rodeo in Lexington with her mother and stepfather. As they walked to and from the stands throughout the night, they kept passing a pitifully small tarp covering the body of a calf that had died during a roping competition.

The West was WON; it wasn't such a brutal struggle for survival anymore. So, why did people insist on reliving it?

It was especially offensive in light of the relationship she had had with Manny for so many years. Of course, there had been times that they didn't agree on the correct way to get something done (i.e., Manny could NEVER see the sense of the 'trot in place' show movement called piaffe, which they had to perform in their dressage tests – he did it, but without the brilliance he could have accomplished if had put his heart into it), but for the most part they had an amazing partnership, a union, that few other people were able to achieve with their horses.

Then, as Kate reviewed the various BLM documents that gave the reasons for removing herds from various public lands, she was even more shocked. Kate had minored in wildlife biology in college, and had spent many hours doing fieldwork as an undergraduate. Most of the BLM's documents were sloppy beyond belief; methodology appeared to be nonexistent.

Kate didn't know much about mustangs. A couple of her friends rode mustangs; both were endurance riders, and the wild horses (once trained) seem to be marvelous at the long distances demanded by endurance. They were surefooted, with wind and ability to cover miles quickly and easily, but the horses seemed to be pretty much like any others temperament-wise. Both were affectionate and devoted to their riders, and were very, very steady.

Then she went on to read that while the BLM had once had a relatively successful adoption program, it had lost momentum for unknown reasons (Kate smelled a political shift within the agency during an administration change). Now, tens of thousands of wild horses were warehoused at various sites in the U.S. The taxpayers paid for these animals who had once roamed free to now be penned in small pastures, where they received food and water, but that was about it.

"Kate! KATE!" John yelled. Kate just about jumped out of her skin.

"What?"

"Dinner! What's the matter with you – you're in another world!"

"Sorry, was just doing some research for a story."

"Well, time to eat."

Reluctantly, Kate left her laptop on the kitchen island, picked up her glass of wine, and followed John into the dining room. His Thai dinner tonight actually smelled good and looked quite edible. She began eating, her mind still focused on the wild horse issue.

"So, Katie," John said, clearly trying for pleasant conversation. "What are you researching so intently tonight?"

"Meyers wants me to do a story on wild horses. He wants me to go to Nevada. Apparently, a couple of wild horse advocates have disappeared and some old friend wants the paper to look into it. I told him I wouldn't go," she said matter-of-factly.

John looked at her and smiled. Something about the smile irritated her. It seemed patronizing somehow.

"Well, of course you told him that. You are a bride-to-be! A wedding to plan!" After she didn't respond, he continued, "I've got some news, Katie. Big news."

"Really, what?"

He reached out and took her hand. "They want me to run for Michael's Congressional seat in Michigan in the next election. Justin's got the petition going right now in the district, and is working on getting the campaign financing lined up," he said.

Justin was John's cousin and the family campaign manager.

"So, I guess you told them you'd do it?" she said, pulling her hand away.

"Of course. You know it's always been the plan," he said, smiling at her.

"Of course," she responded, looking at him coolly. She carefully picked a piece of cilantro from her mouth and sucked her teeth loudly and indelicately.

"And, I guess, as your new bride, I'll be expected to be in tow while you're stumping in Michigan?" she continued.

John gave her a bit of a sidelong look, then continued eating unconcernedly. "Well, yes. I'll want you there by my side, Katie."

"I have a job, John. I hope you didn't forget about that," she said.

"Oh, I think Meyers would be willing to give you a little sabbatical. Plus, we have a wonderful project for you that you'll just love. You always wanted to write a book. Justin wanted to hire a ghostwriter to write about my time in the Peace Corps, but I said why do that when we have one of the best writers in the country right in our own family?"

Kate didn't respond to the flattery. She just looked at him steadily.

"Plus," John continued, "when one spouse goes into public service, it's just standard procedure that the other has to put their career on the back burner for a while. Look at Maria Shriver. She gives her husband the support he needs out there in California. And, it's the same all over. It's just standard procedure.

"Besides Kate, its time we started thinking about having a family. This horse thing you had with Manny, which was wonderful – what an amazing relationship the two of you had!

Anyway, I think we both know that it was a once in a lifetime thing, an adolescent infatuation that you quite sensibly outgrew. We're not getting any younger, Katie, time to plan for the future."

He reached out, took her hand, and smiled at her appealingly. "You are going to make a beautiful mother," he said.

Kate stared at him; it seemed she was really seeing him for the first time. Tall, lanky, relaxed, confident John; her partner for nearly 13 years, and she felt she had never really known him.

"I'm going to bed. I have a splitting headache," she said, pulling her hand away abruptly.

"Anything I can do? Can I get you anything?" John asked, with concern in his voice.

"No. I just want to lie down. I am going to sleep in the spare room so I won't bother you."

"Are you sure you're OK?" he continued.

"I'm fine. I just need a bit of time to myself, to deal with this headache."

"OK dear, good night," John said.

He watched as she walked out of the room. He had thought that she might be difficult when he gave her the news, but she would come around. Kate had been much more tractable and easier to deal with now she was no longer distracted by her foolishness over that old horse.

John took another sip of wine and continued eating his dinner. The dish had turned out even better than he had expected.

*

Kate went to the spare bedroom, taking her laptop and a trashy novel. She loved their little spare room; it had a futon in it and was very cozy and quiet. She and John lived just a few blocks behind the Supreme Court, on 4th Street, NE. The room's windows overlooked a small park on the corner. Sometimes she could see people walking their dogs at night under the streetlights and, for some reason, she found this comforting.

She set the novel and laptop on the bed, then went over to an antique bureau that stood against one wall. She opened the top drawer and dug around for a moment, then pulled out a large pearl earring; a pierced earring that had been set in diamonds. The back was missing from the post. She had found it under their bed the year before, when she had been searching for a lost slipper. She looked at it for a long moment, then put it back in the drawer.

Kate didn't have pierced ears.

She lay down in the bed and continued reading some more about Lindy Abraham and Julia Evans, but the more she read about the wild horse situation, the more depressed she became. She looked at a small picture in the bookshelf in the spare room; it was a picture of her and Manny after one of the Eventing competitions in Lexington. They both looked tired and content.

Kate set the laptop aside, and opened the trashy book. She read about ten pages, then fell into a deep sleep.

She found herself standing on a high mesa in a twilight land. She knew she was dreaming. She also knew she was in the desert in this dream. There were tumbleweeds, and low growing sage; the wind was blowing across the colorless landscape. She heard a noise and turned, and there in the distance she could see the image of a horse running towards her. He trotted up to her and stopped just at arm's length. She reached out and touched his proud neck, and he shook his pale mane and snorted softly. She stroked him and he arched his neck in pleasure, looking at her with emerald green eyes.

She choked a bit as she realized that this was the same horse she had dreamed about the night that Manny had died.

He started to walk away, then turned, and looked at her, and she felt herself drifting beside him. He took her to the edge of the mesa and they looked down into a vast canyon. There, at the bottom of the canyon, were hundreds of horses, trapped in a river valley where a great rush of water was rising inexorably, dashing them against the walls of the canyon, overwhelming and drowning them. The silver horse looked at Kate, and back down at the canyon, and she sighed heavily in her sleep.

The next morning, she woke early and called David Meyers at home (taking a certain delight that she had woken him up) and she told him she would be taking the assignment in Nevada. Meyers seemed sleepily glad. He told her he would talk to her later and give her the details on her contacts and other information.

Kate heard John in the shower, getting ready for work. She decided she would pretend to be asleep until he left, pack a suitcase, and call him from the airport to let him know she was leaving. *Rather cowardly, but I don't care.* She didn't want to deal with him this morning.

Chapter 4

Jim Ludlow woke up quickly, as he did every morning, and stared at the small ceiling fan as it whirred in its soothing, breezy silence over his bed. Today, he had to move cattle up from the south pasture, do some fence repair, then go down to the Center to help with a new load of horses that was coming in that afternoon. The singlewide Ludlow lived in had once been the residence of his sister, Sharon White Owl, and her husband, Hank, who were his partners in the ranching operation. Sharon and Hank had built a new ranch house a few years prior, but had kept the single wide with the intention of renting it out to ranch hands, or Tribe members who fell on hard times.

When Ludlow had fallen far and hard, they had offered it to him, and he didn't think he would ever be able to repay their kindness. When he had come back to the ranch, he had often thought about something his father had said when given the news that Ludlow had been accepted at UCLA. They had been sitting at sunset on his grandmother's porch outside of Elko, Nevada. His dad, John Ludlow, worn and thin from drink, had only looked at him and grinned coldly. He had swigged a beer and said, "Be careful how high you fly, son. Just remember, it's a long way down to the ground. It's always that sudden stop that gets you." And he had cackled evilly.

His dad had been more right than he knew, but Jim never got a chance to tell him. A few months after this conversation, John Ludlow had passed out drunk outside a bar in Elko and had frozen to death in a Blue Norther blizzard. There had been a time Jim had envied him for that, but he was past that now.

Ludlow pulled on a clean pair of Wranglers and padded into the kitchen. He had set the automatic coffeepot the night before, and, as always, felt pampered and rich to have hot coffee waiting for him in the kitchen. The smell itself seemed to give the promise of a bright and energetic day. It was a keen pleasure, and he smiled as he poured the strong, black liquid into a plain white mug.

Ludlow suddenly remembered that he had promised to try to track down a lost mare and new foal that had wandered away from the Reservation herd earlier in the week. He would do that before he moved the cattle. He smiled at the thought of getting to spend some time riding Jerry – he and the mustang gelding hadn't had any quality time for more than a week.

Chapter 5

"Bobby, don't make me call Meyers. I need that satellite phone and I need it 15 minutes ago," Kate said, exasperated. The Gazette's telephony specialist, Bobby Patel, was infamous throughout the company for being an anal nitpicker who took his job way too seriously. Kate stared at him in his tiny cubicle, the only one she knew of at the company with its own locking half door. It was locked now, effectively preventing her from storming into his cube and throttling him. That was probably why the door had been installed to begin with.

"I didn't receive the proper authorization for you to be able to take that phone, and it's the last one we have. We have gone through this more than once, you know," he droned, without looking at her.

"OK, Bobby, yet again, I will tell you that I am sick of this bullshit, and I am holding up my cell phone right now to call Meyers, and he will call your boss, and he will yell at you, and you will give me the satellite phone, as you have done every other time we have had THIS SAME FUCKING CONVERSATION."

Patel looked at her soullessly and sighed heavily. Kate held up her phone in front of her face and theatrically started pressing numbers on the screen.

Patel disgustedly tossed a clipboard onto the little ledge on the locked door.

"Please fill out your corporate charge card number here, and a secondary charge card here, and then sign that you have given me permission to allow the company to bill your credit card for any minutes used. You will also agree that if your corporate card limit is exceeded your secondary card will be billed and you are responsible for all unapproved charges, he said. "In addition, …that device you are using currently is NOT approved for general use throughout the company, and, technically you should turn it into this office.".

Kate scribbled her name on the clipboard, snatched the satellite phone case from Patel's hand, turned on her heel, and shot him the bird on her way out.

"Piss off, Bobby!"

Patel just shook his head and turned back to his computer screen. Reporters were all alike.

Kate did stop to call Meyers on the way out of the building. She was wheeling her large, hard-sided, long-term suitcase behind her (The Beast, she called it), her bulky laptop case strapped tightly to its extended handle. She was surprised when he actually answered his cell phone.

"David – who do I talk to out there in Bumfuck, Nevada anyway?"

Meyers laughed.

"That's Elko, dear. Elko. Never been there myself, but I am sure you are going to have the TIME OF YOUR LIFE. MY GUT NEVER LIES."

"Fine, David, fine. You have crowed about your GUT enough, thank you. Can you please tell me if I have a contact out in Bumfuck, otherwise referred to as Elko, or what?"

"Yes dear, of course. Your contact is the PR specialist at the BLM's Elko office. His name is Mark Johnson, and I am sure he is a excellent example of Western civilization at its finest. Marielle has already sent him your travel schedule, and he will be picking you up at the airport. Marielle booked you into the Travelodge," Meyers said. "Yee-ha, $50 a night. I just love it when you guys go to the cheapie places."

Marielle was Meyers' hyper-efficient assistant, and Kate was convinced that life as everyone at the Gazette knew it would cease to function the day Marielle departed for good. She liked Marielle immensely.

"No doubt, David. Hopefully, the worthy hotels of Elko have managed to escape the ravening bedbug epidemic. But, what else can you give me on this story?"

"Marielle sent you an email with a list of contacts, including Harlan Finney, executive director of the Wild Horse Squad. I would start with him first. And Katie," Meyers paused, and Kate sensed a change in Meyers' tone, "you can trust Finney, I think, but don't believe too much of what you hear coming out of the mouths of those people that work for our government out there. Sometimes things outside the Beltway aren't that much different from things inside the Beltway."

"OK, David."

"And, be careful. Something about this thing makes me a little nervous."

"Don't know why you would feel that way, with two women vanishing into thin air out in the middle of the desert, and you're sending another one out to track them down. I'm the one that should be nervous, and, just so you know, I am."

Meyers laughed a bit.

"So, what did John have to say about you leaving?" he asked.

Kate hesitated and said, "Gotta go, David, cab.," and she hit the 'end' button.

A few minutes later Kate flagged down a cab and soon was on her way from downtown DC out to the Dulles International Airport in Virginia. Right after they crossed the Potomac, she called home and waited for the answering machine to pick up.

"John, Meyers insisted on me taking this story in Nevada, so I pretty much had to do it. It's a great story and he didn't really have anyone else, not with my experience. I am on my way to Elko, Nevada, now. I probably won't be available for a while, so I will catch up with you when I can."

She spent a few minutes feeling cowardly and gnawing on a knuckle. She saw the engagement ring, angrily took it off, and stuffed it into one of the pockets of her handbag. Then she put the setting on her Smartphone to send any calls from John's office, cell phone, Blackberry, and the home phone directly to voice mail.

She shook her head to shake John out of her mind, pulled out her laptop, and started researching the Wild Horse Squad again. It would take 45 minutes to get to Dulles, so she had just enough time to get a little more research finished on the BLM's documentation on the wild horse herds in the Elko region.

*

Kate was experiencing a severe feeling of displacement on the connecting flight between Salt Lake City and Elko. The flight was booked solid, with a variety of different types of people. Most seemed to be engineers, all intent on working on their laptops, oblivious to everything else. There were about half a dozen individuals she easily recognized as Native Americans, a few of whom had long black glossy braids in their hair, men and women both. Kate secretly envied them that hair. Her own hair was a limp, difficult to control auburn string mop. It had been the bane of her existence for most of her adult life. Overhead compartments were crowded with cowboy hats, and everyone had to crouch down and sidle along crablike down the aisles when they were trying to negotiate getting on and off the plane. Kate idly wondered (as always) when the airlines would have the technical ability to slide people into some sort of garment bag that inflated on impact (with tiny breathing holes of course), and hang them up like neatly laundered shirts in a closet (or sides of beef in a slaughterhouse – an image that Kate did not want to dwell on too much) in order to save space and extract the last fraction of a cent of profit per passenger.

She looked out the window at the Nevada desert and what she saw took her breath away. In the early morning light, the desert was bright with glowing ambers, umbers, and pastel pinks. Elko lay in a small valley between mountains and foothills, an orderly, tiny square of green in a vastness of sand and scrub. She had no doubt that Elko from the sky was much more attractive that Elko up close and personal.

She had had a layover the night before in Salt Lake City, and had spent the night at the Marriott near the airport. She had finally called John to talk to him about the trip. It had been a short, tense, monosyllabic conversation. Clearly, he was furious with her.

She remembered how, at one time, she would have put a lot of effort into bringing him out of his mood. Now it was just too much damn work. He had become cutting and sarcastic when she refused to give him an idea of when she would be flying back to DC. At that point, Kate decided she had had enough of him. She simply said goodbye and hung up the phone. She knew he was probably calling her back, but she still had the settings on her phone routing all of John's calls directly to voicemail. If there was an emergency, the Gazette could contact her. It had been a long day and she was too tired to deal with him.

On the trip out, she had spent a good bit of time on the phone with Harlan Finney of the WHS. He was a passionate and intelligent man; at one time, he had been one of the most successful labor litigators in Texas. However, he had abruptly sold his thriving law practice and opened one of the largest horse rescues in the United States on an enormous ranch located between Austin and Houston (the WHS worked on all types of equine welfare issues). Over the years, hundreds of abused, abandoned, and neglected horses had been saved by his rescue and most relocated to good homes. The rest lived out their lives on the ranch. Even though the WHS had a large staff, both paid and volunteer, most of the success of the group was primarily due to the ceaseless efforts of Harlan Finney. He had testified before Congress many times on wild horse issues, and was called as an expert witness in equine welfare court cases around the country. In her brief experience with him, she had come to realize that Finney was simply a force of nature.

He was a gruff, plainspoken, but charming Texan, who clearly had enjoyed being 'on the stage' as a litigator. And even though he was working in a completely different game now, he had not lost his flair and sense of the dramatic.

"Kate – I am hoping you won't mind me calling you Kate–" he had said during their first phone call, "I'm glad that Charlie Markett got Meyers off his ass to send someone out to look into this. I have called the FBI at least 100 times, and they are doing less than nothing to find out what happened."

He had grown silent, and Kate heard him choke a bit.

"I fear those girls are dead, somehow, someway. In fact, I know it, but we owe it to them and to their families to find out what happened. That Lindy, she gave her soul for those wild horses, and she deserves better than to be lying somewhere out there in the middle of nowhere where her boys can't even pay their respects, and the same goes for Julia. Julia had her whole life in front of her. She was a good kid," he said.

Kate had allowed Finney to vent and grieve a bit on the phone, then she had begun asking the hard questions, trying to dissect facts from emotion.

"Harlan, can you tell me exactly why you feel the FBI has been less than helpful?"

Finney snorted. "Oh, you just have to speak to Special Agent Mike Williams, who has less sense than my second ex-wife, who was the dumbest woman that ever walked this earth (no offense intended). Every time I have called him, he has assured me that he is working on following up every lead, but when I ask him about the ones that I had sent him the week before, he can't remember what it is I'm talking about. He always says he has to 'check his files' to refresh his memory, and when I call him the next day to see if he has 'checked his files,' I have to start the same conversation all over again to remind him what lead it is he is supposed to be checking. I even flew up to Carson City and met with the governor, who is slightly more intelligent than Special Agent Williams and my second ex-wife, but not by much.

"I will give the good governor credit for sending out a detective from Nevada State Police, who had some semblance of a brain, but the FBI and BLM security ran him off, saying it wasn't in his jurisdiction since the disappearance happened on public lands. THAT was a real shame, because, as I said, that fellow did have at least a partially working brain. He didn't take too kindly be being run off either."

"And what was this gentleman's name?" Kate asked.

"Antonio Deer, and a fine man he is, a good cop. I just wish he hadn't been run off."

"Do you think it was just a jurisdictional issue, or something else?"

"Well, I'll tell you this," Finney replied. "Detective Deer is a professional; a good law enforcement officer, but the last time I talked to him, just to follow up on what HE found when he went up to Elko, he was mad enough to spit nails, I could tell. Something about the entire situation in Elko bothered him immensely, but apparently there was nothing he could do about it. He wouldn't tell me details, of course; he just told me that going forward I would have to work with The Brilliant Genius, Special Agent Williams. These cops clam up and protect each other when facing the general public, but I could tell he wasn't happy with whatever he had found out in Elko. Hopefully, you might have better luck with him. Just so you know, he is a Native, and sometimes the Non-Natives have a little problem with that."

"You mean Native American?

"Yes, but a lot of them just prefer to be called Native now, and all things considered, I don't blame them a bit for leaving off the American part," Finney said.

Kate got Deer's contact information from Finney, and gave him her email address so that he could send the detailed call records of Lindy and Julia's cell phones from the day they had disappeared.

"Kate, I don't believe Special Agent Williams is a liar, but there is a REASON he is out there in Elko, and it ain't because he's the sharpest knife in the drawer. As far as the BLM goes, I have being dealing with those assholes for more than ten years now, and never saw such a bunch of liars – not even when I was practicing law, and that's saying a lot. Every lawyer I ever met is a liar, including myself. But I've reformed."

"That's good to know," Kate replied, laughing. "I will give you my word on something, I will do my best to make sure I find out what happened to these two women, my VERY best, and I assure you that I am not a liar, and do not go back on promises.

"But I have to ask you something, was there anyone who had anything against Lindy or Julia any enemies like stalker ex-boyfriends or something? Was there anyone who might have followed them and just seized the opportunity to get some revenge while they were out in the middle of nowhere?"

"Trust me, Kate. The only enemies that Lindy Abraham ever had all worked for the BLM – she has had so many heated battles with them, out there in the field at their roundups, on her Internet blog, and also in the courts. She has been named as a plaintiff on every suit we ever filed against the BLM, and there have been plenty of them, believe me. Julia was more of a worker bee in the beginning, when she first started volunteering with us. But she had started going with Lindy more and more in the field. She was good at working with the BLM and defusing tense situations. She was also becoming a very good videographer. Her mother is just heartbroken over this."

"I'm sure she is. I can't imagine what all the families must be going through."

"Or what we all are going through. This has hit us all so hard, all across the country. You just don't know, Kate, you just don't know."

"You have my word, that I will do my very best to see if I can shine a light on what happened, or why they haven't found out what happened," Kate said.

"Thanks, honey."

When the plane landed at the Elko airport, there was the usual anxious rush to get off; seatbelts clicking, overhead bins being slammed against the roof of the plane, quiet curses and apologies. Then, on the way off the plane, people walked trying to make themselves small just to get to a place where they could actually stand up and feel like humans again, instead of some sort of canned seafood. Kate pulled down her laptop case and crabbed out with the rest, nodding and smiling like always at the steward standing at the exit, who wished them a good day and hoped they would come back to the great canning factory in the sky one day soon.

The Elko airport was new, clean, and attractive, although very small. She walked down the ramp past security, a little anxious about whether her contact from the BLM was actually going to show up or not. She needn't have worried. Once she passed the outside of the metal detector in the airport security area, she saw a pocket gopher of a man in the light green shirt/dark green pants uniform of the BLM standing a few feet away, holding up a sign that said 'Wyndham, Washington Gazette.' He was grinning proudly, nodding at some of the engineer types, clearly glad to have been assigned such an important job as picking up a big city reporter. Kate resisted the desire to walk right past him and down to the rental car counter, but she sighed internally, went up to the man, and smiled.

"I'm Wyndham," she said, "Kate Wyndham of the Washington Gazette, and I guess you must be Mark Johnson?"

He looked at her, as shocked as if she had risen up out of the floor tiles.

"Good grief! They never said you were a girl!"

Kate couldn't help but laugh a little. The little man (he was just a couple of inches taller than her shoulder, but at 5'10" Kate was taller than many men) struggled to gain his composure after what he clearly considered to be an inappropriate outburst.

"Thanks for noticing," she said.

"Geez, I am so sorry. They said I was just supposed to meet a guy named K. Wyndham, that's all they told me. Just give me a minute here to get over the shock, no offense," he said, grinning.

"Well, I hope it's not a problem," she said, staring at him.

"No, no, ma'am! We're ALL about equality here in Elko. We have several women that are great field agents at our office. Some of the best. We are all about equal opportunity here. Just because we are out in the back of beyond, we aren't savages."

"Never thought you would be. Do you mind if I call you Mark?"

"As opposed to what? I'm just joking with you. Of course you can call me Mark, and we really want to offer you every courtesy and help that we can. This has been hard on everyone out here in the Elko office. We are always open to members of the press, always about transparency and doing what's in the best interest of the American Taxpayer. And that's straight from the Director, by the way. We want to cooperate fully with the press on this thing, anything you need from us, you got," he said.

Mark looked at her solemnly, but Kate didn't buy it. Mark Johnson might look like a shop clerk, but he had a slickness about him that seemed endemic to individuals that professional bureaucrats used to interface with the public. Johnson wasn't quite as slick as the ones she had met in DC over the years; he was a rather poor liar. Kate had no doubt he had been told to give the appearance of total cooperation, but to give her nothing of any substance, and to run interference between her and any real sources. She nodded internally in satisfaction. She had dealt with people like this many times over the years.

"Well, that's good to hear, Mark," she said, reaching out to shake his hand. "Good to hear. I have been on the phone with Harlan Finney every minute I had a cell phone signal since I originally got the assignment. He is pretty intense, like most of those people are. Wore my battery down, in more ways than one. My editor's old college buddy is on the board of the WHS, and he called, wanting us to look into the whole thing. You know how it is."

Kate tried to set her tone as one press person commiserating professionally with another; one who would instinctively understand the problem of having to take the lunatic fringe seriously on occasion. Then she topped it off with the universal difficulty of all working people of not agreeing with the boss most of the time. She thought it was over the top, but hoped that Johnson would fall for it.

"Oh, tell me about it," Johnson said emphatically. "I can't count how many calls I've taken from Harlan Finney. Finally, our program manager told me to quit talking to him and just let the FBI deal with him. The FBI found we didn't have anything to do with the disappearance, of course. I hope you are clear on that."

"Of course," Kate said reassuringly. "I think my luggage is probably ready. I'd just as soon get busy if you don't mind. Sooner started, the sooner finished."

"You bet. The luggage carousel is just down here, past the slots."

Kate followed Johnson down to the luggage area. She was slightly surprised that she had to stretch her legs a bit to keep up with Johnson's energetic pace. He might be short and pudgy, but he did believe in getting to where he needed to go. As they walked, Kate looked at him more closely. He had a rather bushy dark moustache, and thick wire-rimmed glasses that attested to lifelong myopia.

"So, Mark, are you from here, around Elko?"

"Me? Oh, heck no," he said. "I'm from Salt Lake. I grew up there, and when I got out of college I started right with the BLM. Been with them ever since. Nearly 22 years now. I was out in Winnemucca for a while, but then they sent me here to the Elko office.

"Do you like it here in Elko?" Kate asked.

"Well, it's a good thing the family and I are quiet types. We have our church here, and that keeps us busy, of course. Not much goes on in Elko, really."

"So, did you know Lindy Abraham or Julia Evans?"

"I knew Lindy," he said, nodding and courteously lifting her suitcase off as it came around the carousel. "I had had to deal with her a few times over the past couple of years at some of the gathers we had out in our Herd Management Areas. She could be very difficult at times. Very difficult. She just never seemed to understand all the precautions that we took were for her own safety and the safety of the horses. But, for the most part, she and I got along OK. She did love those horses, but didn't understand all the rules and regulations we have to adhere to."

"Stubborn, eh?" Kate asked, smiling.

"Oh, she was that." Johnson nodded to the doors leading outside. "I've got the car out there right in the no parking zone. Sometimes working for the federal government does have its perks."

Kate followed him out and helped him load The Beast and her laptop into the rear of the SUV. She then walked up to the passenger door, opened it, and slid in before Johnson could open the door for her. He scuttled around to the driver's side and pulled himself in.

"So, it's nearly lunchtime now. Do you want to go to the hotel, get some lunch, or go back to the office or what? I am 100% at your disposal, 100% and that's straight from the Director."

"That's wonderful, Mark. Always makes my job easier if the folks I'm working with are willing to cooperate," she said. "I'm starving. Lunch would be great."

"Yes, ma'am," Johnson said, slowly pulling away from the curb.

About a half hour later, Kate and Johnson were sitting in a booth in a small Mexican restaurant. Johnson looked over the menu with the interest of a man who genuinely loved working lunches. Kate had to admit that the smells from the kitchen were heavenly. She hadn't eaten since lunch the day before and suddenly found herself ravenous.

"Kate, this place may be small, but it is the best in town. Do you like guacamole? Theirs is the best, and their tamales are homemade right there in that kitchen."

"That sounds pretty good. Tamales and guacamole will work for me," she said.

The waiter came with a couple of glasses of water, took their orders, and left. She and Johnson talked of inconsequential things, mainly about her trip out, and a trip he had made to Washington once. The waiter brought their food and they began eating.

"You're right about these tamales," she said, after taking a bite. "They are wonderful."

Johnson smiled and nodded.

"So, Mark," she said, casually, after a bit, "just what do you think happened to those girls?"

Johnson took another couple of bites and chewed a few mouthfuls, then he began speaking, motioning with his fork for emphasis.

"Well, if you want to know the truth," he said, "I think they got out there in the middle of nowhere and just ran into the wrong bunch. Not many people around here talk about it, but there are a lot of illegals in this area, working on ranches and such, and a lot of the Indians have drug and liquor problems. There's been trouble before, you know. Usually it's the Indians and the Mexicans that wind up in jail over it. Terrible, just terrible. Those girls didn't have any business being out there, none whatsoever. They should have stayed home where they belonged."

Although sorely tempted, Kate didn't mention the fact that the entire reason that Lindy and Julia had been out in the middle of nowhere was to meet one of Johnson's BLM co-workers who had never bothered to show up.

"So, were there any suspects, illegal aliens or Natives questioned?" she asked instead.

Johnson stopped chewing for a second, and looked at her evenly, his chatty manner suddenly growing cautious.

"I wouldn't know about that," he said. "Any questions along those lines you need to talk to the FBI agent. We don't have police powers, you know, except for our enforcement section. And they turned over all their notes to the FBI. That's who you need to talk to about any details of the investigation."

Kate smiled and nodded again, not surprised. She expected this from Johnson, but his slip about the Mexicans and Indians told her a little more about the man and the environment in Elko.

They finished up their lunch, and there was a brief disagreement about who should pay the $15 tab, but Kate laid a $20 bill on the table, which ended the discussion. They walked out to the Blazer and got in.

Johnson looked at Kate as he started the car.

"So, I guess you probably want to go back to the hotel, check in with the boss and all that, before you get started?" he asked, hopefully.

"Not really. I would like to talk to the fellow that Harlan Finney mentioned to me yesterday, Sam Conner? I believe he is the BLM law enforcement officer that was supposed to meet Lindy and Julia the day they disappeared."

"Well, that's a problem, because Sam is off in Ely today – not sure when he will be back."

"I see," Kate said carefully. "So, could I at least talk to him on the phone, do you think?"
"I don't think so. He's out in the field – no cell coverage."

"Ah, I see. No satellite phones then?"

"Not usually, budget and all," Johnson said.

"So, who might I be able to talk to that is around today? County Sheriff?"

"The sheriff turned all his information over to the FBI. And anyway, I talked to Mike Williams this morning – he's the FBI agent that has been heading up the investigation – and he said he would be around this afternoon, so we could go right over there."

Inwardly Kate sighed, but didn't allow it to show on her face. She nodded briefly and said, "Sure, sounds like a good place to start to me."

The FBI's resident office in Elko was located in a small nondescript office plaza about 10 minutes away from the restaurant. They pulled into the deteriorating parking lot and parked in a place that had once been delimited by two white lines at some point in its history. Kate grabbed her laptop case and followed Johnson inside. He opened the door and she walked into a rather grim office that was lined with cheap dark paneling and lit by fluorescent ceiling lamps.

At the front desk sat a fat, matronly woman, working away at a computer screen. She had large, green pastel colored plastic rim glasses (expensive designer frames, 15 years out of date), and clearly had her bleached blonde hair styled at the local beauty parlor once a week. It looked lacquered on. She stared malevolently at Kate and Johnson when they came in.

"Hello, Mark, and what can we do for you today?" she asked.

"Oh, Josie, I thought Mike would have told you we were coming by," Johnson said. "This is Kate Wyndham. She's a reporter from the Washington Gazette. She's here to look into what happened to those two wild horse advocates that disappeared."

Josie scowled then snorted. "Mike did not say a word about it. I will have to CHECK his AVAILABILITY, we are busy here you know. And, just so you know Miss," Josie said, looking pointedly at Kate, "there's some people that think those girls got EXACTLY what they had coming to them. Prancing around out there in the desert, chasing around after horses OR so they say. Ridiculous!"

Kate stared open-mouthed for a brief second, not knowing how to respond, then she heard an office door slam down at the end of the small hallway behind Josie's desk. A tall, slim, dark haired man in a golf shirt and slacks walked quickly down the hall and held out his hand to Kate.

"Hi, I'm Mike Williams," he said, shaking her hand. He looked at Josie nervously. "Hey, Mark, glad you guys made it today," he said to Johnson.

Mark nodded happily, shaking the agent's hand in turn, "We had lunch at El Charito. You should have come over, Mike."

Williams looked at Kate, puzzled.

"Mark, I thought you said it was a guy that was coming out."

"Hah! Well, the boss said I was supposed to meet a K. Wyndham, so I just naturally assumed..." Johnson said.

"Oh, yeah, I get it." Williams looked nervously at Josie again.

Mike Williams reminded Kate of many of the high school athletes she knew when she was growing up – popular, not too bright, and not too stupid (although she had doubts about the stupid side of the issue). He also had the same look as most FBI and Secret Service agents she had known – not too good looking, but good looking enough.

"Well, let's go back to my office and chat a bit."

"Coffee pot's broken," Josie said, turning back to her computer screen.

Williams motioned down the hall and walked along quickly, Kate and Johnson in tow. As they entered the small office, Kate noticed a picture on his desk of a smiling attractive plumpish woman sitting with three young boys. She and Johnson sat down in a couple of cheap office chairs. Williams sat down behind his desk and leaned forward on his elbows.

"Sorry, about Josie," Williams said. "She's having a bad day, and she has had to field a lot of mean phone calls about these missing women. A lot of people are saying on the Internet that we aren't doing our job, and that is hard.

"Not a problem," Kate said noncommittally, and shrugged, thinking that nothing would make Josie happier than having someone 'talk mean' to her on the phone. She shook her head to clear it and moved on.

"So, Agent Williams..." she began.

"Please, call me Mike..."

"All right then, Mike," Kate said, smiling slightly, "what can you share with me about this case? There are a lot of people interested in it, you know."

"Well," Williams responded, "it is an ongoing investigation, so there is only just so much I can say. We do know that the women were out on BIA 19 until around 4 or so on June 19th, which was confirmed by two men that stopped to ask them if they needed help. Then, according to the cell phone records, Julia Evans made one phone call to Harlan Finney just after that, which was verified by Mr. Finney, and then no contacts were made after that. The two men that saw them only asked if they needed help, and that was the end of it."

"Who interviewed these two men?" Kate asked.

"Sam Conner, the security officer of the BLM. I have all the transcripts of the interviews, if you want to see them."

"This is the same Sam Conner that was supposed to meet the women to begin with; the same one that left them sitting out in the desert for two hours?"

"Yes. It's the same man, of course. It's standard procedure for him to take a statement if someone comes forward directly to him with information," Williams said, looking extremely uncomfortable. "The two men came to the BLM. He took their statements, and that was that."

"I see. That was that," Kate said. "And, do we know where these men might be now, their names, etc.?"

"Oh, I can't give you that information as it's an ongoing investigation. Can't give out the names of potential witnesses. Bureau privacy policy."

"Of course," Kate said tersely, sighing.

Kate sat, tapping her foot for a few minutes, looking at the ceiling, then she turned back to Williams.

"So exactly what CAN you tell me, Mike, about what might have happened to Lindy Abraham and Julia Evans?" she asked.

Williams frowned, leaned back in his chair, put his hands behind his head, and stared thoughtfully at the ceiling himself. Johnson leaned forward, ready to hang on every word.

"Well, generally, what we have found when people go missing in the desert like this is that they've just run into the wrong bunch at the wrong time," he said pontifically. "It can be risky to go tooling around out there, especially two women, alone like that. All kinds of dangerous types of criminals running around out there in the desert, ready to take advantage of two women alone. Cellular phone coverage is spotty, if it exists at all, so there is not even any real way to call for help if you get in trouble. They were in an old car. They could have broken down in the backcountry and simply died of exposure. Any number of things like that. St. Martjin was blasting up in that area that day. They could have wandered into a closed area and had an accident."

Kate stared at him levelly. "I would think that if they had had an accident like that the employees of St. Martjin Mining would have noticed, don't you think?" she asked, a bit tartly.

Williams looked at her slightly alarmed and leaned forward again. "Why sure they would have! I was just naming some common scenarios, that's all."

"I think it's extremely curious that the FBI accepts it as routine that Sam Conner, BLM security officer, left these two women sitting in an area overrun with dangerous criminals for two hours. And that Conner's interview of the last people to see them alive is taken as gospel, without further follow up by the FBI," she said, staring at Williams.

"Well, I took Sam's statement myself. He's a law enforcement officer and I trust his integrity," Williams said indignantly.

Kate shook her head slightly and sighed. "OK, so, basically, we have a phone call and a pair of nameless witnesses that place both women on a highway at 4 p.m. on June 19," Kate continued ruthlessly, staring Williams in the eye. "They made one last phone call at that time and were never heard from again. Have I got that right?"

Williams looked uncomfortable again and squirmed a bit in his chair. "Look," he said, "we have been working long hours on this, and there just aren't any leads out there. We have followed up on every single phone call and tip we have received and it looks like they just vanished. Probably find their bodies out in the desert in a couple of years."

"No doubt. Seems like the most convenient outcome," Kate responded coldly, "What documentation are you able to give me?"

"Well, I can give you my interview notes with Sam Conner, and the redacted transcripts from the interview with the witnesses that saw the women last, and the cell phone records. I have that all ready for you right now, as a matter of fact."

Williams reached into the lower drawer of his desk, pulled out a pitifully thin manila envelope and handed it to Kate, smiling again. Kate glanced at the envelope that looked like it might contain 8-10 pieces of paper and gritted her teeth, trying to contain her fury.

"Thank you so much. Always happy to get the usual cooperation from the FBI," she said tersely.

Williams nodded and grinned at her. "We like to help out the press anytime we can, but a lot of time our hands are tied, you know."

Kate shook Williams' hand, stood up and quickly walked out. Williams and Johnson, both shocked at her abrupt departure, hopped up and scurried after her. Kate didn't say a word to Josie as she walked out onto the parking lot. The September sun was shining brightly on the crumbling parking lot and Kate reached into her laptop case and pulled out her sunglasses. She turned to see Mark Johnson leaving the FBI office, saying goodbye to Williams, Josie, or both through the door.

"How far is it to this place on BIA 19, where Lindy and Julia were last heard from?" Kate shouted out to Johnson abruptly, as he approached her with his quick, short-legged stride.

"Well, it's about 45 minutes to an hour away, I guess, but you don't want to go all the way out there do you? It's a very bad road, and it runs through the Reservation," Johnson said, sounding alarmed.

"I certainly do want to go all the way out there, and I don't care if it's on the Reservation. Do the Natives have an issue with someone driving into their country temporarily?"

"Well, no," he said. "No, they won't interfere, or probably even notice to tell you the truth...but..."

"So, what's the problem then, Mark?" Kate snapped.

"Well, the local county Sheriff, the BLM law enforcement, the FBI and the Nevada State Police have gone over that area with a fine toothed comb and didn't find anything, as far as I know."

"Mark," Kate said tersely, "remember when you picked me up this morning you told me I was to receive total cooperation, whatever I needed, straight from the Director, 100% cooperation. Do you remember that?"

"Sure, sure," Johnson responded quickly, in a placating tone. "I wasn't saying we couldn't go. I just don't see the point, that's all."

Kate shook her head and walked around to the passenger side of the SUV, opened the door, got in, and slammed it hard. He could see her staring at him through the window. It was a look very much like the one his wife gave him when he didn't move quickly enough when she required he do something for the family.

She never said anything, she just looked, which was an excellent method of motivation for someone like Mark Johnson.

Johnson sighed and pulled himself into the driver's side and started up the SUV. He hated working with difficult women. It was bad enough just dealing with a difficult woman at home, but most of them at work were difficult also. And this one was particularly bad. Not only was she difficult, but she was tall and red headed and, though good looking, she was totally intimidating, at least to him. But there was a bright side; she would more than likely be on a plane back home tomorrow or the next day, so at least the terrorization was temporary.

"BIA 19 it is…" he said, pulling out of the parking lot.

The drive out to the area where Lindy and Julia Evans had spent what Kate was becoming more and more convinced was the last afternoon of their lives was a silent one for the most part. Johnson made a few desultory attempts at conversation. Kate answered distractedly, but without anger. She was past anger. She was desperately trying to figure out the next steps to take in order to find out what might have happened to them. She had glanced through the ten pages of documents that were in the manila envelope (two pages of which were cell phone calls) and, as she had suspected, there was nothing in them that she didn't already know. Conner's statement was just what Harlan Finney had told her. He was supposed to meet the women, but got tied up in an area with no cell service and missed out on getting over to the rendezvous point. Two men saw them where they were supposed to meet Conner, asked them if they needed help, and then left when the women said they were fine.

Something in that part of the transcript bothered Kate, although she couldn't put her finger on what it was. She read that part of the document over and over again to try figure out what it was that bothered her, but just couldn't grasp it. She placed the documents in her laptop case. She would review them later back in the hotel room, and maybe it would come to her then. The cell phone records jived with the ones she had received from Harlan Finney.

This part of Nevada was stark and beautiful, and she looked around with interest for the first time since they had left Elko. The road they were driving on was unpaved, smooth, and straight for the most part. Only occasionally did they hit a pothole or two.

The BLM vehicle rode surprisingly well, all things considered. Mountains rose in the distance, but the area was mainly desert, although she knew there were some reservoirs in the area that were used for irrigation purposes. Where there was irrigation, there were prosperous looking farms.

Kate looked about in wonder, reveling in the clean air and open space. She felt her spirit drinking it in, like a person would drink clean, cool water after a long thirst. The desert seemed pure and pristine, in a manner she had never seen before, even in some of the more remote areas in the world.

"Will we see any wild horses where we are going?" she asked suddenly.

Johnson looked at her oddly.

"Here? No, no, not here, they're up in the hills, or over on the Rez."

"So, where was this roundup that Lindy and Julia were looking for?" she asked.

"Oh, there wasn't any roundup," Johnson said matter-of-factly. "The gold mine up there was just making sure that no wild horses got injured or killed in the area where they were blasting. They are very environmentally sensitive up there."

"No doubt," Kate said with thinly veiled sarcasm, considering the fact that open pit mining, especially gold mining, was one of the most environmentally devastating activities on the planet.

"But tell me something, Mark," Kate said, smiling at him thinly. "Why did Sam Conner tell them there was a roundup, if they were just pushing some bands of horses out of the area temporarily?"

"Oh, I'm sure Sam told them exactly what was going on, and was just offering to escort them to watch as the helicopters moved the horses – making sure everything was on the up and up, that's all."

"That's not what Harlan Finney said the women told him."

"Well, sometimes those advocates just like to make mountains out of molehills, you know. And, they are usually not too good about remembering details," he replied, smiling back at her.

Kate fought the urge to bang her head on the padded dash of the SUV. They drove for a long while in silence.

"Well, here we are. BIA 19 and Shelley Road. This was where they made that last phone call to Mr. Finney," Johnson said.

Johnson slowed as he pulled past an intersection of a blacktop highway and the dirt road they had been traveling on (Kate wondered if he had taken her on this dirt road the entire way just to prolong the process of getting here, and prove a point about how remote and inaccessible the area was). It didn't make much difference to Kate, except for the fact that the sun was beginning to set and she knew they only had two hours or so of daylight left. She looked at her watch; it was about 4 p.m. local time. About the same time that Julia Evans had made her last call from her cell phone the day they disappeared. Kate got out of the SUV and started walking around. On impulse, she pulled her Smartphone from its case and started taking some pictures.

"Kate, you be careful walking around out there. This is the time the rattlers come out!" Johnson said. She noticed that he hadn't stepped off the blacktop and was looking around nervously.

"Well, if they are anything like the cobras in Africa, they come out onto the highways to catch the last of the day's heat," she responded blithely, not looking back at him.

"Hah! That's a good one. How would you know about that?"

"Spent a lot of time in Africa," Kate said, looking back over her shoulder. "It's no joke."

"Well, if you're just taking pictures, I think I'll wait in the car, if you don't need me for anything," Johnson said.

Kate laughed to herself and walked out into the desert to look around. She found it extremely ironic that an employee of an agency charged with taking care of the environment on public lands was terrified to walk across the desert at dusk.

There wasn't much to see, and yet there was everything to see; sand, sagebrush, tumbleweeds, more sand, rocks, hardpan dirt, and various types of low growing bushes that she didn't recognize. Some had tiny bright yellow flowers that stood out cheerfully against the general drabness of the other plant life. The sky was so clear and blue she felt with enough of a bounce, she could dive right into it, like diving into clear blue ocean water.

Up to the north, the mountains loomed a dusky rose, fading to purple in the approaching twilight, and here and there she could see the slightly greenish glow of security lights of some of the local farms and ranches – old mercury vapor lamps just starting to shine a bit as the light dimmed. There was no traffic, and it was very, very quiet. The air had a sharp, slightly herbal smell to it, and Kate's light boots kicked up little puffs of dust as she walked. About 20 feet away, she actually did see a medium sized rattler out hunting for his supper, but Kate didn't pay him much mind. She knew rattlers minded their own business, for the most part. Occasionally, a grasshopper or locust buzzed in the distance, an oddly comforting sound in the stillness.

Kate thought about what it must have been like for Lindy and Julia, sitting for two hours out here in the desert, in the heat, in June, and she felt a strong sense of admiration for their determination. They had been committed to their ideals, to their mission to save the wild horses. For some reason, the thought made Kate uncomfortable and she turned to go back to the car. There was nothing here for her except emptiness. She could see that Johnson visibly brightened with her return.

"So, Mark," she said, sliding back into the passenger seat and slamming the door, "I guess the next person I need to talk to is your boss, if Sam Conner is not available."

"Well, I'm sorry, but Jerry Stills, the program manager out here, was called into the Reno office to deal with some emergency. I'm not sure what it's all about, and he may not be back until next week sometime. And, with Sam, it's the same thing. I just called into the office, and he's stuck off in the Winnemucca area and is not sure when he'll be back."

"I thought he was in Ely," Kate said, looking at him with a raised eyebrow.

"Well, he was, but then he had to go over to Winnemucca."

"And, let me guess, Mr. Stills is also unavailable by phone," she said tiredly.

"In meetings all day, and is not to be disturbed. That's what his secretary said," Johnson said.

Kate closed her eyes and took a deep breath, counting to ten.

"All right, let's just head back to Elko then," she said, between clenched teeth.

"You bet," Johnson responded, clearly happy to be leaving the marauding rattlers. He turned quickly onto the blacktop highway, and began speeding back towards the slight glow in the distance that was Elko.

Night settled quickly in the desert, and by the time they got back to Elko, it was fully dark. Johnson pulled up at front door of the Travelodge, and hopped out to get The Beast from back of the SUV.

"So, what time do you want to get started in the morning?" he asked Kate brightly.

"Well, let me call my editor first thing and see what he wants to do. I can't see much use in me staying here, as all the people I need to talk to are conveniently absent."

She looked at her watch; it was about 6:30 p.m. local time.

Johnson glanced off in the distance, sighed, then reached into his back pocket and pulled out his wallet. He dug around in it for a moment, then handed her his business card.

"I'm sorry that it looks like you made a long trip for nothing, but we have these types of emergencies out here all the time. Staff is just spread so thin, you know. Budget and all."

"Well, what time do you usually get going in the morning?" Kate asked wearily.

"Oh 8:30, right on the dot. I'll be here bright and early! Don't you worry about that."

"All right, I just need to get in touch with my editor and see what it is he wants me to do now, under the circumstances," she said. "We do have his old college buddy to keep happy, you know. So let's plan on meeting at 8:30."

"Sure, sure, here, let me help you with that luggage."

"No thanks," Kate said, taking The Beast away from him, and quickly strapping her laptop case to the retracting handle skillfully and quickly, from long practice. "You've done more than enough to help me today."

Johnson nodded at her, and grinning, got into the SUV and left. Kate wagged her luggage into the Travelodge, and tried not to feel defeated.

Chapter 6

Once she got into the hotel room, which was less bad than she had expected (and seemed to be bedbug free – a huge relief), Kate did her usual routine of getting a few things out of The Beast and setting them in the bathroom. Then she pulled out her laptop, got on the hotel's wireless network, and began checking her email. There was an email from John, which she ignored. When she checked her Smartphone, there was one voicemail from him also, another voicemail from Meyers, one from Harlan Finney, and surprisingly, one from a Detective Deer at the Nevada State Police. He left her a cell phone number to call. He said that Harlan Finney had called him and said that she would be in Elko today, and that if she needed any additional information to please call him. He would be available until 11 p.m. local time.

Kate looked at her watch. It was nearly 8 pm. Getting a little late to be calling the East Coast. So she hit Deer's number on the phone screen for a redial. He answered on the third ring.

"Well, Ms. Wyndham, I was hoping you might call. And, by the way, I have read some of your work – you're a good writer. I was just wondering how things were going for you up there in Elko?" he said.

"Well, so far I might have just as well stayed in Washington, Detective. Aside from a relaxing ride out into the desert, I don't know any more now that I did when I left."

"Ahh, the Federal Stone Wall..." he said wryly.

Kate laughed in spite of herself. "Well, I do have that flat spot from beating my head against it, now that you mention it."

"No doubt," he replied, laughing in turn. He had a deep voice, and a laugh that you liked to hear. "I have had my own frustrations up in that area. And not just with this case, but I won't get into all that."

"So, what is it I'm sensing here, a crack in the wall?" she asked.

There was silence on the phone for a few seconds, and Kate wondered if she had lost the connection.

"Let's not call it a crack in the wall, but I may be able to point you in the direction of a window."

"I beg your pardon?" Kate asked, puzzled.

"Ms. Wyndham."

"Please, call me Kate; no need to be so formal."

"All right, Kate. There is some issue of jurisdiction as to where Lindy Abraham and Julia Evans disappeared," Deer said, "and personally, I have had some issues with the efforts and depth the FBI, BLM security, and local authorities have put into the investigation."

"Uh, you mean the lack thereof, I take it."

"Yes. For one thing, I don't think they researched the cell phone records as thoroughly as they could have. There were many problems with the interrogation and I felt there were inconsistencies in Sam Conner's statement. You understand this is all off the record, of course, but I also want you to know that I did everything I possibly could before the situation became...complicated."

"Absolutely. But, what can be done? They're running the show over here in Elko," she said.

"Not completely," Deer said and Kate could almost see the grin on his face. "Lindy Abraham and Julia Evans were in and out of the Antelope Valley Indian Reservation while they were driving on BIA 19. It stands to reason that they could have disappeared within the Reservation itself. It is a conclusion a reasonable person would reach, I think."

"A reasonable person, as in a juror," Kate said, smiling. "OK, I am starting to get the idea, I think. But what can be done? Am I missing something here?"

There was a brief silence on the phone.

"Indian Country has its own law enforcement," Deer finally said. "Some work for the Bureau of Indian Affairs, but some of the tribes have their own police force. Antelope Valley has its own Tribal Police Force, and it was the Antelope Valley Reservation that they were traveling in."

"OK, so how do we get the Tribal Police Force interested in what happened to Lindy Abraham and Julia Evans?"

Deer chuckled evilly on the phone. "Already done. You drive up to Antelope Valley tomorrow and go to the City Hall – it's right in the center of town, you can't miss it. You'll see the wing that houses the Tribal Police Force. Go in and ask for Police Chief Sharon White Owl. I talked to her this afternoon and she's expecting you."

"And why should she be willing get involved?" Kate asked.

"Because she feels that justice is not being served for two people who have disappeared in the desert. Sharon was a Chicago Homicide detective herself, before she came back to the Reservation to take over as Chief of Police; her husband runs the operations on the family ranch. She's a good cop. She's also just happens to be my cousin.

"Plus, she likes nothing better than to stick it to the man every once in a while. And, that means the WHITE man. She and Sam Conner don't see eye to eye on many things, and she liked the idea of maybe poking him in the ass a time or two. Or three."

Kate barked out a laugh at that. "At least she can find Mr. Conner. He did nothing but hide from me.".

"The BLM protects its own. Anyway, I have Sharon's contact information for you."

Kate grinned happily as she jotted down the info for Chief White Owl. She wouldn't be flying back to DC tomorrow after all.

After the conversation with Detective Deer, Kate called Meyers, Harlan Finney, and John, in that order. Of the three phone calls, the one with John was the least pleasant, of course. He was no longer sulking, but seemed indifferent, which Kate found to be oddly gratifying. They spoke of inconsequential things, and when she said she had no idea when she would be coming back to DC, John only grunted noncommittally. By the time all her phone calls and email checks were done, it was nearly 11 pm. She realized she hadn't eaten dinner, but was too tired to do anything about it. So, she lay down in bed, exhausted, but spent some time on her laptop watching videos that Julia Evans had uploaded to Youtube over the past six months, until she fell into a restless sleep.

The next morning, Kate woke up around 7, still on Eastern Time, and starving. As she jumped into the shower, she smiled at the plan she and Meyers had come up with during their phone conversation the night before.

Sometimes payback was a bitch. Although Kate didn't usually go in for the whole 'get even' mentality of some people, this time it was going to be totally enjoyable. Her only regret was that she really wouldn't get to see the aftermath up close and personal; she would probably only hear about it second hand, if it all.

But you couldn't have everything.

Once she got The Beast repacked, she went down to the complimentary breakfast bar (which was surprisingly decent) and ate so much that she noticed that the few people in the small dining area were staring at her surreptitiously. She went for her 3rd cup of coffee (Kate was an unashamed pure black coffee addict – the stronger the better – and thought the Cafe Mocha Latte Light drinkers and their ilk were an abomination). She placed a couple of phone calls while she was waiting, and relaxed while watching CNN on the TV. Promptly at 8:30, she heard a familiar short rapid step and she smiled. She turned to see Mark Johnson walking quickly into the hotel, looking around in a nervous, bird-like way. Clearly, he did not look forward to another day with 'Big Red,' as she was sure he named her in his mind. She'd been called worse.

"Mark, here I am," she said, waving. He walked over to her, clearly anxious about what this day might bring. She looked at him and nodded, taking another long drink of coffee.

"Good morning," he said tentatively. "Hope you slept well."

Kate nodded quickly. "I did, I did. And I have some good news for you, Mark."

He looked at her suspiciously. "What?"

"Well, I talked to my editor and he feels that the Gazette has done its due diligence as far as favors go for an old college buddy. I booked a flight out at 10 a.m., so if we leave right now, we should make it just in time for me to get through security and on that plane, and you can get on with your day. I don't want to take up any more of your time."

Johnson looked at her, clearly flabbergasted. This was the last thing he expected her to say. He was fully convinced that she was going to pitch an enormous fit and make him drive her to Winnemucca, or Reno, or the North Pole, or wherever it was she wanted to go, to pursue this ridiculous hunt of hers. He had been up half the night worrying about it. The two horse advocates were dead; just another two people who stumbled into a land that could be harsh on those who were careless. Though tragic, he could never get his head around why this was such a big deal. Now, she had given him a reprieve and he didn't know what to think.

"Well, I do have to admit this was about the last thing I expected to hear you say this morning!" he said.

Kate shrugged and looked at him, trying to look a bit sheepish. "Well, I can be like a bulldog when I get onto something, and also somewhat ...abrasive. But it is absolutely nothing personal. You have been more than helpful, 100% cooperation, just like you said when we met yesterday, and I really do appreciate the effort you put into making sure I had all the information I needed to get to the root of what is really going on here. I know I was rude, and I apologize for that."

And Kate gave him her most brilliant, winning smile.

Johnson blushed and looked down at his feet, missing the thinly veiled sarcasm in her voice.

"Oh, no worries there," he said. "I'm just sorry we didn't find out more than we did. It's a tough case, even the FBI is struggling with it."

"Clearly," Kate replied, noncommittally. "So, shall we make our way to the airport?"

"You bet," Johnson said happily, reaching for The Beast.

There was not much discussion during the short ride to the airport. Johnson was so glad to be rid of her he didn't even make a rudimentary attempt to fill the awkward silence, he just hummed some tunes to himself along the road. Kate assumed they were hymns of some kind. She had no doubt that he was thanking God that he would soon see the last of her.

He pulled up to the Departures ramp at the airport and hopped out of the SUV to get Kate's bags for her. She took The Beast and her laptop case from him, then held out her hand. He looked at her, surprised.

"No need for you to see me inside," she said. "I have done this about one million times before and I'm used to handling things on my own. I'm sure you have better things to do than babysit me at the airport, and, quite frankly, I have some work to catch up on. So, I want to say thanks for all your hospitality, and that excellent meal yesterday."

"Well, all right, if you're sure," Johnson said, highly uncomfortable with this development. His boss had said to watch and make sure she got on the plane when she did decide to leave.

"Got everything booked and ready to go, got my confirmation this morning. I'll be glad to get back home. I'm getting married in a couple of months and I have more things to do than I even want to think about."

"Married? Congratulations! Oh, I completely understand about having too many things to do," he said, grinning. "You brides always get in such a fluster before a wedding. Don't I know it!"

Kate was still standing there holding her hand out, and finally Johnson shook it.

"You're sure now?" he asked. "I don't mind helping you get these bags checked at all. No skin off my nose."

"No, you go on. I took up enough of your time yesterday. I just don't know what got into me. I was rude, and I'm really sorry about the way I treated you."

Johnson looked at her and nodded, placated by her apologies. "All right then, see you in the funny papers!" he said, waving as he got back into the SUV.

Kate watched him as he drove away. "Or in jail," she said, under her breath.

Quickly, she got The Beast rolling and went through the automatic doors of the airport, took a sharp right and went straight to the rental car counter. If she got started right away, she could be at the Rez by 2 p.m.

Chapter 7

Kate carefully put in the coordinates in the GPS application on her Smartphone and made sure she also had written down directions to the Rez independently, just in case things went wrong with the gadget. The lady at the rental car counter had said that the trip to Antelope Valley would take a little more than two hours, depending on traffic. It was a two-lane road for most of the way, and Kate was actually looking forward to seeing more of the Nevada landscape. The mid-sized sedan she had rented was boring but reliable, and surprisingly cheap. She had tossed The Beast in the trunk, and pulled out onto the busy roadway going north to Antelope Valley.

Kate turned on her favorite XM satellite station (fossil rock) and lost herself in the music for a while. The Rolling Stones were on with "Wild Horses," which she thought was very appropriate. The area around Elko was sandy, dry desert, without much green, except where there was watering and irrigation, but off in the distance she could see green trees and farm crops. Some of the trip wound through breathtaking canyons, and she was grateful that she was able to see them in the daylight (and not have to negotiate some of the unfamiliar sharp curves in the dark.) Occasionally, she saw free roaming cattle, and once, in the distance, she was excited to see what looked like a band of wild horses. There was quite a bit of traffic; lots of slow-moving trucks carrying construction supplies and also heavy equipment. When she was about 30 miles from Antelope Valley, she ran into some extremely extensive road construction, and she saw that the road was being widened in places from two to four lanes. She took the inevitable delays with some impatience, trying not to be apprehensive about her meeting with Sharon White Owl.

Kate had never been on an Indian Reservation before (aside for one brief trip as a child to the Cherokee Reservation in North Carolina) and didn't know what to expect. She had heard for years that some of them had the poorest populations in the United States, and were plagued with drug and alcohol problems. She did know that casinos in Indian Country had helped to bring in more income for the tiny nations, but she wasn't sure how that was working out for the tribes as a whole. She had looked up the Antelope Valley

Reservation and had noticed that the northern part of the Reservation had a large casino and golf course, which looked posh enough to rival some of the better casinos in Las Vegas or Reno. Not being much of a gambler, Kate had no intention of spending any time in the casino, unless the story took her there, but the pictures on the Internet had looked impressive. The golf course had hosted a few high dollar tournaments over the past couple of years; some of the big name acts had even come up from Vegas for various shows. She had noticed that the casino was far away from what seemed to be the main town of the Reservation (also called Antelope Valley) up in a scenic lake area. For whatever reason, be it the casino or something else, it seemed that Antelope Valley was prospering, just from the amount of activity she saw along the roadway. Once she crossed into the Reservation proper, there were many polite signs with the Reservation logo that said, 'Pardon our progress, we're moving Antelope Valley into the 21st Century.'

The last fifteen miles into Antelope Valley were slow going. Dump trucks carrying loads of gravel stopped traffic at will and the road was dotted with Natives in hard hats, with radios and handheld stop signs. Some had long braids or ponytails and Kate noticed that there were several women operating the heavy equipment. The whole area was such an impressive beehive of activity that Kate forgot to be aggravated. She could only imagine what the town would be like.

As she crossed into the city limits of Antelope Valley, she was so busy gawking that she forgot to pay attention to her driving and nearly rear-ended a car that had stopped short in front of her. The main street was crowded with traffic and the sidewalks with people, both Native and non-Native, all of whom seemed to be doing an extensive amount of shopping. There were many expensive looking arts and crafts stores, all brand new and attractively designed. Kate saw one thing that was quite a surprise; two Hassidic Jews were walking down the street talking animatedly to a Native man, then they turned and went into an expensive looking jewelry store.

The GPS began nagging her to turn left to get to City Hall. She absent-mindedly told it to shut up, for all the good it did.

She stopped and waited until the oncoming traffic had cleared, then took the left to go down to City Hall. Within a few blocks, she found it. It was a beautiful new building, designed by an obviously talented architect in flowing stucco that was painted with an intricate repeating design of turquoise and desert pink. Over to the left, she could see the headquarters of the Tribal Police Force and noticed a couple of uniformed officers leaving the building, chatting amiably with each other. Kate watched as one got into a new Toyota Prius and drove away, while the other pulled a mountain bike from a rack and rode off quickly in the other direction.

Kate pulled into a parking spot across the street from City Hall, got out, slung her laptop case over her shoulder and made her way across the street to the building. She reached for the glass door, noticing the colorful logo of the Tribe: an Eagle rising from a lakeshore, over the words 'Shoshone Tribe – Antelope Valley Indian Reservation.'

When Kate entered the building, a young woman in uniform with French manicured nails, a tiny nose stud, and straight white teeth smiled at her pleasantly and professionally.

"Ms Wyndham?" the woman asked.

Kate was a little nonplussed, both by the young woman's sunny manner, as well as the difference between the greeting she had received yesterday from Josie at the FBI's office.

"Yes, that's right. How did you know?" Kate asked.

"Lucky guess. Chief White Owl said a non-Native woman would be driving up from Elko today, and would be coming in to meet her. I know how long the drive is. I saw you park across the street in a rental car…" the woman shrugged eloquently.

"Good police work. Better than what I've recently become accustomed to," Kate said.

"I'd heard something about that. Chief White Owl is back with our IT technician right now; they are expanding our wireless network and are working on security. Let me see how much longer she will be. My name is Lelinda Shaney, by the way, Officer Shaney."

Officer Shaney reached up, lightly tapped an unobtrusive earpiece, and spoke into a small translucent microphone that curved around her cheek.

"Chief, Kate Wyndham is here now." She waited a few seconds while she received a response, then said to Kate, "They're finishing up. She asked if it would be all right if you two talked over lunch? She's starving."

"Sure, I'll just sit down and wait until she's done."

Lelinda Shaney nodded and relayed this message, then turned back to her computer screen.

Kate didn't have to wait long. Within ten minutes, a very tall Native woman in uniform came walking at a brisk pace down the long curving hallway that ran along the outside wall to Kate's left. She walked right up to Kate and held out her hand. Kate took it, noticing that the woman's hand was strong and a bit calloused. This was a woman who was not afraid to do manual labor from time to time.

Sharon White Owl was moderately attractive, with slightly slanted dark eyes, an oval face, and flawless dusky skin. At first glance, she looked to be a bit on the plump side, but Kate quickly noticed that there was far more muscle than fat. Formidable was the word that came to Kate's mind.

However, clearly she was also a woman with a sense of humor. As she watched Kate, her eyes were dancing.

"So they ran you out of Elko, did they?" she said, grinning.

Kate grinned back in spite of herself. "I guess you could say that. I do know they weren't sad to see me go – although they currently believe I'm on a plane back to Washington. I gave their press liaison the slip at the airport."

"Hah! Good for you! I guess you were dealing with that little ground squirrel, Mark Johnson."

"That's right."

"Poor woman," Sharon said. "Well, let's go get some lunch and you can tell me what you know. There's a place around the corner that makes great buffalo burgers. They come from the Tribe's own herd. You can leave your laptop with Lelinda."

Kate nodded, quickly removed the thin manila folder she had gotten from the FBI, stuck it in one of her handbag pockets and handed the laptop case over to Lelinda, who stowed it underneath her desk. Karen followed Sharon White Owl out the door and down the street. Sharon turned into a small restaurant on the corner that was packed with people. It was called 'The Buffalo Barn.' When Sharon walked in, a couple of men nodded to her and offered her their table.

"Don't leave on account of me. I don't plan on arresting you today…" Sharon said.

The two men just waved and walked out the door, grinning at Sharon and tipping their cowboy hats politely to Kate.

Sharon and Kate slid into the chairs the men had just vacated and Kate picked up the menu from behind a napkin holder and started looking through it. It seemed like it consisted of many varieties of buffalo burgers. Kate asked Sharon to order for her.

A highly efficient waitress came over, quickly cleared the table of the few items leftover by the departing men, wiped it down, and took their drink orders (water for Kate and a Coca-Cola for Sharon).

"The two guys that left are Tribal Elders, very respected here in Antelope Valley," Sharon said.

Sharon had an odd accent that Kate found pleasant. She rolled her 'R's' a little harder than most people, and the 'S's' in her speech were a soft whisper. Her voice was also a bit husky, deeper than a woman's voice normally was. Kate liked her.

The waitress came back and Sharon ordered in another language, which Kate assumed was her native Shoshone. It was a soothing language to listen to.

Sharon took a drink of water, peering curiously over the rim of the glass at Kate for a moment. "So, tell me what you know. Tony has filled me in on a few things, but I would like to hear your take on it."

In less than five minutes, Kate had told Sharon everything she knew about the disappearance of Lindy Abraham and Julia Evans. Sharon listened carefully, watching Kate's face, then held out her hand for the manila envelope Kate had stuck in the outer flap of her handbag. Kate handed it over. Sharon opened the envelope and spent a few minutes quickly reading through the documents. She lingered over the cell phone records and the testimony of the two nameless witnesses.

She looked up at Kate and shook her head. "The cell phone records weren't thoroughly researched, which is something that Tony had mentioned to me. These were just completed calls. At the cellular provider's Network Operations Center, there are engineers that can do a detailed search on incomplete calls – calls that people make that may turn up on a distant cell tower, but don't make it all the way through to the called party. I don't see any information here that shows that they asked the cellular provider to do this level of research. This is just a basic dump of billed calls."

"Also," Sharon continued, "this transcript of the witness testimony – I think it has been altered. Let me show you what I mean."

Sharon laid the transcript in front of Kate and pointed to a paragraph down at the end of the second page.

"Look at the language here, can you see how it has changed just slightly? Reading this transcript, even though it is overly redacted, you can sense a change in the language if you pay close attention. I'm guessing that these two witnesses are Hispanic, not unusual around here; probably a couple of *vaqueros* on their way to do some work on one of the ranches. But, just the way this reads 'We asked them if they needed any help, they said no, so we went on into Elko, like boss said.' Prior to this, these gentlemen apparently gave a lot of details about where they were going and what they were doing (you just have to guess on this as most of it is redacted), then suddenly, no details. Plus, the transcript indicates to me that these gentlemen spoke English well, until you get to that one sentence. All of a sudden they are dropping a pronoun...it just doesn't jive. I know it sounds thin, and it would never hold up in court, of course, but that's my gut feeling.

"I also noticed that Sam Conner took their statements." Sharon looked out the window of the restaurant for a moment. "Kate, I want you to know that unless I tell you differently, any conversation we have between us is off the record. If you have a problem with that, just tell me straight up and we can go our separate ways."

"No problem. You have my word on that, Sharon."

Sharon looked Kate levelly in the eye for a moment, nodded her head, and sighed. "I have never trusted Sam Conner. Never. Not from the first time I met him. I have nothing to base it on but a few isolated incidents and instinct. He's a dirty cop. I would bet my next year's salary on it." Sharon shook her head and sighed heavily.

"Well, I can't give you my impression of him. They managed to hide him from me quite effectively," Kate said, ruefully.

"Just damage prevention on their part," Sharon said. "Sam has been known to be a bit of a loose cannon in the past."

"He has connections in the area. Old and respected ranching family. One of the original non-Native settlers here..." she continued.

"I take it they don't care for the original inhabitants too much," Kate said.

Sharon shook her head sadly. "Old hatreds die hard in some people."

"So what can we do? Seems like they hold all the cards," Kate said.

Sharon looked up and smiled at the waitress who brought two excessively large burgers on homemade buns, together with hand cut fries.

Sharon poured some ketchup on her burger, took a bite, chewed carefully, and then set it down.

"Well, if we do a search on the cell phone records, a THOROUGH search, and we find out that they made some calls AFTER this last phone call at 4 p.m., and these calls were made inside the Reservation, there may be something we can do."

"Any help you can give would be appreciated by whole lot of people, not the least of which are the grieving families of two dead women," Kate said.

"I know, but don't get your hopes up," Sharon said. "It may take a day or two to get that information from the cellular provider. It just depends on how busy their engineers are. There are a couple of managers I know that might help to push the matter along given the circumstances. I've developed a relationship with them over the past few years; we sometimes have tourists wandering off into the desert thinking they are on some kind of 'vision quest' or something. They get lost and we have to go fetch them. We use the GPS coordinates to track them down whenever possible."

Kate smiled, nodded and took a bite of her buffalo burger. It was delicious.

"May I keep this for a bit?" Sharon asked, holding up the manila envelope and the documents Kate had given her. "We can make copies for you."

Kate nodded, her mouth full of food.

"Where are you staying?" Sharon asked.

"Well, I just figured I would go up to the casino and check into the hotel there. I noticed that most of them here seem to be full."

"You won't find a hotel room in this town, honey," Sharon said, grinning. "We are having our annual fall festival, pow-wow, golf AND fishing tournament, and there is literally no room at the inn."

Kate felt a small surge of panic. This was an unexpected development.

Sharon grinned at her, setting her burger back down on the plate.

"I've heard that you're a horse person. Is that right?" she asked.

"Well, I used to be," Kate said, looking away and feeling a slight tightening in her chest.

"I knew you would be in a jam, so I had one of my daughters clean up the apartment in our barn. We use it when one of our mares is foaling, and my oldest daughter lived in the apartment for a while, prior to getting married and moving off on her own. It's just a studio, but it's clean, and it's free."

"The Gazette will be glad to pay you the going rate…"

Sharon held up her hand in denial, and shook her head.

"No, the only payment we require is that you consider helping out with some of the barn chores," Sharon said. "Kimama, my oldest daughter, is about eight months along with her first baby and she will greatly appreciate anything you might be willing to do. She has been our barn manager in charge of our horse breeding operation for several years, and is having a bit of a hard time getting everything done that needs to be done. Nothing too difficult, mind you, or too time consuming."

Kate swallowed the lump in her throat and nodded her head mutely. "I'll be glad to help any way I can," she said quietly.

After lunch, Kate followed Sharon back to the police station. When they walked in, Lelinda was waiting for them.

"We have you a temporary office set up, Ms. Wyndham," she said, glancing at Sharon and nodding, "and I moved your laptop over there. Semilla, our IT technician, will help you get onto our wireless network whenever you are ready. I just need to give her a call."

Kate stared, her jaw slightly agape at this generosity and efficiency. She knew she had planned poorly for this trip, as so often happened when she had to jump because a story took an unexpected twist. She had grown a bit Blanche Dubois-like in her expectations at times. Strangers always seemed to be willing to help those who were apparently helpless.

But this cooperation in a police force was unprecedented and although Kate was ecstatic at the level of access, a little part of her grew suspicious. It was like they were being TOO cooperative.

Sharon White Owl seemed to have the uncanny ability to read minds, however.

"Don't think we are going to monitor your Internet doings, or intercept your emails, or expect anything but fair and honest reporting," Sharon said, patting her on the shoulder, then she turned to walk back down the hallway. "I'll come get you around 6, and we'll go to out to the ranch, and I'll see you get settled in," she called back over her shoulder as she left.

Kate nodded to her retreating back and turned to Lelinda. "OK, if you can get me set up, I'll start to work. I'm behind on a lot of things."

Lelinda smiled and Kate followed her down a hallway of real offices instead of cubicles. In the center of the building was a cleverly designed and relaxing series of rooms, with gently curving walls painted with a subdued version of the same pattern that was on the outside of the building. One or two police officers worked quietly at computer terminals, along with a couple of support staff. It seemed the Tribal Police Force was pretty small. Lelinda led her to one of the last rooms along the hallway.

"This building is so restful and beautiful. Who designed it?" Kate asked.

"One of our Tribe members who is currently living in Los Angeles did. He has a degree in architecture from Notre Dame, but he works as a painter and has his own gallery in Bel Air. When the Tribal Council decided to build a new City Hall they contacted him and asked him to design something that was functional, beautiful, and that fit in with our culture. He came up with the design remarkably quickly. And here we are. He actually came out and oversaw the construction himself. Gave the contractor that built it nightmares, but we achieved our goals: beauty, form, and function."

Lelinda went on to explain that the designer had worked with an environmental engineer to incorporate cutting edge technology with the design. The building was 100% solar and wind powered. Kate was interested to learn that the Tribe actually sold surplus electricity back to Nevada Energy.

Kate nodded, a little overwhelmed and lost in all the technical explanations, but she was pleased that the Tribe had gone to such efforts to build Green. Lelinda ushered her into her new digs, and she set Kate's laptop case down on the floor. Kate noticed that the office even had small curved openings in the wall that let light into the room, and gave a view not only to the hallway, but also to a floor to ceiling window that overlooked a desert garden. She had a hard time believing that this was even an office, much less a police department.

She had had just enough time to get out her laptop and power it up when a short, plump, cheerful young Native woman came bustling into her new office.

"Hi, I'm Semilla, from Tribal Information Technology. Lelinda asked that I come over and make sure you get on our wireless network. It's not too complicated. I just need to get your wireless interface up on your laptop and enter in our security code. If you could just login with your normal ID, please?"

Kate nodded and logged into her machine, then gave her laptop over to the girl. Her fingers tapped a series of commands with dizzying speed. Then she turned the laptop back to Kate.

"There, all done. You are on our Wi-Fi network now. We have fiber broadband here, so you should have very good speed." Semilla turned to go, but Kate stopped her.

"Where did you go to school?"

"UCLA, then I worked for a couple of years in Silicon Valley. My husband had lived in Antelope Valley as a boy, and we hooked up at UCLA. After graduation, we both worked at Google for a while. Not too long ago the Tribal Council asked us to come back; I work on the IT side, and my husband is the technical director of the Tribal Internet and Radio station, which is on the other side of City Hall."

"You look happy," Kate said, smiling.

"Best decision we ever made. The best. When we left here, a good part of our spirits were left behind, but they were waiting when we returned. It's good to be whole again."

Kate nodded, a bit confused.

Semilla looked at her and smiled warmly. "If you have any problems or questions," she said, "just ask anyone around to give me a call and I will come over as soon as I can to give you a hand."

"Thank you so much, Semilla."

"No problem," Semilla said, waving as she walked quickly away. Kate noticed that she was soon talking into the small earpiece that everyone here seemed to use for communication. Clearly, this Indian Reservation had decided to embrace technology with a vengeance. The Gazette wasn't even this advanced – they didn't even have a Wi-Fi network.

Kate sat down and began checking her email. There were no emails from John, but several from Harlan Finney and Meyers. Kate went through them quickly, answered what she could, and then moved onto researching the Antelope Valley Reservation.

It was interesting reading. Twelve years prior, Antelope Valley had been one of the poorest communities in the United States, with an unemployment rate of 65%, widespread drug and alcohol abuse, domestic violence – a community that seemed spiritually and emotionally bankrupt.

Then, something unprecedented happened. One man by the name of Martin Levi, who was currently the Shaman of the local Native American Church, had gone to Israel, attended rabbinical school, and spent time in kibbutz. He worked very hard and learned how a small nation survived among enemies. Martin Levi came back to Antelope Valley with new ideas, and once he shared them with the members of the NAC congregation and Tribal Council, the people of Antelope Valley began to make changes.

One of the first things they did was to start calling on Tribal members living outside the Reservation for help on various projects, the primary one being the approval for construction of a new airport and casino in the scenic northern area of the Reservation. Investors were courted (apparently many were Israeli), and they soon had the airport and casino projects going. The casino had now been operational for five years, and was wildly successful.

Tourists who wanted to experience the beautiful scenery of the Reservation, as well as gamble and play golf at the world-class golf course, flocked to the resort. One thing that helped was that the entire resort was about half the price of most other similar venues, and aggressive negotiations with airlines had made flights from Las Vegas, Boise, Salt Lake City, and even Seattle very inexpensive. The new road construction would open up another avenue for people to easily drive to Antelope Valley.

Much of the casino was powered by solar panels and the wind, and with the Green Movement finally making headway in America, these innovations gave people a sense of smug satisfaction that they were helping the environment as they gambled, drank, ate in the 4-star restaurant, and played golf in a place where antelope could sometimes be seen on the greens. The bi-annual Native powwows were extremely popular. The tourists and guests loved anything they perceived as being 'originally Native' (and Kate had to admit that the casino management seemed to keep the exploitation of Native culture to an absolute minimum). The new road construction would not only bring in more tourists, it would also provide even more jobs.

Martin Levi and the Tribal Council began to call the scattered Shoshone tribes people home with offers of a new life in the place where many would have preferred to live and raise their families had there been job opportunities.

Well, Antelope Valley had opportunity now – in spades. In fact, Kate decided that now they probably were suffering from a labor shortage, if anything.

It was one of the most amazing examples of bootstrapping that Kate had ever seen or heard about. The Tribal Council, under the guidance of Levi, brought home Native accountants and CPAs who worked to carefully spread the money between infrastructure, public works, social programs, and educational improvements, as well as a well-managed distribution of funds to the poorest families on the Reservation.

In addition, there was some indication that the local Native American Church was having phenomenal success with helping people with drug and alcohol addictions by engaging people in what they called 'habilitative' programs.

A group of people, all working together towards a common goal – surviving – and surviving well, and doing it with their honor and respect intact. And making efforts throughout the project to leave the lightest footprint possibly on Mother Earth, as bespoke their ancient heritage.

What a concept.

Kate also found it interesting that the Shoshone had learned so readily from Israel. She guessed that Holocaust survivors must speak a universal language.

Kate spent the rest of the time researching the Reservation's development and history. It was disturbing to her to see that it was currently only a fraction of the size that was given to the Nation in the original treaty – some of it had been sold off by Tribal Councils that were either unethical, desperate, or both. In other cases, the United States Government had simply reneged on the treaty and seized land for various purposes. An incident of this nature had happened relatively recently, when St. Martjin Mining had bid on mineral rights in an area that bordered on the Reservation, then slowly encroached more and more into Reservation territory.

The Tribal Council was pursuing numerous legal challenges to this violation of their sovereignty, but so far, the case had been held up in court. In one alarming incident, when a judge had issued an injunction for St. Martjin to stop work in the contested area, the company had ignored the judge's order and just kept on working. This had happened in the past year, and tensions between the Tribe and St. Martjin had increased dramatically. Someone had begun sabotaging St. Martjin's mining equipment, and in answer, St. Martjin had brought in an armed security force from the infamous U.S. Security Services, who provided security and armed protection for many United States government contractors overseas. There had been much controversy over the use of U.S.S.S. by the Federal Government in the recent Middle Eastern conflicts.

Kate considered them to be mercenaries, pure and simple. Tough, ruthless mercenaries. She had run into them in Africa, and though the experiences had been brief, they had been far from pleasant.

"Well, Kate, are you about ready to follow me out to the ranch?"

Kate jumped, startled. She had been so engrossed in the Internet research she hadn't even heard Sharon approach. Sharon grinned at her.

"You surprised me, I didn't hear you coming!" Kate stammered.

"Hah! Ancient Indian Secret – stealth is in our DNA."

Kate laughed and shut down her laptop and packed it into the case.

"Well, it's been a long day," Sharon said, "and I'm ready to head home. Are you ready to call it a day?"

"I may still want to do some work tonight."

"Don't worry about that. If you want to work out in the barn, we have Internet access there. Kimama uses it to monitor mares when their time is getting close, and also to watch the new babies for the first few days. All our foaling stalls have Internet cameras."

Sharon waited patiently while Kate got her belongings together and then the two women walked side by side out of the building.

"What kind of horses do you have?" Kate asked.

"Medicine Hat Paints –," Sharon said. "Some of the best in the country, if I do say so myself. Most of our young stock is in the money on the cutting and reining circuits right now. Kimama runs a very good operation – she has a Masters in Animal Genetics from the University of Arizona, and it is finally starting to pay off. And Kimmy doesn't overbreed either: 90% of the foals we have wind up, if not champions, good money makers and they ALL have good minds. We always leave open the option that we will take any of our horses back at any time in their lives if the owner no longer wants it, or can't care for it, and we mean it. I think it has actually helped our reputation in the industry."

Kate nodded. She had read Marguerite Henry's famous children's book 'San Domingo, the Medicine Hat Stallion' when she was a girl, and had been fascinated with this specific type of pinto horse for many years. Native Tribes of the Plains had a great deal of mythology surrounding the Medicine Hat horses. In Native lore, Medicine Hats were believed to have magical powers to protect their riders in battle, and also special skills in helping to find wild game. Traditionally, Medicine Hats were mainly white, but had colored patches covering the ears and the top of the head, although they could also have other markings. Most commonly, Medicine Hats now had a 'War Bonnet' on their ears and the top of the head, as well as a 'Shield' of color on the chest. Kate knew that to be able to breed to get this specific combination of color markings, as well as getting the body type for the demanding stock horse sports of cutting and reining, took a great deal of knowledge and skill on the part of the breeder. She was also impressed by the fact that Sharon's ranch was always willing to take back horses that it sold.

"And my brother has several mustangs that he works with," Sharon continued, "He won the Extreme Mustang Makeover in Ft. Worth last year with one of them. Jerry – that's the horse – is one of the best horses I have ever seen in my life. Of course, it doesn't hurt that Jim is ALSO about the best horseman I've ever seen. He starts all our young stock now. We send them out to the trainer once Jim gets them started."

"I've never been around mustangs much, but I've always been curious about them. I have heard a little about the Extreme Mustang Makeover, but can you tell me more about it?" Kate asked.

Sharon explained that the Mustang Heritage Foundation and BLM organized competitions across the country, where 100 trainers trained 100 wild horses for 100 days. The ones that successfully got their horses to the events competed for some pretty big prize money – six figures usually. Kate was interested to hear that children also participated in the event, with yearlings. From Sharon's description, it sounded like an amazingly entertaining horse show. After the competition, the horses trained by the adults were put up for adoption to the highest bidder, while children got to keep their horses if they wanted.

"Anyway, Jim won the Makeover competition in Ft. Worth last year, and he was able to outbid everyone to keep Jerry," Sharon said. "It was a good thing. It would have broken his heart to give up that horse. And probably would have broken Jerry's heart too."

"How hard are the mustangs to work with?" Kate asked, fascinated.

"Well, I think they are just like other horses," Sharon said, "some good, some not so good, some pretty, some not. Jim says they are a dream to work with because they come to us pure, never being handled by a human hand. There's probably something to that. Anyway, I will say they are hardy, healthy, and easy to take care of, overall. Jim's horses never seem to get sick much, although he told me yesterday that Cactus – that's one of his mares – had a hoof abscess. It happens to all horses I guess." She shrugged.

They had gotten onto the sidewalk and Kate pointed to her rental car. "That's me."

"OK, I'm in one of our Prius squad cars, which does give me a bit of advantage in all this traffic we have right now. I'll swing by and you just follow me, OK?"

"Sure."

Kate threaded her way across the busy street and soon saw Sharon pull up in the police car. Sharon flashed the lights a couple of times and whooped the siren briefly. The traffic magically parted and Kate was able to follow her out of town. They drove west for about 15 miles and the busy town of Antelope Valley soon gave way to neat ranches and circular irrigated fields. The mountains loomed in the distance in the twilight. Night was falling quickly, and the full moon was rising in the east, huge and orange. Kate could see it in her rear view mirror. In their infrequent stops, she turned and looked at it. Although this country could seem stark to the point of sterility at first glance, there was no doubt it was breathtakingly beautiful at times.

Kate followed Sharon as she turned up a wide gravel driveway, then waited while an electric gate opened on the road that Kate assumed went into the ranch. She had seen a gate header with some sort of sign or symbol on it, but she hadn't really been able to make out the name of the ranch. She had seen a large carved wooden sign that was painted with a Medicine Hat horse head with four feathers hanging on both sides and a mountain peak in the background.

They drove down the road for more than a quarter mile, passing a neatly kept singlewide mobile home, a small house of painted cinderblock, and a sprawling ranch house. As they passed the ranch house, Sharon turned to the right and headed towards a large new-looking stable. Under the security light, Kate could see another sign that said Toyakoi Stock Horses. The lights were on in the barn and Kate could see someone moving around inside. It looked like they were bringing some horses into their stalls for the night. Sharon pulled up and parked in a graveled parking area at the end of the stable. Kate pulled in next to her and got out.

"Well, here we are. Hope it will suit," Sharon said.

"I'm sure it will be fine." Kate felt the familiar tightness in her chest when she saw the horses in their stalls, but choked it down, grabbed her laptop case, and wrangled The Beast out of the trunk. As she followed Sharon into the barn, she was relieved that the barn aisle was brushed concrete, because The Beast's wheels had made a racket while rolling across the gravel outside. Kate had been afraid that it would scare the horses. However, the horses were being fed in their stalls and didn't even look her way as she made her way down the stable aisle. The building was big; it looked like it would hold 20-25 horses, and it was immaculately kept. Kate noticed that the person she had seen in the barn was a heavily pregnant young woman. She looked quite a bit like Sharon, and Kate realized this must be the daughter, Kimama. The young woman expertly put a lively younger horse in a stall, then turned to look at them. Sharon stopped, and Kate stopped behind her.

"Our new houseguest, Kimmy: Kate Wyndham. Kate, this is my daughter, Kimama," Sharon said.

"Most people call me Kimmy," the young woman said, smiling. She reached out and shook Kate's hand, then reached behind to rub her back, clearly uncomfortable. Kimmy was a large woman, like her mother. She was also in the latter stage of pregnancy and it seemed to be taking a toll on her. She looked tired and had large dark circles under her eyes. Her long hair was braided and hung down her back; she had been sweating even in the cool night air, and strands of black hair clung untidily to her face.

"Back aching?" Sharon asked.

"Not too much. The baby was kicking when I was bringing Little John in."

"You should get Jim or Marshall down here to help you," Sharon said.

"Uncle Jim is out today, went up to the Northside to help someone with a problem they were having with a horse, and Marshall ran into town to get to the feed store before it closed. I guess I should have waited until he got back. I won't make that mistake again."

Sharon patted Kimmy's shoulder and grabbed a chair that was sitting a little further down the aisle and pulled it up next to Kimmy.

"Have a seat. I'll show Kate the apartment," Sharon said.

"Thanks, Mom," Kimmy said, gratefully sinking into the chair.

Kate followed Sharon as she made her way down to the center of the barn aisle. She turned at an intersecting aisle way and started up a set of steep wooden stairs.

"Here, hand me either the laptop case or that other monster," Sharon said.

Kate handed her the laptop case and then followed her up a rather steep set of wooden stairs. Kate tried to lift The Beast as much as possible to keep the noise to a minimum, but it banged alarmingly a few times, and she fully expected to hear horses slamming into the walls of their box stalls, spooked by the noise. However, they all seemed unconcerned by her flailing about.

"We just have to get through this hayloft," Sharon said. "The apartment is down at the other end."

Kate was very thankful that there was a sturdy, smooth plywood floor. Generally, when she traveled, she carried a backpack inside The Beast so that she could repack and wear it if she went out into the field, but she hadn't brought it this time. She had never expected to have to drag The Beast around so much, plus she had packed in a hurry anyway.

They made their way through the neatly stacked square bales of hay until Sharon reached a large wooden door set in a wall at the end. She opened the door with a tug (Kate noticed that they had tightly weather sealed it to keep out dust and keep in the heat), and stepped inside.

"Well, here we are," Sharon said.

Kate stepped inside and nearly gasped in shock. The apartment was a good sized studio with a full kitchen, and sturdy furniture that looked handmade, but what caught her so by surprise was a complete wall of floor to ceiling windows at the far end that gave a magnificent view of the mountains in the distance, now clearly lit by the moon. The scene was positively breathtaking. The entire place would have cost a fortune to rent in DC, even without the windows.

Sharon laughed when she saw her face. "I never get tired of seeing the look on people's faces when they come up here for the first time," she said, setting Kate's laptop case down on the floor. "Kimmy insisted on these windows. Hank, my husband, hissed at her a bit about the added expense, but she dug in her heels, and she got her windows. They are some sort of specialized energy efficient windows that the contractor found for us. Anyway, now, every time Hank comes up here, the first thing he does is to walk to the windows and look at this magnificent view. Most of the furniture came from Tribal artisans, and I have to say, I think it is quite lovely. Of course, you can close the drapes if you want, but people rarely do."

"It is all gorgeous," Kate said earnestly. "How many square feet is this 'studio' anyway?"

"I guess about 700 square feet," Sharon said. "We have another hay barn down on the other side of the outdoor riding arena, which you can see below, so we had the luxury of building a good sized place here. Kimmy did live here for about a year, but mostly we use it for out of town buyers who come to look at horses. Everyone loves Kimmy's view."She went on to show Kate the bathroom, thermostat, and kitchen items. She also asked that Kate be conservative with the thermostat, as the barn was solar powered and they didn't like to waste energy.

"We have several blankets and quilts in here, made by my mom, so you shouldn't get too cold, I wouldn't think, plus this time of year the weather is relatively mild. And the bed is behind that screen over there, which was also made by a local artist."

Kate walked over and marveled at a standing screen that made a visual separation between the living and sleeping area. It was made of some dark, medium weight wood that almost looked like stone. A talented artist had carved petroglyph type artwork into the panels. She looked behind and saw a king sized bed, with a headboard that matched the screen. It was layered in soft looking pillows, blankets, and quilts in subtle colors of teal, brown, and cream. The entire room smelled slightly of cedar.

"This is wonderful, I can't thank you enough," Kate said.

Sharon just smiled. "That fireplace over there does put out heat but no flame," she said, motioning to a small fireplace set into the wall in the sleeping area, "It is just a fake flame really – we are all scared to death of barn fires around here."

Kate nodded in agreement. Barn fires had always been one of her biggest fears when she had had Manny.

"By the way, you may not be thanking me so much when I give you the next bit of news. All guests are expected to report at the main ranch house for dinner – breakfast and lunch too, unless they can figure out a way to get out of it. Dinner is mandatory though. You have to suffer through the ruckus that calls itself our family."

"No problem," Kate said. "What time?"

"Eight o'clock – we have a late dinner because Hank and I always get home late, and please be on time. My mother is in charge of dinner, and she gets mad as a tom turkey when people are late. You can just walk up; it's not far."

"I'll be there. Do I need to go downstairs and give Kimmy a hand? She looked worn out," Kate said.

"No, you just get settled. I will take care of Kimmy. All the barn chores are done for now, and she just needs to put her feet up for a while. Her husband Marshall will be along shortly to pick her up and take her home. Kimmy and Marshall have received a special dispensation from Mother and they don't have to come to the family dinner. She says that Kimmy needs her sleep. Much to Kimmy and Marshall's relief, I think. The kitchen door is around back of our house; you can knock if you want or come right in, doesn't matter. We usually have at least six or seven for dinner every night, depends on who's around. Anyway, just try to be there around eight, and save yourself some grief from Mother. She doesn't take prisoners, strangers or no," Sharon said, smiling. She waved briefly as she walked out the door.

Kate sat down heavily in a chair at the small kitchen table and spent a moment collecting herself. It had been a long, rather intense two days and she felt a little breathless. She looked at her watch. It was a little after seven; she had a bit of time before dinner.

She got up from the table and walked over to 'Kimmy's View.' The mountains could be seen with great clarity in the eerie and beautiful moonlight.

She looked down at the riding arena for the first time and looking at it, felt a sudden yearning to ride for the first time since Manny had died. Someone, she assumed Kimmy, had taken great pains to make it a GOOD arena to ride in. Kate could see that the footing was good and even, and the fencing around it was both horse and rider friendly. At the far end, she saw some simple chairs and a patio table, and then she noticed there were actually lights and loudspeakers on either end. The arena was obviously well used. Sharon had also mentioned something about an indoor arena on the other side of the barn. These were very serious horse people.

Kate pulled The Beast up onto the longish sofa and undid the clasps. She quickly unpacked her clothes and other items, put a few things in a large chest that was located along the wall near the sleeping area, and set her toiletry items in the small bathroom. She considered taking a shower, but decided against it. She hadn't done much but sit all day long. She walked over to the kitchen, and opened several cabinets until she found a glass. She then got a glass of water, and took a long drink, suddenly thirsty. The water was pure and clean, with no chemical taste at all.

She looked at her watch; it was about 7:45, She decided to go ahead and walk up to the 'Big House' and see if they needed any help at dinner. Kate dreaded it. She hadn't been to a true extended family gathering in some time. She hoped this evening wouldn't be too awkward.

She changed from the pullover she had been wearing to a pale pink silk shirt that she liked for traveling because it didn't wrinkle. Her jeans and sensible shoes she had worn all day would be acceptable for a family dinner she thought. She brushed her hair (which had become unruly and tangled as always), put on some lipstick, and considered herself ready to go.

Sharon had not said anything about locking the door to the loft, nor had she left a key, so Kate didn't worry about it. She made her way through the hayloft and down the stairs. As she walked out, she found herself relieved that no horses came up to the 'gossip gates' – large v-shaped metal panels in the stall doors that allowed them to safely hang their heads out in the barn aisle to visit passersby and observe stable activity. She had not laid a hand on a horse since the last time she saw Manny alive; the very idea made her distinctly uncomfortable. However, all the horses were either intent on eating their dinners or napping quietly. Kate walked quickly past them, glad that none of them looked at her.

She stepped out into the moonlit night and walked up the driveway. It was a bit cool and she wished she had grabbed a jacket, but it was a short walk so she just hugged her arms closely to her chest and walked faster. Sharon's ranch house was long and low, with a porch that ran along the front of the house and wrapped around on the one side. When Kate approached more closely, she could see various chairs and one or two hammocks. A couple of dogs were lying on the porch; they looked like some type of cattle dog. One yipped briefly as she walked past, but for the most part they ignored her. Kate guessed they had become accustomed to strangers walking up to the house from the barn and didn't see her as a threat. The porch looked to be a very comfortable and peaceful place to sit.

Following Sharon's directions, she walked around to the back of a house. As soon as she turned the corner, she saw a lighted kitchen with several people moving around through a double glass patio door. Kate also noticed that a large flagstone patio ran along the back of the house for some distance. Clearly the White Owl family enjoyed their time outdoors.

Feeling very shy, Kate walked up to glass door and watched the scene in the kitchen a moment before tapping politely. The people in the kitchen were talking animatedly; an elderly woman stood at a large stove on the far side, alternatively scowling, talking, and waving a spoon at one person or another as she made emphasis on a point. A Golden Retriever sat at her feet, cleaning up anything that dropped from the spoon. A young girl, no more than six or seven, saw Kate, trotted over quickly and opened the door. She was obviously another one of Sharon's daughters; she was very pretty, with short cut black hair, large dark eyes and long lashes.

"Hi," she said brightly. "I'm Missy! Melissa, but everyone calls me Missy or just Mo. Are you really a reporter from Washington, DC?"

"That's right," Kate said, stepping past Missy into the kitchen. "I'm a reporter and I'm from Washington."

"I have a lot of questions then," the girl said pertly, taking Kate's hand. "Mom didn't tell us you were so pretty. I love your red hair! You have to sit by me!"

Kate stood there for a moment, feeling very awkward. All the people in the room were staring at her, expecting some kind of response. Gamely, she squeezed Missy's hand and squatted down beside her.

"I'll be glad to sit beside you. Tell me something, are you married?"

Then it was Missy's turn to look shocked; then she started giggling. "No. I'm not married. Are you?"

Kate shook her head, and stood up embarrassed. Everyone was still staring at her.

"Enough, Missy, enough," said a plump, plain middle-aged Native man who had been standing at the other end of the kitchen. He came over and held out his hand to Kate and she shook it gratefully.

"Hank White Owl. Sharon is just getting out of the shower. She will be down shortly. Now let me introduce you to the rest of our brood," he said. "The lady at the stove is Annie Ludlow, Sharon's mother."

The old lady turned for moment, looked at her with keen dark eyes that didn't show a bit of age, nodded briefly, then turned back to the stove and continued cooking. It looked like she was making a stew of some sort.

"This young lady," Hank said, pointing at a pretty teenage girl sitting at a large round kitchen table with a laptop, apparently working on homework, "is our daughter Dove, and she is Missy's older sister." Dove looked up briefly at Kate, smiled and went back to work.

Kate heard some footsteps coming through the house, and Sharon appeared, wearing a gray sweat suit. Her hair was damp.

"Well, I guess Jim is late as usual," she said. "Dovey, would you mind setting the table? I'll get the drinks."

"Uncle Jim called and said he was on his way," Dove said, shutting her laptop down and folding it up. "I talked to him just a few minutes ago. He went up to the Flying L to help with that new stallion they just got in."

Sharon shook her head and walked into the kitchen.

"I saw that stallion last week. Horse looked loco to me," Hank said. "Sometimes I wish Jim would go back to being a lawyer. It's a safer profession."

"Not for Jim," Sharon said obliquely, then she turned and started grabbing glasses out of the cabinets.

"What can I do to help?" Kate asked.

"Best thing is to just get out of their way," Hank said, motioning for her to come stand next to him. "They have their little routines worked out and don't like being interfered with. Cleaning up is a different issue; that's when we let the guests demonstrate their skills."

Kate grinned and moved over to stand next to Hank. He was a couple of inches shorter than she was, and seemed to be a man that was always in a good humor.

Kate and Hank talked for a bit about the weather, the flight out from Washington, and other inconsequential things. Just as Sharon put the last ice-filled glass on the table, Kate heard the patio door slide open and a man stepped into the kitchen.

Kate turned from Hank to look at the man and felt the world go still. For the rest of her life, she would never forget the first time she saw Jim Ludlow walk into that kitchen. It was as if there was a great bell ringing in the distance, one that could not be heard but only felt down deep in the spirit. She suddenly felt like a ship's captain, long at sea, who sets foot for the first time on the sandy shores of a beautiful undiscovered country and looking about, becomes awash with feelings of fear and wonder at the vast unknown lying at his feet. She shook her head slightly to dislodge this disturbing thought, and looked more closely at the man.

He stood there; calmly smiling, while the old woman at the stove scolded him in rapid Shoshone (Kate assumed it was for being late). The Golden Retriever trotted over to him, and the man squatted down lithely to rub the dog's head. When he stood up, Kate noticed that he was a good bit taller than anyone in the room, even topping her by several inches. He was lean and fit looking, in well-worn Wrangler jeans and a slightly dirty tan work shirt. His hair was clean and blue-black, tied by a leather thong into a ponytail that hung down his back.He   was   not   classically handsome; his cheekbones were too high and broad, his chin bit too strong; but he was incredibly striking, and Kate could not pull her eyes away from him for a moment. Something about his face was vaguely familiar.

"Jim, this is Kate Wyndham. She works at the Washington Gazette. Kate this is my always late brother, Jim Ludlow," she heard Sharon say.

Ludlow looked at her and nodded, still with the same calm smile on his face. Their eyes met briefly. His eyes were large and a lighter color brown than most Natives she had seen so far. He looked at her with calm interest, and Kate felt the tips of her fingers start to tingle, her mouth went dry, and her hands and forearms went icy cold.

She nodded quickly and dropped her eyes to the floor and turned back to Hank. She noticed Missy went to Ludlow immediately and began chattering at him like a magpie. He listened and nodded occasionally, his eyes coming back to Kate several times.

Annie Ludlow put the stew into a handmade pottery serving bowl and held it out to Ludlow. He kissed his mother briefly on the forehead (which brought a slight smile to her face, Kate noticed), took the bowl from her, and sat it on the table. Annie reached into the stove and pulled out a platter covered with a type of puffy flat bread that Kate had never seen before and also set it on the table.

Hank sat down at the table nearest the entryway that went back into the house, and Ludlow moved to a chair beside him. Kate stood awkwardly for a moment, not knowing where she should sit.

"Sit down at Hank's right, Kate. That's the seat we usually reserve for guests," Sharon said.

Kate slid into the chair and moved aside a bit as Missy hurried over to sit beside her. Dove sat on the other side of Missy; then Sharon sat next to her. Once everyone was seated, they all reached out to clasp hands; Kate awkwardly took Hank's large calloused hand in her right, and Missy's small plump one in her left. Everyone closed their eyes, and Annie said a few words in Shoshone, which Kate took to be a prayer or giving of thanks of some sort. Then, Sharon motioned for people to pass their bowls down to be served, and she began dishing up the thick, brown stew. The smells from the bowl were very rich and flavorful, and Kate realized her stomach was growling a bit.

Dove picked up the bread and tore off a small piece and started passing it around. When it came to Kate, she ripped off a small piece also and set it on a small saucer to her right. It also smelled delicious.

Like everyone else, Kate had passed her bowl down, making a concerted effort not to stare at Jim Ludlow. When she got her bowl back she took a bite of the stew. It was quite delicious, with a slight tangy flavor she had never tasted before.

"This stew is wonderful," she said, "but it has an unusual flavor. What is it?"

"Oh, Mother never gives out her recipes," Sharon said offhandedly.

Annie glanced at her daughter, then turned back to look at Kate.

"Juniper berries," she said simply, and went on eating. Kate noticed that she had few teeth, and chewed slowly. But, she had a dignity about her that Kate admired greatly.

Sharon laughed. "Kate, you should feel honored. Mother must like you. That's the first time I've ever heard her share her cooking secrets with a guest."

Annie gave Sharon a slightly venomous look, motioned at Kate, and rattled off something in rapid-fire Shoshone. Sharon and Dove looked from the old woman to Ludlow to Kate, their jaws slightly dropped. Missy giggled. Hank focused intensely on eating. Ludlow stared at his mother with wide eyes. Everyone sat in silence for one long moment.

"What?" Kate finally asked. "What is it?"

Ludlow had mercy on her. "Mother said you had the spirit of the 'Woman Who Became a Horse.' It's an old Indian legend, with a lot of variations. Basically, it is about a woman who left her husband because she loved her horse so much. After a time, she became a horse herself."

"That's not what she said, Uncle Jim," Missy said, giggling again.

"Missy, you hush up!" Dove said, glaring at her little sister.

Annie continued eating quietly, obviously pleased with the uproar she had caused with her observations.

Oh, please just let me die right now, Kate thought fervently. She tried to eat, but the food seemed to stick in her throat.

"Kate, you probably don't remember, but we actually met one time before, years ago," Ludlow said, smoothly changing the subject.

Kate looked up at him in shock. "What? Where?"

He smiled. "You were riding in a Point to Point steeplechase in Middleburg, Virginia."

Kate looked at him, stunned. "That's right, I rode with the Middleburg Hunt off and on for a couple of years. I don't remember where we might have met though," she said, puzzled.

"You had a fall on a jump, your horse got away. I caught him and returned him to you," Ludlow said, looking at her with the same easy smile on his face.

Now she remembered where she had seen him. She had gotten thrown that day, and there had been much confusion on the course. She had been searching frantically for Manny, who had run off after she fell, and then suddenly a good looking dark haired man had appeared, Manny in tow. He had had on a sports jacket and had short hair then, but the face was the same. She only had a chance to say thank you at the time, but she had often wondered who the man was; he had seemed so kind. She had asked John Ridley about the man, but he hadn't been forthcoming. She hadn't thought about that incident in years.

"I DO remember that. My mount got hit pretty hard in the shoulder by another horse and I fell. Manny, my horse, didn't care for steeplechase that much. I don't think I had much of a chance to thank you at the time. That was quite a while ago. It's a small world isn't it?"

"Yes, it is," Ludlow said, clearly pleased that she had remembered him. "That was a very nice horse you were riding that day."

"Yes, he was," Kate, said, feeling the familiar knot in her stomach whenever she thought of Manny. But she was grateful to Ludlow for changing the subject from the 'Woman Who Became a Horse' business, even though this was also another unbalancing turn in the conversation.

She noticed Ludlow looking at her thoughtfully for a few seconds. Somehow, she knew that he sensed that Manny was a painful subject and he did not pursue it.

They all ate in silence for a bit; then Missy spoke up, giggling again.

"Uncle Jim, don't you think Kate's pretty?" she said, her wide black eyes sparkling. Clearly, this one took after Grandmother Annie as far as mischief went.

Dove looked daggers at her sister.

"Missy, really," Sharon said exasperated.

Ludlow looked at Kate unperturbed. "Missy, I think everyone at this table is gorgeous, each in their own way," Ludlow said, smiling at Kate.

Again, Kate felt a rush of gratitude towards the man, and, thankfully, the rest of the meal proceeded without further awkwardness.

Once everyone had finished, Hank ushered the dog, Missy, and Dove into the living room; Dove grabbed her laptop off the kitchen counter as she left the kitchen. Dove looked briefly at her mother, but Sharon made shooing motions toward the living room.

"Go on, Dovey, finish your homework. Miss Kate can help out in here," Sharon said. "You don't mind, do you Kate? She's got a paper due this week."

"Of course not, Sharon. No problem."

Annie Ludlow stood up without a word and walked majestically out of the kitchen through the patio door. She had spent all afternoon cooking; cleaning was beneath her. Ludlow closed the patio door behind her as she left.

"Going out for her one cigarette of the day," Sharon said.

Kate looked around and saw Sharon and Ludlow quickly clearing the table. She pitched in and helped Ludlow clean the plates and seal up leftovers and put them in the refrigerator. Sharon rinsed the dishes and put them in the dishwasher. They all worked quietly and efficiently. Kate was grateful to have something to do with her hands. Within a few minutes the kitchen was clean, and Kate found herself standing awkwardly, leaning against a counter, trying to make a decision on what to do next. Did they expect her to go sit with the family? That thought was remotely terrifying. She just didn't do family well.

"Well, I guess I'll go back to the barn," she said, a bit lamely. "I'm pretty beat, it's been a long day."

"Suit yourself," Sharon said. "You can come down here for breakfast if you want, but there is some decent coffee up in the apartment. I think that tomorrow morning we may have the report from the cell provider about those poor girls' last locations, so maybe we'll get some good news, and the Tribal Police can look into this. You can ride in with me if you want, or come in on your own. I will warn you that I leave early, around 7 usually, and Hank is up and about before that with ranch chores."

"Sharon, I can't thank you enough. I just can't."

"Don't worry about it. I'll either see you in the morning or later on at the office, totally up to you. That office we set up is yours until you leave."

"Well, then, I'll guess I'll say good night. And tell Mrs. Ludlow thank you for wonderful dinner," Kate said.

Sharon nodded and smiled slightly.

"Kate, you don't mind if I walk with you up to the barn do you?" Ludlow asked suddenly, sliding open the patio door for her. "My mare Cactus is in a stall up there. She's had a hoof abscess and I need to check it and see if I can turn her out."

Kate felt a combined rush of panic and elation, and prayed fervently that it didn't show too much on her face.

Stop it, she thought, *just stop it. You are not fourteen years old!*

"OK, sure," she said, surprised that her voice sounded so normal.

Ludlow closed the door after her as she stepped through. They walked out into the bright moonlit night. As they came near the porch, Kate noticed a tiny orange glow of a cigarette hovering ghost-like on the porch. She could see Annie Ludlow dimly in the porch shadows, the dogs lying by the old woman's feet.

"I think that's more than one, Mother," Ludlow said as they walked past.

Kate heard what she thought were Shoshone curses from the porch and she laughed a bit. Ludlow looked at her and grinned companionably, his teeth very white in the moonlight.

"The doctor told her she shouldn't smoke at all," he said. "But we choose our battles with her, and now we have got her down to one to three after supper. Although she always tells us it is just one."

Kate just smiled a bit, not quite knowing what to say.

"I know you felt pretty embarrassed in there at supper, but no one meant any harm," he said.

"I know. It was fine. I survived."

He nodded and they walked for a bit in silence.

"What were you doing in Middleburg, anyway? When you saw me in that steeplechase?" she asked suddenly.

Ludlow looked away for a few seconds, then sighed.

"I lived in Washington for almost ten years," he said quietly. "My wife had friends that were Hunt members; they would invite us to Meets, and sometimes we would go when we had time."

Kate felt crestfallen when she heard the word 'wife,' but couldn't help but be interested in this information. Jim Ludlow was not just some redneck Nevada cowboy. Hank White Owl had even mentioned something about him being a lawyer, but she sensed this was a source of pain for Ludlow and she decided to give him the same courtesy he had offered her and not pry further. It was difficult. She desperately wanted to know more about this man.

As they walked into the barn, Ludlow snapped on the aisle lights. The horses stood in their stalls, squinting their eyes, and blinking rapidly. Clearly they had been sleeping. The barn smelled of the clean richness of pine shavings, grass hay, and distantly of the earthy smell of horse manure.

"Sorry, guys," Ludlow said, as he passed the first stalls.

As they walked down the barn aisle, several horses came out and looked at them with sleepy interest, pushing their heads through the gossip gates as they walked by. Ludlow gave a couple of them a few pats, but Kate only stood by awkwardly. As they approached the stairs, Kate turned to say good night, but Ludlow reached out and gently touched her elbow. His brief touch immediately got her focus.

"Why don't you come down here and see my mare? I could use a little help, to tell you the truth," he said.

Kate stared at him, her mouth a surprised round 'O,' but he gently took her arm and the next thing she knew she was walking beside him down the barn aisle. It was almost like he had willed her feet into motion before she could flee upstairs.

Cactus' stall was the last one, and Kate noticed several rolls of the stretchy 'vetwrap' bandages, sterile cotton batting, and other veterinary-type items sitting on a small wall shelf just outside the door. The door to the mare's stall stood open, and a simple rubber covered chain stood across the doorway. Ludlow's mare watched them alertly as they approached, ears pricked forward.

She was a pretty thing, a dainty black, brown, and white pinto with a long white blaze down her face. She was taller than Kate had expected, and she looked to have some Thoroughbred or Arab blood. She nuzzled Ludlow's hand a bit, clearly looking for either a treat or some petting. Kate stood back a pace, again feeling the tight knot in her stomach.

Ludlow took a well-worn rope halter from a hook on the door and skillfully slipped it over the mare's head. He then dropped the stall chain and led the mare out into the barn aisle. He handed the lead to Kate without asking, and leaned over to look at the horse's bandaged right foot. Kate stood holding the lead rope stiffly, as Ludlow removed the wrapping. She felt a bit sick when the mare looked at her with her liquid brown eyes. The mare began nuzzling her hand and Kate flinched away as if she had been scalded.

Ludlow looked up at her.

"Cactus is more than a little spoiled, I have to say," he said. "We treat her like a pet really; she has such a sweet disposition. She won't bite, though, if that's what you're worried about."

Kate just nodded and looked at the horse again.

The mare looked back at Kate with a quizzical expression, as if she couldn't understand Kate's stiffness. Then she bumped her nose against the back of Kate's hand a few times, which was what Manny used to do when he greeted her.

Kate felt tears come to her eyes and without thinking she reached out to stroke the mare's neck.

It felt like coming home.

Kate stood still as the mare softly nuzzled her neck, ears, and hair. She felt the hard shell she had built around her heart start to crack then crumble entirely. How did she ever think she could give up something that had been so much a part of her life for so long? The emotion was overwhelming and she had to work hard to keep from crying outright.

She looked down and noticed that Ludlow was watching closely.

"See what I mean, Cactus is really just like a big dog," he said. "She has a lot of love to give."

He turned back to the bandage on the mare's foot. Kate saw that he had applied some sort of brown, mushy looking poultice inside the bandage. Ludlow wiped off the poultice and looked at her hoof carefully.

"Looks like I caught it in time," he said, pulling the foot slightly away from the mare's body to take advantage of the aisle way lights. "I used a poultice that really seems to work wonders on abscesses, although I don't quite understand why."

"Is it some Native treatment?" Kate asked, choking down the tears. She was determined not to cry in front of this man and was grateful to have something to take her mind off her emotions.

Ludlow smiled and shook his head. He set the mare's foot back down on the floor and stood up, brushing his hands off against the seat of his pants. "I don't think so," he said, "although an old Native taught me about it years ago. It's a combination of wheat bran and flax seed, boiled, and applied when still warm. I usually leave it on for an hour or so, twice a day. Clears an abscess up within 24 to 48 hours every time."

"I'd like to turn her out, of course. I think that would be the best way to work the poison out of that foot, but I would like to see how lame she is. Cactus would rather be out with her pasture mates, but that probably wouldn't be for the best if she were too sore. Those girls can get a little rowdy sometimes."

"She's really nice. I never would have thought a wild horse could be so, well, gentle," she said, scratching one of the mare's ears. Cactus leaned against her slightly. This had been one of Manny's weaknesses also.

"It was difficult in the beginning, but I was finally able to connect with her with some persistence," Ludlow said. "Kimmy was actually riding her in endurance competition up until she got pregnant. They were doing really well too. Now Kimmy wants to see if she can start a quality line of endurance horses by crossing some foundation quarter horse stock with some specially selected mustangs. Cactus here is the first mare she wants to use in the program."

Kate stroked the mare's soft nose, then looked up at Ludlow.

"You said you needed some help?" Kate asked, lifting an eyebrow.

Ludlow ran his hand over his head, then looked up at her sheepishly. Kate noticed that his fingers were long and slender, browned by the sun.

"Well, I was hoping you could give me an idea of how lame she is if I trot her down the barn aisle," he said. "You know it's really a tough thing to do on your own."

"Ok. I'll give it a try if you want."

Ludlow nodded his thanks and took the mare's lead from Kate. Cactus alertly lifted her head and followed him as he jogged briskly down the aisle. Her hooves made a brisk clip clop noise in the barn aisle as she moved. The other horses watched with interest, a couple of them snorting in pretended alarm as they passed.

"She looked OK, but bring her down again, let me see her coming forward," Kate called out, once he reached the end of the barn aisle. Ludlow waved and started jogging again towards her.

Kate kept her focus tightly on the mare's footfalls, watching and listening carefully for any irregularities in the rhythm as Cactus' feet hit the concrete aisle.

Ludlow slowed and brought Cactus to a walk, then stopped in front of Kate.

"So, what do you think?" he asked.

Kate smiled shyly, looked at the floor, and shook her head.

"Looks like she'll be fine for a night out with the girls. She seemed to be a tiny bit off when you first started out, but she quickly worked out of it."

Ludlow nodded in relief. "Thanks, Kate, that's kind of what I thought, but it's always good to get a second opinion. I was struggling with whether to turn her out tonight or not."

Kate looked at him, not believing a word of it. She could tell that this man had probably forgotten more about horses than she would ever learn. But, somehow he had sensed that she was in pain and wanted to see what he could do to help. By just giving her the opportunity to connect with Cactus, Ludlow had enabled her to take the tiny first step to start getting past the iron grief that had seized her since Manny's death.

Why he had done it, she had no idea. Maybe he was just one of those people who was a natural at fixing things that were broken. She didn't know, but she was grateful. He stood there, in the soft golden light of the stable, looking at her patiently, as if he somehow sensed what she was thinking.

Kate just smiled and nodded. "All right, Jim. Good night. I was glad to help, and I'm sure Cactus is going to be fine."

"OK, many thanks," he said. "I hope these horses don't keep you up too much tonight."

Kate gave Cactus another pat and smiled to Ludlow as she walked past to head up to bed.

Ludlow stood stroking Cactus' neck, and watched as she walked away, glad to see that some of the tenseness and unhappiness he had sensed in her had dissipated.

When he had walked into the kitchen earlier he had been slightly shocked at her appearance. She had stood by Hank, hunched forward and pale, her gingery shoulder length auburn hair seeming to drain the color off her face, which was milk pale and sprinkled with faint brown freckles. Her gray-green eyes had been downward looking, almost as if in shame, after they had had their brief introduction.

It was always surprising to him that the memory of their brief encounter in Middleburg had remained so clearly etched in his mind. So much of the ten years he had lived in Washington had vanished in an alcoholic haze. But Kate Wyndham had been in his mind off and on many times since that afternoon so long ago.

When Sharon had told him that Wyndham was coming to do a story on the missing wild horse advocates, he had felt a sense of elation, quickly followed by nervous anticipation, for Kate Wyndham was something of a minor obsession of his.

The afternoon they had had their brief encounter in Virginia, he and his wife Madeleine had been attending the steeplechase as a 'workable,' as Madeleine called them. He remembered it had been a warm sunny April day. They had arrived just after the third race, and were standing with a crowd of Madeleine's friends waiting for the next race to start. In one break in the conversation, Madeleine had taken his arm and pointed out a tall man standing just a few feet away from them.

"There's John Ridley, Jim," she had said quietly in his ear. "I know you've been trying to get in to talk to Senator Dotson for a while and haven't had much luck. He's the guy you need to connect with. He's an analyst in Dotson's office and Dotson listens to him. You won't get a better opportunity than this."

And Madeleine had turned back to her friends.

At the time, he had been a lobbyist and had been trying to get together with Dotson for a couple of weeks. He wandered over to the man and stood next to him for a moment.

"Do you know what the next race is?" Ludlow asked the man politely.

"Fourth Maiden race," the man responded, then he looked at Ludlow for a moment.

"Have we met before?" he asked.

Ludlow held out his hand and shook John Ridley's hand with a smile.

"Just briefly, not too long ago, at a fundraiser for Congressman Brighton. I'm Jim Ludlow."

"Now I remember, from American Minerals, right?"

Ludlow nodded and gestured out onto the field. "What's your interest here, John?" he asked.

"Probably about the same as you. To see and be seen. But, my girlfriend is riding in this next race."

"Really? She must be quite a horsewoman."

Ridley rolled his eyes and shook his head in exasperation. "For years. You may know her, Kate Wyndham; she's a journalist at the Gazette."

"I haven't met her, but I love the work she does. She's a great writer."

Ridley nodded, and the two men talked legislative shop for a while. Ludlow was just getting around to seeing if he could get an appointment with the Senator when a young woman came up to Ridley and kissed him on the cheek.

"Sally! Good to see you," Ridley said. He motioned to Ludlow. "This is Jim Ludlow of American Minerals. Jim, Sally Mason; she's working as an intern over at Federated Securities."

Ludlow nodded towards the girl, then tactfully looked out towards the course as Sally Mason whispered something in Ridley's ear. Ridley laughed and gave the girl a hug. Ludlow noticed his hand strayed close to the woman's pert bottom in a very familiar fashion. A womanizer, then. Ludlow filed that information away for future use. It was always helpful to know these little details about people on the Hill. Sally walked away with a soft goodbye and a fluttering of lashes at Ludlow. Ludlow shook his head ruefully and smiled. Sex was one of the coins of the realm in DC. Ludlow had no problems staying faithful to his wife, but he knew for many others that was not the case; too many temptations and too many Sally's.

Suddenly, there was a thunder of hooves and Ludlow saw the next race had started. The horses were coming down the jump course in brightly colored waves as they took each fence. The riders had on jockey silks and were jewel-bright in the blazing Virginia sun.

"That's Kate there," Ridley said, pointing down towards the group. "She's in the green and white silks."

Ludlow watched as the riders came closer, and he saw the woman Ridley had pointed to. He couldn't tell much about her under her helmet, but she looked tall and was whipcord thin. Her horse was a big, solid chestnut, clearly a Thoroughbred.

"So, are you a horseman, Jim?" Ridley asked.

"Once. Long ago. Now I don't have the time," Ludlow responded.

"Don't I know it," Ridley said then he turned back to the race. "Here they come."

As the group approached the fence, up course from where Ludlow and Ridley were standing, Ludlow saw a horse swerve into the big chestnut Kate was riding and he almost went down right on the brush fence as they were sailing over. Kate fell, hit the round coop underneath the brush, and slid to the ground, barely escaping getting trampled. Her horse continued to run with the pack for a moment, then broke off, clearly panicked, and ran uncertainly on the course between the two jumps.

"Oh hell," he heard Ridley say in a disgusted tone.

Ludlow quickly ducked under the course barrier, and approached the horse slowly. Running after him would only increase his fear. The horse looked at him, wild-eyed, but Ludlow talked soothingly to him and he finally allowed Ludlow to take the reins. The gelding reared and plunged a few more times, but Ludlow continued to talk in quiet tones to him, and eventually the horse began to calm. He moved him to the side of the course and stroked his neck gently.

"Oh Manny! God, is he OK?" he heard someone say. He turned and saw Kate Wyndham coming towards him. She was walking slowly, taking care not to frighten the horse further.

She was a mess. Her face was scratched and bloody; her now filthy jockey silks were ripped; the strap of her helmet was loose and flapping around her face. Bright auburn hair hung untidily from underneath her helmet and her white breeches had a long green grass stain on them. But when she looked at the horse she called Manny, Ludlow thought she was the most beautiful woman he had ever seen. For a few seconds, he stood dumbstruck, marveling at her large gray-green eyes so filled with concern and worry for her horse.

"I think he's fine," Ludlow managed to say, as she came up and took the reins from him.

They stood there for a moment looking at each other, both stroking the big horse's neck. Their eyes met, and Ludlow felt an odd resonance in his spirit, as if he and this woman were somehow notes on some exquisite, joyful, harmonic chord; a chord that he never even knew existed within himself. It was a deep and profound feeling, unsettling and wonderful, and he hoped the moment wouldn't end.

"Kate! Kate, for God's sake, are you all right?" John Ridley yelled from just behind them.

Kate turned to face Ridley and the moment passed.

"I'm fine, John, just a little banged up. Manny's fine. This nice man caught him for me," she said.

"Well, they want to clear the course and you're a disaster," Ridley said. "Let's get somewhere and get you cleaned up. Jim, just call the office on Monday; let's see if we can get together for lunch."

Ludlow had nodded then watched the pair as they walked away, leading the now calm horse. Kate looked back over her shoulder at him for a moment and smiled. He had thought his heart would stop. Then, he heard Madeleine calling him and he had turned and gone back to her.

He had kept up with Kate over the years, read her stories online, and followed her career as much as he could. Once he had listened to a National Public Radio report she had recorded while on assignment in Africa five times, just to hear her voice. When he thought of John Ridley with his hand on the young intern's rear, he was seized by a fierce anger that was completely out of character for him. How could anyone who had a woman like Kate Wyndham ever think of looking at another?

Now she was here. Against all odds, she was here in Nevada on his ranch.

Something had changed in Kate Wyndham though. Her reluctance to talk about her horse told Ludlow that the horse was no longer with her; clearly he had either been sold or had died. He couldn't imagine her ever selling the horse, so he had assumed that the horse had died. For some people, the grief at these losses could be terrible.

But there was something else amiss with her; the pale, awkward woman in his sister's kitchen was not the woman he remembered. She was just as pretty, but now she seemed cowed and defeated. Like most little daydreams, his memory did not jive with the reality, but he realized that he had a very deep level of concern about her. He found the very thought of her being unhappy profoundly disturbing.

His rational mind fought against this. He had to remind himself that he wanted no entanglements as the last one had nearly destroyed him.

For most of Ludlow's adult life, he had frequently been the object of feminine interest. In his younger years, taking what they offered seemed as natural as breathing, and also like breathing you never grieved or wondered about a breath once it was done. Then he had met Madeleine. Sparkling, beautiful Madeleine. She had settled in him like the clearest and purest mountain air. Even now, there wasn't a day that went by that he didn't think about her, though their relationship had been destructive in so many ways.

Part II
Ludlow

Chapter 8

Ludlow and Madeleine had met during their first year of law school at UCLA. She had come from UC-Berkeley, but Madeleine Greenstreet had been from old money San Francisco and had nothing but disdain for the so-called 'granola nuts' as she called the majority of the Berkeley student body. While not a fiery conservative, she clearly leaned very hard to the right politically.

Somehow the two of them had wound up in the same study group in their first year, and Ludlow had been fascinated with the beautiful, vivacious Nob Hill blonde with the razor wit and legal mind to match. She had been a superb Constitutional scholar, and was very traditional in how she felt the courts should apply the Constitution to present day legal challenges. They had spent many late nights arguing the law, but she never showed the slightest interest in him sexually until their final year. One night, after a mini-celebration after midterms, she had followed him up to his tiny bedroom in the small group house he shared with some other law students. She had very matter-of-factly taken off her clothes, kissed him long and hard, told him that she loved him, and had since they first met. It had seemed to him that even with his previous experience with women, he had been a virgin until that night.

They had lain awake all through that amazing night, alternatively making love and talking. Madeleine told him she wanted to marry after graduation. Again, Ludlow was stunned at her boldness, but as he had been in love with her for nearly three years, he didn't argue, only agreed wholeheartedly. He talked to her about his love of the ranchlands of Nevada and how he would always consider it to be home. He told her of his long and deep love of horses, which had had to be set aside during law school. Madeleine had listened intently, her blue eyes bright in the light of the streetlamp outside, her small hand resting lightly on his bare chest. She had said she wanted to know everything about him. So he had told her.

When he was growing up, he had always worked on the family ranch and had been the one that broke and trained the ranch horses for stock work once he was old enough. He had learned much of the 'way of the horse' from Annie Ludlow's father,

Johnny Elk, a phenomenal horseman. Johnny Elk had taken the place of Ludlow's father, whom Annie had run off the ranch with a shotgun when Ludlow was six (Ludlow's father had never come back after that for obvious reasons, although Ludlow did see him from time to time when he visited his paternal grandparents on their ranch outside Elko). Annie had no tolerance for drunkenness, and John Ludlow had come home drunk one too many times.

His grandfather had taught Ludlow that, for a Native to get ahead in the world, he needed to have a white man's education. Ludlow was intelligent and had been a very hard working and thoughtful student in the Reservation school. The scholarships to UCLA and law school had come relatively easily to him.

As an undergrad at UCLA, he had kept his hand in by working part-time as a wrangler on some of the movie sets. He had even managed to get some minor non-speaking parts in a couple of successful films, which paid well, but that was a rare occurrence. In the summers, he had gone back to Antelope Valley and helped his grandfather on the ranch. Johnny Elk was slowing down a bit, and needed the help. His sister, Sharon, and her husband had moved to Chicago a few years before; she had become a police officer while Hank had driven an 18-wheeler for a manufacturing firm. Ludlow offered several times to quit school to come back and help on the ranch, but Johnny Elk had repeatedly insisted that Ludlow should stay at UCLA and become a lawyer, as they had planned. That would be the best way to help their people, Johnny Elk had said.

When he had started law school, he worked as a legal intern in the summer, and part-time at a small legal firm on one of the California Indian Reservations during the term. His trips home had been brief and infrequent.

Ludlow still missed Nevada deeply, and hoped one day he could go back, even though he knew there were few opportunities there.

Madeleine had hugged him hard when he finished his story, and gave him a penetrating kiss that stirred Ludlow in a very strange way, different than any other woman. Madeleine was like the wild rivers he knew in the West, beautiful and thrilling, but once they caught you in their complex currents, the best thing was to ride it out. And Ludlow was caught; fighting against something so powerful would only bring destruction.

When the two of them had graduated from law school, Johnny Elk, his wife Sarah, Annie, Sharon and Hank had come to the graduation ceremony.

When the ceremony was over, Ludlow's family came over to hug him. Johnny Elk had been so proud; he did not cry outright, but he clutched Ludlow's hand in his own well-worn ones, wordlessly, with tears in his eyes. This was a great moment for him; one that he had never thought he would live to see.

Madeleine came over with her parents, who were still as polished and stiff-necked as Ludlow remembered from the first and only time he had met them in San Francisco. To Ludlow, they were like the polished silver tea set they kept on the antique sideboard in their massive dining room; pretty to look at, of exquisite construction, but high maintenance, and not much use to anyone. They had made it clear in a very politically correct way that they did not approve of Madeleine's fiancé, but didn't really have enough interest in the matter to interfere.

However, when they stood next to Ludlow's family, it was a jarring contrast. Johnny Elk was dressed in clean pressed Wrangler jeans, his best cowboy shirt, also clean and pressed, and a bolo tie he had had made from the Silver Star he had been awarded for gallantry as a Marine in WWII. His long thick graying hair was braided in two neat plaits that hung well below his shoulders, and he sported a new black felt Stetson that Sharon had bought for him. Sarah and Annie had worn their two nicest cotton dresses and Sharon a fitted pantsuit, while Hank had worn a suit that he must have bought in high school. Ludlow had thought it was much to Hank's credit that he could still get into it.

Madeleine and her parents, in their designer clothes and expensive jewelry, made Ludlow's family look dowdy and hickish, even primitive. It was the first time he could ever remember being even a little bit ashamed of his family.

Madeleine took it all in stride though, and was as bright and vivacious as always. She had made a reservation for all of them to have dinner at one of the trendy restaurants in LA, but her parents begged off, saying they had a benefit they had to attend the next day and needed to get home right away. Ludlow saw the hurt in Madeleine's eye when they said this, but she covered it quickly from long practice, kissed them both on the cheek, and was soon talking to Sharon animatedly as they worked out dinner logistics.

Once they were settled in their large booth in the restaurant, they were surprised when a well-known actor (two Academy Awards for best actor, and many other honors) came over to their table, introduced himself, and asked politely if he could shake Johnny Elk's hand. Johnny Elk had stood up, pleased, and greeted the man warmly, although he had no idea who he was. Johnny had always been a gracious and friendly man, but far too busy for movies and celebrities. He asked the man if he would like to join them for dinner.

The actor shook his head, a bit embarrassed and abashed, then went onto explain that he was an advocate for Native American rights, and felt it was a privilege to see an Elder like Johnny Elk in Los Angeles. Then he noticed the bolo and asked about it.

Johnny Elk had sighed and looked away. "Oh, they gave me this a long time ago, on Okinawa, in that Big War," he said, touching it gently and almost reverently with his right hand. "I am still not sure why, I was just doing my job, like a bunch of other guys. I didn't like that war much, but I come from many generations of warriors, so it was my duty, that's all. I wear this in their honor. For them and those other Marines that didn't come home. My friends. I lost many friends on Okinawa."

The famous actor looked at Johnny Elk with what looked to be real tears in his eyes (Ludlow had a poor opinion of actors as a rule, from his time working on movie sets but in this case, the man's emotion seemed genuine).

Then, Johnny Elk had pointed to Ludlow and smiled broadly. "This is the newest generation of warrior. He just graduated today from the California Law School. He will be a new kind of warrior, a better kind. Without all those bullets! Much better for him, I think." And Johnny Elk had chuckled.

The actor looked at Ludlow for a moment, then pulled out his wallet and dug around in it briefly. He pulled out a business card and handed it to Ludlow. "This is my agent. Please, call him. If you need a job, you have one."

The actor shook Johnny Elk's hand again, nodded to the women and Ludlow, then said again, "I am quite serious, call Cy tomorrow – his cell number is on the bottom of the card. He won't mind you calling on a Sunday. He'll find you a place on our team."

With that, the famous actor had left, after courteously wishing them good night. Ludlow had noticed that most of the people in the restaurant were staring, and when the actor returned to his own table, there was a low level buzz of discussion about what had just happened.

The rest of the evening had gone very well after that, at least for Ludlow and his family. Sharon and Annie had known exactly who the actor was, and they were very excited and star struck. They chattered happily about how lucky they had been that the man had come to talk to Johnny Elk. Johnny Elk, much to his pleasure (and embarrassment), was treated as something of a celebrity himself. Service, though already good, improved dramatically and one shy, very plain young woman had even come to ask for his autograph. Johnny Elk had been very puzzled by this, until Sarah had told him irritably in Shoshone to sign his name on the woman's napkin so they could have some peace and quiet.

Madeleine, however, had been very quiet and subdued throughout the meal, and had only toyed with her food. When the waiter told them that the famous actor had picked up the tab, she had been stonily silent in a way that puzzled Ludlow. He thought she would have been pleased to save some money, and was a bit worried about her. He reached for her hand one time under the table, and she had clasped it gratefully, but then Annie said something very amusing in Shoshone, and Ludlow had laughed and Madeleine's hand had gone limp in his.

"OK, everyone, Maddy doesn't speak Shoshone, so let's not be rude," he had said quickly.

Madeleine had only looked at him wanly and clutched his hand, then turned and smiled gamely at everyone else. They were all looking at her with concern.

"No! No problem at all," she had said. "We're all here to have a good time!"

After that, dinner had been less animated, and Ludlow's family made a concerted attempt to include Madeleine in the conversation, but her responses, though courteous, had been brief and distracted.

Finally, the meal, which all agreed was excellent, was done and they made their way from the restaurant. When they stood up to leave, people nodded to Johnny Elk, clearly convinced that he was a person of note, and he smiled back at them with enthusiasm, even stopping at a couple of tables briefly to chat on the way out.

"Sharon," he said, touching his granddaughter briefly on the arm, after he picked up his new hat from the coat check, "it must be this fine hat you got me. Everyone notices when a man has a fine hat."

Sharon had smiled and hugged him. There was no one in the world like Johnny Elk to make a person feel good.

"He'll be wanting to be a chief next, the old fool," Sarah had said irritably to Ludlow in Shoshone. She never liked it when her husband got too much attention. She didn't want him to become spoiled, as she had told Ludlow repeatedly over the years.

As they walked out onto the street to get cabs for Johnny Elk and the rest, his Grandfather had said, "Jimmy, I can't understand why you have told me that these people are not good people. This is the friendliest town I have ever been in. Why, that man that gave you his card, he was a good man, a very good man. He said he would give you a job! I think this is a good place."

Ludlow had laughed at that, and patted his Grandfather on the shoulder. "For you, it probably would be, sir," he said.

Ludlow's family had headed back to the hotel where they were staying, and they all made arrangements to meet in the morning for breakfast, before Johnny Elk and the rest had to drive back home. The valet brought Madeleine's BMW sports car and she took the keys from him and slid behind the wheel. But all the way back to Madeleine's apartment, where for all intents and purposes Ludlow had been living, she kept jerking violently at the gearshift, making the car lurch. She also was driving far too fast, and Ludlow stared at her, shocked. Madeleine was a cool and competent driver, always in control.

"Do you want me to drive?" he asked tentatively. Madeleine had told him early on that she always preferred to drive if there was ever any choice. She loved to drive her little sports car in LA traffic. Ludlow didn't mind; he had never really cared for driving anyway, especially in California, although he did have a small used car that he drove when he had to.

"No!" she said sharply. He looked at her, stunned to see that she was crying.

"Oh, Madeleine," he said. "What is it? What's wrong, honey?"

"Never mind."

"Please, please, just pull over for a minute and tell me what's wrong." Ludlow had reached and put his hand over her small one that was on the gearshift.

She turned to him angrily. "So, I guess everything is OFF now! Everything! Just because you lucked out and a Hollywood icon took an interest in a stupid fucking old Indian!" she yelled.

Ludlow had been too shocked to speak for a moment, but as Madeleine's driving became more erratic he finally grabbed her arm. "Madeleine! Pull over right now – right over there is a parking lot. You are scaring me with this crazy driving. Please. Let's talk this out."

So she had pulled into the parking lot of a busy Target store, and parked in the very back of the lot. By the time they stopped, she was sobbing uncontrollably, and Ludlow had taken her in his arms.

"Honey, please tell me what's wrong. I know this can't be about my grandfather – why would you say such a thing about him anyway?"

"Oh Jimmy," she said. "I've been offered a wonderful job in Washington and I want to take it! Please come to Washington. I need you there with me. I will just die if I had to stay in California. I've GOT to get out of here. You are the only person in the world that loves me for who and what I am. Without you, I don't know what I would do. I love you so much. I didn't mean that about your grandfather. I was just jealous. So jealous."

She sobbed against his chest and Ludlow had been extremely surprised. He had never seen her this way before; she was nearly hysterical. So different from the calm, bright, always-in-control Madeleine he had known for years.

"What job? What job are you talking about?" he asked.

"At the Conservative Caucus. They want to hire me on as a legislative analyst. It's a huge opportunity, Jim. Just huge."

"Well," he said coolly, "when did you plan on discussing that with me?"

"Oh, Jim, don't be like that. I just got the call yesterday and I was still thinking about it myself. I didn't realize how much I WANTED to go to Washington until tonight, I think."

Jim held her at arm's length, and took a close look at her face. She sniffed and wiped at her nose with the back of her hand like a child. He had never had anyone look at him with such pleading before.

"This doesn't have anything to do with the way your parents acted tonight, does it?" he asked.

"No, no," she said, wiping her eyes, smearing her mascara, "I don't think so, or I don't want to think so. They have been doing the same thing to me my whole life, Jimmy. Today was nothing new. I was surprised they even bothered to show up for graduation."

She went on. "Washington, Jim, just think about it. A place we could really make a difference." She looked at him appealingly and placed her hand on his knee.

Jim sighed and looked away for a moment. "You may have a job in DC, but I don't." A few law firms had expressed an interest in Ludlow over the past few months, but he felt that none of them had really been a good fit.

"I don't think that will be a problem, Jim, I really don't," Madeleine urged, instinctively moving to strengthen her case. "Mr. Gonzaga, he's in charge of legal affairs at the Caucus, he said that he was pretty sure he had a friend that was looking for someone with your qualifications to fill a lobbying position. He said he thought it would be a perfect opportunity for you. I think you should at least talk to this guy. What can it hurt?"

Jim had looked at her a long moment then nodded. "All right. I promise you I will consider it, and we'll find a way to work this out somehow. I can't bear to see you this unhappy."

She had hugged him fiercely and they had driven home in silence.

They married soon after, in a quiet civil ceremony attended only by a few close friends. Just as she had said, Ludlow had been offered a lobbying position with a trade group that represented minerals interests in Washington. The man that hired him said that they not only considered his outstanding law school record and his internships, but also his Native heritage, which would give him a certain degree of credibility on Capitol Hill for their lobbying efforts.

When he had told Johnny Elk about his decision, the old man had been confused at first, as he had thought that Ludlow would be coming back to Nevada. But when he understood that Ludlow would be going to Washington, DC, he became very proud.

"Yes, that is the place you can do the most for the people, it is the best place," he had said. But Ludlow had felt like he had not been completely honest with his grandfather and it had bothered him for a time.

So, he and Madeleine had rented a small apartment in a high rise near DuPont Circle, he had cut his hair, and Madeleine helped him pick out some conservative, well cut suits (he shuddered at the expense; he had never bought a suit before). They both started to work within a week of moving to Washington. For the first few years, he had been a good lobbying soldier, selling the ideas on Capitol Hill that benefitted the people who paid his salary. He didn't really have much time to think about what it was he was doing.

Once they hit Washington, his life had become an overwhelming whirlwind. He and Madeleine were constantly being invited to cocktail parties, dinners, and political meetings and fundraisers. They both worked 12-hour days, then had evening activities as well. Madeleine thrived on the pace and the constant drama that was Washington. Ludlow always felt slightly out of place, more like one of the pieces of Indigenous artwork that many Washington residents liked to display on their walls to prove how cosmopolitan and open minded they were. Even though he worked very hard, and his bosses were pleased with him, he always felt that to them he was an Indian first, with a special type of political coin that came with that designation. And they spent him accordingly.

From what he could remember, it was after he first reached that conclusion that the drinking really started to become a problem. Madeleine had always liked to drink and drank heavily at times throughout law school. It had bothered Ludlow, of course, considering what had happened to his father. He never drank at all when he lived in Antelope Valley, nor as an undergraduate. But Madeleine never really seemed to get drunk, and while they were in law school, having a couple of beers when they went out with friends had seemed natural.

DC was very different though. Heavy drinking in the town seemed to be a universal recreational sport. Wine, beer, and even 'light' martinis at lunch were an accepted and even seemed to be an expected practice at times. Soon one, then two, then three drinks became the norm in the evening. At first, Ludlow convinced himself it was just to relax, but then it became more and more critical that he have a certain amount of alcohol just to help numb himself against all the stress and feelings of displacement he was experiencing. As the years passed, he found that more and more often he was pressured to convince members of Congress and the Senate to vote for legislation that was taking away, piece by piece, what little bits of Indian Country the Tribes still held. Madeleine had no patience with him when he tried to discuss the matter with her. She felt that, under the Constitution, there was enough justification through eminent domain to legalize these piecemeal thefts.

Ludlow had little time to go back to the West to visit his family. He talked to his grandfather, grandmother, and mother infrequently and Sharon only on holidays. Sometimes, on Sunday mornings, he managed to call if he wasn't too hung over, but very often he missed connecting with them, as they were busy around the ranch and had no answering machine. Madeleine only spoke to her parents at Christmas and Thanksgiving, if then. Once, on their way to Europe, the Greenstreets had spent the night in Washington and they all had dinner together. It had been a strained, uncomfortable affair, and Ludlow was thankful that Mr. and Mrs. Greenstreet lived on the other side of the country and seldom came East.

Ludlow had been in Washington about ten years when he got the call from Sharon, telling him that Johnny Elk had died. The old man had been out gathering cattle and had a heart attack and fallen from the saddle. They had found him in the west pasture; the reins of his horse lightly wrapped around one hand, the horse grazing placidly beside him.

Ludlow had been devastated by the news and had flown home alone for the funeral. Madeleine had been teaching at a conference and could not come with him, which, he had to admit, was almost a relief. He knew she would never be able to understand the overwhelming grief and sense of loss that he felt and explaining Shoshone traditional funeral customs to a non-Native would have been wearisome.

Madeleine, he had come to realize over the years, was in her own way as high maintenance as her parents, but it was something he had learned to live with. For one thing, Madeleine had never gotten over her jealousy in regards to his relationship with his family. She covered it well, but it was always there, threatening to raise its ugly head whenever she began to doubt his loyalty and focus. At times, she could be insanely possessive; not overtly jealous, just possessive and protective. When he challenged her on any of these things, it quickly erupted into bitter argument, which she always won. Madeleine did not take prisoners when it came to arguments. Ludlow still had the scars from the deep wounds she had inflicted over the years.

So, it was a relief that he could attend Johnny Elk's funeral alone.

When he had driven into Antelope Valley from Elko, he had been a bit taken aback by the changes that he saw. He knew they had just opened the new casino up by the lake on the north end of the Reservation, but now the entire town was a beehive of construction activity. Antelope Valley had always been a poor, sleepy little town of about 500 souls when he was a boy. Now, there were traffic jams, dozens of tractor-trailers hauling in equipment and construction materials, and more cars than he ever remembered seeing in Antelope Valley in his entire life. A Starbucks was going in, and what looked to be a mall devoted to Native artists. But even though he gaped at the changes as he drove through town, all of it quickly moved to the back of his thoughts as he drove out to the little house where he had grown up.

He had stashed a bottle of vodka in the glove box of the rental car, and took a quick swig before he pulled onto the ranch driveway. Just to steady his nerves. Johnny Elk's death had come as a hard blow to him, and when he saw the traditional funeral tipi set up near the house, it begin to sink in that the old man was really dead. He saw Hank and Sharon sitting outside the tipi by the ceremonial fire, and breathed a sigh of relief that they had gotten here before him. The more family around, the better.

He pulled up outside the house, parked, got out of the car then walked over to Sharon. She stood up and gave him a hug, and he shook Hank's hand.

"Where are they?" Ludlow had asked quietly.

"Sitting with him, inside," Sharon said. "I am glad you were able to get here so quickly. They want to bury him as soon as they can, of course, but they wanted to give you a chance to say goodbye."

Ludlow sighed, and fervently wished he could go back to the car for another slug of vodka, but he took a deep breath and walked into the tipi. Annie and Sarah sat on a blanket on the ground on one side of the plain pine coffin. Steam from the dry ice was rising, as traditional Shoshone beliefs forbid embalming of the dead, and the local funeral home provided special arrangements for those that honored the old ways.

Although the light in the tipi was dim, Ludlow could see Johnny Elk's body. They had dressed him in his best clothing for this last journey and Ludlow choked a bit when he saw the Silver Star around his grandfather's neck. His head was pillowed on an American flag that was folded in a traditional triangle, and Sarah had laid Johnny Elk's favorite rawhide lariat, which he had made himself, on his chest. He looked at peace, Ludlow realized, and he hoped that his grandfather had had a gentle passing.

Ludlow squatted down beside the two women and reached a hand out for his mother, but she looked at him strangely, then abruptly got up and left the tipi. Ludlow didn't think much of it. Annie Ludlow could be extremely erratic at times if she was emotional, and he knew she grieved his grandfather's passing deeply. He didn't take her departure personally. He reached out and took Sarah's hand, and just held it. He noticed a small cut on her arm that still had a little dried blood. Sarah had made a grief cut, in the old way. They sat together for a bit, then Sarah started quietly singing a Shoshone grief song, and Ludlow joined her, surprised that he could still remember the words.

He knew that people would be coming soon to say goodbye to Johnny Elk and would be expecting the traditional funeral feast, then there would be drumming and singing to honor Johnny Elk's life. And while many people would be bringing food with them, he knew Sarah would want to make Johnny's favorite dishes in remembrance.

"I'll sit with him if you want. I know people are coming," Ludlow said.

She nodded and walked out of the tipi.

After she left, Ludlow reached out and briefly touched the dead man's hand. It was icy cold and stiff, and he realized that he had not seen Johnny Elk in nearly a year. Things just kept getting in the way. Flying to Nevada was very time consuming, and it had been a demanding year work-wise. He sat, head bowed, overwhelmed with guilt and regret. He should have been here, helping, even though Johnny Elk had insisted that he go to Washington to help their people.

Ludlow reflected on that belief of his grandfather's and realized that, for the most part, what he had done had been exactly the opposite. He had become a master of soft-pedaling the importance of Native lands if they got in the way of mining or energy interests, and had also become very adept at working with the Bureau of Indian Affairs to convince Tribal Councils that giving up just a little more of the land they had been granted via treaty was in the best interest of the tribe as a whole.

He didn't know who he was anymore.

He loved Madeleine as much as ever. Every morning when he woke up to see her either asleep beside him, getting ready to go to work, sitting at her laptop, or doing any number of things, he felt a bit of awe that a woman like her would love someone like him. When she turned to him and smiled, or took his hand at one of the innumerable cocktail parties they attended, every bad thought he had about living and working in Washington was blasted right out of his brain. She was a daily miracle that made life worth living, and he had made whatever compromises were necessary to keep the miracle alive.

Now that he was away from Madeleine with her infinite charm, beauty and demanding love, he began to wonder if it was all worth it. He knew he would have given almost anything to have spent more time with Johnny Elk, instead of having it all end so abruptly.

He sat with his head bowed for a time, until Hank came in and quietly said that people had started arriving to say goodbye to Johnny Elk. Ludlow nodded and stood up. As Hank held back the tipi door, he saw that a goodly number of people had gathered outside, and wanted to come in to pay their respects. He also saw a notable group of drummers and singers had arrived. The ceremony would be starting soon. Two of Johnny Elk's good friends came in to sit with him and to say their goodbyes, when Ludlow left with Hank.

He walked out, speaking quietly to people he had known when he was growing up. He was surprised at the number of people that had come to honor Johnny Elk. Ludlow went around behind the house to come into the kitchen. There were several women in there, helping, occasionally patting Sarah or Annie's shoulder, and setting out an impressive variety of food on the kitchen table and on the kitchen counter. Sharon was helping them. Hank stood in the living room, talking quietly to some men. Ludlow heard more and more cars coming in. He desperately wanted to go to the car for another shot or two of vodka, but didn't dare with so many people around. He wished he had planned better and parked down by the old barn where he could drink in private.

He looked up and saw Annie glaring at him as if she could read his mind. Then she turned away to respond to a woman who was trying to get her attention about something.

The house became more and more crowded, and then Martin Levi, dressed formally as a Shaman, came into the room and greeted Sarah. Ludlow had known him since he was a boy, of course. Martin was about 15 years Ludlow's senior, and his father Willie Levi had been a big crony of Johnny Elk's. Like Johnny Elk, Willie had felt that education was of primary importance for Native children, and he had driven that point home to his own three while they were growing up. Because of this, Martin Levi had obtained a Masters degree in Psychology from the University of Nevada, but then in a move that surprised everyone, spent a year in a Rabbinical School in Israel, and also had spent three months in kibbutz. Martin Levi's grandfather had been Jewish, and he felt a certain kinship with that faith because of his relatives in Israel.

Then, in yet another surprise, Levi came home to study under the Shaman of the NAC in Antelope Valley, and had eventually taken over as Shaman, when the Elder Shaman, Black Wolf, had died. And from what Ludlow had been told, Martin Levi was the driving force behind many of the changes that were happening in Antelope Valley. Rumor had it that his Israeli friends and relatives had helped back the casino, and were functioning as business consultants in the venture.

In any event, Martin was highly intelligent, shrewd, not above being manipulative if it fit his agenda, and extremely forthright. He was also the first one to come when someone in the Tribe was sick, the first one to stand up if the Tribe's rights were being violated, and the first one to assist in an intervention if a family needed help with drug or alcohol problems. His name had come up several times in Washington at Ludlow's lobbying group, as a person of 'concern' that might have to be 'smoothed' in regards to certain agendas. Ludlow had been infinitely grateful he had not been required to do any 'smoothing.' He never wanted to match wits with Martin Levi. His scalpel tongue could match Madeleine's any day of the week.

Levi had shaken Ludlow's hand briefly, then went into the kitchen to talk to Sarah. They stepped outside for a moment, and Ludlow knew that the official ceremony would start soon. He dreaded it. For that would mean that Johnny Elk was really and truly gone from this world.

When he heard the drumming start, Ludlow went out and joined the group that surrounded the tipi where Johnny Elk lay. The drumming and singing went on for a good while, and then Martin Levi spoke briefly of Johnny Elk and all the good things he had done in the community, in the war, and for his friends and family. Then he did a brief cleansing and healing ceremony with burning sage and an eagle feather he had brought. After this, there was more drumming and singing, while the people circled the tipi, chanting a grief song. People patiently took their turns to go into the tipi to say their final goodbyes to Johnny Elk. Finally, after what seemed like days to Ludlow, it was over and everyone had gone home. It was late, past 2 a.m., and he was exhausted.

He was surprised when Annie came to him and took his arm angrily. She had hardly spoken to him all night, only taking the time to glare at him periodically. He had no idea what it was he had done wrong.

"I want you to come with me to sit with Poppa," she said, her black eyes glowing slightly in the light of the campfire that was still burning outside the tipi.

Annie poked her head in the tipi and motioned peremptorily for Hank and Sharon to leave. Family members had to maintain the vigil all night with the body, and they had volunteered to sit through the night, as they knew Sarah and Annie were exhausted. They looked at her with surprise when she waved her hands at them, but they left immediately.

She ducked through the opening and motioned for Ludlow to follow; then they sat down by Johnny Elk's body. Annie turned and looked at him. Her eyes were cold.

"I know the drink has taken you," she said simply. "The drink and that woman. I am ashamed, and I am glad Poppa did not live to see this."

"I don't know what you're talking about," Ludlow said, a bit shocked.

Annie stared at him. "You have lost your spirit," she said. "It's wandering. It was always wandering, but now it may never come back. It has wandered far away and is lost. As you are lost. Poppa loved you very much. Maybe he will help your spirit find its way back. I hope so. You are my son and I love you also despite your foolishness." Then, without another word, she got up and left.

Ludlow sat stunned, staring after his mother as she had left. There had always been a rumor that Annie was a bit of a shaman herself, but he had never believed it until that night.

He sat staring at Johnny Elk, thinking of what his mother had said to him.

After about a half hour, Sharon came in, sat down beside him, and took his hand, wordlessly. She looked at him and smiled. "Hank and I are coming back home, Jimmy," she said. "Martin and the Tribal Council want me to come home and take over the Police force – they are transitioning over from the BIA police and want to do everything on their own. Hank wants to come back and work the ranch anyway. It's what he has always wanted to do. We want to keep Poppa's stock horse line going and have a lot of other plans. You know we had only planned on Chicago being temporary, if there was any way we could come back here and make a living."

Ludlow had looked at her expressionlessly then nodded. "That all makes good sense, Sis," he said. "Grandmother and Mother will need Hank's help and you would make a great police chief, or sheriff, or whatever they plan on calling you."

She had then looked at him curiously. "Plenty of room, Jimmy, if you're ready to come home. Even though it's been a while, I still think you are probably about the best horseman I've ever seen."

He had smiled and had shaken his head. "Those days are over now. Madeleine and I have a life in Washington. We're very happy there."

"Really?" she had asked, with one eyebrow raised. Then she had turned to look at Johnny Elk.

"We were lucky, Jimmy, to have someone like him in our lives. Things could have gone the other way pretty easily, considering how dad was," Sharon said quietly.

Ludlow just nodded and sat silently, thinking about what she and Annie had said as they sat together through the night.

The next morning, the funeral home came and picked up Johnny Elk's body, and he was buried in the Antelope Valley cemetery. After it was all done, Ludlow left as soon as it was politely possible, telling everyone that he needed to get back to Washington for work.

That was not a lie, of course. He did have work waiting, would always have work waiting, for the work never ended. Madeleine had called several times on his cell phone and had also called Sarah and Annie to express her condolences. She had offered to fly out as soon as her conference was over, but Ludlow had discouraged her, saying that he would be home soon. There was no sense in her coming to Nevada, just to turn around and go right back to DC again.

Sarah and Sharon had hugged him, and Hank had shaken his hand, but Annie had only smoked a cigarette and glared at him balefully as he took his departure.

Once Ludlow got back home, he found that something in him had changed or shifted somehow. Every morning, he had to drag himself into the office, and then the work just sat on his desk. He began mixing a little vodka with orange juice in the morning, just to get through the day, then a little more, and a little more. He started bringing vodka bottles into the office in his briefcase. One day, in the middle of the afternoon, he woke up to find himself lying on a park bench in one of the city parks near his office, a kindly DC cop leaning over him asking if he was all right. He had no memory of how he had gotten there.

Things at home had also been deteriorating. While Madeleine had not commented on his drinking (he was taking pains to hide the vodka bottles from her), she constantly scolded him for not listening to her and being off in outer space.

She was not without feeling, of course. Many times, she said she understood that he was grieving for his grandfather, and asked repeatedly if there was anything she could do. She offered to fly back to Nevada with him, or to take a vacation, whatever it was he wanted. The emptiness and indifference in his eyes frightened her more and more, she said. Ludlow didn't care. If she wanted to go, they could go. As long as the place they went had a bar, that's all he cared about.

But they never went anywhere.

Eventually, he quit bothering to hide the vodka bottles and began calling in sick to work more and more. He went to fewer and fewer parties and dinners with Madeleine and, after a time, she would call from work and say she would be going straight to whatever event was critical for that night. Ludlow didn't care. Eventually, he just stopped answering the phone.

In fact, for all practical purposes, Ludlow had stopped speaking at all. What good did words do anyway? He said very little to Madeleine, and when his boss came into his office on the one day in two weeks he had managed to make it in to work, to tell him he was fired, he had simply gotten up and left. He had sat in the park again that day in his fine suit that Madeleine had bought for him, enjoying the fresh air and sunshine. He watched the pigeons as he pulled steadily at a fifth of Jack Daniels. He had given up the pretense of vodka and had just decided to drink what he liked.

Of course, Madeleine had heard about him getting fired very soon after it had happened. She had come home and screamed at him, telling him over and over that he was ruining not only his life but hers as well. He only stared into space silently as she had screamed, even when she had finally collapsed in a chair across from him sobbing. At the time, he distantly felt that perhaps he should care that Madeleine was upset, but he couldn't remember exactly why.

Days and weeks passed and each day revolved around whether he would have to walk to the liquor store to get another bottle or not. One day, he had an unpleasant surprise to find that his credit card no longer worked and, after that, he found he had to work a little harder for money to buy liquor. Madeleine had closed the bank account with his name on it and closed their joint MasterCard. However, he just took some of her jewelry and pawned it and opened two more credit card accounts in her name. It would take her a while to discover these things and Ludlow had stopped concerning himself with the future.

He came to believe that Madeleine was having an affair. She often didn't come home at night and he found that he really didn't care. It was easier just to drink. It took care of all your worries. One weekend, she said she would be going to the Eastern shore for a retreat with the Caucus, and, as usual, he just stared at her wordlessly as she packed her bags to leave.

"Jim, I don't know how much more of this I can take. I can't just stand by and watch you destroy yourself," she said.

Ludlow had only gotten up and walked to the living room and sat in a chair he had pulled near the window. He liked to sit there sometimes and look outside. It was very restful. Much more restful than listening to Madeleine talk about her problems.

The next day, Ludlow had started out the day as usual, stumbling into the kitchen around noon to fix himself a mixer of orange juice and vodka; he didn't usually switch to bourbon until later in the day. There was some fruit in the refrigerator, but it looked like it would be too much trouble to eat, so he skipped it.

He was in the same sweatpants and sweatshirt he had been wearing the day before; he had slept in them through the night. He tried to remember the last time he had taken a shower, but couldn't. It was just too tiring to try to remember.

It came as a shock when the door opened and some people came in without knocking. It was even a further shock when he saw Sharon and Martin Levi, as well as a couple of other people he didn't know. They walked right into the kitchen and stood staring at him, as if he were a bug of some sort. Ludlow felt a bit irritated that they should barge in so rudely.

"Oh, Jimmy," Sharon said and then she shook her head and turned away.

Ludlow saw she was upset and felt bad that he was irritated. He took a long drink of his 'orange juice' and immediately felt better.

"Hi, Sharon. I didn't know you were coming today. Did you tell me? I have trouble remembering things lately. And, Martin, what are you doing here? Maddy's gone I think. She said she was going somewhere…" he said.

Martin looked at Ludlow for a moment and smiled. He picked up the orange juice, and vodka bottle, and set them in the sink, along with Ludlow's glass. Then he sat down beside Jim and laid a friendly hand on his arm.

"Jimmy, do you trust me?"

"Why, sure I do, Marty."

"And I know you trust Sharon, right?'

"Of course, I do. Hey, what's going on? I wish I had known you were coming, I'm kind of a mess this morning."

"Jimmy," Martin said, "if I asked you to do something for me, just a simple favor, would you be willing to do it? Even if it was something you might not want to do at first? Just as a favor to me, and to Sharon?"

Ludlow looked from one to the other then looked at the bottle of vodka in the sink. Ludlow knew what they wanted and he sighed. "I am so tired," he said, rubbing at his face.

Sharon came up and put her hands on his shoulders. "We know, Jimmy. We want to help with that," she said gently.

"All right," Ludlow had said simply. "I want to come home. I'm tired of this place."

"I'm not surprised," Martin Levi said in Shoshone. "There are many walking dead here. This city if full of them and you have become one too."

Ludlow looked at him, wide eyed and frightened.

"But there is hope for you, I think," Martin said, then he patted Ludlow on the shoulder. He continued, in English. "We want you to come home, but you have to understand, no more drinking. That is the condition. We want you home, but we want you alive. Do you understand, Jimmy?"

"Yes. I think so," Ludlow said, confused, "but what about Madeleine – shouldn't we talk to her, shouldn't she know?"

"Jimmy," Sharon said, crouching in front of him and taking his hand, "Madeleine called me. She knows we're here; she's the one that gave us the key to the apartment. She wants us to help you."

"What we would like," Martin Levi continued, "is for you to go with these fellows here. We'll follow along but we would like you to go with them. They are going to take you to a hospital for a few days, where some very good doctors are going to give you some medicine to help get the alcohol out of your system. Then, once it is safe for you to travel, we will take you home, and you will stay at a treatment center for a while. A new one we have just started. I'll be there to help, along with a very good doctor who has come to work on the Reservation. Are you willing to do this, Jim? You have to understand, once you come back home, there can be no drinking at all.

"You have to make a choice, death or life. No one can make that decision but you. And once you make it, we will do everything in our power to help you," Martin said when Ludlow didn't answer.

Ludlow looked at both of them and at the two men in neat blue uniforms who were standing quietly by the front door, smiling at him in a friendly way. He looked at the vodka bottle, and thought about Madeleine for a moment.

"Well, I am willing to give it a try," he said hesitantly.

Martin Levi then took his hand in both of his and said very strongly, "Try means no, and both of us know this to be true," Levi said in Shoshone. "If all the effort you are willing to make to start living again is to 'try,' then Sharon and I will waste no more time with you. You can stay here, and continue in your living death. It is your choice."

Ludlow looked at him for a minute, and, he knew that Martin was right. It would be a very hard thing though. A very hard thing. It was easier just to fix things with liquor so you didn't care anymore. So you did feel dead. Sometimes being dead was preferable to being alive.

Ludlow looked at the sun shining outside then turned to Martin in shame and nodded. Martin had patted his shoulder soundly.

"Don't be ashamed, Jim," he said quietly in Shoshone. "There is no shame here. Only life."

Then, Ludlow had looked at Sharon and had begun to cry a bit. It was embarrassing.

"I don't want to end up like Dad, Sis. I don't," he said, clutching at Sharon's hand.

"You won't, Jimmy. Not you. Come on, let's get out of here," she replied, smiling at him.

He had stood up and was surprised to find that the room was spinning a bit.

"Come on Jimmy, you can lean on me," Martin had said. And he had slipped his arm around Ludlow's waist.

*

And, so began Ludlow's recovery. It had been neither a short nor an easy process.

He spent nearly a week in the treatment unit in DC. It was the hardest thing he had ever done. Martin and Sharon came to see

134

him at the end of the week, when he was stable enough to see visitors. The detoxification process had been very painful and intense, and when Ludlow had come out on the other end, he was so tired and disoriented that he barely even knew where he was.

He still remembered the first time he had looked at himself in the mirror after he had been sober for a few days. The sight of his thin, pale body in the mirror had made him cry. He had cried a lot since he had been admitted to the clinic. It was shameful to him that he could not control his tears. He was a man. He should have better control. One of the counselors, a black man named Judah who was an ex-heroin addict, told him later that it was one of the most difficult withdrawals he had ever seen. Even with the best and most diligent of care, Ludlow had suffered greatly. Judah said many times he didn't blame Ludlow for crying.

But once the physical withdrawal was finished, he had to deal with an emotional emptiness that was far worse. It started to sink in that most of his life was gone, everything that he had worked for, everything that he and Johnny Elk had planned was gone, as Johnny Elk was gone.

And then there was Madeleine. He knew that their relationship was in a shambles, and it was his fault. But he also knew that he could not stay in Washington; the town was killing him. The day before he was to check out of the rehab center, he talked to Martin Levi about it.

Martin had looked at him evenly when he had asked about Madeleine. "Madeleine wants you to get well," he had said. "That's of primary importance to her; she is the one that called Sharon, remember? She wants you to be whole again, Jim. She really has you best welfare at heart. As well as her own," Martin had continued after a brief pause.

"So, I'm going home then?" Ludlow asked quietly.

"Yes, sir!" Martin said cheerfully. "We have a new center where you are going to stay for a while. How long you stay is up to you, of course. But, Jim, I'm telling you, we could use your help with one of our new programs. I think it's right up your alley. Anyway, we're kind of struggling with some of the concepts and could use some new ideas."

"What is it?" Ludlow asked tentatively.

Marin looked at him and smiled mischievously.

"You'll find out when you get there. We've got a flight booked tomorrow, for you, Sharon, and myself. She's gone back to the apartment to pack some things for you, so you don't have to worry about it."

"I would like to talk to Madeleine before I leave, of course," Ludlow said.

Martin shifted in his chair, ill at ease. Ludlow could see he had something he needed to say, but was having a hard time getting it out.

"She doesn't want to talk to me, does she?" Ludlow asked quietly, feeling very small.

Martin shook his head. "I think Madeleine has made some decisions about what she wants out of her life, as is her right. Your illness has been very, very hard on her, Jim. I think you might need to come to grips with the fact that your lives have come to be on widely divergent paths. We will need to spend some time working through this at the Center. But, one thing, Jim, I know you are feeling a lot of guilt and remorse right now. I don't want you to ignore it, and we will be talking about these feelings a lot at the Center, but try not to get too weighed down by any 'might have beens.'"

"What I want you to understand," Martin continued, leaning forward and looking at Ludlow intently, "is that you have started a new life. And you are going to be a little wobbly starting out, like a newborn calf. But there are many people who care about you, probably more than you know. And we are committed to helping you, as long as you commit yourself to living this new life and giving up that living death you were trapped in. You can't go back, that bad time is gone now, never to be relived again. You made mistakes, some bad ones, but we want to help you learn from them and move on.

"There may come a day that you will be able to apologize to Madeleine, or there may not. But I don't want you to worry about that right now. Just worry about today. OK? Madeleine is fine, and we will keep in touch with her to let her know how you are doing. I'm asking that you trust us to have both of your best interests at heart."

Ludlow sighed and lay back down on the bed. He felt very tired all of a sudden. Madeleine had been so much a part of his life for so long, the thought of leaving without even speaking to her was upsetting. He felt very strongly the need for a quick shot of booze, as this whole situation was just too painful to deal with. He was surprised when Martin slapped his arm with his open hand. It stung.

"Get up," Martin said. "We're going for a walk."

"What?"

"You heard me. Get your sorry Indian ass out of bed, we're going outside for a walk," Levi said angrily.

Martin dug around in a small chest of drawers across the room then tossed some clean underwear, blue jeans. and a T-shirt at Ludlow none too gently. Ludlow grabbed for them to keep from being hit in the head.

"Go on, get dressed. You've lain around long enough feeling sorry for yourself."

"I wasn't…"

"Don't give me that shit, and don't even get me started on your emotional laziness, or cowardice might be a better word… Put on those clothes and meet me out in the hall. And don't dawdle."

Martin stalked out of the little room, leaving Ludlow staring after him in shock. He had no idea what he had done to anger the man so, but he quickly pulled on the clothing and put on the old pair of running shoes he had worn when they had checked him in. When he stood up, he felt a little weak, but it passed and he walked out into the hall.

Martin looked at him and gave him a sharp nod. "It's a start," he said. "Come on, it's a nice spring day outside."

Ludlow followed Martin down the hall to a set of double doors that led to a quiet garden. He was a little unbalanced at first, but Martin caught his arm and steadied him.

"I guess I'm going to have to get back in practice walking," Ludlow said.

"That's right. Walking and everything else," Martin Levi responded, laughing.

Chapter 9

And that had been the start of Ludlow's life. Today, looking back on it, he felt that it was the moment that his life had really begun. A rebirth.

They had flown back to Elko the next day, as Martin had said they would. Ludlow found that sleep pulled at him a lot these days, so he slept most of the way to Salt Lake City and then again on the puddle jumper to Elko. There were a couple of tense moments when the steward had offered Ludlow and Martin a mixed drink (Sharon was sitting across the aisle from them), and Ludlow had felt the old temptation, but Martin had waved the man past and the craving had passed.

Martin Levi had watched him from the corner of his eye when this happened, and was glad to see that the anxiety Ludlow seemed to feel when offered the drink was relatively low, compared to others had had worked with over the years. That was a good sign. Levi was convinced that while Ludlow probably had a genetic disposition towards alcoholism, it was the emotional imbalances in the man that led him to drink so heavily. That and the destructive relationship Ludlow had with Madeleine Greenstreet. She had become the type of woman who seemed to pull all the oxygen out of the air whenever she entered a room. But she was so charming and beautiful; it would be easy to ignore the fact that you were being slowly suffocated. If you were a man, that is. Martin Levi had been happily married for more than 25 years, and even he had momentarily felt a strong attraction towards the woman. But he had been around the type enough that he recognized her for the narcissist she was, and treated her accordingly: politely, firmly, and non-challenging. She was not an evil woman; at some level she did care what happened to Ludlow, but she would never put him before her own interests.

Sharon, on the other hand, had been hard-pressed to keep her temper in dealings with her.

Ludlow considered his stay at the Medicine Wheel Center for Life as one of his more treasured memories. The building was new, set out in the desert a few miles away from town. It was also small, with accommodations for only 10-12 people. While Martin Levi was the associate director of the facility, the director was an older psychiatrist, a woman named Dr. Josephine Balcer. She had been Chief of Psychiatry at Beth Israel Hospital in Manhattan for 15 years and had done her residency at Bellevue. She had even spent 5 years in Bethesda, MD, at the National Institutes of Mental Health, as a research fellow prior to taking the job as Chief of Psychiatry at Beth Israel. She was a tiny woman with white hair and a whisper quiet voice. She loved to dress in bright gaudy colors reminiscent of the 60's. Martin said she had leapt at the chance to move to Nevada when he had called her. She was divorced, her children were grown, and she had been ready for some new challenges (and was sick of New York City).

When Ludlow met her she had only smiled and nodded her head. "So, this is the one, eh, Martin?" she asked, when they walked into her office. Ludlow noticed it was pleasantly decorated with cool, calming colors.

"This is him."

The woman looked him up and down momentarily then nodded. "I think he'll do," she said, and Martin had chuckled.

"Well, we are glad you're here with us, Mr. Ludlow, and I trust you plan on making the most of your visit?" she asked.

"Yes ma'am," Ludlow said.

"Humph," she responded, staring at him over her bifocals with penetrating blue eyes. Her gaze made him feel distinctly uncomfortable.

Then she just nodded briskly and turned back to a pile of papers on her desk.

Martin took him to a tiny room and he set his suitcase down on the floor. Ludlow's room had a huge picture window that looked towards the mountains, a bathroom, a twin bed and a nightstand. He was drawn to the window. Looking at the desert and the mountains was like food for his soul. After a few minutes, he began wondering how he had ever had the strength to leave so many years ago. He took a deep breath and sighed. He felt a strong urge to feel the desert sand under his bare feet.

Martin looked at his watch. "Well, dinner is in about an hour, at 6, then there is group therapy afterwards. Attendance is mandatory, by the way. And, just so you know, there are no locks on the doors here. No secrets. You can walk out of here anytime you want to."

"My cell phone?"

"You don't have one anymore, Jim. I'll see you at dinner."

Martin left, closing the door quietly behind him.

Ludlow sat for a minute, then slowly unpacked the few belongings Sharon had brought from his apartment. Three pairs of jeans, two nice shirts, some underwear, his shaving kit, several t-shirts and a leather jacket that Madeleine had bought him when they had first moved to DC; one pair of running shoes, which he was wearing, and one pair of nice shoes. Not much to show for nearly 18 years of work.

He sighed and sat on the edge of the bed for a moment, staring at the mountains. It was April, and the desert was starting to green up. In another month or so, some of the desert flowers would be blooming. He wondered how his mother and grandmother were doing. He hadn't talked to them in weeks. He hoped he would get to see them soon, but Martin Levi hadn't said anything about visitors. He felt very lonely.

There was a knock at the door. It opened and an elderly Native man stepped in.

"Jim Ludlow?" he asked.

"Yes, sir?" Ludlow said.

"My name is Daniel James. Martin sent me to get you for supper. He said you're new, and wouldn't know the way."

"Thanks, Mr. James," Ludlow said, rising to follow the old man out of the room. "Are you in treatment here?"

"Me, no, no. Not anymore. I went through the program last year. My wife died and I had a hard time. When I got healed, I asked if I could stay on. I generally do whatever needs doing."

"You're not from here are you?"

"Oh, no. I came up from Phoenix. This is one of the best treatment programs in the country, I think. Even though it's a new program, it is getting to be very popular. Natives can usually get in here without waiting, but there is a waiting list of non-Natives, they tell me. I think everyone will have to wait soon. They work miracles here," James said.

Ludlow only nodded as he followed the old man down the hall and into a spacious room that contained a couple of long folding tables and chairs. It was a busy place, with about a dozen people, both men and women. Some were seated; others were setting the table or bringing out steaming plates of food. Ludlow realized that probably for the first time in months, he was actually hungry.

The old man sat down at the table, then motioned for Ludlow to sit beside him. Within a few minutes, the table was set. Martin Levi came in, said a brief prayer in Shoshone, and everyone began to eat. Ludlow ate heartily; the smells were wonderful and he felt ravenous. Occasionally, he looked around surreptitiously at the people sitting at the tables: twelve men and women, a few Native, but most were non-Natives, including one very well dressed African American man and one attractive young Asian woman. Once dinner was finished, people quickly cleared the tables and took the small amount of leftover food to the kitchen. Daniel James helped clear things away, then waved to Ludlow briefly as he left. A couple of the men moved the tables to the side, and everyone started pulling chairs into a circle. Ludlow, feeling a little lost, just did what everyone else did.

Ludlow noticed for the first time that a true medicine wheel had been painted onto the floor. It was brightly colored in the wheel colors of Red, Black, Yellow and White, with a small green circle in the center. He hadn't seen one in a long time, and he found it oddly comforting when he looked at it. People pulled their chairs up around it and sat down.

Martin Levi looked around at the group, smiled, and sat down.

"Hoka hey," he said formally. Ludlow was a little shocked to hear him speaking in Sioux. "It is a good day to die."

"Hoka hey," was the universal response.

"OK, everyone, we have a new member tonight. This is Jim Ludlow," he said, motioning at Ludlow. "Jackie, could you please explain to Jim why we begin each of these meetings with that phrase?"

"OK," the black man said, looking at Ludlow. "This is from something that Crazy Horse reportedly said to his warriors before battle. It can be translated in a number of ways, but we interpret it as 'It is a good day to die,' as Martin said. What this means to us is that if we were to die today, we could do it with no regrets, knowing that we had done our best to honor and respect not only ourselves but others as well."

Levi nodded, and looked at Ludlow.

"As a Native, Jim," Levi began, "you are familiar with the Medicine Wheel, and its Seven Aspects: the East with the color yellow, which represents the Emotional aspect of ourselves; the South with the color red which represents the Mental; the West with the color black, the Physical as it relates to our bodies; North represented by the color white represents the Spiritual. There are also Sky and Earth, which can't be represented in a flat circle, as they are three-dimensional. Sky that is above us represents our relationship with a higher power, and Earth, below us, represents our relationship with Mother Earth. The last direction is the Green circle in the center of all, which represents the individual when he or she is centered and balanced with the other six aspects. Our goal is to teach you to always be able to find that green center when you are pulled off balance in one of the other directions."

"Easier said than done," Levi continued, and several members of the group chuckled.

"So, Jim, for tonight, I would like you to listen to the others in the group, to help you get your bearings with where they are in the Wheel right now. I think you will find there are many things you can relate to. Why don't you start, Susan?" Martin said, nodding to the young Asian woman.

And so, Ludlow listened as his fellows spoke of their lives and their addictions. Susan, a successful software developer, had come close to losing everything because of a gambling addiction. Jackie, the black man, a documentary producer from LA, was recovering from an addiction to prescription drugs, two people were recovering from crystal meth (Ludlow was horrified to hear what they had gone through before they came the MWCL), most of the others had alcohol addictions. As he listened to them talk about their feelings in regards to their addictions, he found some small comfort in the fact that he was not the only one who had the same feelings of helplessness as well as exhaustion with life. Ludlow sat quietly in the session, trying to pay attention as the others talked, but not saying much. The meeting went on for three hours. At the end, Ludlow felt exhausted, even though he hadn't done much of anything. When they were finished, Martin walked him back to his room.

"Tomorrow, Jim, you have to start to work on getting well. You have a session with Dr. Balcer at 9 am, right after breakfast. It's a two-hour evaluation session. Then lunch at 11:30, an afternoon session with our nutritionist and physical trainer – weather is good tomorrow, so that should be outside. Then dinner, then another group session."

Ludlow nodded but said nothing.

"Breakfast is from 7-8:30. Up to you when you show up; just be sure to be on time for your appointment with Dr. Balcer."

Ludlow nodded again, and moved to open the door to his room. He felt like he could sleep for a week.

"Martin, who is paying for all of this?" he asked, before he stepped inside.

"Well, Madeleine's health insurance policy, which is very good, plus we have grants from various agencies for substance abuse rehab for Natives. Don't worry about the money, Jim."

Ludlow nodded again, relieved. He didn't want Sharon and the rest of the family to get stuck with the bill.

He slept very hard that night and had a difficult time getting up the next morning. He had set the small alarm clock in the room and when it went off he dragged himself out of bed, took a shower, and went to breakfast. He ate alone; he had no idea where the others were.

His first session with Dr. Balcer was uneventful. She asked questions, he answered. He volunteered nothing, but obediently and honestly answered everything she asked. He enjoyed the exercise in the afternoon, which mainly consisted of walking on a trail through the desert. While he was outside, he took the opportunity to feel the sand beneath his bare feet, and it felt wonderful.

In group therapy that evening, he sat and listened, again volunteering nothing. It was a different leader that night, one of Dr. Balcer's assistants; she was calm and professional, and Ludlow answered her questions when asked. He tried to listen attentively to everyone else, but found his mind often wandering. For the most part, he just sat and watched the clock. He constantly wanted to lose himself in sleep.

This became the pattern of the first month at MWCL. He made no friends among the other addicts. He answered politely if addressed directly, but did not actively engage anyone else in conversation. Just the thought of talking was like heavy work; it was so hard.

He knew Martin Levi was frustrated with him. Dr. Balcer had told him that she felt he might need antidepressants, but Ludlow had said no. He didn't see much sense in it – trading booze for pills. They kept expecting him to do something, but he didn't know what. It was like some force had locked him inside himself

143

and it was determined not to let him go. He didn't have a horrible craving for alcohol that some of the others at the Center had described, he just felt empty. He wanted to ask if Sharon, his mother, or grandmother were coming to visit, then he decided that probably, like Madeleine, they didn't want to have anything to do with him.

He didn't really blame them, so he didn't ask.

One day, at lunch, Ludlow noticed that a few of the other people in the group seemed particularly animated and excited. Apparently, from what he could gather, there was a guest therapist coming in with a new type of therapy they had signed up for. Ludlow was puzzled. He hadn't been informed of any change in the routine. They hustled outside, talking and laughing among themselves, while Ludlow just sat, confused. The others in the group began leaving also; apparently they had opted to take an afternoon off and were heading into town for a small field trip. Ludlow felt irritated. He would have liked a trip to town.

Ludlow just sat for a minute still puzzled and annoyed, then Martin Levi came walking to the room. He was carrying a large paper bag with him.

"All right, Jim," he said, grinning. "This is the little program I was telling you about that we needed some help with. Are you up for it?"

"I guess so. Is that what's in the bag?"

"Nope. Just some old things of yours."

He handed the bag to Ludlow and he peeked inside. He was surprised find an old pair of boots he had worn when he used to work the ranch with Johnny Elk. He'd left them at home many years before. He set the bag on the floor and gazed up at Martin a bit suspiciously.

Martin leaned on a chair and looked at Ludlow, still grinning. "Do you remember a fellow by the name of Mike Patterson?"

"Mike Patterson?" Ludlow said, even more puzzled. "Well, we had a guy named Mike Patterson that came to work on our ranch one summer. He was a rodeo cowboy that wanted to learn the 'Indian way' of working with horses, as he called it. He had heard Johnny Elk was the best there was; that's what he told us anyway. I guess I was about 12 or 13 when he came. I remember when I was home a couple of years ago, Poppa and I watched him on TV once; he had managed to get his own TV program. He was traveling around the world teaching people how to work with horses. Grandfather said must have he married a smart woman, because he didn't have enough sense to do all that on his own, but he was probably rich now, thanks to a smart woman. Johnny Elk thought it was a great joke."

"Why did he think that?"

"He always said that Mike had too much vanity and boasted too much. The horses sensed it, and did not respect him because of it. We had some trouble with him on the ranch once, and Johnny Elk gave him a sharp lesson. Mike was much better after that," Ludlow said.

Martin quit grinning and looked intrigued. "Tell me about it," he said.

Ludlow leaned back in the chair, remembering. "Well, Mike came to us and begged Johnny Elk to let him work for a summer and to teach him about horses. Johnny Elk agreed reluctantly, and put him up in that old bunkhouse behind the barn. Anyway, Mike turned out to be a fair hand, surprising everyone, although Poppa often corrected him for being too rough with the horses. Plus, he did like to show off, and that's why Grandfather felt he needed the lesson.

"One day Grandfather and I were bringing in some cattle for worming, and we saw Mike roping a calf for no good reason. Threw him down on the ground and tied his legs, like they do in the rodeo. Then we saw that Sharon was sitting there with a couple of her girlfriends, and Mike was showing off for them."

Ludlow shook his head at the memory.

"Poppa looked at me and said, 'Jimmy, lope over there and heel that fool and drag him around a bit to teach him some manners. Just a bit. I will be right along behind you, as soon as I get these cattle penned. Just don't drag him over no big bushes or yank his leg off. We still got six weeks of work to get out of him.'

"So, I did. Mike had turned the calf loose and was walking towards the girls, and I loped over and heeled him. He went down pretty hard and I dragged him around some. He got kind of scratched up, but his pride was hurt more than anything. When I finally stopped, he was yelling and screaming, telling me all the things he was going to do to me as soon as he got me off my horse. And the next thing I knew, Poppa was just THERE. He came at a full gallop and slid to a stop, just missing Mike's head by inches, it seemed like. I can't remember that I ever saw him that mad before or after.

"Mike rolled out of the way quickly; he was really scared, and he got to his feet and tried to run, but Poppa wouldn't let him. Every time he tried to get away, Poppa was there with his horse. Anyway, he would turn the horse and put its shoulder into Patterson, until he finally knocked him down on the ground again.

"Grandfather got down from his horse and yanked Mike up by his shirt with one hand. Then he said, 'You touch this boy and I will plant you, law or no. I told him to rope you. Let me ask you something. How does it feel to be a calf?'

"Mike just looked at him a minute, not understanding. Poppa rolled his eyes and said, 'Now look, I have known white men even dumber than you that managed to figure it out. So, I will ask again, in a different way. Now that you know how a calf feels, do you think people have a right to treat you this way for fun? To show off for girls? Or some other prideful reason?'

"Mike looked at him, finally understanding, and he said, 'No sir, Mr. Elk.' Poppa brushed some of the dirt off Mike's chest, none too gently. 'We take care of our stock here, boy. They provide us with a living, and we respect them accordingly. As long as you are on this ranch you will do the same, or you will get out.' Mike nodded, and that was the end of it. After that, his work with the horses improved dramatically. I think Grandfather actually developed a fondness for Mike, even though he never thought he had much sense."

Martin shook his head. "That's pretty much the same story Mike told me. Anyway, come on. I want you to see something. Put on those boots."

"I don't know what you're up to," Ludlow said grumpily. "I haven't done anything with a horse in over 10 years. I forgot most of what I thought I knew."

Martin shrugged. "I don't recall saying anything about horses. I do recall saying something about boots. If you notice, I'm wearing mine."

It was true. He did have on a pair of well-worn cowboy boots.

Reluctantly, Ludlow pulled off his old running shoes and pulled on the cowboy boots he had had since he was in college. He was surprised they still fit.

Martin quickly put the running shoes in the bag and folded

down the top tightly. "We'll drop these off in your room on the way out," he said.

"Where are we going?"

"Another part of the Center you haven't been to yet. No more questions. Just come on."

Ludlow reluctantly followed Martin down the hall. Martin stopped at his room briefly and unceremoniously opened the door and tossed the bag inside without missing a step. They walked out into the bright sunshine. It was early May, and was starting to get warm during the day.

There was an old golf cart parked outside. Martin got in and motioned for Ludlow to get into the other seat. They drove down a dirt road for about 15 minutes, until they came to a large barn and corral area that Ludlow recognized as once belonging to a former Tribal Council member who had moved to Elko some years ago. There was also a bunkhouse, and some men were painting it a pale yellow color.

"What's all this?" he asked, as Martin pulled up by the barn.

"We have a program that we're starting with the Nevada Department of Corrections," Levi responded. "It's a type of work release. Those guys over there, all non-violent offenders, are in the program, and they're finishing up painting their accommodations. But, that's not why we're here. We can talk about that later if you like. Come on down to the arena.".

Ludlow followed Martin down past the barn and into a covered riding arena. As they neared the arena, he heard a familiar voice. Mike Patterson, much older now, stood with the rehab patients in the middle of the arena, giving some guidance to Susan Wong, who was tentatively holding the lead rope of a bay horse.

"Now turn around, holding that leadline lightly in your hand, and walk away. Don't think about anything, just walk away, normal-like," Patterson said.

Susan looked at him, then turned and walked away. When she took her first few steps the horse threw up his head and resisted following her, yanking at her arm, then he came along at a slow walk.

"OK, that's good," Patterson said. "Now, the reason he didn't follow your right away is he didn't understand that you are the one leading in this little dance, and he just didn't know what to do. So, let's work on fixing that. Remember, a horse's behavior is often

147

the reflection of what's going on inside us, so it's best we pay attention. That's what this type of therapy is all about."

Ludlow nodded to himself. Johnny Elk had said this many times as he was growing up. Martin slipped quietly into an old folding chair near the door, and motioned for Ludlow to do the same. They both took care not to distract the small group of people that was standing in the arena.

Ludlow watched Patterson as he worked with each of the six people. They worked on nothing else but having the horse follow them in a free and calm manner. It was interesting to watch the change that came over people when they got it and the horse trotted along behind them happily and freely. Having experienced the joy of the connectedness with horses himself many times, he knew what they were feeling. He envied them.

After the session, the rehab patients left to take one of the Center vans back to the main building. A couple of them waved to Martin and Ludlow on the way out. Mike Patterson stood holding the horse and watching as they left, then he walked over, the bay horse following quietly along behind him. It had been more than 20 years since Ludlow had last seen Patterson. He had put on weight and was now sporting a large graying walrus moustache. He had on a black felt cowboy hat, cowboy shirt, jeans, and an old pair of leather chaps. When he walked up, he held out his hand to Ludlow.

"Hello, Jim, it's been a while," he said, smiling.

Jim stood up and shook Patterson's hand.

"It has. Good to see you, Mike."

Patterson toyed with the lead rope a bit, staring down at the ground.

"I'm sorry about Johnny Elk, Jim. I would have come to the funeral, but I was in Australia."

Ludlow only nodded, feeling very uncomfortable.

Patterson looked up at him keenly. "I think Johnny probably saved my life, you know. I learned a lot that summer I spent on your ranch. If it hadn't been for him, I probably would have wound up dead in a bar fight or locked up. He was quite a man."

"Yes, he was," Ludlow said quietly.

Patterson stared at him a moment, then nodded to Martin. "This was a good session today, Martin. I thought they did really good all things considered. I think this new idea of yours definitely has got potential."

"I'm glad you were willing to come down to help us get started, Mike. I know how busy you are," Levi said.

"Pleased to be able to do it and it's not that far a drive from my place in Idaho. I'll be going back out on the road again in about a month, so if you decide you want to make this permanent, we'll have to come up with another plan, find someone else to take over."

"Oh, I'm sure that things will work out somehow," Martin said quickly, "one of your associates, maybe?"

"Sure. I'll ask around," Patterson said then he turned to Ludlow. "Jim, I hate to put you on the spot, but I was wondering if you might be willing to help me out with a problem I have right now?"

Ludlow stared at him a minute. "I don't know, Mike. What is it?"

"Come on out back."

Ludlow looked at Martin, who shook his head, then shrugged.

They both followed Patterson as he walked across the arena. Patterson stopped at a small temporary corral at end and turned the bay horse loose inside. The horse immediately went over and started eating from a pile of hay in the corner.

"Sonny does enjoy his groceries," Patterson said, chuckling a bit.

The three men walked out the far end of the arena into the sunshine. There, adjacent to the arena, was a round corral. In it stood a paint horse, looking over the top rail out into the desert. The horse did not turn or glance towards the men, even when Patterson walked up and set his foot on the metal panel of the corral, making a bit of racket. It was a pretty horse; tall, flashy and an interesting blend of brown, white, and black.

"This is my problem," Patterson said, pointing towards the horse. "This mare was brought to me by one of my credentialed instructors. She's a mustang that came from a herd out in Western Nevada, one that the BLM rounded up. They adopted her out to a lady that fancied herself a horse trainer. The mare threw her and the lady wound up in the hospital with a concussion. Then my instructor got her; she threw him and he got bunged up pretty bad, and now I have her. If I don't find a way to get through to her, she will basically fall into the '3 strikes you're out' group, and these horses stand a good chance of going to Canada or Mexico for slaughter so that the people in Europe and Asia can dine on horsemeat."

"But I thought the wild horses were protected," Ludlow said, frowning.

"Well, that was the case up until a couple of years ago. Then a Senator from Montana snuck an amendment into some legislation that basically allows 'incorrigible' wild horses to fall outside the protections of the law so that they can go to slaughterhouses or wherever. This mare is probably on a one way trip to a Belgian dinner plate unless I can figure out a way to get through to her."

Ludlow remembered this piece of legislation now. He was not at all surprised that this particular Senator would do such a thing.

He watched the mare speculatively. She did not look at them, or even acknowledge their existence. She just continued to stare out into the desert. She was a beautiful horse and he liked the way her ears pricked forward alertly when she saw a car passing in the distance. He also liked the depth of her chest and her long legs that had plenty of bone – she would be one that could run all day, as long as she was conditioned properly. She also had good feet, like most wild horses.

Patterson looked at Ludlow. "Jim, I've worked with this mare for three weeks and she has not changed one bit from where she was when I got her. She can go through some of the motions; I think the woman that first got her must have round penned her to death, so she can run around in a circle, but that's about it. I don't want to turn her back to the BLM, but I'm all out of ideas. I can't keep her – she really needs some close attention, and I'm going back on the road here real soon, and I've got my own colts I have to get started. When Martin told me you were back in Antelope Valley, I figured I would see if I could get you to give it a shot."

Ludlow looked at him for a long moment, and then shook his head. "I can't help you," he replied firmly, turning and walking away. "I haven't had anything to do with a horse in over 10 years."

Patterson called after him. "Johnny Elk told me once that even as a kid you were one of the best hands with horses that he had ever seen. He said you never gave up on a horse; you were always willing to take whatever time it took to get a horse on the right path.. Never thought I'd see the day that Jim Ludlow would walk away from a horse that was in trouble."

Ludlow walked on a bit, then turned back to face him, suddenly furious. "Goddamn it, what's wrong with you? Don't you understand English? I can't help you! That PERSON doesn't exist anymore."

"How do you know that if you aren't even willing to try?" Martin called back.

"I'm not asking for myself, Jim," Patterson said in a reasonable tone, not reacting to Ludlow's anger. "This is a good mare, I can sense it in her. Please. Even if you don't do no good, you can't do more harm than what's already been done."

Ludlow looked at the mare again. "Can't you understand that she doesn't want to be here? She wants to be out there," he said, pointing to the desert, and speaking loudly. "Free. Why don't you just turn her loose?"

"You know better than that, Jim," Patterson said. "There's no place for her to go. She's still BLM property, so we can't just turn her loose. Her own herd was rounded up and wiped out. If the BLM gets her, that's it. They'll ship her off to one of their holding facilities, and the private contractor will probably sell her to slaughterhouse buyer the first chance he gets. That's the way it works now. She's a 3-striker, don't you get it?"

Ludlow was trapped and he knew it. He looked at the mare, who still staring off into the desert. "Did you have anything to do with this?" he asked Martin angrily.

"Me?" Martin said, surprised. "Why, no."

Ludlow paced a bit, then stopped and looked at Patterson. "All right. I will try, but no promises."

Patterson nodded and smiled. "So, you want her history or anything?" he asked.

"No. Not from you!" Ludlow knew he was being rude, but he was still angry at the situation and didn't care. Patterson only grinned and shook his head.

Ludlow opened the gate to the round pen and walked inside. The mare glanced at him once when the gate opened, then turned away. He walked slowly from one side of the pen to the other; the mare ignored him completely. He walked within about ten feet of her and she quickly turned her hind end towards him and raised a rear foot in a clear warning not to come any closer. She continued to stare out into the desert.

Ludlow sighed. The horse was completely shut down, the worst kind to work with. Once you got a reaction, got the feet moving, then you had something you could build on to start developing a partnership. When they wouldn't even recognize your existence, it made the process extremely difficult, if not impossible.

He slapped his leg a couple of times to see if that noise would evoke a reaction. Nothing. He took a lariat that was hanging on the side of the corral and slapped his leg a couple of times. Still nothing. He tossed the rope towards her flanks, and she sidestepped a bit, but didn't move. She still continued staring out into the desert.

"Mike, do you have a flag?" Ludlow called out.

"Yep," Patterson said. He walked over to a dually truck that was parked nearby, opened the door, and pulled out a long stick with a small wedge of orange plastic taped to the end of it. He brought it over and Ludlow took it from him.

Ludlow lightly tapped the ground with the flag, making a bit of noise, and noticed that he got the flick of an ear towards him, as well as a brief wary look. He took the flag in his right hand and pointed it towards her inside hip. She moved to his left in a slow, sullen walk, as far away from him as she could get. She still refused to look at him. It was not much, but it was a start; at least she was walking.

"How did you get her in the trailer to get her here?" Ludlow called out as he moved the mare around.

"Well, we used a war bridle, and flagged her. Plus she likes Sonny, the horse we used in the session today," Patterson said.

Ludlow just shook his head. He knew why Patterson had done what he had, but it didn't make things any easier. War bridles, halters that used pain from a wire or cord run across the gums of the horse to force the horse to lead, were equipment you used when everything else failed. Johnny Elk had hated them and had not allowed them on their ranch.

"Is there any sweet feed around here?" Ludlow asked.

Patterson again went to the dually and pulled out a small white bucket and brought it over. Ludlow took a good handful of the feed and put it in both pockets, then set the bucket just behind him. He noticed that the mare's ears flicked forward when she heard the noise of the feed rattling around in the bucket. Another hopeful sign. Some horse trainers refused to use feed when training a horse, but Ludlow knew that it was a tool, just like any other tool, that could be either used correctly or misused. In certain cases, it could help get a concept across quickly to the horse that might be struggling.

"What's her name?" Ludlow asked.

"Well, we've been calling her Cactus, since she has such a prickly disposition," Patterson said.

Ludlow laughed a bit, in spite of himself.

He kept his eyes focused on the mare and continued to move her forward. She had a nice clean walk and, to Ludlow, she didn't seem to have any physical problems.

"She looks to be about 5 years old, is that right, Mike?" he asked.

"That's right," Patterson said, shaking his head. Not many people could judge a horse's age by just looking at them from across a corral.

Ludlow kept the mare moving forward, carefully watching her inside eye and ear. She had her ear slightly flicked toward him, but she was not really 'with' him; she simply just keeping an eye on the noisy flag. He was just a nuisance as far as she was concerned, something to be ignored once the irritation of the flag was removed.

He put the flag behind him against his leg to keep it quiet and she stopped, still not facing him. Then he reached behind and got the feed bucket. She turned her head to look at him and her ears pricked forward.

"Well, young lady, I think we know what your Achilles heel is now, don't we?" Ludlow said quietly. Ludlow approached her with the feed bucket and she turned to face him. He held out a handful of sweet feed, which she delicately took from his flattened palm. When she was done she turned quick as a snap to kick. Ludlow had expected this though, and he quickly tapped her on the rump with the flag. Shocked, she bolted off to the other side of the corral, where she finally turned and looked at him with an indignant expression. It was the first honest look he seen from her.

He continued to work with her, trying to find a balance between getting her to move forward and turn inwards towards him. Sometimes, the only thing he got was a slight ear flick in his direction when he dropped the pressure from the flag and stepped back. An hour passed, and then another. Finally, Ludlow pushed with the flag very hard, trying to drive her forward into a lope. This time she whirled to face him and reared, striking out with her front feet. Ludlow easily sidestepped her and banged the flag on the ground several times. She whirled and took off, kicking out at him for good measure, but again he moved aside. Then, she turned to face him, watching him carefully; her ears pricked towards him.

"Well, that made her mad, didn't it?" he called out to the two men on the side, chuckling a bit.

"Good girl. Good girl," he then said in a soft soothing voice, smiling. She was looking at him and paying attention. It was progress.

"Mike, could you toss her a little hay?" he asked.

Mike waved assent, and again went back to the dually, grabbed a good-sized flake of hay, and tossed it in the round pen. Cactus walked over to it and started eating, still keeping a close eye on Ludlow until he stepped out of the corral.

Ludlow saw a water bucket sitting outside the pen. He picked it up, opened the gate and set it inside. After he walked away, Cactus came over and took a long drink, then returned to her hay, pointedly ignoring the men standing just outside the corral.

Ludlow looked down at the ground and laughed. It didn't occur to him that it was the first time he had laughed in months. Then he turned, set the flag down on the ground and looked at Patterson and Martin.

"This is going to take some time," he said. "She's nearly totally shut down as a defense mechanism, and if you try to push past it, she fights you, as you and these others have already found out. This mare has a strong will and she has no trust of people. I also think she's pretty sensitive, but I don't think she's beyond hope."

"So, what do you plan on doing about it?" Martin asked.

Ludlow looked at him strangely. "Me? Martin, remember, I'm in rehab myself," he said, glancing at Patterson.

"Yes, and this is the first time since you left Washington that I have seen you act like a living, breathing human being instead of a zombie," Martin said tartly.

He roughly grabbed Ludlow's arm and turned him towards the mare.

"You are NO DIFFERENT than this horse," Martin yelled, gesturing towards Cactus. "NO DIFFERENT. Shut down, just waiting to die because LIFE hasn't been fair."

Ludlow looked at him, shocked. Mike Patterson stared at the ground and shuffled his feet, clearly wishing he were somewhere else.

Martin picked up the flag and started banging Ludlow's legs with it.

"If I had known this was what it would take I would have gotten one of these things a long time ago!" he said.

Ludlow and Patterson both looked at him as if he were daft.

Then Martin stopped and chuckled a bit. "Look, Jim, I believe in using whatever type of therapy works for any particular individual. I think working Cactus through her problems is the best thing you could do right now."

Ludlow stared at him suspiciously for a minute. "I don't understand what you're telling me," he said.

"I mean," Martin said, rolling his eyes theatrically, "that the therapy we've tried hasn't worked with you, so I want to try something else. I think that if you help this mare work through her problems, you will work through your own. I don't know how I can make it any clearer than that."

"So, no more sessions with Dr. Balcer, no more exercise, no more three hour group sessions?" Ludlow asked.

"Dr. Balcer, those you still have to attend, exercise – I think you'll get enough exercise here, group session – since you've been sleeping through them anyway, I don't see that missing them will be that much of a loss."

Ludlow stared at Cactus for a long while, remembering what Patterson had said about the equine slaughterhouses.

"OK. I give up," Ludlow said, shaking his head and smiling, "I'll see what I can do with her. I may need a riding horse to work with her; can we do anything about that?" He looked at Patterson.

"I'll leave you Sonny; I think he'll work for you real good," he said.

"I guess I'll need my saddle and a few things from our ranch," Ludlow said, looking at Martin.

"Just tell me what you need; I'll get Sharon to bring it over."

Ludlow nodded and gazed at Cactus a minute.

"Well boys, I need to be getting back home. I'll leave you

plenty of hay and feed, I brought a good bit with me," Patterson said.

Ludlow looked suspiciously from one man to the other. "I'm not going to ask any more questions, I don't think," Ludlow said. "Just set the hay and feed out beside your truck. I'll move it and make sure the horses are well bedded down this evening."

"OK. See you in a few days when I come back for another session. Call if you need anything or have any questions. Martin has my number," Patterson said.

He waved and walked off to his truck. He set out two good-sized bales of hay and a bag of feed at the side of the barn, then drove off, towing his large horse trailer behind him.

After he left, Ludlow turned to look at Martin. "Can I ask you something?" he said.

"I thought you said no more questions."

"Different subject. Is there some reason I haven't had any visitors?"

Martin looked uncomfortable. "They wanted to come, but we generally don't allow visitors for the first 30 days. Sharon wanted to see you today when she dropped off the boots, but I wanted to wait."

"Wait on what?"

"Wait to see if you decided to come back to the world of the living."

*

The next morning, Ludlow got up at 6, grabbed some coffee from the kitchen, hijacked the golf cart, and drove down to the barn to check on the horses. He fed them, then headed back to get some breakfast and have his 9 a.m. with Dr. Balcer. He found himself talking about Cactus and her problems, while Dr. Balcer only listened and nodded, occasionally taking notes. Then it was back down to the barn. Ludlow was stiff and sore from the exercise the day before, but he made up his mind to work through it.

Johnny Elk had told Ludlow many times that horses had to mull concepts over in their minds for a day or two before really accepting something new, and he found that with Cactus. This time, when he walked up to the corral, she turned and looked at him, ears pointed attentively towards him for a few minutes, before she turned back to look at the desert. He nodded and smiled to himself. Progress.

Ludlow was surprised when Sharon showed up around lunchtime with a couple of burgers, as well as his saddle and saddle blanket, a couple of bridles, and a few other items of tack.

She gave him a big hug.

"Good to see you, Jimmy. We've been worried sick," she said.

"I'm sorry, Sharon. I really am. I never wanted to cause anyone any trouble."

"I know that. But anyway, I'm glad you're back with us again. And this mare," she said, pointing towards Cactus, "she's a pretty thing."

"She is," Ludlow replied, "but she's had some rough breaks. I think I can get her going again."

Sharon nodded and grinned. "Well, if anyone can do it, you can."

They sat down in a couple of the old folding chairs and started on the burgers. To Ludlow, they tasted delicious. He couldn't remember the last time he had had a hamburger. Finally, he looked over at Sharon.

"Have you heard from Maddy?" he asked tentatively.

Sharon glanced at him a second, then took the last bite of burger, and put the paper wrapping in the bag she had brought them in. "I talked to her last week."

Ludlow looked at her, he could tell that she really didn't want to talk about Madeleine, but he pressed her anyway. "What did she say? Is she coming out?"

Sharon shook her head. "I'm not sure we need to be talking about this right now."

"Look, I'm going to find out sooner or later, whatever it is you're holding back. I prefer sooner myself," he said.

"All right," she said, looking at him evenly. "I know Martin is probably going to be pissed at me for telling you this, but I don't care. Madeleine won't be coming out. She says she felt so betrayed by your drinking that she doesn't want to try to put things back together; she just wants to get on with her life. She said she'd keep you on her health insurance policy until you get out of rehab, and send you whatever personal items you want if you get her a list. But she doesn't want to talk to you. She says it just hurts too much."

Ludlow sat back in the chair a bit, feeling winded. Even though it hadn't been unexpected, hearing Sharon say it was still a blow.

"Look, Jimmy," Sharon said, putting her arm around his shoulders, "you've tried to do what Johnny Elk wanted you to do, and then you tried to do what Madeleine wanted you to do. Maybe it's time to do what Jim Ludlow wants do to. Quite frankly, I wish you'd never left the ranch, although the extra education didn't do you any harm, knucklehead that you are."

Ludlow looked at her, pleased that she was teasing him again as she used to when they were kids.

"Madeleine will want a divorce, I guess," he said. He was surprised that he actually felt light, as if a great weight had been lifted from him.

"Probably. Although she didn't say that."

"Well, if that's what she wants, I won't stand in her way," he said and shrugged, surprised how little the thought bothered him.

Sharon stared at him a moment, mouth agape, and then shook her head. "You never cease to amaze me," she said. "Mother and Grandmother will be coming over this weekend to pay you a visit. And, Jim, I'm glad you're back, in more ways than one."

Gradually, Ludlow's life at the MWCL began to center around Cactus and Sonny. Martin came by one day and asked if he could give guidance to one of the trustees in the work release program. The poor man was charged with getting the old barn cleaned out and refurbished and he didn't know what he doing. Ludlow was the only one at the Center who had any real ranch experience and Martin felt he could provide some desperately needed some guidance.

Ludlow began working with Justin Angelo, the trustee, and soon the barn and other buildings got cleaned up and repaired.

He had started riding Sonny as soon as he got his saddle and bridle from Sharon. He began taking him out on long trail rides through the desert. Sometimes he ponied Cactus behind them, making sure both horses got adequate exercise. Ludlow grew lean and fit again as the weeks passed. Patterson came once or twice a week to conduct his 'equitherapy,' as they were beginning to call it. At first, Jim only watched, but then he agreed to take over the sessions when Patterson had to go back on the road again for his clinics.

The day that Ludlow rode Cactus for the first time, there was quite a crowd in the arena, which he would have avoided if possible. But Cactus was actually shaping up to be a solid, sensible horse and she wasn't bothered at all by the people. Ludlow had been so pleased with her he told Patterson that he could take Sonny back home; Cactus was doing just fine.

Dr. Balcer had reduced the number of morning sessions to 2-3 a week, and sometimes even those were conducted down at the barn area. She often watched the equitherapy sessions.

Ludlow's family had started visiting regularly. He was distressed to see that Sarah was starting to become frail and weak, but Sharon had told him that she had taken Johnny Elk's death very hard, and often talked of the day she would see him again. Annie hugged him, grinned, and frequently pinched his cheeks, as she had done when he was a boy and she was pleased with him. They were all there the day that he first rode Cactus, along with most of the people from the rehab center (many he had been with initially had gone home; there were new people coming in all the time).

Then, one day a tractor-trailer pulled in with a load of horses, which were released into several paddocks adjacent to the large barn. They were wild horses, recently captured out in Western Nevada. Martin had finally got around to telling Ludlow that the MWCL had successfully bid on a contract with the BLM and State of Nevada to develop a work-release program where non-violent pre-release inmates would gentle and train wild horses so they would have a better chance of being successfully adopted out to good homes. Martin Levi had asked Ludlow if he would be willing to design a training program that would fit within the BLM/Nevada Dept. of Corrections guidelines.

"How long has this been in the works?" Ludlow asked when Martin told him about the program.

"Over a year, so don't think we planned this just for you," Martin said a bit caustically.

Ludlow shook his head, chuckling, and agreed that he would do whatever he could to help.

Ludlow found now that his days were filled from the time he got up until he went to bed, which was sometimes very late. He only slept at the Center; usually he ate with the work-release team at the barn because there was just so much work to get done with the horses.

He found that he had become attached to Cactus and worked with Mike Patterson to approach the BLM to see if he could adopt her. Patterson called someone he knew in the BLM office in Idaho, they sent out some paperwork, and it was done.

One day, Martin came looking for Ludlow down at the arena. Ludlow was just starting to train Cactus to be ridden without a bridle, something he had always loved doing on the ranch, and she was doing very well. Ludlow thought she was one of the smartest mares he had ever seen, and delighted in working with her. When Ludlow saw Martin down in the far end, he pushed Cactus into a fast lope and had her come to a sliding stop right in front of him. Then Ludlow patted her proudly.

"Have you ever seen such a mare, Marty?"

Martin Levi laughed and rubbed Cactus' neck. She had come to love humans and was very affectionate, a real pet. She touched her nose to Levi's face in a 'kiss' and he laughed.

"Amazing transformation, Jim. Simply amazing," he said. Then he looked at Ludlow keenly. "Got news for you Jim. Dr. Balcer says she's done all she can for you. You've made a lot of progress; you're out of the woods so to speak, now it's time to move on. Time to go home."

Ludlow looked at Martin, and then swung down off Cactus. She waited at his shoulder patiently while he stood in front of Martin. "Where's home, Marty? And what about these programs here? I've put a lot into them, you know."

Martin held up his hands. "You know as well as I do where home is. You're going back to the ranch, and you've got a job here as long as you want it, and guess what, we'll actually PAY you to do what you have been doing as therapy. Hank, Sharon, and the rest of your clan are looking forward to having you back home. That new house they have been working on for the past year is far enough along for them to move into. Annie and Sarah are going to stay in the old house. The mobile home that Hank and Sharon and the kids have been living in is going to be available, so it's yours if you want it."

Ludlow looked at him and shook his head in wonderment.

"I recommend you getting an AA sponsor and attend meetings. We have several good ones who would be glad to sponsor you. And you always can call me, you know."

Ludlow smiled and looked down at the ground a moment. "I'll take your advice, but now that I am alive again, I'm finding I like it. Probably more than I ever did," Ludlow said, with a slow grin. "And I've got you to thank for that, Marty."

Marty pointed at Cactus. "And her. And yourself."

"Thanks, Martin. I won't ever be able to repay you."

"Stay sober, that's payment enough," Martin said, placing a hand on Ludlow's shoulder.

Part III
Kate

Chapter 10

When Kate got back up to the studio, she collapsed on the small sofa that looked out towards the mountains. She was as tired as she could ever remember being. She sighed and took a deep breath.

Her mind, of course, inevitably kept swinging back to the man who was probably still downstairs in the barn. She could never remember having such a profound reaction when she had ever met anyone for the first time before. Of course, Jim Ludlow was gorgeous, and seemed to be a genuinely nice guy (and he loved horses which was a HUGE plus). There was something else though. She had been around plenty of good-looking men before over the years and there had never been this sense of disorientation. She felt as if some giant hand had reached down and wrenched her life onto a completely different path.

All because of one man? I'm becoming too silly to be believed. Must be hormones, she thought.

She looked at her watch. It was about 10:30, which meant it was almost 12:30 in DC. Too late to make a phone call.

Kate had some questions she had been too afraid for months to ask. Suddenly, she wasn't afraid anymore.

She was finally ready to get some answers. Tomorrow morning, she would start.

*

The next morning Kate woke up after a surprisingly peaceful night's sleep. The bed had been comfortable, and she had been so exhausted from the past few days that sleep had come easy. When she got up, she muddled her way into the kitchen, found the coffee and coffee maker that Sharon had told her about, and made a pot of coffee. She checked her watch; it was 6:30. She gave Sharon a call on her cell phone and left a voicemail saying she would meet her later down at the office. She had some things to take care of this morning.

She went over to Kimmy's windows and looked out towards the mountains. They were just starting to glow with the dusky dawn pink of the morning. The ambrosial smell of coffee caused her to drift back to the kitchen. She poured herself a good-sized cup and sat down, took a long drink, and picked up her Smartphone. She looked through her contacts until she found

Maria Nuncio's name. It was nearly 10:00 am in DC; Maria would be at work now. Kate took another long drink of coffee, and breathed deeply to try to steady her heart rate. This conversation, the one that she had been avoiding for months, would be where the rubber met the road.

Kate pushed the button and Maria's cell phone started ringing. Kate held her breath, hoping that Maria would pick up. She felt that if she had to leave a voicemail message, she would lose the courage she had finally gathered together. But then, Maria picked up.

"Kate, hi! What's up?"

"Hi, Maria, don't know if you heard, but I'm out in Nevada right now."

"I heard that. Rumor had it that Meyers sent you out on one of his 'GUT quests.'"

Kate paused a minute, took a deep breath, and decided just to spit it out.

"Maria, I want to know what happened with Manny," she said. "The night he died, I mean. I hope you have time to talk right now, because I don't know if I can work up the nerve to call and ask again."

"Oh, Kate," Maria said, "I don't know how many times I can tell you I'm sorry."

"It's OK, Maria, don't worry about it. I don't blame you, but I need to know what happened."

She heard Maria sigh.

"Well, there's not much to tell really. I came home from work and checked on Manny and gave him his dinner – I fed him exactly at the same time and gave him the same grain as always. While I was there and finishing up, John showed up."

"John came out?" Kate asked, surprised.

"Yeah. He said that he had had a terrible day at work, and just wanted to get of town for the night. I told him that he didn't need to worry about Manny, and I would come back in the morning to feed and turn him out."

"About midnight, I got a call from Dr. Leonard," Maria said. "She called to tell me that Manny had colicked and asked what I had fed that night. I told her it was just the usual mix that you fed, nothing special. She said Manny was in really bad shape and some hard decisions needed to be made – either to take Manny to the equine hospital at New Bolton or put him down. I asked if there was anything I could do, she said no. She told me that John was trying to call you in Africa to see what you wanted to do. The next morning, I called Dr. Leonard back, and she told me that you had made the decision to put Manny down. And, that's all I know. I am so sorry, Kate. I know how much you loved that horse."

"Leonard said that I made that decision?" Kate asked.

"That's right. I was surprised that she told me that. I guess vets have client confidentiality like everyone else."

Maria was silent for a minute.

"Kate, don't tell me John didn't talk to you about it before it happened," she said.

"Maria, I don't want to get into that right now in any detail, but, no, he didn't talk to me. He called me after it was done."

"But," Kate continued after a pause, "maybe Leonard got it wrong."

"Maybe. I just know what she told me when I called. Again, Katie, I feel sorry about what happened."

"Maria, it wasn't your fault. Just don't worry about it."

"Are you sure? You haven't really talked to me since it happened; not until today."

"I was afraid what you might tell me," Kate said simply. They talked a few more minutes, and then agreed to get together when Kate got back to DC.

Kate ended the call and sat for a moment. She had another decision to make now. Call Dr. Patricia Leonard, and find out what exactly happened that night, or just let it go. Put it behind her. She could probably patch things up with John, even though he was royally pissed at her right now. She dug around in her purse and found the ring he had given her. She carefully set it down on the table, picked up her phone again, found Patricia Leonard's number and called. She got the vet's office, but wheedled Leonard's cell phone number out of the receptionist. She had known Patricia Leonard since she had moved to DC. Leonard was also an Event rider, but Kate didn't normally use her as a vet. She had never cared for the way Leonard treated her horses in competition, and she had an arrogance about her that set Kate's teeth on edge. Kate usually used another veterinarian, Bobby Marklinson, but he hadn't been available the night Manny had died. Or, at least that's what John had told her.

Patricia Leonard picked up on the third ring.

"Hey, Patty. It's Kate Wyndham."

"Hello, Kate, how are you?" Leonard's tone was definitely cool, Kate noticed.

"I'm OK, Patty. Listen have you got a minute? I want to talk to you about Manny, about the night he died."

"Well, I'm on the road, between clients. I guess I can give you a few minutes. I don't know what I can tell you that you don't already know."

Kate sighed. "I think you can tell me a lot that I don't already know," she said. "First thing, I want you to know that I never knew anything about Manny even being sick until after he had been put down."

"What? Jesus, Kate...I want you to know that your boyfriend told me that this was YOUR decision, that you were fully informed," Leonard said defensively.

"Look, Patty, I'm not holding you responsible. Can you please just tell me what happened that night?"

"Well, your boyfriend, John, that's his name, right? He called me, said that Manny was down, rolling in the stall," Leonard said. "I got there as quick as I could, and he was right. Manny was down, and in quite a bit of pain. We gave him two shots of banamine, which helped with the pain. He got up again and we started walking him. I tubed him and he did pass some poop, so I was feeling pretty good about things. His gums were pale, which was a concern, but then he suddenly started groaning with pain and was getting weaker. I gave John the choice, put him down or give him another shot of banamine and see if we could get him to New Bolton for a more thorough workup. John had told me that he would try to get you on your satellite phone in Africa. He walked in the house, was gone for about 10 or 15 minutes. He came back and said he had managed to get you on the phone long enough to tell you what was going on, and that you made it very clear you didn't want Manny to suffer. If he was in pain, to put him out of his misery immediately. He said you were not in favor of taking him to New Bolton. I asked if I could talk to you, and he said that the connection had dropped and he hadn't been able to get you back. So, as far as I was concerned, the decision was made, and I followed through with the client's wishes."

"Jesus, Patty," Kate said, without thinking.

"Kate, I'm sorry. I don't know why John would lie about such a thing. Maybe he just wanted to spare you."

"Do you think they could have helped Manny at New Bolton?"

Leonard paused on the phone for a moment, then said, "I don't know. This was a very unusual colic. I could have sworn he was pulling out of it when we got him up and moving, but his gums were almost paper white, as if he had internal bleeding."

"But what would cause sudden internal bleeding in a perfectly healthy horse?"

"Any number of things really, injury, poisoning, cancer, dietary 'indiscretion' come to mind. Hard to tell without an autopsy."

"Well, it's way too late for that now. Thanks Patty, I want you to know I appreciate everything you did for Manny and I'm sure you only did what you thought was right."

"All right Kate, I'm sorry all this happened."

"Me, too. See you, and thanks again."

Kate hit the end call button on the phone and set it down on the table. She hugged her arms to herself and walked over to the window and looked out. She felt very cold.

She thought back on the past few months and remembered John had said repeatedly that Dr. Leonard had told him she suspected it was Maria feeding Manny incorrectly that had caused him to colic so badly. John also had complained several times about how arrogant and difficult Patricia Leonard had been, and he understood why Kate didn't like to use her as a vet. He had cautioned Kate not to talk to her about that last night, because it would do nothing but upset her further. Manny was dead, Kate needed to move on with her life.

John Ridley wasn't as clever as he thought, however. He had overplayed his hand.

She sat in the armchair near the window and stared out at the mountains, thinking about her relationship with John Ridley, and how she had come to be with him to begin with.

*

Kate's childhood, up until she was about 10, had not been an easy one. Her mother and father had been the darlings of Berea High School in Kentucky. Her dad, Anders Wyndham, had been a good-looking star basketball and football player. Tall, auburn-haired and green-eyed he had been considered 'quite the catch' by the high school girls, her grandmother had told her once, with a disapproving curl of her lip. Kate's mother, Cynthia Moore, had been the slim blonde cheerleader, editor of the student newspaper, homecoming queen, and voted 'most likely to be famous.' Cynthia Moore and Anders Wyndham had been the dream couple their senior year at Berea High.

According to her Grandmother Moore, her mother had big plans. She had dreams of being a 'woman of consequence,' Grandma Moore told her sourly many, many times. However, Grandma Moore had usually spoken in sour tones about any subject other than herself, the Bible, the Berea First Baptist Church, and the IGA grocery store (which itself was marginal). But, in any event, Cynthia's (she refused to answer to the diminutive Cindy) magnificent plans came to a screeching halt when she discovered she was pregnant.

Anders had stood up to do the right thing and married Cynthia Moore the day after graduation. But many wondered how the marriage would work. Anders Wyndham had a questionable background. He and his family had moved to Berea from Union City, Tennessee and no one knew anything about them. He lived with his grandparents, and while they seemed to be decent, hard working people (his grandfather worked as a pharmacist in the local chain pharmacy), there was always the question as to why young Anders didn't live with his parents like a normal boy. Plus, they were Catholics.

Grandmother Moore had mentioned to Kate several times that it could have been worse, of course.

They could have been Jews.

Kate Wyndham came into the world in mid-November. She was a fat and happy baby, with her father's red hair and gray-green eyes. As she grew, her chubby legs shot out until they were small replicas of Anders'; by the time she was seven she was nearly 5 feet tall and skinny as a rail.

Anders and Cynthia tried to make a go of it as a young married couple. They both did all the right things. They went to church on Sundays, (to the correct Baptist church– Cynthia had scotched the Catholic nonsense early on in the marriage) and Anders worked hard delivering car parts for a local distribution center. Cynthia was determined to be a 'woman of consequence,' even as a mother. She always made sure Kate had the most darling dresses and was always clean and adorable-looking. Never mind that the scratchy pinafores left a bleeding rash on Kate's thighs.

"Beauty knows no pain, dear," Cynthia would say, brightly, when Kate was old enough to complain. That was on the good days. On Cynthia's bad days, which became more and more frequent as Kate grew older, a quick stinging slap across the face usually followed any complaints. Kate learned early on to endure.

When Kate's permanent teeth came in, some real trouble started. Anders had a slight overbite, but his wide eyes and strong jaw offset it, and it actually made his face even more attractive. In Kate, the overbite was much more pronounced, with two protruding buckteeth. With her nearly carroty red hair, she looked like Howdy Doody, which was what other children usually called her.

And it was also at this time that Cynthia and Anders' marriage began to fall apart.

Kate could still remember hiding in the small closet under the stairs during the worst of the fights. It was always the same, her mother yelling, throwing things across the room and striking Anders with her fists.

And then, one day, Anders struck back.

Kate never knew what it was that set her father off that night; she only remembered peeking out from her hiding place after hearing a loud scream, followed by a heavy thud. She could just see her mother's head, with her long blond hair fanned across the worn linoleum floor in their rented house. Cynthia Wyndham was unconscious, blood running from her perfect nose. Her arm lay at a sickeningly unnatural angle.

Then she saw her father, the man that took her for piggyback rides, bought her ice cream cones at the Dairy Queen, and helped her to sneak away for her first pony ride. His face looked sick, like her friend Debbie when she saw a truck hit a dog on the road while they were walking to school.

He looked at her and she remembered that his face was wet and shiny.

"I'm sorry, Katie-girl, but I can't take any more of this. If I stay, I'll kill her," he said.

And she heard him go upstairs, she heard drawers slam, then he came downstairs with a suitcase. He went and put his hand gently on her mother's throat, like the doctors on television did when they wanted to see if someone was alive, went to the phone, and made a call.

Then he walked over to her, picked her up and gave her a hug and a kiss.

"You just remember this. You're a good girl, and I love you and I will always love you. You be good for your momma, now."

And he had walked out the door. A little later, some policemen came, then some other men that put her mother on a rolling bed and took her away. The policemen took Kate to live with Grandma Moore while her mother was in the hospital.

She never saw her father again, or any of his family after that. Anders' grandfather had died the year before. His grandmother was rumored to have moved in with a sister in Cincinnati, but no one knew how to get in touch with her. Anders' grandparents had never had much to do with Kate over the years anyway.

Kate's Grandpa Moore had died several years prior (Kate had heard someone say once that it was the only surefire way he could escape Grandma Moore, although that didn't make sense to her), so it was only Kate and Grandma Moore in the drafty old house in the country until Kate's mother came home from the hospital. When Kate's mother did get out of the hospital, she and some friends from the Baptist church packed up her belongings from the house she had rented with Anders and she showed up on Grandma Moore's doorstep.

"It's only temporary, Mother," she had said as she walked in the door, awkwardly carrying a suitcase as her right arm was still in a cast. Grandma Moore had glowered at her daughter, but had not objected.

Once her arm healed (Cynthia's broken nose had been well repaired by a local surgeon in Lexington, cousin to one of the women in her Sunday School class) Cynthia went out and got a job as an administrative assistant in a small law firm in Lexington called Weed and Harrington. She worked long hours, and Kate spent most of her time with Grandma Moore when she wasn't in school. Although Grandma Moore was very stern and strict, Kate liked living in the country. Their neighbor had two gentle draft horses that would come to the fence and eat grass that Kate pulled and stuck under the bottom rail. She loved to feel their velvety noses when they nuzzled her hands, and she always marveled at

171

their feet, which were as large as dinner plates.

She also developed a great love of reading and would spent every bit of time she could in her small bedroom, curled up in bed with a book she brought home from the school library. Then, there was church of course. Grandma Moore went Sunday mornings and evenings and Wednesday nights, and Kate was required to go also. Kate's mother also went when she wasn't working.

During the course of Cynthia Wyndham's tenure at Weed and Harrington, she began keeping company with one of their premier clients, J. Quincy Montcrief. JQ was quite a bit older than Cynthia, being a widower in his early 60s, but he found the young woman to be intelligent and engaging. When he came to the see his lawyer, Joe Harrington, Cynthia always had a special smile for him and made fresh coffee. JQ found himself coming up with more and more excuses to stop by and talk with his lawyer, and spent less and less time tending to his chain of convenience stores and truck stops. One day, Joe Harrington, who had finally had enough, told him flat out that it would be cheaper just to ask Cynthia Wyndham out on a date, rather than racking up billable hours on bullshit legal questions. Cynthia had been standing outside when Harrington had his little outburst, and she had casually opened the door and told JQ she would be glad to have dinner with him anytime he asked.

"What about Friday?" JQ blurted out, as if he had been poked with a stick.

"Friday will be super," she replied, and smiled her special smile at him.

And so, JQ Montcrief's courtship of Cynthia Wyndham commenced.

Kate always remembered the first time she met JQ. One evening, he had come to her grandmother's house with her mother for dinner. He was kind of a funny looking man, not much taller than her mother, with a crooked nose and big ears. She had also thought he was terribly old. But he had played a game with her of guessing how much change he had in his pockets. She guessed an amount, and looking surprised, he counted out the exact amount and gave it to her. But then he turned and Kate heard his pockets jingling and she giggled.

From that moment she began to love JQ Montcrief.

Cynthia and JQ 'saw each other socially' as Cynthia liked to say, for a little more than a year, then one night JQ had proposed, handing her a big diamond ring that had to be resized for her small hand. They were married in a quiet ceremony in the Baptist church a few months later, with only a few friends, Grandma Moore (who disapproved of her daughter's fiancé, but was tolerant of the marriage because it meant she would get her house back), and JQ's brother. JQ and his former wife had had no children.

And so, Kate moved from her grandmother's small farmhouse to JQ's rambling rancher that lay on one of the many winding roads between Berea and Lexington. And as soon Cynthia Wyndham became Cynthia Montcrief, she began a very well planned campaign to become a 'woman of consequence.'

The first thing she did, of course, was to quit her job at Weed and Harrington, although she made sure she remained on good terms with them. Then she slowly began to use JQ's money to open a wedge into the 'good blood,' as she called it. Not too quick, and not too brash; she knew quite well that any overt push would only earn disdain, so she began very slowly appearing at fundraisers, political banquets, any play or show that would seem popular, and, of course the numerous social events that surrounded Lexington's horse industry. She worked hard at making JQ more presentable. It was no easy task. JQ was a high school dropout who had started life as a mechanic. But he was also a clever businessman and very adept with a dollar. When his aging boss decided to sell the gas station where JQ worked, JQ bought it then added a convenience store to the station. The station was very near an interchange off the new interstate that was being constructed, and soon he had a thriving business from interstate traffic. Then he purchased other properties and expanded; his company was always growing. His wife, Mary, whom he had married when he was 18, had died of breast cancer after 20 years of a relatively happy marriage. JQ didn't see any sense in all the folderol his new wife wanted from him, and insisted on going to work at 6 am every morning like he had always done. But he learned that behind Cynthia's special smile and sparkling blue eyes lay an iron will, and he wanted to make his new bride happy. So, inch-by-inch, party-by-party, club membership by club membership, he began to conform to Cynthia's idea of what the husband of a 'woman of consequence' should be. Generally, it amounted to wearing a tuxedo or suit, going with Cynthia to events, and not saying much.

JQ and Kate, however, developed a deep affection for each other as time passed. Kate's mother paid little attention to her (in fact it often seemed to Kate that it pained her mother to even look at her). One of the first things Cynthia did was to hire a live-in nanny/housekeeper (or *au pair* as Cynthia called her); an illegal Mexican immigrant named Ignatia whom Kate became very close to.

JQ was special though. It was JQ who took her to the orthodontist for braces, and JQ who took her to the dermatologist when she developed severe cystic acne. Kate's fascination with horses only intensified as she grew older, and JQ arranged for her to have riding lessons at a boarding stable whose property adjoined his. He also made provision with Mrs. Keller, the stable owner, for a string of leases of ponies and horses for Kate as she grew up, and went to every horse show she rode in. Cynthia would go to the more important shows, making sure she could be recognized as the doting horse show mother, but other than that, had no interest in the child's hobby. She was now busy with the Junior League, the Republican Women's Caucus, golfing, and the country club, and other events, and only noticed Kate when she did something clumsy in the house (which she usually did when her mother was around). Her voice, though soft, measured, and Southern, stung with scorn most of the time when she bothered to talk to Kate at all. Eventually, Kate began avoiding her whenever possible.

Occasionally, Kate's mother took umbrage with the attention JQ gave her daughter. He had offered to adopt Kate several times, but Cynthia always found reasons to put it off. Eventually, she started becoming angry when he asked about it, so he stopped asking. JQ learned that things in the household ran much more smoothly if he didn't pay too much attention to Kate when Cynthia was home. Kate understood. What she and JQ had was special and private and must be protected.

There was some trouble, though, on Kate's sixteenth birthday. JQ had gotten Kate up early, and had her go out in the driveway. There, parked on Cynthia's manicured zoysia lawn, was one of the small horse vans that the Thoroughbred farms around Lexington used for short haul horse transportation. Cynthia, who was totally unaware of her husband's plans, was still in bed at the time, and only managed to look out the window when she heard the van pull up.

The driver lowered the ramp and out came a horse, such a horse as Kate had always dreamed of having.

He was a 4-year-old chestnut, 16.2 hands, with a white blaze on his face and four white stockings. He had the old English hunter build of 'head like the duchess and bottom like the cook.' He snorted and pranced on the lead, flagging his tail. Kate started walking towards him, tears rolling down her cheeks. Then she heard the front door slam.

"Katherine Anne Wyndham, what do you think you're doing?" she heard her mother bark.

JQ walked right up to her mother and took her arm, none too gently.

"Not today, Cynthia," she overheard JQ say in a stern tone that Kate had never heard him use before. He turned her mother back towards the house. "You go right back in that house and stay out of this. This is my gift to Kate, between her and me, and that's it. We'll have him off this lawn, which I paid for by the way, in a few minutes. This gentleman will take him to Keller's. For this one time, I want you to do as I ask."

Cynthia Montcrief's mouth opened and closed a couple of times, fishlike, but she allowed JQ to lead her back towards the house. She went back inside, slamming the door behind her. The red horse plunged a bit at the noise, but the van driver skillfully turned and calmed him.

Kate slowly approached the horse, who looked at her a little wild eyed, until she patted her leg softly and cooed to him. Then the horse looked at her briefly and reached down to crop at the grass.

"Oh JQ, JQ! He's beautiful, what's his name?" Kate asked.

"What was it they called him again?" JQ asked the driver, a thin, wiry black man.

"Giddy Manitou, but we always called him Manny."

"Didn't make it as a racehorse, Katie," JQ said. "I talked to Angie Keller six months ago, and asked her to be on the lookout for a horse, a PERMANENT horse for you, and this is what she found. She said he'll make a great Eventer, which I guess is what you are determined to do, although I wish you would take up something a little less crazy."

Kate hugged JQ and kissed him on the cheek, and she saw that he had tears in his eyes too. He grasped her hand.

"I didn't buy you a horse before because I didn't want you to get too attached and then have to give him up when you outgrew him. This horse is yours for life, Katie, do you understand? I'll make sure you always have money to take care of him."

"Oh, JQ, I just don't know what to say. No one ever did anything like this for me before. I will never, ever give him up," Kate hugged him again, and he patted her back a bit roughly, becoming embarrassed by so much emotion.

"Well, I think we've relied on your mother's patience long enough, and if he craps on the lawn that will be it for ALL of us," he said, looking at the driver. The man grinned and led the horse back into the van.

"I'll see ya'll over at Keller's," the driver said crawling up into the driver's seat.

"And just so you know," JQ said, putting his arm around Kate, "I understand very well you'll need a new saddle or three, they all have to fit of course, bridles etc. Angie Keller is going to help you out with all that."

Then JQ had hugged her hard.

"Katie, I know this is your dream. And, I am bound and determined to do my best to help you live it. Even though a good part of it scares the shit out of me."

Kate laughed, and hugged him again.

"I promise you I will stay in one piece," she said.

JQ nodded and patted her arm.

"I love you, JQ."

"I love you too, sweetie. Now, let's get over to Keller's and make sure Manny gets settled in all right."

Kate nodded and rushed inside to put on her barn clothes.

*

It seemed that Kate and the big red horse were born to be partners. Both were fearless on the jump course, and extremely competitive, with a high degree of focus and determination. Plus, there was a connection between them that very few riders ever achieved with their horses. Every weekend throughout high school they spent their time together either training for or riding in that most grueling of horse sports: Eventing.

The French were credited with the refinement of three-day Eventing, a type of horse triathlon, in the 1800's. In the beginning, it was officially classified as a 'Raid Militaire', which was a comprehensive test for cavalry horses. Then, over the years, it evolved into a competitive equestrian sport. It became an Olympic sport in 1912 and in 1964 women were allowed to compete against the men equally in all sports venues. Eventing has three phases: dressage, where a horse and rider are tested on precise movements within an arena of a particular size; cross-country, a timed race similar to steeplechase, with jumps and other obstacles; and stadium jumping, another timed jumping event held in an arena or stadium.

In Kate's senior year, she and Manny won the regional Eventing championship and they finished twelfth in her division at the internationally famous Rolex 3-day event held every spring in Lexington. Competing in Rolex had been the crowning achievement in Kate's high school years. She had done well in high school, but had very little social life, except for hanging around the barn with her horsey friends she had grown up with. She only had two dates the entire time she was in high school, both miserable and tense affairs with the sons of two of her mother's friends.

It wasn't that she was excessively homely. The braces had made a world of different in her face, and the acne had cleared up as the years past. But, she was tall, nearly six feet, with long gangly legs and large hands. She was relatively flat chested, which she didn't care about; she had too many big-breasted riding friends who complained about their chronic back pain (and more jokingly, black eyes). Her knobby knees sometimes stuck out oddly in her riding breeches, but fortunately she was leggy enough that the snowy white breeches she had to wear during competition actually looked attractive on her. But the Howdy Doody and Pizza Face jokes of her early adolescence had done their damage. There were a couple of boys she had major crushes on early in high school, but she was so shy and awkward that she never spoke a word to either of them. Having a beautiful, always perfectly put together mother didn't help. Cynthia attempted a few times to take Kate shopping for clothing, but Kate only bought whatever she told her to buy, then put it in her closet and would only wear the clothing if forced.

In any event, between competitions, looking after Manny, and going to school, she didn't have much time for a social life. Her mother still dragged her to church when she was at home on Sundays, but that became less and less frequent. The year after JQ bought Manny for Kate's birthday, he bought her a truck and trailer so she could haul herself to competitions. JQ went with her whenever he could, but he was nearing 70, and starting to slow down a bit. He planned on retiring when Kate graduated from high school. She had been accepted at the University of Michigan and would be moving to Ann Arbor at the end of the summer. She planned on majoring in journalism. JQ had driven up with her to Ann Arbor and helped her find a barn for Manny. They checked out the dorm where she would be staying; she planned on trying out for the UM Equestrian team in the fall.

The day Kate left for college, Manny in tow, everything all packed into her truck, JQ and Cynthia had stood in the driveway, JQ with tears in her eyes, Cynthia merely smiling coolly. She hugged JQ, and bussed her mother's cheek, got in the truck, and headed north.

College opened up a whole new world for Kate. Although she missed JQ (she spoke to him at least a couple of times a week), she found it incredibly liberating not to be living under the oppressive presence of the 'woman of consequence' in her life. While her mother had pressured her to join a sorority, Kate wasn't interested. It seemed too structured and superficial to her. Her roommate, Marty Stuart, was a bit of a party girl, and while Kate wasn't much for drinking, she did go to a few fraternity parties with Marty and it was at one of these parties that she met John Ridley.

He was the first boy who had ever paid the least attention to Kate. He was older than she was by four years, and seemed mature and worldly to Kate, from his time in the Peace Corps in Sierra Leone. The first night they met, he told her about his dreams of going to into politics to make 'a difference.' Politics was the family business, he had said, only half-jokingly. John was an excellent listener, and Kate shared some of her most secret dreams with him. She said she wanted to write stories about animals. She wanted to write about people like Dian Fossey and Jane Goodall, and travel the world.

She and John began to spend more and more time together, but their relationship remained relatively chaste. A few kisses and awkward gropings and that was about it, but they talked at least daily and it was through a Washington contact of his father's that she got her first internship at the Washington Gazette. She was grateful to get the job. JQ and her mother had been in Europe and planned on staying there throughout the summer. Kate had no interest in summer school or staying at the house in Berea by herself while they traveled. John had worked in his father's constituent office in Dearborn that summer, but they still kept in touch over the phone. Kate left Manny at the boarding stable in Ann Arbor when she went to Washington. It was the first time she had been separated from him for any length of time and she found she missed him greatly.

It was during these three months in Washington that Kate lost her virginity to a handsome, elegant Frenchman who was a Washington correspondent for the French liberal magazine, Le Monde. Jacques Du Berrier taught Kate many things, about what wine to have with dinner, how to choose and wear clothing with style, and, most importantly, how to stand up for herself in a newsroom.

"You must speak up to your editors, Kate dear," he said many times. "Don't argue enough to get dismissed, but to make them respect you. You can't hide in the background, not if you want to be a successful journalist."

Kate took his advice to heart and found the courage she had on the cross-country course was there when she needed it to stand up to a junior editor who was trying to run over her, or a rude waiter, or one of her catty fellow interns.

In one such interchange, Kate had caused a bit of a scene with her editor (who was not much older than she was). They were in a heated discussion concerning the fact that Kate would not refer to chimpanzees as 'monkeys' in a story she had written about the Washington Zoo. The editor thought the term monkey 'sang' better on the page. Kate told him flat out that she had no idea what that meant, and she preferred her stories to have accuracy than to 'sing.' When she said that, she heard someone clear his throat, and she turned to see that the Gazette's City Editor, David Meyers, was observing the exchange with a smile on his face.

"She's right, Mr. Tyndale. The story runs as is," Meyers said.

From that point on, David Meyers made a point to say hello to her whenever he saw her, and she saw that what few feature stories she was allowed to write (her internship consisted mostly of copy editing) were actually run pretty much as she had written them.

Kate was hurt, of course, when at the end of the summer Jacques told her about his wife and three children who lived in

Paris. But once she got back to Ann Arbor, she realized that Jacques had never made any promises to her, and he had given her a great gift.

Self-respect.

When she returned to college in the fall, she and John Ridley picked up where they left off, but this time Kate wanted more than gropings and kisses. John never inquired as to how she had acquired her skills as a lover, he was just profoundly grateful.

And so their relationship continued to develop. They got along well; they rarely had arguments, and John supported her riding and seemed to enjoy coming to Eventing trials she rode in on occasion. She spent Thanksgivings with his family in Dearborn, and he went with Kate the couple of times she went back to Berea at Christmas. Cynthia had decided that she preferred to spend Christmas in the Virgin Islands, so she and JQ were rarely home around the holidays. Kate began to see them infrequently as time passed. When she did see them, she found she was becoming more and more concerned about JQ. He seemed to have lost much of his zest for life once he retired, and he just seemed content to go through the motions and do what his wife required of him. It was too much effort to do otherwise, Kate guessed. He was still generous with Kate's college allowance; Kate often wondered how much that cost him as far as Cynthia was concerned. But she was glad she didn't have to scrimp along like so many other students did. When she and John got an apartment together, JQ never said a word. He liked the boy, and hoped that Kate would be happy with him.

Kate continued to intern at the Washington Gazette in the summers, and in the summer prior to her senior year, she actually worked as a reporter, complete with a salary. David Meyers had taken an interest in her career, and at the end of that summer, he asked her if she wanted to work at the Gazette full time after graduation. Kate was stunned, but not too stunned to immediately say yes. When she called John later to tell him about the job, they had one of their rare fights. He was upset that she had not discussed it with him first. He had spent the summers working in his father's constituent office in Dearborn, and the goal had been for him to work on the campaigns, then eventually ease into Michigan politics. Kate's decision did not fall in well with his plans.

That evening, though, John called her back and apologized. Kate was bothered by the argument, but didn't dwell on it too much going forward. One evening, about half way through their senior year, John took Kate out to dinner at a nice restaurant and announced to her that he had gotten a job in U.S. Senator Bryce Dotson's office after graduation, so he would be moving to Washington with her. Kate had smiled happily and kissed him, as this had been the elephant in the room between them since she had come back to Ann Arbor. But later, while they were eating, John stopped and looked at her quizzically.

"Kate, do you think we ought to get married or anything?" he asked tentatively, toying with his napkin.

Kate stared at him a moment. When she was growing up, she had never been particularly interested in romance or romantic notions like other girls. She had a practical nature and always felt the huge weddings that were becoming more and more en vogue were a waste of money. Better to invest the money in a house, or something else that endured. Nevertheless, this struck her as an odd way to propose marriage.

She shrugged; the subject made her uncomfortable, although she wasn't sure why.

"Why don't we just wait and see how it goes, OK? We have a lot of changes coming up. I don't think we should add one more complication. Things are good now, right?" she asked.

"Right," John said, clearly relieved, "That was my thought exactly. There's plenty of time."

Kate smiled and nodded, only pausing to wonder briefly why the subject made her so uncomfortable.

After they had moved to DC, they were both too busy to think much more about it. Kate began to travel more and more, and John worked long hours in the Senator's office. John also began to change in small ways, disturbing to Kate, but the changes were so gradual that she didn't realize how much he was truly changing as a person.

She realized now that John had simply stepped into the role that he had been groomed for since birth. He had become the consummate politician. He had gotten all the training and behavior reinforcement he needed in Washington to develop the required presence to smoothly manipulate people with lies and half-truths to get what he wanted. At one time, John had evidenced that he knew the difference between right and wrong; now, what he considered being right was what was best for HIM at any given moment, and he was willing to do whatever it took to get it. She was well aware that this was an arrogance John had always had to a certain extent, but now, living in a town full of egoists, this arrogance had bloomed into something poisonous.

She realized she had been becoming more and more aware of it for the past few years. Since they moved to DC, their social life seemed to revolve exclusively around John's job and the contacts he wanted to make on the Hill. What few friends Kate had, she made at the Gazette, and with her own work schedule and John's socializing, she had little time for them. It was John who insisted that she join the Middleburg Hunt for two years, although she hated fox hunting, and Manny was getting a bit up in years for anything so strenuous. When JQ died and left Kate half his estate, her mother had (of course) contested the will. It was John who insisted that Kate hire a law firm in DC to fight tooth and nail for every penny (which was considerable; JQ Montcrief had been a multi-millionaire when he had died). Kate grieved JQ deeply and would have been perfectly content to let her mother have the money since it meant so much to her. Kate was making a good salary at the Gazette, and while money was always nice, she could have gotten along without her inheritance from JQ.

However, in another one of their bitter fights, John had ruthlessly reminded her of all the things that her mother had done to her over the years, and Kate had finally given in and hired the lawyer. Now, it had been three years since Cynthia and Kate had spoken.

And then, there was the incident of the pearl earring under the bed. She had heard other rumors off and on about John's infidelity, but she had closed her ears. *Cleopatra, Queen of Denial, that's me all over*, she thought bitterly.

Now she was convinced that John had killed Manny. She wasn't sure how he had done it, but she knew in her heart that he had.

And now, she wanted to murder John. If not murder him; then hurt him as much as he had hurt her. Kate had never hated anyone as much as she hated John Ridley at that moment, and she was grateful that she was in Nevada and well out of arm's reach.

She made another phone call to June Tolson, one of her

friends in the Gazette office. June had recently gone through a nasty divorce and had hired one of the best divorce attorneys in town, who had helped her immensely. He also worked on property divisions in 'palimony' cases. Kate thought to herself ruefully that a mortgage was far more binding that a marriage license, and she knew that John would fight for the farm in Maryland. She had no intention letting him have it. She got the attorney's number, called his office, and got an appointment. The first opening he had was in three weeks – she jotted down the date and time then entered it on her Smartphone calendar. She took a deep breath, let it out, walked to the window, and looked out at the mountains. The sun had come up and was shining brightly, making the desert dew shine like diamonds.

At that moment, Kate made a pledge to herself. She would do whatever it took to find out what happened to Lindy Abraham and Julia Evans. Unlike her, they had stood by their principles to protect something that they loved. Perhaps this could provide some atonement for her failure to protect Manny.

Part IV
The Search

Chapter 11

Kate showered quickly, put on jeans, hiking boots, a plaid shirt and jacket, and then checked her watch. It was about 8:30 a.m., so she actually had managed to get a good start on the day. She grabbed her laptop case and handbag and went down into the barn. A youngish, heavyset Native man was cleaning the stalls. She saw Kimmy working on sweeping the barn aisle. She was moving slowly and Kate walked up to her and took the broom away from her.

"Sit," she said. "Let me do that."

Kimmy smiled at her thankfully and sat down.

"Kate," Kimmy said, pointing to the man cleaning the stall. "That's my husband, Marshall Sams. Marsh, this is Kate Wyndham. She's the journalist I told you about."

Marshall nodded shyly at Kate and kept cleaning the stall. Kate quickly swept the barn aisle clean, then set the broom against the wall.

"What else do you need me to do?" she asked.

"I know mother said that you should help me out in the barn to pay for room and board, but that's just silly," Kimmy said. "If you're around, and there's something to be done and you've got the time, we'd appreciate the help, otherwise don't worry about it."

"I don't mind helping," Kate said.

"I know. But I think you have other things to do that are more important," she replied, looking at Kate evenly.

"All right, then. I'm heading into town now. I hope your mother will have some good news for me this morning."

"Me too," Kimmy said.

Kate nodded her goodbyes to Kimmy and Marsh and went out to the rental car to drive to the police station. She caught herself looking to see if Jim Ludlow was about anywhere, but she didn't see him. She mentally scolded herself for being a fool. This was about the worst time ever to develop an infatuation, and she worked hard to compartmentalize her feelings. But on her drive into town, the memory of his face, his slim hands, and voice bubbled up to the surface of her thoughts in a very distracting fashion.

She pulled into the police parking area, as Sharon had told her to do the night before, and parked in one of the Official Visitor spots Sharon had told her she could use. Kate was glad. Even this early in the morning, Antelope Valley was a busy place.

She went into the police station and said good morning to Lelinda.

"Oh, Kate," she replied pleasantly. "Hi, I'll tell Sharon that you're here. She wanted to know right away when you came in."

Lelinda tapped her earbud, spoke quietly for a few moments, and then turned back to Kate.

"Do you remember your way to that office we set up for you? She'll meet you there," she said.

Kate nodded and quickly made her way down the hallway. She was a bit excited – maybe she would finally start getting some answers.

Sharon was waiting for her in the office when she got there, along with Semilla, the IT tech. Kate stepped past them into the office and set her bags down on the floor.

"I've got good news and bad news," Sharon said without preamble. "My contacts at the cellular provider worked faster than I expected – seems like one of the engineers is a horse lover and took a personal interest in the issue. She worked until 1 a.m. this morning sifting through data in the phone switches and she got us quite a bit of information.

"There was a lot more data than what the FBI gave you, as we expected. These ladies tried to make a lot of calls that never went through because of poor signal quality, and in at least some of the cases, we were able to pick up their GPS coordinates. So we do have a rudimentary record of their movements up to a certain point, then it's like they just dropped off the map. But it's more than you had yesterday."

"Well, that's great news. Were any of the calls made on Tribal land, to give you the jurisdiction to investigate?" Kate asked.

Sharon sighed and looked at Kate seriously. "Oh hell, yeah," she said. "They spent a good amount of time on the Reservation, although I doubt they knew it. But here's the bad news, St. Martjin Mining currently controls most of the area they were calling from. And while we technically have jurisdiction there, we generally have to work with Mine Security to go into those areas. And relations between Antelope Valley and St. Martjin are poor to say the least."

"So what can we do?" Kate asked.

Sharon leaned up against the desk and looked at Kate for a moment. "If you're up for it, I say let's just go as far as we can with it," she said. "If Mine Security gives us a hard time, we'll deal with it when it happens. I'm sure not going to give them a heads up that we're looking into this. But I feel I need to tell you that things could get a little rough, Kate. There has been trouble between Mine Security and Tribal members. Last month, Mine Security shot several head of cattle and brought in a Tribal member to me in handcuffs. They said he was trespassing. He was roughed up, but he refused to testify against those thugs and never even told me exactly what happened. I don't know what they said to him, but he was scared to death." Sharon sighed.

"The Tribe is getting more and more angry at the situation, and I'm worried it's going to blow at any moment. I just wanted you to know that it's a powder keg," she finished.

Kate shook her head. "Don't worry about that. I've been in rough situations before in Africa, I'll be all right," she said.

Sharon grinned at her. "My kind of woman," she said, "but here's another problem I have. With everything going on this week, I can't take time off to follow this trail of breadcrumbs, and it's the same with all my officers. We've got everyone working double shifts just to deal with all the 'guests' we have on the Rez this week. And you're going to have to have someone who knows the area."

"The Gazette will be willing to pay for a guide, if that's what you're asking," Kate said.

"Well, we might be able to get my brother to help," Sharon said, "although he is pretty busy right now. He would be a good choice; he knows the area around here better than just about anyone. He's usually the one we get to track down tourists who either get lost or decide go on those stupid vision quests I was telling you about yesterday. He's been deputized in the past, so he can act for the Tribe in an official, but not too official, capacity."

"So, what's the problem?" Kate asked, although she did feel her stomach do a little flip, "Let's call him. The Gazette will pay him just about whatever he asks."

"Just wanted to run it by you first. Some people would think I was just pitching my brother a job."

Kate shrugged. "I'm not worried about that. If he's available and up for it, he can just about name his price."

"Another thing about Jim," Sharon said, grinning and shaking her head. "He's got a cool head and can usually slick talk his way out of just about anything, stinker that he is."

Semilla laughed at that.

"Anyway, I'll give him a call. I think he might be willing to help out," Sharon said. "Semilla is going to take this list of coordinates and try to generate a route for us. I thought you might give her a hand. I think it would help develop an idea of their movements in your head, which might help when you're out in the desert. That kind of thing has always helped me anyway."

"Great idea," Kate said. "And, I really appreciate this help, guys. And just so you know, I am going to make sure Harlan Finney and the families know what you've done, no matter what."

Sharon just shook her head and smiled. "Just doing our job, Kate. I'll catch up with you later, and I'll let you know what Jim says.". She turned and hurriedly walked out of the office.

"I don't know how she manages to keep up with everything," Semilla said, watching Sharon leave. "Anyway, let's go to my office, Kate. The computer I have in there will be perfect for what we need to get done."

"Lead the way," Kate said.

A couple of hours later, Kate and Semilla were both crouched over Semilla's computer. Semilla was plugging the GPS coordinates into a mapping program, and was painstakingly putting in the times each attempted call was made. Kate was helping her keep track of all the numbers. They had made it about two-thirds of the way through the list when Semilla received an email from Sharon saying that Jim Ludlow had agreed to help with the search, and would be coming by later in the afternoon. When Kate got that news, she was both relieved and apprehensive.

Semilla suddenly sat up straight and stretched.

"I've got to take a break or I'm going to go blind," she said. "Let's go get some coffee."

"Sure."

Kate followed Semilla down the hall to a medium sized break room. There was a coffee pot and refrigerator, but none of the snack machines you usually saw in the workplace.

"The Elders said if people want to poison themselves, that's their own business, but the city's not going to make it easy for them," Semilla said, when Kate commented on it.

They sat at a table and sipped the coffee, which was surprisingly good. *Someone must have just made it*, Kate thought.

"So," Semilla said, looking at Kate a bit mischievously. "Have you met Sharon's brother yet?"

Kate nodded. "Last night at dinner."

Semilla sighed, and leaned forward, lowering her voice a bit.

"How a *duibichi'* like him can be such a nice guy is beyond me."

"A what?" Kate asked.

"A *duibichi'*. It's a Shoshone word for a good-looking guy. A hottie."

Kate nearly choked on a sip of coffee.

"There are some girls on the Rez who would pay good money to spend time alone with Jim Ludlow out in the desert," Semilla continued blithely.

"He said something to me last night about a wife."

"Oh, her. Yes, he was married for a while, when he lived in DC," Semilla said. "He had some problems while he was living there, and they got divorced. I don't know that much about it."

Kate got the distinct feeling that Semilla DID know more than she was saying, but didn't press her on it.

"Jim is the one that helped my husband and me get into UCLA. He wrote letters and helped us get scholarships. He was really great," Semilla said quietly.

"So he went to UCLA?"

"Yes. Undergraduate and UCLA law. He did well there. It was after he moved to DC that he started having problems," Semilla said. "He's fine now, though," she added hurriedly.

Kate didn't attempt to pry any more information out of Semilla, although it was difficult to keep her mouth shut. She had a ton of questions about Jim Ludlow, but didn't want to appear to be too interested. Antelope Valley was a small town with small town gossip (as Semilla was so aptly demonstrating). That was something she would just as soon steer clear of.

She and Semilla went back to work after their short coffee break, and were again huddled over the computer, getting the fine details on the map squared away. They had just about finished and Semilla was getting ready to print it out and also email a copy to

Kate's Smartphone. They were deep in conversation when they were interrupted.

"You girls are making me tired just watching you."

They both jumped, completely startled.

Ludlow stood leaning in the doorway, his arms crossed, wearing old jeans, well-worn cowboy boots, a plaid work shirt, and a leather jacket. He was smiling at them, clearly amused. Kate had no idea how long he'd been standing there. She hadn't heard a thing.

"Jesus Christ, Jim!" Semilla scolded. "Don't you bother to knock?"

"Knock on what? The door's wide open," he said, grinning.

"Well, you're in a police station. There's no need to sneak around, " Semilla said grumpily.

"I wasn't sneaking. I was looking for Kate, and I was told she was in your office. I just walked up and stopped in the doorway for a minute watching you two. You just seemed so engrossed in that map on the computer I hated to disturb you."

"We were. Check it out, Jim. We got the Lats and Longs from some of the cell phone call attempts of those advocates that went missing and we were able to kind of get a rough trail of where they went before they disappeared," Semilla said.

Ludlow stepped in and looked at the computer screen.

"So I guess you want to retrace their steps, Kate?" he asked. "That's what Sharon said."

"That's right. No one else has even bothered to look at this information."

Ludlow sighed and shook his head. "Been a long time since they disappeared, Kate. It's not like we can follow a trail or anything. Plus, I think a great part of this has been closed off by Mine Security anyway."

"I feel like I have to make the effort," Kate said tightly. "They deserve that much from someone."

Ludlow stared at her evenly for a moment, then nodded. "Come on then, we might as well get started."

Kate nodded, thanked Semilla, and grabbed the map off the printer. She also checked to make sure the route was also on her Smartphone. Semilla winked at her as she walked out the door.

"You behave yourself now, Miss Kate," she said.

Kate shook her head in exasperation and followed Ludlow out

the door. They stopped by her office to get her things. She started to get her laptop case, but Ludlow stopped her.

"We won't need it, and it would be best if it weren't with us," he said. "We might have to leave the truck for a while and I wouldn't want it to disappear."

"OK," Kate replied. Her handbag converted to a backpack; it would be no trouble to carry if they had to go on an impromptu hike.

They left the building and Kate found that even she had a bit of trouble keeping up with Ludlow's long stride. He was clearly someone who liked to get to where he was going.

"Had lunch yet?" he asked.

Kate shook her head.

"Or breakfast either probably. Neither have I. I had some coffee and that's about it. It's been a hectic morning. Let's eat, and then we'll head out to the first point on the map."

"OK, sure. But I guess we need to discuss your fee for all this," Kate said.

"We can talk about it over lunch. We can go to one of my favorite places; it's just down the street here."

Kate fully expected another buffalo burger, but surprisingly, Ludlow led her past The Buffalo Barn then turned down an alleyway. They came out on another street and he led her into a small café. It had about six tables in it and only one was free.

Ludlow pulled out her chair for her as she sat down. She was a little startled at such a display of manners. JQ was the last man who had ever done such a thing for her.

"I've found, as I've gotten older, that I don't like to eat as much meat as I did when I was younger," he said, sitting down across from her, "and this place has a great squash casserole. Their frybread is good too."

A pretty blonde woman brought two menus, smiling brilliantly at Ludlow, and more coolly at Kate. Kate decided that Semilla was right about Ludlow's female lust-worthiness in Antelope Valley.

"Hi Jim, good to see you again," the waitress said.

Ludlow nodded and ordered some water and Kate did likewise.

"How's Cactus?" Kate asked.

"She's doing just fine. You have a good eye for lameness."

Kate just shrugged then looked out the window for a moment.

"So, Jim," she said, deciding to get the money out of the way, "how much is this going to cost the Gazette?"

Ludlow nodded and frowned in a very businesslike way. "Very practical. Let's get these negotiations concluded. How does $20,000 a day sound?" he asked.

Kate laughed in spite of herself and shook her head.

Ludlow sighed. "In law school, they taught us that the opponent should always open with an offer, but I've found I just like to throw out an outrageous figure. You never know, someone might be willing to take me up on it. But I guess you aren't that person."

"No."

The waitress came back with their water, and they ordered two squash casseroles.

"Oh well, nothing ventured," Ludlow continued after the woman left. "I'll make you a deal: what if you pay for gas, and maybe buy a meal or two, then we do our best to find out what happened to these women? How does that sound?"

"It sounds like you aren't making any money for your time."

Ludlow shrugged. "Money's a funny thing. I had a job once where I made a lot of money, and I was miserable. I have several jobs here around the Rez and I don't get paid that much, and I'm happier than I have ever been. So, I've decided what makes me happy doesn't really have anything to do with money. And I would like to try to help find out what happened to these women. They were only doing what their hearts led them to do, and that shouldn't be a fatal exercise. It just feels like the right thing for me to do at this point in time." He took a drink of water, shook his head then looked at her ruefully. "I guess that must sound strange."

Kate didn't think it sounded strange at all. In fact, she thought it was one of the most sensible things she had heard anyone say in a long time.

"Are you sure? I am going to take some time out of your life that you're never going to get back. That should be worth something to you," she said.

Ludlow smiled again, and shook his head, and then he looked at her in a way that made her fingers tingle. "I don't consider it a waste. I hope you'll tell me a little something about yourself and your life. When I lived in Washington, I followed your work quite a bit. I still do. I always thought you were a gifted writer."

Kate felt herself blushing, and took a long drink of water. "Thanks. I am always glad to hear someone say that," she said. "I do try."

"You succeed. But anyway, Sharon has told me some of the information you have on these two women we're tracking, but why don't you fill me in on everything you know. Who knows, I might turn out to be something more than just a taxi driver and be able to provide useful help."

So Kate told Ludlow everything she knew about Lindy Abraham and Julia Evans. She found that Ludlow was a good listener and she wound up doing most of the talking while they ate (and he was right, the squash casserole, served on a trencher of frybread, was excellent). He asked pertinent, probing questions, which brought in a different insight or point that she hadn't considered. When she brought up her experience in Elko with the BLM, Ludlow shook his head.

"I know those guys down there some," he said. "I dealt with Sam Conner before, during a slight disagreement we had last year over whether the BLM had any claim on the Reservation herd, which has some ancient bloodlines that need to be preserved. He's not an easy man to negotiate with. He's weak, and like a lot of weak men, tries to make up for his weakness by being implacable on issues that really don't matter in the great scheme of things. I know Sharon has problems with his ethics."

Ludlow looked out the window for a minute, then turned back and looked at Kate intently.

"But those guys in Mine Security at St. Martjin, they are a whole different breed. They brought them in about two years ago when there was some equipment sabotage – our people were guilty of that, although there were extenuating circumstances. But, to be frank, they scare the shit out of me."

"You should be scared. That company they are using, U.S. Security Services, hires out mercenary forces, plain and simple. I ran into some of them in Africa a few years ago. They are very serious about their jobs. Most of them are ex-Delta and Special Forces from the military," Kate said. "And, like your Sam Conner, not particularly overburdened with ethics. At least not the ones I had dealings with. They were very professional, but I also knew they would have very professionally disposed of me if I had gotten in their way."

Ludlow looked at her a moment and smiled again. "Well, I guess you are probably more familiar with the risks than I am, then."

Kate shrugged. "Seems like a hazard of my profession. I've had to talk my way out of more than one sticky situation, but being a reporter from a big newspaper usually provides you a certain amount of protection."

"It didn't help Daniel Pearl," Ludlow said pointedly, speaking of the Wall Street Journal reporter that had been kidnapped and executed in Pakistan by terrorists.

"No," Kate said, toying with her fork. "It didn't help Danny."

"Sorry," Ludlow said. "Sorry to bring that up, I guess he might have been a friend of yours."

"I met him once at a press function when I was still in college. He was a nice guy. We weren't friends really, but his death affected everyone in the business. After Danny was killed, my editor made us all take classes on what to do if you find yourself in a hostage situation. I don't think it would have helped Danny though.".

The waitress came with the check, and Kate reached for her credit card. She noticed that Ludlow was also digging around in his pocket, but she quickly took the check.

"Food and gas, remember?" she said, smiling at him.

"Old habits die hard. Chauvinist that I am; I guess I will never get used to a lady picking up the check."

Kate smiled and shook her head then signed the bill when it came. "Not really me picking it up anyway, it's the Gazette," she said.

"Thanks for saving my fragile ego."

Kate grinned. Even for all Ludlow's stunning good looks, she found herself liking the man above and beyond that. It was just like Semilla had said, unlike a lot of good-looking men, Ludlow seemed to genuinely be a nice guy, and he was pleasant company, very easy to talk to.

"So, let me take a look at this map that you and Semilla put together," he said.

She reached into her purse and pulled out the two sheets of paper that they hoped covered most of the points where Lindy and Julia had made phone calls. They had taken a meandering route from BIA 19, down a few side roads, but always angling further and further into the canyon lands that laced through the mountains.

"It looks like they were very determined women," Ludlow said, looking at the map. "Or they were just hopelessly lost. Or both. Some of these places I'm pretty sure are closed, but we can at least make the attempt to retrace the route as much as possible.

"Well, are you ready to start? I planned on us taking my truck. I don't think your rental car could handle some of these roads out here," Ludlow asked.

"Sure, no problem. Just let me fill up the tank before we go," Kate said.

"I see you are bound and determined to turn me into some kind of kept man. I suppose I could think of worse things," he said, looking at Kate sidelong with a crooked grin.

Is he FLIRTING with me? she wondered to herself, in a bit of a panic. Then she quickly put a lid on that thought.

They walked back to the police station, to his truck parked beside her rental car. It was an old Ford F-250 4x4 that looked serviceable, but it had bits of rust in the body. The interior was cluttered with halters, ropes, and other miscellaneous ranch equipment, and the floor had a good amount of sand on it.

"Sorry about the mess, but this is my work truck," Ludlow said, opening the door for her to climb in.

"No problem. Believe me, I've ridden in worse."

They headed out north. There was a lot of traffic, but Ludlow seemed unperturbed, very often stopping to let people pull out from parking lots and waiting patiently in the long lines of traffic. Kate, who was an impatient driver (as were most people who lived in DC), found herself growing a little frustrated with his slowness, but when she glanced over at his face, he seemed so calm and relaxed she found herself relaxing also. *Getting upset about traffic never did any good anyway,* she thought.

"This place is so busy, I just can't get over it," she said.

"I know. The Reservation has completely changed from when I grew up here. Back then, we struggled with the same problems many others have in Indian Country; poverty, drug and alcohol abuse; unemployment, domestic violence. My family was pretty fortunate. We've been ranchers for a long time and have always been very centered. That's not the case with some, I'm afraid. Things were very tough when I was a boy."

"What happened? What changed?"

"Well," Ludlow said, "I think most of it is due to the efforts of one man. A friend of mine named Martin Levi."

"I read about him," Kate said. "He sounds like an amazing man."

"He is," Ludlow said, smiling fondly. "Some of the Elders say he is Wovoka reborn, only he is having us do a different kind of dance."

"I don't understand."

"Back in the late 1800s, there was a Paiute Holy Man named Wovoka, or, by his English name, Jack Wilson. He was a pacifist who preached that the Indian should learn to live in harmony with not only other Natives, but also the Whites. He encouraged people to live cleanly and honestly, and show kindness to all others. It was through his teachings that the Ghost Dance movement began, and it swept through the Tribes like wildfire. Different tribes interpreted Wovoka's teachings differently, which is usually the case with any religion, I guess. Some of the non-Natives at the time interpreted the dancing as a precursor to violence. It was the Ghost Dance that led to the First Massacre at Wounded Knee. I guess you're familiar with that?"

"Of course," Kate said.

"Anyway, some of the Elders here say that Wovoka walks on the earth again in Martin Levi, and he doesn't argue with them about it," Ludlow said, grinning a bit and shaking his head.

"But you don't think so?"

"I have no idea. Could be, I guess."

"Isn't he part Jewish?"

"Ah, so you heard about the Israeli connection I see. I guess it's no big secret really. Marty's grandfather, old Ruben Levi, was the original Wandering Jew, or that's what he called himself. When he was a young man, back in the 1920s, he decided he was tired of New York so he moved out here and opened up a little trading post in Antelope Valley. He married a local Shoshone girl and they had about nine kids, one of which was Marty's father. While Ruben strayed from his religion quite a bit, they still had a Menorah and Torah in the house, and they observed most of the high holy days. Ruben also stayed in touch with his relatives in New York, several of whom immigrated to Israel after World War II. Marty was always interested in the Jewish side of his family and he kept the connections going after his grandfather died. He never converted though; instead, he became our Shaman here at the local Native American Church. It's through his connections that we were able to raise the money to build the casino, which funds a lot of the improvements we've been able to make over the years."

"Well, I think it's wonderful. And Semilla told me that a lot of the younger Tribal members are starting to come back because of all the job opportunities," Kate said.

"That's right. One thing Marty has been adamant on is that the Tribe's greatest resource is its people, and the more people we have working together towards a common goal, the better the chance we have of success. He also was extremely firm about women being considered as equals in all things."

"I guess that was a hard sell," Kate said. "Even where I work, there are dinosaurs that have problems with that concept."

Ludlow smiled and shook his head. "Not so much as you might think, not with our Tribe at least. The Shoshone have always had a tradition of a strong matriarchy. Sacajawea was Shoshone of course. You've met my mother; I don't think I know a tougher woman than she is, but she's very kind too. Anyway, it wasn't as difficult as you might think. Marty also had the support of most of the Tribal Elders. My grandfather, who was always a very influential man in the Tribe, wholeheartedly supported Martin when he came back from Israel and first started working towards his goals. He helped convince some of the other more skeptical ones. Of course, we still have politicians who have their own agendas. That just seems to be in the nature of politicians, no matter what the ethnic background might be."

Kate found herself getting angry as she thought about this last statement and just sat, stonily silent, thinking of John Ridley.

Ludlow glanced over at her and noticed her clenched teeth and the white knuckles of her hands that were clasped together in her lap. Then he remembered John Ridley had worked in a Senator's office. He assumed he still did.

"I'm sorry," he said mildly. "I didn't mean to offend you."

"What?" she said startled, looking over at Ludlow. "No, no. No offense taken. I had my mind on something else. Just woolgathering."

Ludlow nodded and decided it was time for some quiet. They

rode together for about 20 miles in silence, Kate moodily staring out the window and Ludlow just driving. She looked like she was a million miles away. He slowed down and made a left turn, then an immediate right. They came to a long wire fence with a gate on the road. The gate had a sign saying 'No Trespassing, Antelope Valley Indian Reservation.' The gate was locked, but Ludlow had a key and he unlocked the gate, pulled through, and then closed it. Kate watched him puzzled.

"Is this on the map?" she asked.

"No, we took a little detour, not much of one, but there is something here I think you should see."

Ludlow drove down the road, which was in very poor repair. Kate found herself being jarred repeatedly as they hit holes and washboarding, but she didn't complain. She was interested in where he was taking her. He slowed down, turned off the road, and stopped at the base of a good-sized hill.

"Come on, walk with me up to the top of this hill," he said.

Kate got out and followed Ludlow as he made his way up the hill. When they had turned west, away from the town and the river, the vegetation had become more and more sparse, and the ground more rocky. Kate had a rock on the slope break underneath her foot and she almost fell, but Ludlow reached out and took her arm, steadying her. She found herself both embarrassed at her clumsiness and pleased at his touch.

"Give me your hand," he said, in a soft whisper. "We need to go quietly here."

So Kate put her hand in his with extremely mixed feelings. His hands, which were so slender to be almost delicate-looking, were nevertheless calloused and strong. He carefully chose the way up the slope and Kate followed closely along with him. When they had nearly reached the top, Ludlow dropped her hand and put a finger over his lips for silence. Then he went down on his hands and knees, and motioned for Kate to follow. They finished crawling up to the top of the hill, and Kate peered over a stony outcrop, after Ludlow took a brief look then motioned her to do also.

What she saw was a wide valley rimmed by mountains that became greener as it dropped steadily towards the river that gleamed like a silver ribbon winding in the background. It was a beautiful sight, but as her eyes took in more of the valley she suddenly whispered to Ludlow, "Oh my God, look at them."

Scattered across the valley were several bands of horses, most quietly grazing, but off to the side she could see several yearlings rearing and play fighting with each other. There were probably 100 or more horses all told, scattered out across the wide valley.

Many were dun colored, with a long dorsal stripe down their backs and shadowy stripes on their legs. Kate knew that these would be the 'ancient' bloodlines that Ludlow had told her about. But there were also palominos, paints, and blacks. There were several sorrels, their reddish coats gleaming in the afternoon sun, and mares with nursing foals at their sides. As always, Kate wondered how the babies managed to control their spidery long legs as they trotted along beside their dams. Their long manes and tails blew like silken streamers in the soft breeze. It was all so peaceful looking.

One of the sorrels stood staring at the hill from about 50 yards away. He reminded her of Manny, for he too had had a white stripe on his face and four white stockings. Kate felt tears come to her eyes, but choked them back down.

"Magnificent, aren't they?" Ludlow whispered, leaning close.

"Oh, yes," Kate said fervently.

They continued to watch for another 15 minutes or so, then Kate heard the sorrel snort in alarm. He took off at a trot towards the river. Soon others fell in behind him. Ludlow slowly stood up and the horses moved into a slow lope. They were out of sight very quickly.

Ludlow reached down and helped Kate get to her feet. "I had a feeling they might be up this way today," he said. "We lucked out to see them so close. That stallion though, he was smart, as soon as the wind shifted he got our scent and knew it was time to move on."

"That was that sorrel with the four white stockings?"

"Yes. He's the senior stallion of the Rez wild horse herd. Come on, we can go back to the truck now. I just thought it would be good if you got an idea why these advocates feel what they're doing is so important."

Kate followed Ludlow back down the slope. He took a rather meandering route. *To help keep me from going ass over teakettle down the hill*, she thought. He seemed to have no problem at all; he moved easily, as if the ground actually welcomed the touch of his boots. Kate stumbled a couple of times, but managed to catch herself before falling. It had been a while since she had done any hiking, she realized. She was out of shape.

Once they got back to the truck, Ludlow opened the door for her and she scrambled inside. He turned the truck around and they drove back out. Ludlow locked the gate again after they pulled through it. Soon they were back out on the main road, heading west again.

"You said that you had had some trouble with the BLM over this herd last year; what was that all about?" Kate asked.

Ludlow sighed. "The BLM made the decision to do a 'gather' in this area last year because they claimed the range was being overgrazed," he said. "One of their pilots strayed over into Reservation land and gathered up some of our horses by mistake. We don't brand them, so it was basically our word against theirs that the horses came from our herd. Those duns, the old Spanish horses, can bring a big price on the BLM Internet auctions so it was a little difficult to get them to release them back to us. Sharon and I had to spend a lot of time talking to Conner, as well as some of the other BLM staff. I work with a group of people that keep track of the herd; we have records of markings, births, deaths etc., and we brought all that information, but it was still difficult getting them to give us back our horses. Martin Levi finally called the governor and got him involved. If we hadn't had his support our horses would have been long gone, I have no doubt."

Kate shook her head. "It never stops does it?" she said.

"What?"

"The White Man Screwing Over the Indian."

"No, it never seems to," Ludlow said, chuckling a bit.

Kate looked at him, marveling at his equanimity. "Doesn't it make you mad?" she asked.

"Getting mad about it wastes energy. I'd rather put that energy into finding ways to either outsmart or work around them. Although there are plenty that are still very angry, of course."

They rode in silence for a while, Kate thinking about what Ludlow had said, and also thinking about the wild horses.

"Our church here," Ludlow said after a time, "teaches unconditional forgiveness. It's not an easy concept to incorporate into daily life, but once you do, it can be very liberating."

"Some things are unforgiveable," Kate said suddenly, thinking about Ridley.

Ludlow glanced over at her, surprised at her vehemence. "Is there something you need to talk about, Kate? We're going to be spending this time together, and I've been told I'm a good listener. I'm more than willing to lend an ear, if you have something bothering you. Sometimes it's easier to talk to a stranger than a friend, you know."

Kate looked at him, horribly embarrassed. "No, no, Jim. I am really sorry. I've got some personal issues going on right now, and I'm letting it get to me. I just need to refocus on the job we're trying to get done. I got some news this morning – rather bad news – that I'm still trying to process."

Ludlow glanced at her again and shrugged. "OK, well, I'm right here if you need to talk. And will be until we're done."

"Thanks, but I'll be fine. Anyway, are we getting close to the first spot on the map yet?"

"I think so, but why don't you get out that GPS you were talking about and let's see."

Kate rummaged around in her handbag and pulled out the Smartphone. She turned it on and it went through its start up program, locked onto the satellite, and came up with the screen. She checked the current Lat/Long and saw they were indeed very close. She pulled up her mapping software and entered in the destination lat/long. A route immediately appeared and the Smartphone began speaking directions.

Ludlow laughed. "Well, I don't know what you need me for; that thing seems to know where we're going better than I do," he said.

"Not very accurate out in areas like this, as I have found out more than once," Kate said ruefully. "Why don't we pull over? I want you to see this."

Ludlow pulled the truck over to the shoulder. There wasn't much traffic, but he pulled a good ways off the narrow road. She handed the device to him and he looked at it.

"You can zoom in like this," she said, showing how to 'pinch and stretch' on the screen to zoom into an area.

"Amazing," Ludlow said, obviously delighted by the technology, "but, as you can see, this is just a point on the Bureau of Indian Affairs Road 19. The next point up is also on BIA 19, which shows they were going north, but then they turned off here on Sage Creek Road. It almost looks like they were doubling back, trying to get up close to the mountains, like they may have been stopped at some point."

Ludlow sat for a minute, looking off to the north. "That area up there is one that the Mine closes periodically. That may have been what happened. Want to go have a look?" he asked.

"Sure, how much daylight do we have left?" Kate asked, looking at her watch, it was nearly 4 p.m.

"Two, three hours. We have time to at least get to this point and back to town before dark," he said, pointing to the spot on Sage Creek Road.

"Well, that's why we're out here. Might as well get to it," Kate said.

Ludlow pulled back onto the road, drove a few miles, and then took a right onto a rather narrow dirt road that ran due north, from what Kate could tell. The desert here was very bleak, only sagebrush and low growing bushes. It was very similar to what she had seen the day before, when she forced Mark Johnson to haul her out to the BIA 19/Shelley Road intersection, which she realized now was further south.

They drove about 30 miles up BIA 19, then Ludlow slowed and took a left onto another dirt road that angled off to the west-northwest. Kate saw the lat/longs match up between the map and the GPS on the Smartphone.

"This is one point they called from," she said, staring down at the map.

"And look what's up ahead," Ludlow said.

The road was blocked by a gate with a heavy padlock and a quickly erected t-post and wire fence that ran for several hundred feet in either direction, ending in what looked to be two washed out gullies. A sign on the gate said 'Closed for blasting. St. Martjin Mining.'

Ludlow stopped and got out of the truck and walked up to the gate. Kate followed him.

"I'd heard they had closed off some areas up here," he said, "but this gate and fence was put up some time ago. The t-posts have rust on the top, and the gate's paint been worn down by the sand." Ludlow shook his head and kicked the t-post a couple of times with the toe of his boot. "Technically this is Reservation land, although we don't use this area much. The courts have ruled that if the Mine closes an area on Rez land for safety reasons, it has to be temporary and the Tribal Council has to be notified. I don't remember anything about this closure."

"Are you on the Council?" Kate asked, surprised. No one had mentioned this.

"An alternate. I do try to get to some of the meetings, and I read the minutes when they put them out. I'm sure I haven't seen any notice about this though," he said. "I think we can be certain this was one point that the advocates tried to get to and were turned back. I just wonder why they were so determined to get up near the Mine." Ludlow stared off towards the mountains.

Kate remembered something Sharon had said to her. "Sharon said that she thought the interview transcript of the two witnesses, who were the last ones to see Julia and Lindy, had been altered. Maybe those men said something to them that made them come up this way. Maybe they said something that the BLM didn't want getting out," she said.

Ludlow looked around, thinking. The shadows were getting longer, and the hills were getting a slightly bluish hue, the first feathery touch of twilight. "Didn't you say Sam Conner took their statements?" he asked.

"That's right."

"That's a pretty good possibility then, I think. It wouldn't be the first time Sam did such a thing."

"I wish we could talk to those witnesses," Kate said.

"At this point, the only thing that would do is just tip off the BLM that we are snooping around. Sharon told me that, currently, they believe you're back in DC," he said, looking at Kate pointedly.

Kate merely shrugged. "Girl's gotta do, what a girl's gotta do," she said.

Ludlow grinned and shook his head, then walked around a bit, looking at the ground. He then turned back towards the mountains again. "Well, we know they were here, and probably got turned back by this gate. If I remember right, the next point we saw was further west. So, let's start there tomorrow. We're running out of daylight anyway. I want to think about some of this, and make some calls tonight. I want to find out if anyone knew about this road closure."

"OK," Kate said, heading back to the truck. Ludlow stood

staring at the gate for a moment, then turned and followed her.

About an hour later, he dropped her off at the police station.

"I'll be seeing you at dinner tonight?" he asked.

"Wouldn't miss it," Kate replied, looking at him and rolling her eyes a bit.

"I bet. Tomorrow, we'll just leave from the ranch, if that's OK with you. It'll be Saturday, so things are really going to be crazy in town. Let's try to get away by 8."

"Sounds good," she said, grabbing her handbag and heading into the police station to pick up her laptop.

Ludlow watched her walk away. "Damn it," he said to himself. She had the unconscious grace of the natural athlete and he found himself mesmerized by the almost sinuous movement of her hips as she stepped up on the curb and up the two steps into the building. She had gained a little weight since he had last seen her, and he liked the soft curves her body had now. Ludlow didn't care for the anorexic look that was currently in fashion; he thought it looked unhealthy. Kate Wyndham looked far from unhealthy. *In fact*, he thought, *she looks positively luscious*.

Kate turned quickly and waved at him and he nodded at her. He fervently hoped that she hadn't noticed his ogling.

When they had stopped to see the wild horse herd, he had watched her more than he liked to think about. She had had her reddish hair pulled back in a short ponytail, but the wind had tugged wisps loose on both the sides of her face that kept blowing into her eyes and mouth. He had to squash the urge to push the straying hair back behind her ears. The bright desert sun had revealed some faint scars on her face that looked like old acne scars. To him, it didn't detract from her beauty; it only added character to an already beautiful face. She had a slight overbite, with full lips, which gave her a slightly breathless, kissable appearance when her face was relaxed and unguarded. Her wide clear eyes were honest and open when she looked at him. This was the first time he had had an interest in a woman since Madeleine and Oh what an interest it was.

"Damn it," he said again, shaking his head. Well, she would be leaving in a few days and that would be that. Besides, she clearly had some issues; some kind of personal problems she needed to deal with. He didn't need that sort of complication in his life.

So why did the thought of her leaving generate such a feeling of regret and loss?

"Damn it," he said for the third time.

Later on, at dinner, Sharon had asked very pointed questions about what Ludlow and Kate had found out that afternoon, which was, of course, not much. She was very interested in the gate that was blocking Sage Creek Road, and also Kate's hypothesis that the witnesses who had come forward with information about the missing women had told them something that had made the women go up towards the Mine. The rest of the family took only polite interest in the conversation, except for Annie, who pointedly ignored the discourse.

Sharon also spent some time bemoaning the traffic and tourist problems. "I swear, next time I'm calling Tony to see if we can get some State Police support up here," she said. "Three accidents, one of which required an airlift, and traffic like you would not believe. I heard it is taking three hours just to get into town from the south. Always before, people went right up to the casino and pretty much stayed there. Now, shopping in Antelope Valley has also been added to the weekend agenda."

"Well, we did do all that work to develop a thriving Native artist colony here, Sharon," Hank said quietly.

"Hank, please. I don't want to hear reason tonight, or any 'no good deed goes unpunished' lectures. I want to whine."

"Well, what about the people in casino security, can't they help?" Hank asked.

"You know better than that, Hank. Besides, they've got their hands full anyway – this is the busiest weekend of the year for them too," Sharon replied.

The Reservation Casino had its own private, highly professional security force. Rumor had it that most were ex-Mossad agents brought over by some Israeli investors. Some members of the Tribe even whispered that they were formerly elite Israeli soldiers who disagreed with their government's ill treatment of Palestinians in Gaza. Sharon didn't know nor did she care. In her dealings with them they had always been polite, efficient, insular, and extremely helpful. They rarely got involved in any affairs outside of the Casino, but when they did, they made a significant impact on whatever it was that needed addressing. Which suited her right down to the ground.

"Jim," Sharon said, a little later on, "you know, you could try talking to Bobby Nardo."

Ludlow sighed and looked pained. "I know. I've been thinking about it."

"Who's that?" Kate asked.

"He's a Native who sometimes works the crew that does roundups in this area on government contract," Sharon said. "He's a helicopter pilot; he learned to fly in the military. He and Jim were good friends when they were growing up."

"Long time ago," Ludlow said, clearly uncomfortable with the direction the conversation was taking, "Bobby is a difficult man to deal with these days. Besides, I doubt he would know anything about this."

"I don't know why you say that, Jimmy," Sharon said a bit tartly. "He's the first one the BLM calls when they get into a bind."

"Maybe he could help; he might know something," Kate said, wondering why Ludlow had not brought this up before.

Ludlow set his fork down on his plate, took a deep breath, and then looked at Kate. "OK. If we can find him tomorrow, we'll see what he has to say. Don't get your expectations too high though."

Kate simply nodded. Clearly there was some history here.

"I hear you can usually find him at The Pronghorn down in Elko most afternoons," Sharon said casually.

"Bobby Nardo has been taken by the drink," Annie said, looking at Kate. "He is a bad man now."

"Not bad, Mother, just lost," Ludlow said quietly.

"Bad," Annie said, looking at Ludlow.

Ludlow shook his head and took a few more bites from his plate. "I've got to make some phone calls tonight. I want to double check what information the Mine released on what they are doing over there on the West Side," he said, standing up. "Hope you guys don't mind if I beg off cleanup tonight."

"I'll do it, Uncle Jim," Dove said, looking at her uncle.

Ludlow smiled and nodded his thanks at his niece. "I'll see you in the morning, Kate. Good night everyone," Ludlow said as he left. *A bit abruptly*, Kate thought.

Everyone else finished up their dinner, Annie went out for her cigarette(s), Hank took Missy into the living room, and Kate helped Sharon and Dove clear the table. After the work was done,

Kate said her goodnights and started to head back to the barn. Sharon touched her arm briefly.

"Can I talk to you a minute?" Sharon asked, stepping outside behind her.

"Sure," Kate said. "What's up?"

Sharon shifted uncomfortably on her feet for a minute and then looked steadily at Kate. "There's something you probably need to know about Jim," she said.

Kate's first thought was '*Oh No He's Gay*,' but then she immediately quashed it. *Where are these thoughts coming from anyway?* she thought, disgusted with herself.

"Jim's a recovering alcoholic himself. He's been sober for six years now, but still, I'm sure it's hard for him sometimes," Sharon said.

"I see," Kate said. So this must be the 'problems' that Semilla had told her about.

"He doesn't hide it, but it's also not information he freely volunteers. But I wanted you to know. It's a big thing to ask of him to go and talk to Bobby Nardo. He has bailed Bobby out of jail a couple of times, and has tried to get him into the rehab clinic here, but Bobby's not ready. He may never be ready, and that's hard for Jim."

"So why did you bring it up?" Kate asked.

"Because I think it will help the case," Sharon said, and she sighed. "I may be Jim's sister, but I'm also a cop. Sometimes I'm cop first."

Kate nodded and Sharon squeezed her arm. "Goodnight, Kate. I'm sure I'll see you at some point tomorrow, but who knows when. Tomorrow is bound to be even more crazy than today was."

"Goodnight," Kate said, as she headed back to the barn.

On the way to the loft, Kate stopped and patted a few noses and gave some neck scratches. She went down to the stall where Cactus had been the night before, but it was empty, so she still must be feeling all right. Kate was glad.

She turned and went up the stairs to the loft, thinking about the day.

Once she got into the apartment, she thought about calling John Ridley, and telling him what she had found out that morning. But there was no point in it. She doubted it would make much of a difference to him. She hadn't talked to him since she left Elko, and that was fine with her. She checked her phone and noticed that he had not called, which also was satisfying. But she did know he was probably up to something. She shrugged. He had done the worst possible thing he could do to her. *So why worry about whatever else it was he might be doing?*

She sat down in the chair near the window and spent a good bit of time looking out towards the mountains and thinking about the day.

Ludlow's detour to see the wild horses had accomplished what he had intended. It had helped crystallize her understanding of exactly why Lindy Abraham and Julia Evans had been so passionate about saving the mustangs. When Kate had spent those few minutes watching them today, she had felt her spirit and heart moved in a way she still didn't understand. She only knew that what was being done to them by the BLM was one of the worst imaginable tragedies. The horses were as much a part of the American West as the Rocky Mountains, or, as once the Natives had been. And if the BLM kept up their plans, soon they would be either eliminated, or, as the Natives, proscribed to living on a fraction of a percentage of land they had once roamed freely. And probably, one day even that would be taken away from them, as the special interests and corporations took more and more of public land for their own uses.

Knowing Washington though, Kate had her doubts that something could actually be done. Special interests were too entrenched, wielded too much power.

Well, she would do what she could. She would tell the story. Hopefully, the American people would pay attention. That was all she could do. She tried not to feel defeated at the thought.

Then she allowed her thoughts to drift to Ludlow.

She had an image of him that she couldn't get out of her mind: Ludlow standing on the ridge, tall and straight, looking at the wild horses. Like them, he had seemed so much a part of the land, his black hair softly blowing behind his back like the silken tails of the horses in the valley. At that moment, he had been the most beautiful man she had ever seen in her life.

And she wanted him. Despite all she had learned today and the mess her life was in. She wanted him. Plain and simple.

She had gone through most of her adult life not having much

interest in men, except for Jacques, John, and a couple of brief flirtations that didn't amount to anything. Thinking of Ludlow made her antsy, and she shifted in her chair. It was a bit like having a maddening itch that couldn't be scratched.

To distract herself she pulled her laptop out of the bag and went online. She remembered Sharon saying something about Ludlow winning the Extreme Mustang Makeover the year before, and she decided to see if she could find a video of the finals. She wanted to see what kind of rider he was.

She pulled up the EMM website, and soon found a link to the YouTube video of the finals in the Ft. Worth competition. She sorted through several videos, until she found one that said 'Winner – Freestyle – Jim Ludlow,' and she began watching.

His routine had started with a complicated flute and drum music that she had never heard before; it was lively and very compelling. She thought it must be some type of Native music. After the first few bars of the music, Ludlow came racing in on a big bay horse, no saddle or bridle, and made a perfect sliding stop, then the horse rolled back and turned, did another rundown, and another sliding stop. Then Ludlow turned the horse and faced the judges and nodded gravely. He was dressed in traditional Native clothing of buckskin breeches with five blue and white stripes painted across the calves, beaded moccasins, silver armbands, a necklace, and a beautifully beaded buckskin vest. His arms were wiry and muscular, and his skin glowed in the light a soft nut brown. His hair was loose and flowed down his back. He sat on the big bay gelding, erect and proud, like some arrogant pagan prince returning from a battle won. Once he had saluted the judges, he gave the horse some invisible cue, the horse sprang into a lope, and they began running a wide circle, first a slow lope, and then a fast gallop, then across at a diagonal with a flying lead change in the center, then another circle pattern at different gaits. Kate could not see how Ludlow was giving the horse the cues for all the maneuvers; it seemed like they were one being. They ran to the center of the arena, stopped, did a lightning fast spin to the right, the horse planting its hind foot and practically running with its front feet, then they did the same to the left. After this, Ludlow put the horse into a slow trot, and did a sidepass to the left and to the right. Then, the horse slowed to an extremely slow collected trot, stepping high with each beat of the music. Ludlow trotted the horse to a spot in front of the judges, stopped, and bowed. Then he turned with a loud war whoop, and the horse went into a gallop across the arena, and jumped through a flaming hoop that some hands had brought in and placed near the exit gate.

Kate sat for a moment, mouth agape. She knew that he had trained this horse in a little more than three months, and the horse had been wild when he had started. She had seen people work with horses for years, and they would have never been able to accomplish this. And, to do it without saddle and a bridle?

If she hadn't seen it, if someone had just told her about it, she would have said it was completely impossible.

But Ludlow had done it, and she couldn't help but be awestruck. His connection with the big bay horse had seemed almost mystical. She had had similar feelings with Manny, but she had to admit that she and Manny never had the connection that this man had with his mustang.

Kate realized that she had witnessed a miracle. She sincerely regretted that she hadn't been there to see it when it happened.

She sat looking out the window for a while longer, then went to the bathroom and filled the tub. She sank into the warm water, stretched out in the tub and sighed.

She closed her eyes and thought of Ludlow as he looked standing on the hill with the wind blowing in his hair. Then she let her hand drift down below her waist and did what she could to soothe the maddening itch.

Chapter 12

The next morning Kate got up, showered, and had just finished getting dressed when Ludlow knocked at her door. She had taken special pains with her hair and had even put on lipstick, although she scolded herself as she did it. Her hair would be a mess in an hour and the lipstick would be worn off, so why bother? But she did it anyway.

As she went to the door she grabbed her handbag and left the laptop behind, remembering Ludlow's caution from the day before.

She opened the door and felt a rush of pleasure just at the sight of him.

"You ready?" he asked. He had a travel mug of coffee and took a sip from it.

"Yep. Oh, that coffee looks good," she said.

He smiled and handed her a mug of her own that he had set on the floor when he knocked at her door.

"Thought you might like some. It's black, I hope that's OK. I have to admit that I'm a hopeless caffeine addict."

"Me too. Seems like everyone in the newsroom is. But I can't stand those fancy latte drinks. Too much of a purist, I guess," she said, taking the mug that he handed to her.

Ludlow smiled and started walking through the hayloft, Kate following closely behind him. When they got to the truck Kate was surprised to see a hunting rifle in the rack in the truck's rear window. It hadn't been there the day before.

"Expecting trouble?" she asked, when she looked at it.

"Not really. Just better to have it and not need it, than the other way around. Does it bother you?"

Kate shook her head.

Once they got in the truck and began pulling out of the driveway, Kate took out the map, set it on the seat between them then turned on her Smartphone.

"Do you have that satellite phone with you, too?" Ludlow asked.

"Yes. Why? Do you think we'll need it?"

"Maybe. Most of the area we're going today doesn't have cell coverage, and it would be nice to have some type of communication, I think. Sharon gave me a police radio, but it won't have the range where we're going," he said.

Kate watched Ludlow closely; he seemed a bit worried, and it was clear there was something he wasn't telling her.

"Why don't you tell me what's going on, Jim?" she asked. "I take it your phone calls last night were disturbing."

Ludlow sighed and shook his head. "Well, it has more to do with Tribal politics than anything else."

Kate looked at him with a raised eyebrow, and made a circular hand motion for him to continue.

"There's a Tribal Member who lives in Elko who used to be on the Council. In fact, he used to pretty much run things before we got the Casino and started working on all these changes and improvements on the Rez. He used to pass himself off as the 'chief' here, although he was just a Tribal Council member – a senior one, granted, but he was not a 'chief' by any stretch of the imagination – but he managed to convince some outside the Tribe that he was a 'chief' and could negotiate and sign contracts on the Tribe's behalf."

"I'm taking it that when you say 'some,' you're talking about the BLM and others that have special interests in this area."

"That's right. He was the one who signed the agreement to let St. Martjin Mining do their open pit mining on Rez land years ago. He didn't have the authority, according to Tribal law, but St. Martjin has been arguing that he was a legitimate representative of the Tribe at the time the contract was signed, so therefore the agreement is binding."

Ludlow tapped the steering wheel a few times with his fingers and shook his head.

"It hasn't helped matters any that at the time Tribal law was more of an understanding among our people, based on tradition, rather than something written down that a judge would recognize," he said. "It's been a long, expensive battle in federal court. What's disturbing is that we won the last round and the court issued an injunction for St. Martjin to stop mining on Rez land, but they've appealed and are ignoring the injunction. It's made for a lot of tensions between the Rez and the Mine. Apparently the Mine has been telling Joshua Bann about these closures; he's the fake 'chief' I was telling you about, and they consider that to be sufficient notice for closures and other actions."

"I take it Mr. Bann is getting some sort of payment for these agreements and notifications?" Kate asked.

"We can't prove it, but it's what we all believe. He's always been one of the richest Natives in the area. He has a big house in Elko and he leases about 200,000 acres from the BLM that he runs cattle on."

"So what's with the rifle?"

Ludlow looked at her uncomfortably. "I have a feeling we may run into Mine Security today," he said. "I have no plans to get into a shootout or anything, but I just felt better having it with us. That's why I'd like to have the phone also. And, if you notice, I am wearing my Tribal Police badge today."

Kate looked as he touched a brass badge that he was wearing on his belt. She hadn't noticed it before.

"I'm sorry, Jim," Kate said. "I don't like it that I've put you in a situation that obviously worries you."

Ludlow laughed a little.

"Well, I've been told that I come from long line of warriors, but I think that gene skipped me. I don't like guns, although I was trained how to use them, of course, as a boy. The thought of shooting a human being, or just about any living creature really – well, the thought makes me a little sick. I used to hunt a lot as a boy, but I have no interest anymore. Now, I primarily use the rifle for target practice, so I can kill an animal cleanly if I have to." He paused. "It won't come to that though, I'm just taking precautions.".

"OK. But now I really wish you'd let the Gazette pay you something for your time," she said.

Ludlow just shook his head and smiled.

They drove to the main road north out of Antelope Valley, but instead of taking a left to go into town, they took a right, and then another left on a dirt road that angled its way down to BIA 19. Once they got close to 19, Ludlow stopped and looked at the map closely.

"OK, here is Sage Creek, where we got turned back yesterday," he said, pointing to the last place they had stopped the day before. "It looks like they doubled back down BIA 19, then took this side road that angles back north-northeast. We've got a little bit of a drive ahead of us."

Kate simply nodded. *Seems like getting anywhere in this part of Nevada involves a 'little bit of a drive.'*

"I watched you last night on Youtube," she said, after they had driven for a while, "At the Makeover last year. I watched your Freestyle."

Ludlow groaned and shook his head. "Now who told you about that?"

"Sharon did. She mentioned it to me when I first got into town."

"My sister has a big mouth," Ludlow said.

"No, no. I thought it was wonderful. I never would have believed such a thing could have been done if I hadn't seen it myself. How in the world did you ever get that horse trained to do all those movements?"

Ludlow smiled, with a fond look on his face. "It was easy. Jerry, the gelding I was riding, is about the smartest horse I've ever worked with, and by far the easiest to train. He's athletic and has a lot of focus once he understands what it is you want from him. It was a unique experience, starting that horse. He had a lot of resistances in the beginning, but once I got his trust, he'd do anything for me."

Ludlow smiled broadly and glanced over at Kate.

"I was glad I got to keep him. I didn't know if I would be able to or not, but, since we had won that big pot of prize money, I did have the cash it took to outbid the others that were bidding on him. If I had had to give him up it would have broken my heart."

Kate watched Ludlow closely, and was surprised to see wetness in his eyes as he spoke. She had never met another man like him in her life. It seemed that he had managed to let go of the ego-laden façade so many men felt they had to wear to face the world. She put her hand on the seat and leaned towards him slightly.

"I'm surprised you don't travel and do clinics. Quite frankly I think you're about the most amazing horseman I've ever seen. Better than Patterson, Monty Roberts, or most of those other 'horse whisperers.'"

Ludlow laughed a bit and shook his head. "Traveling doesn't suit me too much these days. That trip to Ft. Worth last year was bad enough, and I had Kimmy and Dove with me to keep me company. I do work with a lot of other people on horsemanship though. I don't just keep all the knowledge to myself. My grandfather, who WAS the greatest horseman I've ever seen, wouldn't want that."

Ludlow went on to tell Kate about the work he did at the MWCL, with the rehab patients and the work-release inmates. He also told her about Mike Patterson, and how he had trained with Johnny Elk so many years before.

"So this is the same grandfather that helped your Martin Levi with this revolution here in Antelope Valley? He must have been quite a man."

"He was. A great man in his own way, although you'll never see his name on a monument anywhere."

Kate sat in silence for a bit as she thought about JQ. He too was a great man, in his own way, whose name would never be on any monument except for his tombstone. She still missed him fiercely.

After they had been driving about an hour on 19, Ludlow slowed down and took a right onto a road that didn't look like much more than a cattle trail. He drove slowly, trying to spare them as many bumps as possible, but continued to follow the road to the north as it angled back towards the mountains. He asked Kate to check to see how close they were getting to the next point on the map.

"We're just about there," she said, looking closely at the GPS.

Ludlow pulled over onto the desert, and rolled down the window. Kate wondered why they had stopped.

"Do you hear that?" he asked.

Kate listened without hearing anything; then in the distance she heard a quick whump-whump-whump that sounded like a helicopter.

"Sounds like a chopper, but I think it's pretty far off," she said.

"Shit," Ludlow said under his breath.

"What's the matter?"

"I was hoping they wouldn't be out patrolling today since it's a Saturday. No such luck."

Kate rolled her eyes a bit, exasperated, when he didn't continue. "What are you talking about?" she asked.

"Mine Security has a couple of helicopters that they use to keep an eye out for any people, cattle, horses etc. that might manage to stray into one of their 'safety zones.' Zones that seem to be getting wider and wider every month, I might add."

He looked at the map again. "Well, we're still clearly on Rez land, but if we get too much farther north we will get into the 'disputed' territory. I was just hoping we could kind of scoot by under the radar, but I should have known better."

"What will they do?"

"Well, the helicopter pilot will probably fly in for a closer look, and watch what we're up to. If we don't clear out, then we will probably wind up having a conversation with the Mine Security guys, who will drive out here and come up with a reason to run us off. That's the way this usually works."

Ludlow still sat, listening to the noise from the helicopter, which was getting louder.

"This is Native land, right?" Kate asked, suddenly feeling angry.

"According to treaty, that's right."

"Fuck 'em, then. I want to finish what we started."

Ludlow stared at her a moment, and Kate felt momentarily guilty for dropping the 'f' bomb into the conversation. But he just shook his head, grinned, and pulled back out onto the road again.

"You're the boss," he said, shaking his head and chuckling.

Sure enough, within 15 minutes or so, the helicopter began shadowing them closely. After a rocky, bumpy drive, they reached another impasse – this time a huge stack of rocks that had been piled up between two steep hills, with a sign that said 'No Trespassing' with the St Martjin Mining's logo. Ludlow managed to get the truck turned around (it took a while, they were in a tight place) and they headed back to 19 again to find their way to the next point on the map. The helicopter kept them in sight the entire time. Ludlow paid it no mind.

However, when they turned north onto 19, they had only driven a few miles when they hit a roadblock. Three brand new pearl colored Lincoln Navigators were blocking the roadway. They had insignias on the doors that said 'St. Martjin Security Services.' There was also a barrier across the roadway with a sign that said, 'Road closed for blasting, St. Martjin Mining.' Several burly armed and uniformed men were standing at the barricade; most were carrying assault weapons.

Ludlow stopped about 25 feet away from the barricade. He put the truck in park, but didn't shut off the engine.

"Kate, would you please get that Sat phone out and call my

sister? I want you to tell her that we are on BIA 19 about 30 miles north of Sage Creek and we've run into a roadblock with Mine Security. I'm going to get out and talk to these guys a minute."

"Are you nuts? Look at them! They'll eat you for breakfast!"

Ludlow gave her a slightly injured look. "Oh Ye of Little Faith. Please, just call Sharon and tell her what's going on," he said.

"Let me go with you then," Kate asked desperately. "I don't want you to go out there alone."

"No!" Ludlow said quickly, looking at Kate and putting his hand on her arm. "Leave this to me. You just get on the phone with my sister and tell her where we are. And make sure these guys can see that you're on the phone. Please."

Kate looked at him a moment and he squeezed her arm.

"It'll be OK. Trust me," he said.

Kate got the phone out and dialed Sharon's cell phone. While the phone was ringing she looked at the rifle sitting in the rack behind her. She hadn't shot a gun since college, when she had shot skeet with John and his father on one of their Thanksgiving trips, but she remembered enough to use this one if she had to. Sharon's phone kept ringing, and Kate hung onto the phone tensely, praying that she would pick up.

Ludlow stepped down slowly out of the truck, and walked towards the men with as relaxed a posture as he could manage. He made sure his Tribal Police badge was visible and waved casually as he walked towards them.

"Good morning," he called out pleasantly. "How are you gentlemen this morning?"

"Just fine, sir, just fine," said a tall man who was standing behind the barrier. He was one of the few without a weapon. He too answered in a pleasant and courteous tone.

"Ah, Mr. Shelton," Ludlow said. He had seen Victor Shelton once before, briefly. Sharon had met with him to talk about the sabotage of some Mining equipment, and she had asked him to ride along to the meeting to see if he could help with tracking the perpetrators. Ludlow had seen plenty of tracks, but hadn't bothered to tell anyone about them.

"Mister?? I'm sorry, I can't remember the name. Is it Mr. White Owl?" the other man asked.

"Ludlow. Jim Ludlow," he said, reaching out his hand, which

Shelton shook.

"Of course. Mr. Ludlow."

Shelton stood looking at Ludlow patiently. He was an inch or two shorter than Ludlow and had an air of lazy watchfulness about him. His eyes were flat black, like obsidian, and when he had smiled, his teeth had had an odd yellow cast to them. Ludlow knew that this patient attitude was just a little game that the man was playing, to see if he could push Ludlow into a reaction. It was a game of dominance, one that Ludlow was long familiar with from his work with horses. He too stood relaxed and patient, with a slight smile, as he carefully watched Shelton's face.

Minutes dragged on, and Ludlow heard one of the guards clear his throat. He also heard two others talking in low tones to one another, although he couldn't catch the words. Shelton glanced back at them in irritation, then turned back to Ludlow.

"So, Mr. Ludlow," Shelton said, "as you can see, we've closed off the road here; we've got some blasting and other work going on up at the mine, and we designated this as a safety zone for today."

"I see that," Ludlow said, still keeping his voice friendly and pleasant, "but we never received notice of this closure, Mr. Shelton. And, as per numerous court orders, unless our Tribal Council is notified of a closure and agrees to it, your company has no right to shut off any part of our land for our use."

"Oh, you'll have to talk to Josh Bann about that. He knows all about this and approved. We always aim to comply with Tribal law."

"Mr. Shelton, surely you are aware that Mr. Bann is not affiliated with the Tribal Council and hasn't held a seat for several years now. He has no authority to approve this or any other closure. So the courts ruled two years ago."

"Is that right?" Shelton said with a pseudo-astonished look on his face. "I had no idea. I'll have to get with my management to ask about that. First I've heard of it."

Ludlow looked at Shelton a moment, and fought the urge to heave a heavy sigh. Instead, he continued to smile pleasantly, as if Shelton was the most reasonable man he had ever met.

"Mr. Shelton, I am on official business for the Tribal Police, and we need to get past this roadblock, as we're on an investigation. So I'd appreciate some professional courtesy if at all possible. We both know Mine operations are 25 miles away to the north and west, and our investigation is going to take us back towards the east, well out of danger, I would think."

Shelton looked at him for a moment with undisguised contempt. "Professional courtesy?" he spat, his voice cracking like a whip. "Well, when I see something other than a jumped-up cowboy who thinks a badge and a beat-up pickup makes him a professional, maybe I will consider offering a little courtesy. Come back with a court order and the sheriff and then maybe we'll talk."

"You're on Tribal Land here under our jurisdiction," Ludlow said coolly, unperturbed by the man's outburst.

Shelton chuckled. "Well, you know what they say, 'Possession is nine-tenths of the law' and right now it looks like Mine Security are the ones that have control of this situation, doesn't it? What do you have? A woman talking on a cell phone? I'm sorry, but that doesn't make much of an argument for 'professional courtesy.' If it did I'd have to be offering courtesy to most every car in the State of Nevada."

Ludlow laughed without humor and stared at Shelton a moment. Then he looked down at the ground and shook his head, taking a deep breath to get his anger under control. Shelton was right. He didn't have any leverage in these particular negotiations at this place and time.

"By the way," Shelton said, leaning forward slightly and speaking in a confidential tone, "the young lady there. It would have really been for the best if she had gotten on that plane back to DC instead of sneaking up here to start trouble between St. Martjin and the Shoshone. This is rough country. Very, very dangerous country in this part of Nevada, especially for women. People like her don't understand how we do things here. She's just here to make a big name for herself, you know. Don't fool yourself into thinking she gives a shit about what happens in Indian Country. She doesn't. Good day, Mr. Ludlow," Shelton concluded, smiling then turning and walking away. "We're very busy today. If you get that court order and the sheriff, you just let me know and we'll talk again."

Ludlow stood watching the man walk away, then he turned and went back to the truck. He opened the door and got in, again taking a deep breath to get his anger under control. And his fear. He hadn't missed Shelton's veiled threat against Kate and it bothered him immensely that the man had known that Kate hadn't gone back to DC.

"What happened?" Kate asked, placing her hand over the phone. "Sharon's about to have a fit."

"Just tell her I was out-negotiated," Ludlow replied, with disgust.

*

Shelton watched from behind the barrier as the old white truck turned and drove back the way it had come. The exchange had bothered him more than he let on. He was glad he had hit the mark in guessing that the woman was the journalist from DC. He had not known for sure, but as soon as he had said it, he had seen the startled look in the Indian's eyes. It had been satisfying that he had been able to extract that piece of information, because the encounter had left him feeling very disturbed.

That had been an unusual Indian. A very cool customer. It took courage for an unarmed man to walk up so casually to a group of men holding assault weapons out in the middle of nowhere. Shelton didn't like it one bit. And the woman. She was obviously clever, although it wouldn't have taken a rocket scientist to give the little BLM PR man the slip. She was also a snooper. He hated snoopers. They did nothing but cause problems for guys like him, who were just trying to do a job.

He was also irritated with a couple of his new staff. They talked too much. They were still talking now, when they should have been keeping their mouths shut, waiting for orders. Time for an object lesson.

"Hey Vic!" one of them said. George, his name was. He'd just come in the week before, and still didn't understand the way things worked on Shelton's team.

"I guess that's an All-American Girl," George said, grinning hugely.

"Is that right? What makes you say that, Mr. George?" Shelton said turning and smiling pleasantly at the man, his hands clasped behind his back.

"She likes Red Meat!" George sallied, guffawing loudly. Shelton stepped towards George and struck with his fist at the man's back so fast the others didn't even see him move. His knuckles hit George just over the kidney. George fell and rolled around on the ground in pain. Shelton reached down into the

221

man's mouth with his thumb and grabbed him by the front of his upper jaw with the rest of his fingers, digging into the unfortunate George's upper palate with his thumbnail. George gabbled in pain, his eyes wide and bulging. Shelton lifted his head and upper body off the ground easily with one hand.

"Now, Mr. George, have a care now. Don't bite me, otherwise I might break your jaw, and we can't have that," Shelton said in a reasonable tone, closing off the man's nostrils with the knuckles of his index and middle finger, causing the hapless George to open his mouth wide to gasp for air.

"Ah, that's much better. Mr. George. You're new, so I'm going to be lenient with you, but you need to understand something. These are not people we are dealing with here. They are jobs. Just jobs. You see, when you make comments like you just did, which was racist, sexist, and completely inappropriate, it affects the attitude, and people become more than just a job. We can't have that, Mr. George. So, my recommendation to you is that you should try to purge yourself of these thoughts. You won't last here unless you do." Shelton had abruptly dropped George back down to the ground.

"I need to get back to the office, gentlemen. I want you to stay here and take care of Mr. Ludlow and the young lady in case they decide to come back," he said. "And please see to Mr. George. He seems to have had an unfortunate accident."

He then turned and got into one of the SUVs, wiping George's blood and spit from his hand onto his pants. George struggled to sit up, blood pouring from his mouth. Shelton had nearly ruptured his upper palate. The other guards just stared at him. They had known Shelton was rough, but they had no idea he was this rough. They were hard men, but they had never seen anything quite like this before.

And they hoped they never would again.

Shelton stared moodily out the window as he and his driver headed back to the office.

Things were starting to spin out of control a bit. He needed to make some corrections to get everything back on track.

*

Ludlow drove south in bitter silence. He knew that Kate wanted him to talk to her about what happened, but he was angrier and more frightened than he had been in a long time, and wanted to

222

wait until he was less emotional before he spoke. She seemed to sense this, and sat quietly, asking no questions. After a time, she reached across the cab of the truck, placed her hand on his shoulder, and gave him a little shake.

"Are you OK?" she asked.

Ludlow smiled and glanced over at her. "Yeah. Just scared."

"You didn't look very scared. You looked like Clint Eastwood in one of those old spaghetti westerns," she said.

Ludlow laughed out loud at that. "Absolutely. That's why we're headed south with our tail between our legs."

"Speak for yourself. My tail is in its normal spot."

Ludlow laughed again, this time harder. He was starting to get past that bitter feeling; he looked over at her again briefly and saw she was smiling broadly at him. "I can't believe it, you seem to be ENJOYING this," he said.

"Not really. I just got tired of watching you sit there and stew. What choice did we have up against armed men?"

"None."

"Well, there ya go. Now we just need to figure out what to do next. For one thing, I'm hungry. To me, that's the top priority right now. What can we do about it?"

Ludlow looked at her, amused at the way her mind worked. "Well, knowing that we would be out here on the west side, with no place to eat, I packed us a lunch this morning. I have a couple of sandwiches and some apples. Also some juice. How does that sound?" he asked.

"Heavenly. Let's find a place to pull over and regroup."

Ludlow looked around until he found a likely spot, and pulled the truck off onto a little rise. Once they stopped he pulled a small cooler out of the back of the truck and handed it to Kate. Then he got out an old, worn wool blanket out of the truck cab. It probably had been red at one point, but it was faded to a medium pink, and was covered with horsehair. He found a flat spot, kicked the rocks aside, and stretched the blanket out. He sank down, crossing his long legs in front of him. Kate set the cooler on the blanket and sat down beside him.

It had turned out to be a beautiful day, the desert landscape was very pale and stark here, and the mountains in the background looked like the shoulders of sleeping giants. Kate knew that Montana was called Big Sky Country, but she couldn't imagine that the sky being any bigger than this white-flecked blue dome over Nevada. The air was dry and smelled clean, with just a scent of sage. She shook her hair lose from its elastic band and let it blow in the breeze. She reached into the cooler, pulled out a sandwich and a bottle of apple juice and handed them to Ludlow, and then she got a sandwich and juice for herself. She took a bite; peanut butter and jelly on some kind of homemade bread. It was delicious. In the distance she could see the same helicopter that had followed them earlier, sweeping back and forth, looking for other people to terrorize, she guessed.

She watched Ludlow surreptitiously, as he thoughtfully munched his sandwich. He had put on a battered cowboy hat, which made him look rakish and exotic to her eyes. He was staring off towards the mountain, his thoughts clearly a million miles away.

"This is the best peanut butter and jelly sandwich I ever had in my life. This bread is wonderful, with the little bits of fruit and nuts in it. Who made it?" she asked.

"My mother did," Ludlow said, turning back to face her. "It's her specialty. I've eaten many a peanut butter sandwich on this bread over the years."

Kate continued to chew contentedly on the thick pieces of hand cut bread. Then she turned to Ludlow and poked him playfully on the leg with her foot.

"I think we should go to Elko this afternoon and talk to that fellow that Sharon mentioned last night. That old friend of yours.".

Ludlow shook his head. "I don't think so."

"Why not?"

"I just don't think it's a good idea. I think we've gone about as far as we can with this," Ludlow said.

Kate sat up straight and looked at him, serious now. "So, you're saying you want to give up?" she asked incredulously.

"It's not about giving up. It's about knowing when you're beat."

"I'm not beat," Kate said. She got up and stalked off into the desert, leaving her half eaten sandwich and apple juice sitting on the cooler.

Ludlow watched as she walked away, then sighed. *Stubborn. Just plain stubborn.*

He finished his sandwich, got up, and followed her. She hadn't gone too far, just down to the foot of the hill, where she was pacing angrily.

"I'm sorry you're angry," he said once he got close enough for her to hear, "but I'm just telling you how I feel."

"The hell you are," she said, turning to face him, her arms were crossed on her chest and her eyes were blazing. "What did that man say to you anyway that made you want to give up?"

This statement took Ludlow aback. *How could she know?*

"If he threatened your family, just say so plainly. Or maybe he threatened your horses or something. Whatever it is, just say so, instead of standing there looking all noble and worried and suffering in silence.".

Ludlow stood in front of her, shocked and speechless.

Kate rolled her eyes and shook her head; the anger seemed to have quickly drained out of her. "The gigged frog expression is not much of an improvement, Jim." She walked up to him, placed her hands on his shoulders and looked him intently in the eye. "Oh," she said in quiet gasp.

She dropped one hand, but the other drifted down to rest lightly on his chest. Ludlow reached up and covered it with one of his own. They stood there for a long moment as the rest of the world fell away. It was if some penetrating breeze passed through them, blowing away an opaque veil that had been holding them apart. Once the veil fell, they each perceived the heart and spirit of the other and realized that no matter what their waking minds told them, there was a bond between them that was both profound and sacred – a bond that, once recognized, created a sense of inexpressible joy, wonder and awe.

However, the moment passed, and they both started, as if waking from a dream.

Kate dropped her hand quickly to her side. She turned away from him and he saw her make an odd shivering movement as if she had a sudden chill. Then she turned back to him.

"So, they said something about me, then," she said. "I guess they figured out I didn't go back to DC. Big deal. So they know. So they're mad. So they're going to be uncooperative. What's different? What's changed?"

Everything has changed for me, Ludlow thought helplessly. *Everything.*

She looked so beautiful, standing in front of him with the wind blowing in her hair, just like one of the wild ones. Ludlow wanted so badly to take her in his arms and hold her, to protect her from those who might do her harm. To feel her warmth against him.

"I don't want to give up," she said.

Ludlow sighed and put a hand on her shoulder. "OK, Kate, OK. I'm sorry. If you want, we can drive into Elko and see if we can find Bobby, but don't get your hopes up. Bobby is not one to stand up to these people. He decided long ago that the easy way was the best way."

"Well, if we don't try, then we'll have removed an opportunity from him to do the right thing. Don't you think?" she said.

Ludlow nodded and turned to walk back toward the truck. Kate noticed that his shoulders slumped as he walked up the hill, and she hated herself for putting him in this position. But, like Sharon, sometimes she had to put the job first.

"We're not leaving until you finish your sandwich and an apple," Ludlow said firmly.

"Deal," Kate said, laughing a bit. She came up, took his arm, smiled at him, and took his hand in hers.

"Friends, right?" she said easily, meeting his eyes. "Don't worry. It'll be all right."

Ludlow nodded and smiled at her. And, at that moment he found that he was happier than he had been in a long, long time.

*

They drove down to Elko, sometimes talking of inconsequential things, sometimes in companionable silence. Kate told Ludlow about some of her trips to Africa and was pleased and happy when Ludlow seemed knowledgeable and interested in the work she had done there.

They spoke easily and happily with each other, often laughing at some joke the other made. Although neither fully understood what had passed between them earlier, they both realized that some sort of emotional wall between them had vanished. Neither questioned it; they only knew they were no longer strangers.

*

It was a long trip and when they arrived, it was nearly 2 pm. Ludlow drove unerringly down the streets of the town, eventually turning into a down at the heels quasi-industrial area. He pulled across some bumpy railroad tracks, drove a few blocks, and pulled into a gravel parking lot adjacent to a row of run down storefronts. There were a few motorcycles in the parking lot, some trucks, and a few cars. Once he pulled up and parked, Kate got out of the truck.

Ludlow gazed at her with a pained look as she walked around the truck with her handbag over her shoulder.

"I guess asking you to stay in the truck this time is out of the question?" he asked.

"Are you crazy? I'm scared to stay out in this parking lot by myself. Even in the middle of the afternoon. I'd rather take my chances in the bar."

"OK. Well, let's stick close together. Safety in numbers."

"Yeah right, all two of us," she said.

They walked about half a block down the street, until they came to a bar on their right. There was an old-fashioned shed roof that covered the sidewalk in front of the bar, and under the roof was a rather ratty looking stuffed pronghorn antelope head. As they opened the door, there was the jingle of a bell, and all heads turned to look at them as the door closed behind them. Ludlow put his arm around Kate's waist, and pulled her abruptly towards him, so abruptly that she was thrown a little off balance. Several biker-types were playing pool and a few other customers were seated at table, most with large pitchers of beer. Some were watching ESPN on a big screen TV. Two or three were sitting at the bar. Ludlow headed towards the bar, making for a skinny angular Native man sitting at the far end.

The man looked at them, eyes widening in surprise as he saw Ludlow. "Well, Hi, Jimmy. Long time no see. Have a seat," he said.

Ludlow nodded and smiled, reaching out to shake the man's hand. "Hi Bobby. Want you to meet a friend of mine. This is Kate Wyndham. Kate, this is an old friend of mine, Bobby Nardo."

"Hi Bobby," she said, nodding and shaking his hand after Ludlow was done.

Ludlow pulled out the stool next to Bobby for Kate to sit down then he sat on the other side of her. The bartender came over and asked for their orders. Bobby ordered another beer, Kate ordered water and Ludlow got a club soda. When Ludlow ordered the club soda, Bobby gave him a pained look. "Still on the wagon?" he asked.

"Six years now," Ludlow said, unperturbed, sipping at his club soda.

"We used to have so much fun in the old days," he said, looking at Kate woefully, "Jimmy Ludlow used to be a real party man, now he's just a party pooper."

"That's harsh, Bobby, very harsh," Ludlow said.

Bobby shrugged. "I just miss those good times, Jimmy, that's all."

"I'd like to ask you something, Bobby, and I hope you'll be honest with me, for old time's sake," Ludlow said.

"Sure, Jim, sure, whatever you need, you just let me know. We used to be good friends, Miss, very good friends," Bobby said, looking at Kate. She noticed that he was at least two sheets to the wind, if not more.

"We used to hunt together, and ride horses together, and go fishing. Those were good times, weren't they, Jimmy?"

"Very good times. Anyway, Bobby, I need to ask you a question, and I want you to think very hard about it. About three months ago, do you remember flying for the BLM or doing work up by the Mine? Any roundups?"

Bobby looked at Ludlow owlishly; then he glanced over at Kate. "That would be back, in, June or something. No, I haven't done any work for them this summer. No sir. Not one thing," he said.

Ludlow placed his hand on Bobby's arm and gave it a little shake. "This would have been about the time those two mustang advocates disappeared. We think they were looking for a roundup, and something happened to them. We're trying to find out what."

Bobby shot Kate another look; a cunning look, she thought. "I don't guess Jim ever told you about his experience with the ladies," he said. "He used to be quite the cutter, back when we were still friends. Back in the good old days."

"No," Kate said, shrugging. "Never mentioned it."

"Oh yes. No telling how many little Ludlows there are running around this part of Nevada, leftovers from those days, eh Jimmy?" Bobby said.

"There aren't any that I know of, thankfully," Ludlow said. "But Bobby, did you do some work for the BLM back when those women disappeared? Do you remember?" he pressed, not allowing Bobby to change the subject.

"I don't know a damn thing about any roundups, I tolt you, I ain't done none all summer!" Bobby said, growing angry. "Now either have a drink with me, for old time's sake, or get the hell out. I cain't stand to be around no teetotalers."

"All right, all right," Ludlow said, clasping Bobby's arm briefly. "You know where to find me if you remember something that might be helpful. But these women who disappeared were just trying to do the right thing by the wild ones."

"I tolt you," Bobby said, raising his voice, and throwing Ludlow's hand off. "I don't know nothing about no roundups or no women. Now leave me the hell alone."

Ludlow nodded briefly and laid ten dollars down on the bar to pay for the drinks. "OK. You call me if you change your mind," he said quietly, then reached for Kate's hand and led her out of the bar.

"That went well," she said ruefully, once they got out into the street.

"About what I expected. I figured it would be a waste of time, but, like you said, sometimes a man may never do the right thing, unless someone gives him the opportunity to do so. Bobby used to be a good person. I still like to think he is, somewhere, down under all that self-loathing."

"Where does he live?" Kate asked, noticing that Ludlow was still holding her hand. She kept her hand quiet and small in his, hoping that he wouldn't break the contact. But he did, and she felt a brief pang of loss as her hand fell to her side.

Ludlow sighed. "He used to live in Antelope Valley. But his family couldn't deal with the drugs and drunkenness anymore. Have you heard the term 'shunning'? It's something I understand that the Amish do as punishment. Our people do something similar. Basically, Bobby Nardo is a social exile. He may come to Antelope Valley, but most people turn their faces away from him because they feel he has shamed them."

"But you don't feel that way?" Kate asked, curious.

"I'm not one to cast stones at anyone for shameful behavior. All those things he said in there, about the women. They were all true, Kate. And I was a drunk, as bad or worse than Bobby, but not when we were young. Bobby didn't drink back then either. Something happened to him while he was in the military that changed him. No one knows what – he's been drinking ever since he came back from Afghanistan. As for me, I became a drunk while I was living in DC. I shamed my wife greatly, and she stopped loving me and divorced me."

Ludlow sighed heavily and smiled a sad smile. "But I found my way back to the world of the living. I believe Bobby can too. I hope and pray that he will one day. That life he's living, it's just walking death. I know. I've walked there myself. But, a person can put his life back together. Madeleine, my ex-wife, has remarried and has two young children. I'm happy for her, but still have regrets that what we had didn't work out. We talk once or twice a year, but it took her a while to get to the point where she could get past the shame and find some forgiveness for me. I can't blame her.

"But, I didn't answer your original question. I don't know where Bobby is living now, I guess somewhere here in Elko," Ludlow said as they turned into the little parking lot and headed for the truck.

Without thinking, Kate slipped her arm around Ludlow's waist and held him close to her for just a moment, then she kissed him on the cheek. "You're a good man, Jim Ludlow. One of the best," and she dropped her arm, walked around, and got into the truck.

Ludlow stood, stunned, and watched her walk away, mouth slightly agape.

As they drove back to Antelope Valley, both sat silently, lost in thought. Kate was pondering if there was anything else she could do at this point as far as the story went, and Ludlow was thinking of Bobby Nardo. Bobby had been lying, of that much he was certain, but whether he would ever find the courage to tell the truth was an open question. Ludlow doubted it was possible; Bobby had been in the walking death for too long.

Kate dreaded going back to Washington. It would be the first in many steps of starting a new life, and she felt overwhelmed at the thought. When it was done, the only thing she would have left would be work. Plus, she still had her murderous feelings for John Ridley that had to be dealt with. The anger had not lessened; it had only changed in form from explosive hot gas to icy cold rage. She wasn't sure she was ready to face him yet.

And now, there was Jim Ludlow. Kate knew that he cared for her; how deeply she wasn't sure, but she had seen it in his eyes earlier when they had stood on the hill. It had been a stunning revelation; one that she was still coming to grips with.

The one thing she did know was that she had come to care for him also, far beyond the intense sexual attraction she had for him. Being with him had become a bitter combination of longing, subtle delight, and unbridled inner joy. This was something she had never experienced before.

But her life was a mess. She had never had feelings like this and her intellect cautioned her that this was just an infatuation manufactured to cushion the blow of the upcoming break-up from John Ridley. She had seen the same phenomena plenty of times with friends – they either used the meeting of the 'love of my life' as an excuse to escape a failing relationship (the subsequent new pairing rarely lasted) or as a band-aid to cover the wounds of a breakup. The rebound effect, Kate knew the latter was called. Rebound relationships were notorious for their disastrous consequences.

Even though her feelings for Ludlow ran deep, she didn't trust them. They had developed incredibly quickly, so therefore were more than likely fleeting. She feared if the relationship was pursued, it would be like throwing dry leaves on a campfire; at first the fire burned hot and leapt high, but then it was gone, leaving nothing but ashes. She didn't want to use Ludlow as a crutch to help her hobble through the aftermath of her own bad decisions. As she thought about it, she realized that Ridley was just a different version of her mother and she had easily stepped into that relationship because of its familiarity. At some level, she had felt she was getting what she deserved.

She looked over at Ludlow, gazing carefully at the smooth planes of his face, his beautiful hazel eyes, and his strangely elegant hands. While he watched the road, she knew his mind was on the man who had once been his friend. The man who was now the 'walking dead,' as Ludlow had described it.

When he had spoken of Madeleine, there was no mistaking the fact that he had once loved the woman, and losing her still pained him at some level. Whether it was just because he had shamed her, or because he still had residual feelings, Kate couldn't determine. Maybe Ludlow didn't know himself. But one thing she did know, she didn't want to put him through more pain because her life was a mess. Better to end it now, before things went any further.

There was no doubt in her mind that things would go further. A clean break early would be best for both of them, she decided.

Now that the decision was made, Kate took a deep breath and turned to Ludlow. "I don't see that we can do much more here, Jim," she said evenly. "I saw how tense things are with that mining company, and I don't want to add anymore fuel to the fire. You and the other people on the Reservation have to find a way to co-exist with these people. I don't. Bobby didn't have anything for us, so that's another dead end. Besides, I've got enough for my story, I think, even though we didn't find out what happened to Abraham and Evans. Maybe if I write what I have now, someone in Washington will take an interest."

Ludlow glanced over at her and she thought she saw a bit of hurt in his eyes. Or was it just her imagination?

"If that's what you think would be best," he said quietly.

"I do. If I stay here any longer it'll just make for a lot of complications," she said, looking at him evenly.

He glanced over at her again; then nodded slowly. "And you've got those personal issues you need to take care of?" he said.

"That's right," she replied, thankful that he seemed to understand without any further explanation.

"I see."

"So, I'm going to call the airline and see if I can get a flight out tomorrow."

"All right, Kate."

She pulled out her Smartphone and called the airline. There was a flight around noon to Salt Lake; it was full, but Kate booked a seat on standby. If she didn't get out on that flight, she would take the next one at 5 p.m. Now that she had made the decision, she just wanted to be done with it.

After she got off the phone, they drove in silence for a bit, then Ludlow glanced over at her and smiled. "Look, it's your last night here, why not have some fun? We're having a pow-wow tonight, why not come?"

"I don't know, Jim. I have to pack then I need to get up early to make sure I make my flight on time. I've got a lot to do," she said.

"Don't you ever have any fun?" he admonished her teasingly. "You may not get this chance again. A chance to party in Indian Country."

232

Kate shook her head and grinned in spite of herself. "This sounds like a date to me. Are you asking me out?" Kate asked archly, then she scolded herself. This man really made sticking to a decision tough.

Ludlow looked a bit abashed, then he laughed. "I'm drumming tonight, so I don't know how good a date I would be. But, if that's what it takes to get you to come, sure, I'm asking you out."

"What do you mean drumming? Do you play in a band or something?" she asked.

Ludlow chuckled again. "Something like that. If you want to find out, I guess you'll just have to come. All the family will be there, except maybe for Sharon; she'll probably be working late. So there'll be people you know there. I think you'll have a good time."

"OK. I'll come, but I'll drive myself. I don't want to stay too late. I need to leave early in the morning," Kate said.

"Fair enough. Basically it starts about 7:30."

"OK. Where is it?"

"At the high school gym. Do you think you can find it?" Ludlow asked.

"I think so."

The rest of the drive back to Antelope Valley passed relatively quickly. Ludlow took a shortcut that avoided town, and Kate was extremely grateful for that. When they got to the ranch, it was about 5:30 and Ludlow dropped her off at the barn.

"When you come into town tonight, just park in that visitor spot at the police station. The high school is just behind there; their parking lots adjoin. You should find it with no problem. I'm going to have to get there a little early to help them set up. I'll see you there," he said.

Kate stood watching him as he drove away, feeling more than a little forlorn. She walked into the barn, spent some time petting the horses and scratching their withers and other itchy spots. It made her feel better. She went up to the apartment and called Meyers at home to tell him she was flying back to DC the following day and that she really was not much closer to getting answers than she had been when she first arrived. He was sympathetic, but distracted, and she didn't keep him on the phone long. She didn't call John Ridley. She would deal with him once she got back into town. She wished she could see the attorney prior to talking to John. Oh well, nothing she could do about it now. She took a quick shower and pulled on some underwear, old pajama bottoms, and a t-shirt, leaving her hair wet. She would get dressed a little later. She began packing her clothes in a desultory manner, just wadding them up and stuffing them into The Beast. She felt a bit teary and was angry with herself about it. It came as a complete surprise when she heard a soft knock at her door. She went to answer and was shocked to find Dove standing there with some sort of garment and other items hanging over her arm.

"Uncle Jim said you were coming to the pow-wow tonight. Grandmother said you needed to dress properly, so she sent me over here with this," Dove said.

"Oh, I didn't know I had to wear something special. I was just going to wear jeans and a nice shirt."

"Grandmother insisted," Dove said and rolled her eyes a bit. "Come on, I'll give you a hand. This is one of Kimmy's dresses, but it should fit, especially with a belt."

Kate took the dress from Dove and looked at it carefully. It was a beautiful light tan buckskin dress with an intricate beaded pattern across the shoulders and long fringe on the arms and hem. Dove held up matching high-topped moccasins that were also exquisitely beaded.

"I hope these fit. Kimmy wears a size 10; she's got big feet," she said.

"I wear a 9 ½, so they should be fine, but won't Kimmy mind me borrowing this? This is about the most beautiful dress I've ever seen. And these moccasins are incredible."

"We asked. She was happy to have you wear it. She sure can't right now," Dove said, giggling a bit.

"Is Kimmy coming tonight?"

Dove shrugged. "She said she might, depending on how she is feeling. I know she'll be glad when that baby comes. Should be any day now."

Kate nodded. "Well, I'll see if I can get into this," Kate said.

She went into the bathroom and pulled off her old t-shirt and pajama bottoms, then wiggled her way into the dress. Kimmy was much more gifted in the bust area, but the dress fit well through the hips. The hem of the dress came to just below her knees, and the fringe hung a few inches past that. The fringe on the arms tickled a bit, but she quickly became accustomed to it. She walked out of the bathroom and raised her arms and turned around for Dove to see how it fit.

"Well, it fits pretty well, it looks like," Kate said.

Dove looked at her critically. "Put the moccasins on, then we'll see what we have to do."

Kate slipped the moccasins on over her bare feet. They were a bit too big, so she took them off, got some thick socks out of The Beast, put those on, sat down in a chair, then put the moccasins back on. The thick socks helped. The moccasins had laces, and Kate struggled with them a bit.

"Here let me," Dove said peremptorily. She quickly laced the moccasins so they fit snugly around Kate's calves. Kate stood up and walked around a bit. They were more comfortable than she thought they would be.

"Come here, let me put this belt on," Dove said.

She had brought a little plastic bag with her and she reached in and pulled out a beaded belt with rawhide ties that matched the dress and moccasins. It had a small pouch on it that closed with a magnetic clasp. Dove wrapped it around Kate's waist and tied it in an intricate knot just over her left hip.

"The pouch is for money and car keys. Not completely traditional of course, but Kimmy never liked carrying a handbag at pow-wows," Dove said.

Dove looked at her critically again. "Now for the hair. Why don't you let me do it? I used to do Kimmy's before she went to pow-wows."

Kate looked at her. "Don't you have to get ready yourself?"

"I'm dancing tonight, Fancy Shawl. I'll get dressed when I get there."

Kate merely nodded. She had no idea what dancing Fancy Shawl meant, but decided not to ask.

"I need a blow dryer and a brush," Dove said in a businesslike manner.

"In the bathroom. I'll get them."

"That's all right. You just sit."

Dove came out with the blow dryer and brush and was soon drying Kate's hair taking special pains to make sure it was flat and straight.

"You hair has a curl to it, but I want to see if I can get it

235

straight for tonight," she said.

"Good luck with that," Kate replied. "I've wanted straight hair for years and have never been able make it happen."

Dove laughed and kept brushing and drying. "You've spent a lot of time with Uncle Jim. He's nice isn't he?" she asked after a time.

"He sure is. You're whole family is nice though. You're a lucky girl."

"I wish you weren't going back tomorrow. I hardly got to talk to you at all. I wanted to hear about some of the places you've been and what Washington is like."

"Well, I have to get back to work. Things didn't pan out here like I'd hoped, with the story and all," Kate said.

"I know. Uncle Jim told us. I think he's a little sad that you're leaving."

Kate didn't know what to say to that, so she kept silent. Dove pulled something out of her bag, and then stepped around to Kate's right shoulder. She clipped it into Kate's hair up near the crown, and then began weaving a tiny braid. She used a small elastic band to secure the braid on the bottom then fussed with the top of the braid a bit. Then she stepped back and nodded, satisfied.

"All done. Come into the bathroom and see what you think."

Kate got up and walked into the bathroom and Dove snapped the light on. They looked in the mirror together and Dove smiled. Kate was speechless at the transformation.

Dove had used the belt to get the top of the dress to drape attractively, but what amazed Kate most was her hair. It still had a bit of curl, but the hairpiece she had braided in was beautiful. It had two small feathers that laid flat at an angle on her hair and Dove had cleverly braided a tiny strand of beads into a long narrow, single braid that lay just in front of Kate's right ear. The bead strand, which matched the beading of the dress, hung down past where her hair ended and had a tiny silver feather on the end.

"Oh! Almost forgot!" Dove said.

Dove went back to her bag again and pulled out a necklace. It was a choker necklace with a turquoise stone set in the center. She handed it to Kate. Kate reached around her neck and hooked the clasp on the ends. It was strung on elastic cord and it stretched comfortably when she turned her head.

"I just can't believe how different I look," Kate said.

"You look great. When you do your makeup, don't use too much."

"I can't thank you enough," Kate said taking Dove's hand. "I just can't."

Dove smiled shyly and shook her head. "Grandmother said you were our guest and we needed to make sure you were properly dressed. She made a fuss about it, to tell you the truth. There's no arguing with her when she makes up her mind about something."

"I can believe that," Kate said.

"Well, I've gotta go. Dad will be wanting to leave soon."

"So, should I drop all this off when I leave in the morning?" Kate asked.

"You can do that, or just leave it up here. I'll come get it tomorrow. Uncle Jim said you would probably leave early. So if you just want to leave it up here, it's OK."

Kate nodded and surprised Dove by giving her a hug. She was a very sweet kid and Kate was grateful for the help she'd given.

After Dove left, Kate was astonished to see that it was almost 7. She went in the bathroom and put on some makeup, taking care to use a light hand when she did so, per Dove's instructions. It was just as well, as Kate's efforts at makeup could be unpredictable if not frightening when she went beyond the basics.

She looked at herself in the mirror again. It was quite a transformation and she felt very shy about going out in public in the beautiful dress. She worried about getting it dirty. Oh well, she would just have to be careful. She didn't plan on staying at this pow-wow very long anyway. She pulled the key to the rental car off its ring, got a small amount of cash to take with her, as well as her driver's license, Smartphone, and lipstick, and stuck it in the little beaded pouch. She wondered briefly what Ludlow's reaction would be when he saw her and she found herself blushing foolishly at the thought.

That all ends today, she told herself sternly.

She left the apartment and went downstairs and got into the rental car. As she slid into the seat, she noticed that the buckskin was buttery soft and sensual on her skin. Once she got into Antelope Valley proper, she was soon in bumper-to-bumper traffic all the way to the police station. She was glad that she was able to use the visitor's spot as the parking lot was filling up fast. She parked and got out of the car, then followed the crowd that was moving towards a large, brightly lit building at the top of a flight of stairs at the back of the lot. She was glad to see that many people, both Native and non-Native, were dressed similarly to her, although others were wearing jeans, long sleeved shirts, and boots. People smiled at her as she walked up the stairs, but no one stared, so Kate began to feel less self-conscious.

She walked in through the double doors to the gym and stepped to the side, out of the flow of the crowd, to get a better idea of what was going on. The place was filling up fast; people were milling around on the gym floor and others were moving up into the bleachers. She didn't see Ludlow anywhere. She stood for a few minutes, feeling out of place and uncomfortable, when she heard someone calling her name. She turned, and saw Hank White Owl standing up in the bleachers and waving to her. Kimmy and Marsh were with him, but the rest of the family was nowhere to be seen. Kimmy was leaning back against the seats behind her, her hands resting lightly on her huge belly. Kate made her way up to them and sat down beside Hank.

"Kate," Kimmy said from behind her, "if I'd known that dress was going to look so good on you, I wouldn't have loaned it out. You're going to be a hard act to follow if I ever get to the point where I can wear it again."

Kate shook her head and laughed a little. "I doubt that. I'm just grateful that you're so generous. I think this is about the most beautiful dress I've ever worn," she said.

"You'll have to thank Grandmother," Kimmy said. "She made that dress herself, as well as the belt and the moccasins. I actually got married in it."

"This is a wedding dress?" Kate asked, slightly horrified.

"Well, technically, I guess you could say that. But I also wear it to pow-wows and other special functions. When you have something like that, you don't just wear it once."

"Oh, I see," Kate said. "That does make sense."

And it did. She had always thought it was ridiculous to spend a bunch of money on a dress that you only wore once.

"Oh look, they're starting the Grand Entrance now," Hank said.

Kate heard a man's voice over the loudspeaker make the same announcement.

A man came in, dressed in a long, feathered headdress and a

specially constructed staff; Hank told her the headdress was a traditional war bonnet and the staff was an Eagle staff. He also told her that the man was Martin Levi. Some flag bearers came next, and the MC called in both Shoshone and English for all people to stand. Kate noticed that most held their hands over their hearts as the American Flag passed. Then came the dancers.

Kate watched as a line of people dressed in various types of Native regalia entered the gym, dancing their way in with complicated steps and rhythmical hand movements. They danced in a long line that flowed across the gym floor; their dancing was quite complex and beautiful. The MC was calling out different names for the dancers, but they meant nothing to Kate. She thought that he must have been asking different groups to come in together at different times.

"Jim's down on the floor on the drum," Hank said, pointing down to the far end. Kate saw him finally; he was sitting with several men around a large drum and they were the ones singing and drumming for the dancers. Ludlow was in traditional Native dress and looked very handsome in the beaded buckskin shirt he was wearing. She watched him as he struck the drum with a curious looking padded stick and chanted loudly with the other men in the group. The rhythms were complex and compelling; Kate's toe was tapping seemingly of its own accord.

As the dancers came in, Hank took the time to explain to Kate what it was she was seeing. There were different types of dances and regalia between men and women. The men's dances consisted of Fancy Dance characterized by vividly colored regalia of usually non-traditional materials (always called regalia, never called costumes, Hank informed her) and dramatic movement, including spins and leaps; a real crowd pleaser, Hank said. He went onto explain that they were the only ones that wore two bustles at their shoulders and hips, a bustle being a round-feathered piece of regalia traditionally made from hawk or eagle feathers. Traditional Dance regalia were based on authentic designs and materials, with a single bustle at the hip or no bustle at all. Movements were very conservative and based on traditional Native dances. The Southern Straight dancers were even more traditional in dress and movement than Traditional, with very strict rules on foot placement and steps. Then there were the Grass Dancers with regalia consisting of long, flowing fringe and designs reminiscent of grass blowing in the wind. Their movements had to be very precise and were often circular, with both feet coming down on the ground during a particular downbeat of the drum.

Women also had a complicated set of regalia and dances, Hank continued to explain. Traditional Dancers wore cloth or leather dresses and were required to perform, precise, highly controlled movements. He said when Sharon used to compete, she did so as a Traditional Dancer. Then there were the flamboyant Fancy Shawl Dancers, who wore brilliantly colored, decorated shawls with long flowing fringe. These dances were performed with rapid spins and elaborate dance steps and required athleticism and precise timing. There was the healing dance called Jingle Dress in which the dancers wore skirts with hundreds of small tin cones that jingled loudly as the dancer moved. Jingles Dress steps were light, precise, and delicate on the floor.

Hank also explained that there were different types of couple's dances, but by this time Kate was completely bewildered by all the information, as well as the details and traditions surrounding them, but she was glad she finally understood what Dove meant when she said she was dancing 'Fancy Shawl.' She looked forward to seeing the girl dance.

Even with all the exotic pageantry, she found her eyes being drawn back to Ludlow over and over again. Somehow the Native clothing, which would look ridiculous on most men, looked natural on him. She had never seen a man so beautiful, or one she wanted more, and it was extremely unsettling. She turned back to Hank.

"So, is Sharon going to be able to make it do you think?" she asked.

"I don't know. I sure hope so. The last I heard, she was trying to tie up some loose ends on a mugging that happened down near the grocery store. She was pretty muddy on the details. I feel bad that she has to work so hard this weekend, when everyone else is having so much fun."

"I do too," Kate said.

Hank chuckled. "She and Jim had some words on the phone earlier. She was mad as hell at him for mixing it up with those Mine Security guys. I don't know why she was so upset, Jim can take care of himself," he said.

"I'm sorry about that. I hope they didn't have too big a fight. He just did it to try to help me out."

Hank shrugged. "It just scared her that's all. Jim's still her little brother in her mind, one that needs looking after."

"Where are Missy and Miss Annie?" Kate asked, noticing that the little girl and the matriarch were not around.

"They're down to helping Dove dress, although Missy is probably causing more aggravation than anything else. I don't see Dove down there in the Grand Entrance, but she may come in later. It's a zoo down there, it looks like. Anyway, Missy's jealous and dying to dance Fancy Shawl herself, but she's too young. She has to wait until she is 10 before she can start competing. It's a family rule. We like our kids to be kids for as long as possible. Some people push their kids into these competitions, but Sharon and I don't think that's healthy," Hank said.

Kate nodded, her gaze drifting back to Ludlow. The last of the people were flowing in through the door and they wound their way through the gym until the floor was nearly full. There were at least 150 of them.

"There a lot of people here," she said to Hank. "I'm surprised there are so many people competing."

"We offer good prize money here, although this pow-wow is really short compared to most. Some last an entire weekend."

"How much money are you talking?" Kate asked.

"For Ladies Fancy Shawl, the prize is $4000 and the same for Man's Fancy."

"Wow, that makes me want to take it up myself," she said, surprised.

"Me too. But I can't dance a lick. Sharon's quite good when she can practice, and Kimmy was Champion at Traditional for several years. Kimmy's like her mother, very competitive," Hank said, looking back at his daughter fondly.

Kate smiled, then noticed that all the dancing had stopped.

"Looks like Martin's getting ready to give the invocation," Hank said, pointing at the man with the Eagle Staff.

The man with the full war bonnet walked out into the middle of the gym floor and held the Eagle Staff up and turned around in a circle, waiting until he had everyone's attention. The drumming stopped, and the gym became very quiet. Kate noticed he was wearing a wireless microphone, which she guessed tied into a PA system.

"*Behne!*" he said. His voice was low and melodious.

"Welcome Friends. May the Great Spirit bless us all this night. For those of you that have traveled far, we give you our thanks for making the journey, and for those people of the Tribe that worked to organize this pow-wow, we thank you for your efforts. We also thank the Great Spirit for the gifts he has given us, with all our hearts. May he continue to bless us with his kindness and wisdom, and may we pass that kindness and wisdom onto others."

There was a pause and Martin Levi looked around at the crowd, holding his staff up in the air. To Kate's eye, there was a bit of mischief in his posture.

"All right everyone, LET'S DANCE!" he yelled. And there was a thunderous roar and applause.

"That's one of the things I like about old Marty," Hank said. "He doesn't go on and on and on like some of these guys do. He gets right down to business."

Kate heard the MC make the announcement, "All right, we need Men's Fancy Dancers, please, we need you out here on the floor. People, please clear the floor to make way for the first competition."

There was a lot of milling around as the dancers who had come in with the Grand Entrance made their way either to the sidelines or up into the stands to sit with their friends and/or families. It looked very chaotic and she was glad she was up in the bleachers.

Kate was looking off towards the near end, watching some children practicing complicated dance steps down to her left, when she noticed someone standing on the next bleacher step down, just to her right. It was Ludlow.

"Hey, Jim. How did you get off the drum?" Hank asked.

"Andy Markum owed me a favor, so I asked him to stand in for me. I told him I had a date," Ludlow replied.

"Andy must of about died from shock," Hank said, chuckling.

"Yes. It was a shock to him. He had mercy on me, said it happened so rarely he wasn't going to rob me of the opportunity to have the company of a female. Then he went onto say some other very rude things that I won't go into. The other guys said I needed to get off the drum anyway, since I wasn't drumming worth a crap. Too distracted by the novelty of a little female attention," Ludlow said.

Hank and the others laughed. Kate wanted to roll up in a ball and become invisible. *Why did I EVER agree to come to this thing?* she asked herself. She stared stonily at the floor.

Ludlow leaned over until she had to look at him. "Katie, have you eaten yet?" Ludlow asked.

She shook her head quickly and silently. She felt like she was back in junior high all over again and could feel her face turning a flaming red.

"Come on then, let's go get some Indian tacos. You don't eat enough," he said.

Ludlow took her hand. She looked up at him, and saw him standing there with a kind and patient smile on his face. He nodded for her to make her way down the stairs to the floor and she smiled weakly and stood up. It was difficult as the place was crowded. Many people stopped to talk to Ludlow, some of them looked at her and made comments in Shoshone. Ludlow usually just shook his head and laughed. They finally made it to the far end and out into the entryway of the gym where it joined the school. Dozens of vendors had set up in this area, selling various types of craftwork, art, medicine wheels and other miscellaneous items. Down at the far end were some food vendors. Ludlow pointed to one that had about 20 people standing in line.

"That's Hiram Levi's stand, Martin's brother. He's got the best food. Let's go get in line, we shouldn't have to wait too long," Ludlow said.

Kate nodded and made her way down to the end of the line. It wasn't easy, not only was the area crowded with spectators, some of the Men Fancy Dancers were queuing up to make their way into the hall and she had to be careful not to get tangled up in feather bustles. But she made it to the end of the food line and heaved a sigh of relief. Standing in line and eating were at least two things she was familiar with.

While they waited, she noticed Ludlow looking at her oddly. She immediately felt uncomfortable and self-conscious.

"I hope I don't look too silly in this dress. I mean, not that it's a silly dress, it's a beautiful dress, and it was nice of Kimmy to loan it to me, but I guess some people might get offended at seeing a non-Native wearing something they probably don't have any right to wear. Your mother was really insistent that I wear it and Dove came up and helped me put it on then she did my hair and was wonderful, I mean she did a wonderful job..." she said. She realized she was babbling, but couldn't seem to help herself. She looked down at the floor, hoping that it would magically open and swallow her.

She felt the light touch of a finger on her chin. Ludlow tilted her face up to look at him. Then he smiled, and shook his head slightly.

"You look lovely. Really, really lovely. Relax, Kate. Let's just have a good time," he said and dropped his hand.

Something in his eyes put Kate at ease, and she smiled too. "Thanks, Jim. I have been pretty nervous," she said.

"What were those people saying to you when we were coming over here?" she asked after a pause. "I know some of them were saying something or other about me."

Ludlow laughed and shook his head. "No need to get paranoid. No one said anything bad about you. They said plenty of bad things about me, though. Along the lines of me being arrested for robbing the cradle, their great–grandmother getting jealous if she saw me with another woman, how much I was paying you to be seen in public with me and other rude things. I apologize; I should have explained it to you."

Kate laughed. It seemed silly now that she should have felt so embarrassed earlier. This was Ludlow after all. Someone she could relax with.

As they got nearer the food stand, Kate started to reach into her belt pouch for money, but Ludlow stopped her with a pained look on his face. "Please. Tonight's on me. If any of these guys see you paying, they'll make my life a living hell. Not that they aren't anyway, but I'd rather not give them any more ammunition," he said.

Kate giggled. They were next in line to the food stand.

"What do you want?" Ludlow asked.

"I don't know, just whatever you're having. And a bottle of water if he has it; if not, a Coke."

Ludlow stepped up and ordered from a cheerful plump Native woman. In short order, Ludlow had two large plates of food. He handed Kate one, then grabbed a bottle of water from a cooler sitting outside the stand, handed it to her, and got one for himself. Kate saw there was a large piece of frybread topped by some sort of chili, then sprinkled with cheese, lettuce, and tomato. She realized she was ravenous. There were several tables scattered around the area, but they were all full.

"Let's go outside and sit by the fountain," Ludlow said. "Too much of a ruckus in here."

"I'm scared to death of getting something on this dress," she said.

"Don't worry about it. We'll take plenty of napkins."

He grabbed a bunch of napkins, wrapped forks and knives in them, and tucked them under his chin, then led her out through the double doors into the night. The high school was a U-shaped building, with the gym running off the end of one of the 'arms' of the U. In the center of the U was a large green, scattered with benches and seats. In the center was a fountain that was lit with soft, white underwater lights. Standing in the center of the fountain pool was a bronze statue of a woman, dressed in traditional Native clothing. She had a baby in a cradleboard strapped to her back. It was an exquisite sculpture – the woman had a strong face, not beautiful, but striking.

"Sacajawea?" Kate asked, as they sat down on the bench that was part of the enclosure for the fountain pool.

"That's right. It's Sacajawea High School. It's new. We just finished it last year."

"That statue is beautiful."

"Tribe member that lives in New York designed and cast it," Ludlow said.

Kate watched as Ludlow skillfully broke of pieces of the frybread, making little sandwiches out of the filling. She did the same, taking special care not to drop any on the dress.

The night was clear and the full moon was riding high in the sky, casting a dim silvery light on the green. The fountain made a sighing sound as a small spray of water bubbled at the statue's feet.

"I like your braids," she said. Ludlow had parted his hair in the center and it hung in two neat braids down his shoulders. She cleaned her fingers carefully on a napkin and reached out and touched the tail of hair that hung down from the rawhide thong that secured the braid.

Ludlow picked up one braid and stared at it a bit sheepishly. "I have to admit that I am a bit vain about my hair," he said. "I hated it when I had to cut it short. Felt like I was losing a part of myself."

"You had to do that when you were in Washington?"

"Yeah," he said, taking another bite of the taco. "I don't like to think about those days too much."

"So I guess you must be a little like Samson then," Kate said, with a soft smile.

Ludlow looked up at her, surprised; then he smiled back. "Well, I never looked at it quite like that before. I think you're right," he said. "Probably more right than you know," he continued, after a pause, and he looked up at the moon.

They ate in silence for a while. Finally Kate raised a question that had been on her mind all evening. She thought she knew the answer, but she wanted to hear Ludlow say it.

"Jim, why did you ask me here tonight? And don't tell me it was just to see a pow-wow, although I am enjoying it."

Ludlow sat his plate down on the bench and looked at her a moment. Then he sighed. "I just wanted to have a nice evening with a pretty lady that I'll probably never see again. For my mental scrapbook, you might say. I do enjoy your company, Kate. Although you do try a man's spirit with all these impudent questions."

Kate laughed at that and Ludlow smiled a slow smile back at her.

"Seems like there are plenty of pretty ladies around that would be pleased to have your company," Kate said, a bit more tartly than she had intended. She'd noticed a certain amount of female fluttering when they had passed through the crowd. Sweet hellos and eye battings at him, and cool smiles for her; that is, if her presence was even acknowledged.

"Jealous are we?" he asked, rubbing his hands together theatrically. "Excellent. I'll have my way with you yet."

Kate laughed nearly choking on a sip of water. "Oh, you're hopeless. Let's go back in. I want you to tell me about this dancing," she said.

They went back into the gym and Ludlow found them a couple of seats where they had a good view of the dancers. He took pains to explain to Kate what the dances meant, and some of the history and tradition behind them. When the winner of the Men's Fancy was chosen, she was surprised to hear that he was a Comanche from Oklahoma.

"He came a long way," she said.

"The Comanche were a branch of the Shoshone Tribe, or

that's what they tell us anyway. Legend has it that it was the Comanche who brought the horse to the Shoshone."

"The Comanche were some pretty rough customers, weren't they?" she said.

"Oh that's just Comanche PR. Their warriors were mewling babes compared to ours."

Kate laughed and laid her hand on Ludlow's arm and shook it chidingly. "Sounds like an old argument to me," she said.

"Oh yes," he replied. Then he picked up her hand and placed it in his free one, lacing her fingers through his. It seemed such a natural gesture that Kate didn't even give it much thought.

The men's dancing continued with the Traditional Dance competition, then the Grass Dancers. Their bright regalia with its long flowing fringe especially fascinated Kate. Once that competition was over, the MC announced that the men's competition was completed, and a couple's dance would be held before the women's competitions started.

"Come on down, ladies and gentlemen, for the Potato Dance!" he called out loudly.

"Let's go," Ludlow said, pulling Kate to her feet. "You'll never get a chance like this again."

"Oh, God, no. I can't dance for shit," Kate said, mortified at the thought.

"Neither can I, so we'll make a great pair. This one's fun though," he said.

Reluctantly, Kate followed Ludlow down to the gym floor. Kate was certain she would fall on her face or disgrace herself in some other manner. She and Ludlow got in a line of people who were queuing up to pick up something, but Kate couldn't see what it was. Finally, when they got to the end of the line; Ludlow took a raw Idaho potato from an Elder who was sitting in a chair handing them out.

"What are we supposed to do with this?" Kate said, looking at the potato skeptically.

"You'll see. Come on. Let's see if we can find a place to dance that's not so crowded."

Ludlow explained that in the potato dance, a couple had to hold a potato between their foreheads and dance to the drum and singing without dropping the potato. Kate looked at him as if he were daft. She then saw other couples laughing and carefully placing the potato between their foreheads, trying to hold it just right to keep it from falling, and she realized that Ludlow was telling the truth. She finally just shrugged.

"I guess I've done weirder things in my life," she said.

Ludlow placed the potato on his forehead and slipped a hand around her waist to pull her forward. It took a few tries to get the potato properly suspended because Kate kept giggling and leaning over to laugh. Finally, she got control of her humor, and they had the potato locked in between their foreheads.

"Watch my eyes," Ludlow said. "And let me lead, although I know it will be VERY DIFFICULT for you to do that."

Kate glared at him, then chuckled (carefully), but didn't say anything.

He held her at the waist, and took her hand as if they were going to waltz. Then the drums and singing began.

Kate struggled at first, but soon she was moving with him in tiny baby steps. Her gray-green eyes were locked on his; at first she was smiling broadly, then she became more serious. She had had to tip her head slightly to the right, so their noses wouldn't touch. He could feel the soft touch of her breath against his lips, which were just a few inches away from his. There were strict rules that the dancer's bodies could not touch, and Ludlow was thankful for that, as one part of his body seemed to have developed a mind of its own tonight.

The first time he had seen her across the gym while he was on the drum, he had missed several beats, which had drawn evil looks from the other drummers. And it was true that the group had good-humouredly kicked him off the drum because he was too distracted to play that night.

But she was so beautiful. It was odd, her wearing Kimmy's dress had helped him really see her for what she was, her shining bright spirit. Something he had known was there, but had only seen in glimpses up until that moment. While Madeleine had been a wild river that could sweep up those foolish enough to stray in too deep, Kate was like the bright sun in springtime, and rain on flowers. A woman who did not keep her spirit just for herself, but gave it freely to those she loved.

As they danced the dance, held apart by nothing but the ridiculous potato, he knew that there had never been nor ever would be another woman in his life like this one. The thought of her leaving the next day brought a blackness to his heart that he hadn't experienced since his time in DC. He knew he would have to talk to either his AA sponsor or someone at the MWCL tomorrow, as he was feeling a need for the oblivion of liquor for the first time since he had come back to Antelope Valley.

Kate must have seen that he was troubled, for she moved her hand that had been resting lightly on his shoulder to his neck. She gently stroked the hair where it was parted at the back of his head. Ludlow felt a slight shiver that came from that touch, and he realized that he needed to put himself in the 'now' and let tomorrow take care of itself. He smiled and squeezed her hand and she smiled back.

How he loved her.

The dance ended and they moved apart slightly, the potato fell but Kate caught it in midair.

"What do we do with this?" she asked holding the potato up.

"Take it back where we got it. They'll bake them tomorrow at the Elder Center."

Kate nodded, then slipped her arm around his waist as they walked back to drop off their potato. He put his arm around her shoulders. He saw one of the Elder women glare at him in disapproval. Most Elders felt that public displays of affection were inappropriate. He knew his scandalous behavior tonight would start a firestorm of gossip, but he really didn't care.

They made their way back to their seats. Neither spoke; both being lost in their own thoughts. As they sat down, Kate slipped her hand back into Ludlow's and he took it, lacing her fingers through his again. He gently stroked the back of her hand with his free hand. It was soft, but he could feel strong muscles and tendons underneath the skin. Kate rested her cheek against his shoulder. It seemed the natural thing to do.

The dancing was starting up again, and the MC called for the Fancy Shawl dancers to come onto the floor.

"There's Dove," Ludlow said, pointing out an elegant dancer stepping onto the floor right in front of them.

Kate would never have recognized her. Dove was wearing purple and lime green regalia, with a rectangular shawl draped across her arms and shoulders. Very detailed appliqués of running horses in golden satin had been sewn at intervals across the back of the shawl. The bottom of the shawl was festooned with purple, lime, and gold streamers that hung nearly a yard off the hem. Dove also had an elaborate headpiece made of tiny purple, lime green, and gold beads, with two eagle feathers at the back of her head. The running horse design had been picked out in golden beads on the headpiece. Her moccasins were soft tan buckskin, but they also were exquisitely beaded with the running horse design. Kate thought she was the most beautiful dancer on the floor and said so.

"You'll have to tell Mother," Ludlow said. "She made that outfit."

"She did? And Kimmy told me she made this dress too. She's incredibly talented."

"She makes her pin money sewing regalia. She used to be one of the best designers with a long waiting list, but she's been slowing down some the past few years. Arthritis in her hands. She learned from her mother, my grandmother Sarah, who was also very good. Grandmother kept sewing regalia right up until the day she died. We lost her four years ago," Ludlow said.

Kate nodded, looking at the intricacy of the beading on her borrowed dress. It took someone with infinite patience to do such work. She guessed that was where Ludlow had must have learned the patience it took to work with horses so successfully.

Kate had not stopped to wonder how Ludlow came to be holding her hand, or why she found it so easy and natural to rest her head against his shoulder. To behave any other way would have been strained and difficult.

She still didn't trust the feelings she had for him, but this was their last time they would have together, and she had decided to make a scrapbook memory herself. She knew it was a good chance she would never feel this way about anyone ever again and she wanted to squeeze every drop of joy out of the night that she could.

She also knew sleeping with him would be a huge mistake and made up her mind that it would not happen. If she slept with him, that would be it; she would have a very difficult, if not impossible time leaving. And she had to leave. She had a life to go back to, some messes to clean up. What if she stayed and later found out that this was just a lustful infatuation or a crutch some part of her ego had manufactured to support itself while she rebuilt her life? She wouldn't risk doing such a thing to this good man.

It was a difficult vow to make. Kate hadn't missed the looks Ludlow got from women (and some men for that matter). He was definitely an extremely desirable man physically. The thought of having to keep him out of her bed was unpalatable, but there it was. It had to be done. But she pushed that thought out of her head; she would worry about that later. For now, it just felt so right to lay her head against his shoulder and feel her hand resting in his.

In just a few short minutes, the Teen Fancy Shawl dance started, and Kate watched, mesmerized, as the girls danced with the grace of ballet dancers, whirling and dipping to the beat and the song, their feet striking the floor with dainty precision, the shawl fringe fanning out beautifully as they danced. Dove was especially good, and Ludlow whooped a bit when she made a particularly good step or spin. When the song ended, there was a bit of a wait, then the MC announced that Dove had won. Kate and Ludlow both stood up and whooped and cheered.

"She deserved it, she was the best," Kate said.

Ludlow looked at her grinning. "Ready to be a judge now are we?"

"Oh hush up. I need to go to the bathroom. Where is it?" she asked.

Ludlow gave her directions, then unashamedly watched the movement of her hips under the soft buckskin as she walked carefully down the stairs, holding the dress up slightly. He sighed heavily as she reached the gym floor and walked out of the far door. He noticed other men were watching her also, and found he was very jealous of their gazes. It was an unfamiliar feeling for him.

He was sitting and considering this when his thoughts were interrupted.

"Hello, Jim!" he heard someone call out.

He looked over to his right and saw Joshua Bann and Sam Conner standing at the end of the row of seats. Ludlow got up and walked over to them. He reached out and shook each man's hand.

"Josh. Sam," he said, nodding easily to each man. "Good to see you here tonight."

"Good to see you too, Jim," Bann said, patting Ludlow on the arm heartily. "You're looking good!"

"You too, Josh," Ludlow said, though in truth he thought Josh

Bann looked terrible. Although dressed in a fine and expensive Western suit, he had a bloated and unhealthy appearance. Jim tried to remember how old Josh was, then came up with an age of about 65. They had been hard years, apparently.

He turned to look at the other man, Conner, who stared at him with thinly veiled contempt. Ludlow gave a mental shrug at this. The Conners seemed to have a genetic hatred of Natives, so the contempt was not a surprise. It even amused Ludlow to a certain extent that the man was so transparent.

"So, Jim, I see you're keeping company with that journalist from DC. Don't blame you, she's a nice looking woman," Bann said, smiling and raising an eyebrow with a man-to-man type familiarity that Ludlow found extremely offensive.

"I hardly think you came over here to talk about my social life, Josh," Ludlow responded coolly. "We haven't spoken since Johnny Elk's funeral that I can remember. So why don't we just get down to whatever it is that you want?"

Bann held his hands up, waving them ineffectually, as if trying to wave off his gaff.

"I'm sorry, Jim. We're getting off on the wrong foot, here. I've made you mad talking about the young woman and I didn't mean to. But look, I want you to think a minute about all the things that Johnny Elk and I worked for over the years."

"Like what?" Ludlow asked in his most reasonable tone. "I don't recall you and my grandfather working on anything together at any time in my life."

Bann sighed, and opened his mouth to speak, but Conner rudely interrupted him. "Look, Ludlow, this woman you've been toting around is only out to stir up trouble. She just wants to make a big name for herself," Conner said. He was a burly, florid man with a large, heavy moustache and seemed to have been born with belligerence in his DNA. Ludlow had heard that the BLM had had some excessive force complaints about Conner, but as far as he knew, they had never done anything about them.

"I know all about women like her," Conner continued. "She doesn't give a shit about anything except getting some big story about those two girls that disappeared. Hell, she'll probably make up most of it. And by the way, as far as you go, why you're just a screw she can tell her girlfriends about over their three martini lunches. I'm sure they'll have a good laugh about it. Seems like you would have learned your lesson the first time around."

Conner stared at him with a cold smile on his face.

Ludlow felt a hot rage boil up inside like he hadn't felt in years; one hand closed of its own accord into a fist. But one thing being a lawyer and lobbyist had taught him was how to quickly compartmentalize his emotions and put on a game face. So he unclenched his fist, and his jaw, then smiled thinly at Sam Conner.

"I appreciate the effort you are making to instruct me on women and the motives behind their behavior, Sam. I had no idea you were such an expert," he said.

This was a finely barbed comment. It was well known that Conner had been thrown out of his house a couple of years prior by his wife and had been living with his mother since. No one knew the details as to why. Rumor had it that the ex-Mrs. Conner had made one too many visits to the Emergency Room after her husband used her face for a punching bag. Conner's other attempts at female companionship had not lasted more than a few weeks at most. It was a common source of gossip and ridicule that no woman in Nevada could tolerate Sam Conner except his mother, who really didn't have much choice in the matter.

Conner's face flushed with fury, and Ludlow immediately regretted his statement. It had been reckless and foolish. Sam Conner was a man who carried a gun every day in an area where people disappeared and were never heard from again. He also held grudges for years. Not a man you wanted to make into an outright enemy.

Josh Bann looked between the two men and quickly stepped in to defuse the situation. "Sam! Jim is a gentleman and doesn't want to talk about his lady friend. Fair enough. But Jim, Sam has a point; this woman's motives are very suspect. And anyway, she just doesn't understand the way we do things out here. People from back East rarely do, you know," Bann said.

Ludlow studied Bann for a moment. He sensed fear in the man. There was something going on here that had Bann worried.

"Look guys," he said in a placating tone, "all this conversation is moot anyway. Kate Wyndham is flying back to DC tomorrow. End of story. I'm just showing her a good time tonight. She's never been to a pow-wow before."

"Oh, flying back tomorrow, like she was supposed to fly back earlier in the week?" Conner said.

"I heard her make the reservations myself," Ludlow insisted, "and she has some business she has to get taken care of in DC. Urgent business. Plus, she didn't find anything here anyway. So, why should she hang around?"

"Good question. Why should she?" Conner asked with narrowed eyes and a leer.

"There is no reason. Like I said. She's going home tomorrow."

There was some noise as some people walked up the bleachers. Ludlow turned to see Hank White Owl and Marsh standing behind him.

"Everything OK here, Jim?" Marsh asked. Marsh was a healthy specimen, just slightly shorter than Ludlow and strapping. He glowered at Conner and Bann.

"Hello, Sam. Josh," Hank said. "Good to see you guys here tonight."

"Yes. Good to see you too, Hank," Bann said quickly. "I hadn't seen Jim in a while and just wanted to say hello. Come on, Sam, we need to get back to Elko. It's getting late."

"You just remember what I said, Ludlow," Sam Conner said, before they turned and walked away. "And also remember, accidents can happen to people who don't understand the way we do things in Nevada."

The three men watched as Conner and Bann walked away.

"What was all that about, Jim?" Hank asked. "That sounded like a threat."

"I'm not sure," Ludlow replied slowly, thinking. "Those two are most definitely stirred up though."

He heard footsteps and turned to see Kate making her way back up the bleachers.

"The line to the ladies room stretched halfway down the hall!" she said, then she noticed the three men were standing tense as wires in front of her.

"What's going on? What happened?" she asked, looking around. "Is everything OK?"

"Fine, Kate, everything's fine," Ludlow said, smiling at her. "Hank and Marsh just came over to talk about Dove winning that last dance. Hank was wondering if she was ready to compete in Las Vegas; there's a big pow-wow there soon."

"Right," Hank said uncertainly. "Right. Well, we'll be

getting back over to the rest of the clan. Marsh doesn't like to leave Kimmy on her own for too long right now."

"Yeah," Ludlow said, looking around at the crowd. "We'll come and hook up with you guys later."

Hank and Marsh turned to leave but Marsh turned back, said a few words in Shoshone, and made an odd hand gesture. Ludlow responded in Shoshone, shook his head, and made a shooing motion at Marsh. Marsh looked at him a moment, shrugged, then walked away.

"What was that all about?" Kate asked.

"Nothing," Ludlow said, rubbing her arm under the buckskin fringe and smiling at her. "We were just talking about Dove. That was a great win for her."

Kate reached up and quickly gave one of his braids a none-too-gentle yank.

"Oww!" Ludlow yelped. "What the hell was that for?"

"For lying," she said, scowling at him.

"Jesus! You are the damnedest woman. I wasn't lying."

He took a quick step backward as she reached for his braid again. "OK. I was lying. Sorry."

Kate looked at him and crossed her arms on her chest, and stared at him with a raised eyebrow.

Ludlow sighed and shook his head. "If you must know, I was just paid a visit by Mr. Sam Conner of BLM Security and Mr. Josh Bann, formerly of the Antelope Valley Tribal Council. They said a couple of things that worried me a little and I didn't want it to wreck our last night together, OK?"

"What kind of things? And don't you dare say 'Nothing to worry your pretty head about.' If you do, I'll slap you into the middle of next week," she said tersely.

"You are a very violent woman," Ludlow responded, in an injured tone.

"Don't change the subject. I like to stay informed, that's all. What did they say that worried you?"

"Something about accidents happening to people that didn't understand the way Nevada worked. It was nothing, probably. Sam Conner said it, and he's just a big blowhard."

"Well, I'm sure that's exactly what happened to Lindy Abraham and Julia Evans. I guess I must be next on their fucking hit list."

"Jesus, Kate," Ludlow said, clasping her arms, "don't even think that."

Kate looked at him for a moment then shook her head. "Doesn't matter anyway, as I'm leaving in the morning."

"That's what I told them."

"I'm sorry that you're having to go through this, Jim," she said. She sat down and her shoulders slumped forward unhappily. Ludlow sat down beside her and put his arm around her. He shook her a little bit.

"Come on, cheer up. Don't let those guys wreck our night," he said.

Kate turned to look at him, and he was surprised to see tears in her eyes. "I'm tired, Jim," she said, and wiped her eyes quickly. "I need to get back and finish packing so I can get away early in the morning."

Ludlow turned away from her for a second, staring down at the crowd. Then he turned back to her and smiled. "OK, Kate, but I don't want you walking to the car by yourself tonight. Let's go and tell the family we're leaving, then I'll drive you to your car. And I want to make sure you get back to the ranch all right, so I'll follow you home."

Kate looked at him, and shook her head stubbornly. "I can take care of myself," she said.

"I know, honey," Ludlow said squeezing her shoulder a bit. "Just indulge me, OK?"

Kate sighed and wiped her eyes again then she turned back to Ludlow and gave him a wan smile. "What did Marsh say to you – when he made that hand gesture?" she asked.

Ludlow looked away quickly. "It doesn't really translate well into English."

"The gist of it will do just fine. I want to know what he said."

Ludlow shifted uncomfortably then shrugged and turned back to her. "He basically asked if I needed help in protecting something, the term he used generally refers to possessions..."

Kate flushed indignantly and started to speak, but Ludlow held up his hand indicating he wasn't finished. Kate closed her mouth, but continued to stare at him with narrowed eyes.

"But the gesture clarified the offer as protection of a loved one. I think it could be literally translated into English as 'beloved.'"

"Oh," Kate said, staring down at her hands, which were clasped tightly in her lap.

The sat for a moment in uncomfortable silence then Kate turned back to him. "All right, Jim. You can see me home if it'll put your mind at ease. But under one condition."

"What's that?"

Kate met his eyes unwaveringly. "That you don't make my leaving any harder than it already is."

"Ah," Ludlow said, taking a deep breath and looking away, "I see." He dropped his arm from her shoulder.

"I've got things I have to deal with, I can't afford any entanglements. I'm an emotional wreck right now. I don't want to be responsible for any collateral damage to someone else because of serious mistakes I've made in my own life," Kate said.

Ludlow sat silently for a moment, then turned to her, nodded and took her hand. She didn't try to pull away.

"All right, Kate. I know you have to do what you believe is best. But understand this, every time I see a potato I'm going to think of you," he said.

Kate laughed in spite of herself. "Such a romantic parting statement," she said. "Let's get out of here."

Ludlow led her down the bleachers and they made their way over to where Hank and the rest of the family were sitting. Dove was there with several friends and they were giggling and laughing. Missy was sitting in Sam's lap. The next group of women dancers was making their way to the floor. Annie was sitting next to Kimmy, and smiled a small smile when she saw Kate and Ludlow coming towards them. Ludlow and Kate said their goodbyes. Kate promised she would stop by the house before she left in the morning. Kimmy said she would be at the barn in the morning, and would see Kate then.

When they were done, Ludlow started moving back through the crowd to the other end of the gym.

"I'm parked out this way," Kate said, pointing to the doors closest to where the White Owls were sitting.

"I know. My truck's near the loading dock, out back on the other side. I'll drive you over to your car from there, OK? And then follow you home?"

Kate shrugged and allowed Ludlow to lead her back through the crowd and out through the far doors. They went down a hallway and through another set of double doors on the right that led onto a loading dock. It had a large overhang to for protection against the weather.

"I'm parked at the back of the lot here," he said.

The back lot was poorly lit, but Kate could see Ludlow's truck about 20 feet away. They walked down the stairs of the loading dock and then along a wall under the overhang. As they stepped out from the overhang, Ludlow dropped Kate's hand and turned towards something he saw along the outside of the wall. Kate realized it was a man in a hooded jacket who was slumped on the ground in the shadows. He looked unconscious. Ludlow walked over quickly and knelt down beside the man.

"You all right, friend?" he asked, putting his hand on the man's shoulder.

Quick as a snake, the man's opposite hand flew up and grasped Ludlow's arm. Kate gasped in shock and fear, then moved towards the two men, although she didn't know what she could do if the man had a knife. Ludlow stayed quite still, however. The man's hood slipped a bit, and Kate saw the outline of his face in the dim light.

It was Bobby Nardo.

He was blinking at Ludlow, but he didn't seem to be all that drunk. He was certainly less drunk than he had been earlier in the afternoon.

"I guess I must have dozed off. You startled me, Jimmy," he said.

The two men looked at each other steadily for a moment, then Bobby Nardo sighed. *"Dehaya'* Canyon," he said quietly, and dropped his hand from Ludlow's arm.

Ludlow stared at him a moment, then nodded his head. "That's where you pushed the horses?" he asked.

"That's right. The day those women disappeared, but I don't know nothin' about that."

"You took a chance coming here, Bobby," Ludlow said.

Nardo grinned a crooked grin at him. "Jimmy, you know damn well if I don't wanna be seen, I ain't gonna be seen."

"Still…it was a risk."

Nardo shrugged then looked up at Kate. "I'm pretty sure they're monitoring your cell phone, Miss. Your phone at home too, Jimmy."

"Sharon will have a fit when she finds out," Ludlow said. "I'm not too happy about it myself either, come to think of it."

Nardo chuckled bitterly. "Won't do neither one of you no good. They don't give a shit about Sharon, or you or anyone else on this Rez. Or the wild ones for that matter," Bobby said, with a catch in his throat. "That's all I'm tellin' you. And just so you know, Jimmy, we never had this talk. And, if the shit hits the fan, I gotta do what the man pays me to do. Things may wind up gettin' rough, Jimmy. You need to know that."

Ludlow nodded and stood up.

"You go on now," Nardo said, pulling the hood over his face and slumping down again. "Once you're gone, I'm gonna get outta here and head back to Elko. I done my good deed for the day."

"You be careful, Bobby," Ludlow said, smiling.

"You too, old buddy," Nardo said, "and look after that pretty lady there."

Ludlow took Kate's arm and led her quickly to the truck without looking back at Bobby Nardo. He opened the truck door for Kate, got in himself, and pulled out slowly from the parking lot. He looked in the rearview mirror several times and headed down to the lower lot. Kate sat across from him silently, tense and worried.

"What did he mean when he said things could get rough?" she asked.

"I'm not sure. Didn't sound good, though."

"Well that's the understatement of the year," Kate said crossly. "Do you think he'll be all right?" she asked, after a pause.

"Oh yeah, don't worry about Bobby. He's right about not being seen if he doesn't want to be seen."

"So, what was he saying about this canyon? Where is it?"

"About a day-and-a-half ride on horseback up the River. That's about the only way you can get there from here, since the Mine closed most of the area that leads to the south end of the canyon. It's rough country."

Ludlow pulled into the parking lot and stopped behind Kate's rental car.

Kate started to say something, but Ludlow stopped her.

"Let's get back to the ranch. There's just too many strange things happening around here tonight," he said.

259

Kate opened the door and stepped out of the truck, then came around to Ludlow's window. "We could…" she said.

"Kate, I need to think about this for a bit," Ludlow said, interrupting her. "We'll talk about it when we get home, OK?"

Kate nodded and quickly got in her rental car, started it, and pulled out of the parking lot. She saw Ludlow following closely behind her.

He's worse than an old mother hen with one chick, she thought irritably.

She ignored him and concentrated on driving and worked through the information they had just received.

The idea of her cell phone being monitored outraged her, of course, but it didn't surprise her. Lots of privacy rights had fallen by the wayside after 9/11, and she wasn't the first journalist to have such a thing happen. She was pretty sure that the Sat phone was safe though; the only people that had that number were Gazette employees and their families, for the most part. It was an expensive phone to use and was only to be used as a last resort, when there was absolutely no other way to communicate. It was also just one of a pool of phones that was under an account the Gazette held at the service provider. She worked through all the information she had been given, and soon had a plan put together in her mind as to what she was going to do. She pulled her Smartphone out of her pouch and used the voice-activated dialer to call the airline to make some flight changes.

*

They pulled into the ranch driveway and Ludlow followed her down to the barn and parked beside her. They both got out and Kate met Ludlow at the back of her car.

"I want to go to this canyon," she said, before Ludlow could say a word.

"Absolutely not," Ludlow replied, in a no-nonsense tone. "The only thing you are doing is getting on that plane tomorrow and going home. They'll be watching to make sure you do this time."

"Who the fuck do you think you are to be telling me what I can and can't do?" she said, furious. "It's my life, Goddamn it!"

"Yes, and I want you to keep it!" Ludlow said, raising his voice.

Kate stepped back and stood there glaring at him, breathing

heavily. The quarrel had erupted so quickly that neither knew quite know how to cope with it.

"I'll go myself after you leave and I promise I'll let you know what I find, Katie," Ludlow said, working hard to speak in a reasonable tone.

"You shouldn't go alone," she urged.

Ludlow stood silent for a moment. She had a point. He really shouldn't do this by himself, but there wouldn't be anyone available to go with him until after all the events of the weekend were over. And that's if he could even convince Sharon to let someone from Tribal Police go with him. *Dehaya'* Canyon was not on Rez land proper, although it had been included in the original treaty signed years ago. He knew Sharon would be against his nosing around up there.

Nevertheless, he felt an urgent need to start at first light. He had no doubt that the Mine and/or the BLM would work quickly to remove any evidence if they thought there was a chance that someone might do some investigating. If there was any evidence to remove, that is.

"Jim," Kate said, interrupting his thoughts, "I called and cancelled my plane reservations."

"Kate, are you nuts? You know they tapped your phone."

She smiled at him thinly. "I'm neither stupid nor crazy," she said scornfully. "Of course I know they tapped my phone, I heard Bobby say that and I understand English quite well. I made another reservation out of Salt Lake for tomorrow evening. Told the airline that I wanted to spend the day driving there to see the country, as I doubted I would be out this way for a while. I even made arrangements to drop off the rental car at the Salt Lake airport, and left a message for my boss at work telling him the same thing."

"Jesus, Kate," Ludlow said, feeling a bit helpless.

"Look, Jim," Kate said. "You know I can handle the ride itself, you've seen me ride before. And this is what I came here to find out. I know you're worried about me and feeling protective, but I've got a right to make these decisions for myself. To remove the option from me just because you're worried is selfish, patronizing, and unfair. I'm an adult. I have a pretty good idea this might be dangerous, and I'm ready to live with that. Believe me, I've been in dicey situations before. I'm prepared to take these risks if there is any possible way I can find out what happened to Lindy and Julia."

"And I have a feeling you're going to need my help," she said, when Ludlow didn't speak.

Ludlow stared at her a moment. *God, she was stubborn.* But she had made some good points. She'd pinked him pretty well with her statement about being selfish and patronizing. "Well, if I've got a choice here, I'm not seeing it. Even if I tried to sneak away, you'd probably follow me, you are so damned pig-headed," he said sourly, "but I don't want to hear any whining. This is not going to be an afternoon hack on a Virginia bridle path."

Kate nodded and gave him a small smile. "You won't. Now, what do we need to do to get ready?" she asked.

Quickly, they worked out a plan that would help keep the trip quiet for as long as possible. Ludlow said he would pack the trail rations and other items they would need. He had done it many times before; it wouldn't take that long, not just for a short trip like this.

"Did you bring any riding clothes?" he asked. "And I don't mean those fancy white breeches, I mean something you can ride in all day?"

"I did, although I didn't plan on doing any riding while I was out here. I just threw in a pair of my trail breeches and my boots at the last minute. They should be fine."

They drove her rental car to the hay shed behind the barn. Ludlow pulled it into a narrow area after they had cleared out some hay, and they covered it with an old tarp.

"Just in case someone comes by to see if your car is still here after you're supposed to leave in the morning," he said.

As they walked back to the barn Ludlow glanced at his watch. It was just past midnight. He would be up for another hour at least getting together the things for the trip. Then he would try to catch a few hours sleep. They stopped at the stairs that led up to the barn apartment.

"I want to get away early, at first daylight, Kate. So we need to be up and moving by 5 at least. Go on up and try to get some sleep. I'll do the same after I get together a few things. And I'll see you early, OK?"

"OK," she reached out and grasped his arm lightly. "Thanks, Jim. Maybe we'll finally be able to figure out what happened to those two women. That's the least we can do for them, I think."

Ludlow looked at her a moment, then patted her hand, smiled and nodded.

"You're right, Katie. It is the least we can do. Now go on up and get some sleep. I'll finish up what I can get done tonight."

"Are you sure I can't help you?"

"Go on to bed. Tomorrow's going to be a hard day for you. Get what rest you can."

Kate went up to the loft and made sure her phones were plugged in and charging. She also made sure the phone connection was turned off on her Smartphone, so she couldn't be tracked. She pulled off the buckskin dress, hairpiece, and moccasins and laid them carefully on the sofa. Then she went to bed in nothing but her underwear.

Sleep didn't come easily to Kate though. She tossed and turned in the night, thinking of Ludlow as well as Lindy and Julia. When she did finally manage to doze off, she had a disturbing dream where she was riding the silvery horse she had dreamed about before. They were racing madly across a featureless plain, alone; something was chasing them, but she couldn't see what it was. She just knew she was terrified. The horse stopped suddenly to face whatever it was that was after them, reared, and silver hooves flashed in the moonlight. He screamed a challenge at the danger, over and over again.

Kate woke to the sound of her alarm ringing shrilly. She sat up in bed. The bedclothes were a rumpled mess from where she had thrashed in her dream. It was 4 a.m., time to get ready to go.

Part V
The Journey

Chapter 13

After a shower and a quick blow dry of her hair, Kate got out her trail breeches. She hadn't worn them in a while and was glad they were stretchy, as she had a bit of a time getting them zipped. She had gained some weight over the past few months, which was disturbing. Not much, but she was clearly out of shape and she knew this trip was not going to be easy. She was glad she had the breeches; they had a deerskin seat and leg protection and really did help cut down on muscle fatigue and soreness in the saddle. She also put on a long-sleeved pale blue cotton button-down shirt and a quilted riding vest. The nights were cool, and she expected it to be even cooler when they got into the mountains. Once she was dressed, she went downstairs into the stable.

Ludlow was in the barn aisle with two horses, tightening up a saddle cinch on one of them. Kate noticed that one of the horses was the big bay that Ludlow had ridden in the Mustang Makeover. Jerry, she remembered his name was. The other horse was a sorrel, shorter than Jerry and very strong looking. When Ludlow saw her, he smiled and nodded.

"This is your horse, Dozer," he said. "One of our best trail horses. He's not speedy, but he can go all day without getting tired and he's surefooted as a goat."

"I see where he got the name," Kate said. The horse did look like a bulldozer. "I just hope I don't have to outrun any trouble."

Ludlow shook his head. He picked up a set of well-worn leather saddlebags and set them behind the cantle of the Dozer's saddle, then tied them on the rings on the saddle skirt. Kate looked at the saddle closely. It looked a little like a Western saddle, but it had no horn and was not made of leather, but of some synthetic material. It looked very lightweight.

"Kimmy's endurance saddle. It should fit you all right, and she's ridden Dozer in it many a time," he said.

"I've borrowed a lot from Kimmy this trip," Kate said ruefully.

Ludlow chuckled. "Don't worry about it. Kimmy's not a stingy person."

Kate petted Dozer a bit while Ludlow tied a set of saddlebags on Jerry.

"This is Jeremiah here. He and I are good friends. He's the

horse that helped me win that big pot of money in Ft. Worth. Jerry is what we call him," Ludlow said.

"Why did you name him Jeremiah?" Kate asked.

"Because he can jump like a bullfrog," Ludlow said, with a completely straight face.

Kate giggled and Ludlow grinned at her. "By the way, I didn't forget about your caffeine addiction." He handed her a rather large Sigg style insulated mug that had a clip attached to it. "Clips to one of the saddle rings, and if you want some coffee you just push this little button, and take a drink."

"Well, it doesn't look like you rough it as much as you make out," Kate said.

Ludlow shook his head and smiled. "You just wait and see. Bend over here a minute. I want to show you how to put these horse boots on Dozer."

"Oh, I see he's not shod. I've seen other people use these boots before instead of shoes, but I've never used them," she said.

"Well, wild horses like Jerry and Dozer have tough feet, but I don't like to take chances. No feet – no horse. We're going to be in some rocky country and I'd rather not risk a stone bruise."

Kate watched closely as Ludlow slipped the boot over Dozer's raised foot and tightened some Velcro straps and buckles. He let her put the other one on, corrected her a couple of times on how she had placed the boot, then once she realized how it fit on the hoof she soon had it on snugly. He then put boots on Jerry with the ease that comes with long practice.

"We'll check them after an hour or so to make sure they haven't loosened up," Ludlow said and Kate nodded.

Ludlow stepped over to a cooler he had brought with him and handed her a sandwich – another peanut butter and jelly. Kate took a bite, and took a sip of coffee from the travel mug. Ludlow's coffee was excellent.

"So what did you tell the family about this trip?" Kate asked.

Ludlow looked at her uncomfortably and frowned. "Not much. I left a note on the kitchen counter. Someone will run across it eventually. I just didn't feel like having yet another argument over this crazy trip," he said, with a pointed look at Kate.

"Don't be grumpy. What else do we need to do here? I brought my phones and a few other things that I need to pack somewhere."

"There's room in your saddlebags; just pack whatever you need in there. I'll tie on the slickers and sleeping bags. I have a feeling we might get some rain, so I got a slicker for you, and a down vest that packs very small is in your saddlebag. Oh, and a hat."

He handed her a well-worn Western hat, then took a couple of rolled up bundles and expertly tied each of them on the rear of the saddles, just over the saddlebags. Kate put the hat on. It was more comfortable than she thought it would be.

Ludlow showed her how to put on the Western bridle, which was less complicated than the English bridles she had always used before. She looked at the curb bit skeptically as she slipped it into Dozer's mouth. She had always ridden with the less severe snaffle bits.

"You ride him with a loose rein. Dozer is a bridle horse; he takes direction from the rein on the neck and your seat mainly. We'll ride here at the barn until you get the hang of it. It won't take long for you to figure it out," Ludlow said.

Kate led Dozer out behind the barn, then swung up into the saddle. The endurance saddle was remarkably similar to her dressage saddle, except that it was more cushy (a fact for which she was extremely grateful), and it fit her reasonably well. She practiced turning Dozer, who was very responsive with a little leg pressure and the rein on his neck.

Ludlow came up leading Jerry, and looked at her questioningly. "Looks like you and Dozer are getting along just fine. How about your stirrups?" he asked.

"I guess they're a little short. I'll get down and fix them."

"Let me," he said. She pulled her foot out and he lowered the stirrup, then took her foot by the ankle and placed her foot gently back on the stirrup bar. It was a strangely intimate gesture to Kate, but she didn't object when he did the same on the other side.

"Better?" he asked and Kate nodded.

Ludlow was wearing an old leather jacket, jeans, and some well-worn tan chaps with fringes down the side that fit him perfectly. He had his battered straw hat on, and an old blue western work shirt with white snaps down the front.

Kate also noticed that Ludlow had a revolver strapped to his leg in an old-fashioned leather holster and the rifle in a scabbard on his saddle. She started to mention it, then changed her mind. She knew very well that they might run into trouble, and, as Ludlow had said before, better to have it and not need it than the other way around.

"I'd like to get started if you're ready. Do you have any questions?" he asked after he had swung up into the saddle.

"Well, I have one question. Where are we going?"

"We're going to follow the creek that runs at the back of the place over to the river, then make our way up to the canyon. I hope we can make good enough time to get to a fishing cabin that belongs to some friends of mine, where we can stay the night. It's a ways. But if we get this rain I think is coming, we'll appreciate being under cover. I didn't bring a tent," he said.

"Let's go then," Kate said.

"All right. I'm going to lead, so if you have any problems, just holler."

"I'll be OK. Let's get going. I don't fancy the idea of sleeping in the rain."

They started off at a walk and wound their way down a trail that went through what looked to be a hayfield to Kate. The sun was just rising in the east, turning the sky a glorious salmon. She remembered the old saying of JQ's 'Red sky at morning, sailor take warning.' Ludlow might turn out to be right about the rain. There was a clean, green smell to the air, and Kate breathed deeply. It was a bit cool, and a thin mist had settled on the ground. As the sun rose, the dewdrops sparkled jewel-like on the blades of the long grass.

It felt good to be riding again. Dozer was very mannerly and moved along with little direction from her. Clearly he was used to following Jerry and knew this trail well. She studied Ludlow as they rode along. He rode differently than most Western riders she had seen; he didn't slump in the saddle, but sat relatively straight. She noticed that he took his feet out of the stirrups periodically and rode with his long legs stretching downward. He moved like he was completely one with the horse and was a pleasure to watch. Kate had always appreciated watching good riders, and Ludlow was clearly one of the best. Jerry was a well-put together horse who looked very fast to Kate's eye.

They had ridden about an hour down the winding trail until they reached the creek. Ludlow stopped and looked at her. "How are you doing?" he asked.

"Fine. No problems," she said.

"Good. We need to check these boots, so climb down and see how old Dozer is doing with his."

Kate swung a leg over and dropped lightly to the ground. Her legs were a little stiff, but not too bad. How they would be at the end of the day was another matter all together. She checked Dozer's boots; the horse stood patiently and helpfully lifted a foot when she leaned over. Ludlow was right. They had come loose a bit. She tightened the buckles, and checked the tightness again. The boots didn't shift. Ludlow also walked over to check.

"Good job," he said, nodding in approval. Kate felt foolishly pleased by the praise.

"OK, Kate, in order to get to that cabin by dark, we are going to have to ride a little harder. Walk in the tricky areas, then trot and lope when we can. Are you up to it? I'm going to set a pretty fast pace, and I want to make sure you're going to be OK."

"Don't worry about me. I'll keep up as much as I can on Mr. Dozer here."

"That's my girl," he said, placing a hand on her shoulder, "but you just yell if you start having any problems."

She turned away from him and quickly climbed back up on Dozer. She didn't want to encourage any physical contact with Ludlow. She had done so last night, and it had been a mistake. It wouldn't happen again.

Ludlow crossed the creek and Kate followed behind him. They went up a cutback in the bank to another hayfield. Once they reached the meadow, Ludlow, good at his word, took off at a trot. Dozer started trotting with just the briefest of a touch from Kate's heels. Dozer had a rough trot, and Kate started posting to the trot out of old habit. She saw Ludlow glance back over his shoulder, then he moved Jerry into a slow lope. Again, Dozer went into a lope with only a minimal cue from Kate. He had an easy lope and Kate found herself settling into the rocking chair motion of the gait.

They kept up the pace for another hour and Kate marveled when the mountains far ahead of them turned a bright rose, then a gray-blue as the morning light broadened. The sky was thick with clouds, but occasionally the sun shown out brilliantly to reveal views that filled Kate with a sense of incredulous wonder. Nevada was beautiful country.

270

The land dropped more and more as the morning wore on, and Ludlow varied his pace according to the terrain. At one point, he slowed Jerry to a walk as he carefully made his way through a rocky descent where the creek ran beside them in a beautiful waterfall. Again, Kate gave Dozer minimal direction as he picked his way down the trail. She really was just a passenger; Dozer knew his business. Though happy that she was able to relax and enjoy the scenery, she deeply missed Manny. They had had a partnership; she wasn't just a load that he carried. She didn't blame Dozer of course; he was a very well trained horse, a good horse. She patted his neck appreciatively, and he shook his head and snorted.

The terrain became steeper and more difficult, always angling downward, and Kate knew they were getting closer to the river. Her legs were aching and she was tired. She had packed away some anti-inflammatory pills in her saddlebags and she surreptitiously took a couple with some now cold coffee. They had been a godsend when she had competed on Manny.

Finally, the creek opened up into a wide gap and they hit the Owyhee River. Kate gasped when they emerged onto a wide rocky beach where the creek fed into the river. Across the river, sheer bluffs towered hundreds of feet over their heads. The rock was striated in various colors of slate, gypsum, quartz, and some other rosy colored stone that Kate didn't recognize. She sat motionless on Dozer, in awe of the sight.

There were aspens, willows, and other trees on the river and in the light autumn breeze the air was filled with bright leaves as they fluttered down to make a golden mosaic in the river shallows. Small birds twittered and chirped in the aspens, and wading birds flew up from the shallows, disturbed by the unexpected intruders. The air had a wholesome smell, as if it had just been washed clean by the crystal clear waters of the river. Kate took a deep breath and held it for a moment; the air even seemed to have more oxygen than normal air.

Ludlow had dismounted and dropped the reins; Jerry moved to the water's edge and was now drinking deeply at the river. Ludlow walked over and lightly caught Dozer's bridle. "Let's rest the horses a bit and maybe eat some lunch," he said.

Kate nodded and swung her right leg over to step down from the saddle. To her great embarrassment her leg buckled a bit when it had to support her full weight on the ground. Ludlow stepped forward quickly and caught her at the waist to keep her from falling. She was horribly embarrassed. Such a thing had never happened to her before.

"I'm all right," she said irritably, stepping away from him.

Ludlow rolled his eyes a bit then grinned at her. "Pardon me, ma'am. But, I do want to say that you've done well this morning. Even Kimmy would have had a hard time keeping that pace. I mean the pre-pregnant Kimmy. And she's an endurance rider, used to spending hours in the saddle."

"Thanks," Kate said, not meeting his eyes. She led Dozer up to the little pool where Jerry had been drinking. She dropped the reins as Ludlow had done and let Dozer drink also. She stood at the edge of the river, looking up at the cliffs, her hands on her hips.

"Beautiful isn't it?" Ludlow asked. He had come up to stand beside her.

"Yes. Gorgeous. Does it have a name?"

"To tell you the truth I don't know. I guess it must, but I don't know what it might be. It's strange. I've been here hundreds if not thousands of times, and I don't know the names the Whites have given to these formations. They may have a name in Shoshone, but I don't know what that is either."

Ludlow sounded a little sad, and Kate turned to look at him. He was staring up cliffs as if he'd never seen them before.

"What do we have to eat? I'm starved. Thirsty too," Kate said to change the subject.

Ludlow smacked his head with his hand. "I've got your canteen. I remembered to get you the coffee, but not the canteen. Kimmy and I always have to tie it on because the holder is designed to hook onto a saddlehorn. Sorry, Kate."

"Well, I should have asked. Don't feel bad. After all you're the one that did all the packing, I guess you're allowed a mistake or two. But anyway, what do we have to eat?"

"Pemmican and water," Ludlow said. Kate looked at him strangely and he grinned. "You'll like it. Come on over here," he said, motioning her to follow him.

He walked over to his saddlebag and pulled out a couple of square bars wrapped in plastic wrap. He also got her canteen, which was hanging on his saddlehorn and handed it to her. She took a long drink of water, then looked at the large tan colored square he handed to her. It looked almost like the blondies she used to eat as a child.

"What is it?" she asked, opening the wrapper and sniffing of the thick bar.

"Pounded cooked meat, with a certain amount of fat, nuts and fruit mixed in. This is my mother's recipe, although I make it myself these days. Try it."

She took a tentative bite and was delighted by the salty/sweet taste and chewy texture.

"This is wonderful. What kind of fruit is this?" she asked

"Chokecherry. We have a lot of it on the property and I dry some every year just so I can make this stuff," Ludlow said, pleased with her reaction.

Kate quickly ate the rest of the bar then started walking around on the beach so her legs wouldn't stiffen. Ludlow stood off near the horses, munching on his own bar of pemmican. The horses took an interest and she watched as he fed Jerry a small bite.

The sun had come out, lighting the river valley brightly. Kate pulled off her hat and vest and set them on a piece of nearby driftwood. She walked around some more, then bent over to stretch her back out a bit.

"Are you OK?" Ludlow asked.

"I'm fine. I just feel like my butt has been in a meat tenderizer."

Ludlow had watched with interest as she bent over; he couldn't help but notice that her butt did look delectably soft and tender.

"What are you looking at?" Kate asked. Still bent over, she was glaring at him from under one arm.

"Just checking out the view, that's all," he replied, looking away and whistling innocently.

"No doubt," Kate responded caustically. "How much longer do we have to ride today?"

"We should be able to make the cabin before dark. We've made good time this morning, better than I was expecting. About four more hours, I guess."

Kate groaned inwardly, but didn't let it show on her face. Hopefully, the anti-inflammatory would kick in soon. She would rather cut out her own tongue than complain.

"It'll be slow going at times, as we are going to be working our way up into the mountains, some areas are pretty rocky. And Katie, we can turn around at any time. We don't have to do this, you know."

"I'm fine. Don't worry about me. I want to see this thing though," she said a little grumpily. She found it highly annoying that Ludlow was standing there looking like he had just gotten up from a refreshing nap. Of course, he probably rode every day, and she hadn't ridden consistently in the past couple of years, but it was still irritating to see him looking so pain-free and relaxed.

He took off his hat and jacket and set them in a dry area on the little beach. He then squatted down easily at the river's edge, dipped his cupped hand into the river and took a long sip of water. Kate watched fascinated as the water streamed down from his fingers into the shallow pool, his lips parting slightly as he drank. The tip of his tongue reached out to touch his index finger and catch a drop of water. He'd taken down his braids and tied his hair back with a rawhide strip; it hung in a long, thick ponytail down his back and gleamed blue-black in the bright sun. It still had little waves in it from being braided, and Kate felt a strange sense of loss when she noticed this. He stood up and dried his hand on the seat of his jeans. Then he turned to her.

"And what are you looking at?" he asked.

Kate laughed in spite of herself. Oh, this man did have the devil in him!

Ludlow grinned like a small mischievous boy, confirming her thought. "Most people would tell you not to drink directly out of the streams here; too much contamination. They're more than likely right. Sometimes I just feel like it's worth the risk," he said. "You need to be careful, though," he continued, looking at her. "I have some of those water purification tablets. You need to use those before you drink any water from this river. Otherwise you might get a case of La Tourista, which is pretty miserable when you're riding."

"I'd say so," she said, appalled at the thought. She checked the canteen, it was getting low on water. "Might as well give me some of them now, I don't want to be without water this afternoon. It's warming up."

"Yes, it is. And I still think we're going to get some weather this evening." Ludlow went to his saddlebag, got some tablets packed in silvery foil and handed them to her. "You know how to use these?" he asked.

"Sure. I always take them with me when I go overseas."

Ludlow nodded, retrieved his hat from the bush and put it on then tied his jacket on top of his bedroll. Kate leaned down, filled the canteen, and then dropped in a couple of tablets. She didn't like the taste of treated water, but she liked the idea of explosive diarrhea even less.

She grabbed her vest and put her hat on then went over and caught up Dozer's reins. He had wandered over to a tasty bush and was pulling off leaves and chewing contentedly. Kate leaned over and checked his boots (making a great effort not to groan in pain); they were still tight and snug. She tied her vest on top of her bedroll as Ludlow had done, then clipped the canteen on with the coffee mug.

"Well, I'm packed," she said looking over at Ludlow. "I'm ready if you are."

"I'm ready," he said, grabbing Jerry's reins and swinging up easily in the saddle.

Kate waited until he had moved off a bit, then she hurriedly led Dozer over to a large rock she had spotted. She scrambled up on the rock and painfully pulled herself up into the saddle.

'I'll feel better once we get moving,' she told Dozer. She pushed him into a trot to catch up with Ludlow; he had gone round a bend in the river and was nearly out of sight.

Ludlow took them along the beach for several miles. The river was wide and shallow in this area, but Kate could see high bluffs on either side further upriver. The scenery was some of the most spectacular she had ever seen, even in her trips to Africa. The river flowed low and wide over rocky scree and made a musical noise as it ran downstream; at other places, where it narrowed, there was some beautiful whitewater. The sky had cleared completely, and the sun was warm on Kate's arms. She was glad that Ludlow had gotten the hat for her. Ludlow stopped for a moment and was looking up at the sky. Kate rode up and stopped beside him.

"Look at that," he said pointing up to an area just over a bluff.

Kate saw two extremely large birds flying in lazy circles over the river. "Golden eagles?" she asked.

Ludlow nodded.

"I wish I could fly like that, don't you?" he asked, turning to her and smiling.

"I do. Today, especially."

Ludlow gave her a sardonic look. "I know you have to be in a certain amount of pain, dear, but are just too obstinate to complain about it," he said.

"You said no complaints, didn't you?"

"I did. But I also don't want you to kill yourself out of pure stubbornness."

"Stop gloating," Kate responded crossly. "I'm fine. Let's get going."

Ludlow grinned and shook his head. They walked along the river for another hour or so then he turned to the left and went up a steep rocky trail that ran beside another noisy waterfall. Kate turned Dozer up the trail also and let him have his head; he scrambled up the rocky slope with no difficulty. They made their way between two tall rocks at the top of the trail, then they were out on a wide flat plain that ran along the top of the bluffs as far as the eye could see. It was covered with sage, knee deep wild grasses of a golden color and juniper.

"This is the last level area we are going to have for a while. We follow along the river for about fifteen miles then take another trail down to the river again then we cross. The cabin is on the Idaho side; some Native friends of mine from Boise built it a few years ago. They hire out as guides and bring people out here for trout fishing," he said.

"How do we know it's not occupied?"

"They're all down at the pow-wow this weekend."

Kate looked at him speculatively. "So, I can see a trail here, is this the one we follow?" she asked

Ludlow nodded.

"Well, we might as well make some good time then!" and she quickly put Dozer into a lope.

Ludlow sat for a moment, laughing then he lightly touched Jerry with his heels and caught up with her easily. As he rode beside her, he realized this was the first time he had seen her look really happy since she had come to Nevada. She stuck her tongue out at him then gave him a heart-stopping smile as he rode beside her. He just shook his head. She was a crazy woman. He doubted she would be able to walk tonight.

They rode through the early afternoon on the mesa, alternating between a long trot and lope when they could. The horses were well conditioned, and while sweating, weren't particularly tired.

Once they ran up on a band of wild horses, which took off at a gallop when they saw the riders. They stopped to watch them. Jerry and Dozer observed with great interest, their ears pricked forward attentively. Jerry nickered a bit and pawed the ground. Ludlow rubbed his neck soothingly.

"Do you think they envy them?" Kate asked.

Ludlow looked at her, surprised to see tears in her eyes. "I don't think horses suffer from that deadly sin, Katie. Only us foolish humans," he said, leaning over and patting her hand. "Jerry and Dozer are interested in what they're doing, that's all."

She smiled and nodded, then they turned and continued at their fast pace along the mesa. After a while, Ludlow moved ahead of her and slowed to a trot then a walk as the land began angling down.

"Kate, we have to take care here," he said, as she slowed beside him. "This is where we have to make our way down to the river again, and it's a little tricky getting down this slope. Just let Dozer find his way. Once we're down to the river, we'll cross through the shallows and make our way up to that cabin. It's only a few miles from here."

Ludlow looked at the sky. Far off to the north and west, he could see an angry cloudbank and the wind was starting to pick up. He was glad they had made good time today.

Ludlow worked his way down the slope, letting Jerry find the best path. He glanced back at Kate several times; she was doing exactly as he had said, letting Dozer pick his way down. At one point, he heard part of the slope give way and he turned in alarm, but Kate had quickly shifted her weight uphill, which allowed Dozer to get his feet back underneath him on a stable part of the trail. She didn't looked frightened at all, even though it would have been about a 50 foot drop for her and the big gelding; she just stayed focused on making her way down.

When she reached the bottom she came up beside Ludlow and stopped, looking around with interest at the river.

"That scared me," he said.

Kate shrugged. "I guess it would have scared me too, if I had thought about it too much. I learned to just think about getting past the obstacle at hand when I was Eventing, whether it was a jump, water jump, or whatever. This isn't that much different."

Ludlow nodded his head admiringly, then rode Jerry into the river. It was very wide and shallow; the deepest area came up just below the horses' bellies. Kate felt water splashing on the bottom of her breeches as she crossed. Once he got to the other side, he turned Jerry up a well-worn trail that wound its way up a slope. The shadows were getting long in the valley, it would be dark soon, and Kate saw that the storm to the west was getting closer. She hoped they didn't have too much farther to go. She turned Dozer up the slope to follow Ludlow, and soon they were on another mesa that climbed about 100 feet above the river.

Ludlow moved Jerry into a trot; Dozer and Kate followed along. In about a half hour, they came to the cabin, which was a longish, rectangular building, painted white, with a deep porch across the front, a small shed attached on one side and an outhouse about 20 feet from the other end. It was set back about 40 feet from the edge of the mesa and was surrounded by a few juniper and small aspen trees. Kate could see the top of some wooden stairs cut into the cliff edge, which she assumed allowed the fishermen access to the river. Ludlow rode right up to the front porch, got off Jerry, and dropped the reins. Jerry immediately began cropping at the long grass in front of the cabin. Ludlow reached under the stairs of the porch and pulled out a key, then went and unlocked the front door. In a few minutes, he came back and pulled his saddlebags off Jerry.

"We lucked out," he said, coming to stand beside Kate and Dozer. "The place is actually pretty clean this time. Let's put the horses in the shed. They've got hay in there; my friends usually keep some for me as I come up here now and again."

Kate sat unmoving for a minute, then gritted her teeth and swung her right leg over Dozer's rump. However, she didn't get her leg up high enough and it got caught up on the cantle. She struggled to get the leg off the cantle then wound up losing her balance. She fell practically on top of Ludlow, who also lost his balance and they both hit the ground. Luckily, Kate had kicked her left foot out of the stirrup, so she didn't get hung up on the saddle. Dozer stared at them for a moment with unadulterated equine disgust, then he began cropping the grass unconcernedly.

Kate found herself next to Ludlow on the ground. He was lying motionless, with his eyes closed, as if unconscious. His hat had fallen off and was lying a few feet away, as were the saddlebags. She poked him hard in the ribs and he gasped and sat up. "Quit playing possum and help me up," she said.

"Well that's some kind of thanks I get for breaking your fall. I think I have whiplash."

"If you hadn't been standing in the way you wouldn't have gotten falled on. It's your own fault."

"I don't think there is such a term as 'falled on.' A journalist should know that."

"Never mind about that. Help me up," she said grumpily.

Ludlow climbed to his feet, then pulled Kate up after him.

She groaned and rubbed her back and posterior and stretched. She took a few wobbly steps, then the blood seemed to get back into her legs and she was able to walk somewhat normally. She picked up Dozer's reins and started to lead him over to the shed. Ludlow stopped her.

"Please, for the safety of all concerned, go inside and sit down, if you can. I'll take care of the horses," he said.

Kate glared at him a moment, then grinned ruefully and nodded. She walked over and pulled the saddlebags, her bedroll, and vest off Dozer, then made her way into the cabin.

When she opened the door and walked in the light was dim, but she could see an ancient heavy sofa, as well as a rag rug in front of a stone fireplace. There was just one large room with walls of rough wood paneling; on one side to the left of the door there was a sink with a large galvanized bucket turned upside down in it, and a long wooden counter running down one wall with cabinets above and below. There was a four-burner gas Coleman cook stove, as well as a Coleman gas lantern on the counter. Kate went over and looked around, found some matches, pumped up the lantern and lit it. She had used similar ones many times in Africa. Once she adjusted the brightness of the lantern, she saw there was a large round table with six chairs at the back of the room, and behind that there were several backpacking style inflatable mattresses up against the back wall. There was a long line of windows at the back of the cabin that looked out on the mesa. She could see a rough looking road, which she assumed provided access to the cabin on the Idaho side. Any fishing trips here would be pretty rustic. She gave a mental shrug – these were luxurious accommodations compared to some she'd had over the years.

She set her saddlebags and vest down on the floor and walked over to the fireplace. There was a goodly amount of wood stacked to the side and she had also noticed a stack on the front porch. It was starting to get cool; she decided they would need a fire. She went and got the lantern and set it on the mantelpiece. With the improved light, she found that someone had thoughtfully laid in some fatwood type fire starters along with the hardwood. She laid the wood carefully in hearth, checked to see that the damper was open, and lit the kindling. The dry wood caught quickly and with a little help from a bellows lying on the hearthstone, it began burning nicely. The chimney had a good draft.

Every time Kate moved, it was painful. She was paying the price for showing off this afternoon. She had a competitive nature though and sometimes it got the better of her. It had become important to her that she prove to Ludlow that she was independent and competent. She wished she had been less vigorous in her proofs; now she worried she might have trouble riding the next day.

Ludlow came in a few minutes after she got the fire going well. She stood in front of it, with her backside towards the warmth, hoping against hope that the warmth would help to dissipate the soreness.

"You got a fire going. Good work. I think it's going to get a bit chilly tonight, as well as wet," he said.

He had his saddlebags over one shoulder, and was carrying the rifle. He set his saddlebags down on the floor of the kitchen. He went over to a wall rack by the door, leaned the rifle up against the wall, then took off his gun belt and chaps and hung them up. Then he returned to the kitchen and took the bucket out of the sink.

"I'll go get some water. There's a pump out by the shed," he said. "And let's make sure we hang our slickers up here by the door. Better to do it now than have to fumble around in the middle of the night."

Kate found a long yellow slicker rolled up inside the sleeping bag that Ludlow had loaned her. She went over and found his slicker rolled up in the same manner and she took both of them and hung them up by the door. She shook out both sleeping bags and laid them near the mattresses against the wall.

Which brought to her mind the thought of spending the night alone with Ludlow in this cabin. One thing about her soreness, it did make the idea of having sex much less attractive. She made up her mind that if Ludlow got too friendly, she would just tell him no and mean it.

Then she sighed. The 'meaning it' would be the tough part. She went back to the fireplace and started warming her backside again.

He came back in with a bucket of water and set it in the sink. He then walked over and sat down on the couch, crossing his legs and resting one ankle on the opposite knee. He looked up at her pensively.

"Thanks for taking care of Dozer, Jim. This is the first time I haven't done something like that on my own," she said, not meeting his eyes.

"Katie, you've been grouchy and out of sorts off and on all day. Are you angry with me about something?"

Kate opened her mouth to speak, but words wouldn't come out. He just sat there, watching her carefully, his face pleasantly neutral.

"No, no, Jim. I'm not angry. Not at you, anyway."

"Well, who then? There are only two people here that I can see."

Kate shifted her weight, feeling extremely uncomfortable under the steady gaze of those hazel eyes.

"It's complicated," she said, looking at the floor.

"Hmmmmm. Complicated. I see. Are you worried about me crawling into bed with you?"

Kate almost said, 'No, I'm worried about ME crawling into bed with YOU', but she didn't. She just stood there, silent and miserable.

"Kate, I won't lie, I'm mighty interested. But only if you think it's the right thing to do. Please, relax. You're wound up tighter than a watch spring."

Kate looked him in the eye and found only concern and gentleness there.

She gave him a tentative smile, then moved over and sat down carefully on the other end of the couch. "I'm sorry, Jim. I know I've been a bitch today. I've got a lot on my mind, but that's no excuse. I'll do my best just to put it aside. I can't do anything about it right now, anyway."

"Good. Friends, then?" he asked.

"Of course, always," she said, smiling at him warmly.

"Well, feel up to helping me make dinner? If you sit there, you'll just stiffen up."

"Sure."

They walked over to the kitchen. Ludlow picked up the saddlebags and set them on the counter. He started rummaging around in one of them. Soon he had some plastic bags laid out on the counter; each one had some different kind of dried foodstuff in it.

"In one of these cabinets is a pot about this size," he said, measuring the size with his hands. "Can you find it and fill it about halfway with water and set it on to boil? I'm going to make us some stew. There's another large pot in there we'll need also for cleaning, so if you could get that and get some water in that also."

Kate opened various cabinets (finding plates, glasses and silverware in the process), until she found one with the two pots he had requested. She got them out, then checked to make sure the fuel tank for the stoves had enough fuel, and then she lit two burners. She dipped the smaller pot into the bucket to fill the larger one about half full, then filled the small one halfway and set both on the burners.

"Looks like you've had plenty of camp experience," Ludlow said.

"I have. John and I used to camp in college quite a bit, and I've had to do a lot of it in the field in Africa, of course," she said. "That's John Ridley. The man I've been living with for the past 13 years," she said quietly, after a pause.

Ludlow watched her carefully. He sensed that the source of her tension and unhappiness probably revolved around John Ridley. He must be pretty far up in the Washington Food Chain by now, Ludlow realized. Ludlow had disliked him from the first time he had met him at the race, and the man hadn't done anything in the subsequent contacts they had to improve his opinion. The man was too much of a clever political animal, always seeking the advantage.

Suddenly, Ludlow also recalled something Madeleine had told him once. She had said that John Ridley was one who kept himself 'occupied' when Kate was on assignment. She had told him this during an angry rant about the firing of a Conservative Caucus intern who had been having an affair with Ridley. Madeleine was furious because it made her conservative group look bad, as Ridley was an important staff member of a liberal senator. Ludlow also remembered Ridley's interest in the young intern when he had seen him at the steeplechase. He had no intention of mentioning this information to Kate, but the memory made him angry. He quickly put the feeling aside.

"I met John a few times when I lived in DC," Ludlow said in a neutral tone, hoping that it would encourage her to open up a bit. He didn't look at her, just kept carefully examining the dried items in various bags, deciding which would be best for the stew. "I was talking to him that day in Middleburg when I caught your horse for you."

"I think John's met about everyone in that town," Kate said bitterly.

Ludlow decided not to respond to that. Kate walked over to the fireplace, put on some more wood and used the poker to stir up the fire. Then she just stood gazing moodily into the flames.

This would not do, Ludlow decided. Right now Kate reminded him of some horses he had taken on for retraining over the years. The horses had suffered different types of human mishandling and abuse (Cactus was only one of many he had worked with), and it took careful and persistent work just to get them to the point where they would trust again. He hated to see her so unhappy. Tonight, he would do everything he could to get her to tell him whatever it was that was making her so miserable. Maybe it would help. Even though Ludlow was basically a non-violent man, right now he felt if John Ridley walked through the door he would have cheerfully shot the man's head off without batting an eye.

Soon he had the stew bubbling and he added in some dried onion. He took a spoon and sampled it critically. It was about done. Kate was still staring into the fireplace.

"Kate," he said, "would you mind going out and getting some water? The hand pump is out by the shed. We need it for the lemonade."

She came over and took the bucket out of the sink and went out the front door without a word. Ludlow stirred the stew some more then set out some bowls and spoons. When she came back in with the bucket, he filled a pitcher he had found the cabinet and added some powdered lemonade mix. He stirred it, poured the lemonade into a couple of glasses, and handed her one. Then he put stew into the bowls, and gave her one also. They carried them to the table, sat down, and began eating.

"This is really good," Kate said. "I was hungrier than I thought."

"Thanks," Ludlow said. "I do enjoy cooking."

"So does John," Kate said, with the same bitter tone she had used previously. "You're a better cook though."

"Thanks again," he said. "Try the lemonade."

Kate took a long drink. It was very good and a nice break from the plain water they had been drinking all day.

She knew that she was poor company, but for some reason the thought of John Ridley and everything he had taken from her was growing inside her like a festering wound. She ate the food Ludlow sat in front of her, but she only tasted the first few bites. She dutifully ate all of it, though, then sat staring out the windows at the back of the cabin. Darkness was falling. Far in the distance, she could see some dim flashes of lightning, followed by faint thunder. Ludlow picked up her bowl and glass and carried them to the kitchen.

"There's a little left if you want some," he said.

"No thanks."

Ludlow finished the stew himself, then set the dishes in the big pot that was now boiling. He turned off the heat. When the water cooled a bit, he would wash them. He repacked the dried food into his saddlebag then walked over to stand behind Kate.

"Are you feeling OK?" he asked.

She glanced at him quickly, then looked down at the floor and nodded her head. "I'm fine. Just a little tired I guess."

Ludlow stepped past her and grabbed a couple of the backpacking mattresses and the sleeping bags, then took them and spread them out in front of the sofa.

"I'm a little tired too. Why don't we watch the fire while the storm comes in? Might take your mind off what's bothering you," he asked gently.

He walked in and sat down on one mattress and leaned his back up against the sofa. He made a point to sit at the far end, giving her space. She came and sat down at the other end. Ludlow noticed that she moved slowly and painfully as she sank to the floor.

"Can I get you anything? I can see that you're in pain. I have something that might help," he said.

"I'll be all right. Thanks for asking though," she said, smiling at him weakly.

They sat in silence for a long while. Ludlow called on the patience that had served him so well with horses over the years and sat quietly with little movement. Finally, he got up and added wood to the fire and turned down the lantern. He would light it again when he did the dishes. When he turned, he saw that she was now facing the sofa, had curled one arm on the seat, and was hiding her face against the fabric. He saw her shoulders shaking slightly, and he realized she was sobbing. He walked quickly to the kitchen, got a small, clean washcloth he found in a cabinet under the sink, dipped it in the cool water in the bucket then walked back to Kate, and sank down beside her. He rested his hand on her head and stroked her auburn hair.

"Katie, what has John Ridley done to you?" he said in a soft tone.

Kate looked up at him and the pain in her eyes wrenched his heart. He gently wiped the tears from her face with the cool cloth.

Kate looked carefully at Ludlow's face. He smiled encouragingly, his hand still stroking her hair.

He looked so gentle and kind; she suddenly felt she could tell him anything. He would not judge her.

"He killed my horse, Jim. He killed Manny. I can't prove it, but I know he did. Just because he didn't want me 'distracted' anymore, so I could be a good little wifey and broodmare for him while he runs for Congress. I denied it for months, but I called the vet and my friend and asked, and what they said told me everything I needed to know. Manny was the only creature in my whole life that loved me for who and what I was. Manny and my stepfather, JQ."

Now that she had started telling the tale the words came out in a rush.

"JQ gave me Manny when I was sixteen. My mother hated it, but he did it anyway. I loved JQ so much, and now he's gone too. And John, he may have loved me a little in the beginning, but now, he thinks I'm just a political asset to use as he sees fit. He wants me to be Maria Shriver to his Arnold Schwarzenegger."

She told the story of her father, and how her mother had hated her for so many years because she was a living, breathing reminder of Anders Wyndham. Kate was ugly, Kate was clumsy, Kate was useless, and so many other messages she had gotten from her mother, either directly or indirectly. And now, embattled in the fight over JQ's money, they only spoke through their lawyers.

She turned away from him and stared into the fire. "The worst thing is, I believe at some level I knew that John couldn't be trusted. And when I got back from Africa, I didn't even have the guts to ask Maria or the vet what happened. I didn't do it until I got here."

"I'm a coward, Jim, and because of that, Manny's dead. I should have split from John years ago, when I first realized what Washington was doing to him. If I had done that, Manny would still be alive. But, I didn't, because I was too damn scared of being alone for the rest of my life. I didn't want to marry John, not really, although I said I would when he asked, because I just didn't see how anyone could ever love me. So I stayed.

"Now my life's a wreck, and I have to put it back together all alone. And I'm scared, Jim. I'm really, really scared."

Ludlow sat quietly watching her, just taking in all she was telling him. His family had been the cornerstone of his existence; he couldn't imagine living in the bitter isolation that Kate had suffered for most of her life. His heart ached for her.

She turned and looked at him with a soft, sweet smile. "You've given me a great gift though, Jim. I hadn't touched a horse since Manny died, not until I came here. And somehow, just being with the horses, Dozer and Cactus and Jerry and the others, has helped me to face these hard facts I've been hiding from for months."

"Horses are natural healers, Kate. I know from experience," Ludlow said.

He sat aside the washcloth, reached out and cupped the side of her face with his hand, and wiped a tear away with his thumb. She closed her eyes, and pressed her cheek against his palm with a soft sigh. His hand drifted down the side of her face, his thumb lightly touching her lower lip. Her lip had the same softness and texture of a desert rose, and she sighed again. Her breath moved across his skin like a gentle mesa breeze and he inhaled sharply at the sensation.

Kate opened her eyes and looked at him. There was deep love there, and longing, and need, and fear. She reached up and took his hand and gently pulled it away from her face. "I'm not worth it," she said looking at the floor. "You've already been through enough in your life."

Ludlow sat back against the couch and took a deep breath. He placed both hands in his lap and stared at them a moment. "Yesterday, when we were having our argument about this trip, you made the statement that to remove an option, a choice, from someone because you want to protect them is selfish, patronizing, and unfair. I also think it's arrogant. I am a grown man, I think I can make my own decisions," he said in a quiet tone.

They sat in silence without looking at each other.

Finally, Ludlow sighed and stood up. "I'm going to go check on the horses," he said. He walked over to the front door and stopped. "Kate if you don't want me, fine, I can understand that," he said without turning around, "but don't ever think you are unworthy or unlovable. I know a lot of people made you believe that, but it's just a lie. A huge lie. And John Ridley is a fucking bastard. Don't blame yourself about what he did to Manny."

Kate watched as he walked out the door. When the door closed, she felt a door was closing on her life and she almost called out for him to stop, to come back. But she didn't.

She sat, staring into the fireplace, thinking about what Ludlow had said. Minutes dragged on like hours, and he didn't come back in. Then she heard the sound of his boots on the wooden floor of the porch. She turned expectantly when he neared the door, but the door didn't open, he walked on for a bit, then stopped. More long minutes passed.

Suddenly she found herself standing up and walking toward the door. It seemed that a decision had been made at an almost cellular level – she would not let that door close on her life forever. When she stood up, she felt suddenly light and joyful. She turned back to where she had been sitting, almost expecting to see some dried out husk she had shed lying on the floor. She nearly ran towards the door. She had hurt him and she couldn't bear it. She must make things right again between them.

She stepped outside and saw Ludlow standing at the end of the porch, looking out towards the approaching storm. The wind was starting to pick up and the lightning was getting more frequent now and brighter; she could see his outline in the flashes and the thunder was getting closer and louder. He was leaning against one of the support posts of the porch, one long leg crossed in front of the other, the toe of his boot resting on the floor. His arms were crossed in front of him. Without a word she walked across the porch, slipped her arms around his waist and rested her forehead on his back. Ludlow didn't respond, and Kate felt a moment of despair. She was too late; the gulf that had opened between them couldn't be crossed. She'd wounded him too deeply.

*

Ludlow stood transfixed for a moment as her arms went around him. His own feelings towards Kate he was very clear on, but when he had seen the same feeling reflected in her eyes, it had been a sobering moment.

Ludlow knew that Kate found him physically desirable. She had given him the same looks that women had been giving him since he was 15 years old. Johnny Elk had noticed the looks and repeatedly warned him not to become vain, nor to become a shallow person who sees nothing but the outer shell. He had explained that those who only saw the housing, and not the spirit of a person, were doomed to unhappiness. When Ludlow had been a young man, he had thought that the old man's advice was frivolous, and had taken what the women had to give. But after a time he found these experiences empty and meaningless. Then Madeleine came along, and everything changed. But now, looking back, he sometimes wondered if Madeleine too had been more enamored of the shell than the spirit.

Now he and this lovely woman stood at a crossroads. If they took the path their spirits led them, it would take them into unknown, and because it was unknown, frightening territory.

Kate pressed her face into Ludlow's unyielding back and started to drop her hands and go back into the house. Before she could, though, he caught one of her hands and turned to face her. Kate smiled at him tentatively.

Ludlow reached up and stroked her face, then pulled her to him in a tight hug. She buried her face on his shoulder; his worn cotton shirt was soft against her cheek and smelled slightly of clean soap and horses. He held her like that for a moment, just happy to have her in his arms.

Suddenly, Kate turned her face towards him, placed both

hands gently on the sides of his face, and kissed him. It was a tentative kiss, then she became bolder, wrapping her arms tightly around his neck, kissing him more deeply. Ludlow responded, probing her velvety lips with his tongue. Kate moaned and began unsnapping his shirt and rubbed her fingers lightly along his ribcage. Ludlow felt a bit of madness at her touch, ran his hands down to her hips, and roughly pulled her against him.

Kate cried out in agony.

Ludlow looked at her in horror. He had hurt her. Fool that he was, he had forgotten how much pain she was in. "Oh,   Kate honey, I'm so sorry," he said contritely.

She rested her forehead against his chest for a moment. "I guess we're just going to have to be careful tonight," she said in a small voice.

"Things were going too fast anyway. I want to treasure this, not rush through it," Ludlow said, gathering her gently in his arms.

She looked up at him shyly, and smiled. "Well, you know if we stay out here too much longer we're liable to be struck by lightning," she said.

"Too late. For me at least," he said, grinning slowly and leaning his forehead against hers.

Kate laughed at that.

Ludlow took her hand and led her slowly back into the cabin.

When they got inside, Ludlow noticed Kate wincing as she walked "You're hurting pretty badly aren't you?" he asked.

"Well, some. But not enough to keep…"

Ludlow shook his head. He was amused to see Kate look a bit crestfallen. "Will you do something for me if I ask?" he said.

"Of course."

"I'm going to see if I can do something about that soreness. I don't want you hurting while we make love. I couldn't bear it. Take off your clothes and lie down there on your stomach in front of the fireplace, on the sleeping bags."

Kate looked at him quizzically then walked over in front of the fireplace and started to unbutton her shirt. She suddenly felt very shy. "Are you just going to stand there and watch?" she asked indignantly.

"No. I think I'll sit on the couch and watch," Ludlow said, moving around and sinking down onto the sofa. He looked at her appreciatively.

"Men!" she said a little crossly after a moment. "I guess I should be glad there's not a stripper pole in here."

"Might be a good addition. I'll have to speak to my friends about it," Ludlow said with a bit of a leer.

"I don't see how it could help the fishing any."

"All depends on what you're fishing for. Anyway, quit dawdling. I think this was what you were planning on doing anyway, wasn't it?" he asked, grinning at her impudently.

Kate glared at him a moment, then rolled her eyes. She unbuttoned her blouse and set it aside. She had on a lacy powder blue sports bra that Ludlow found to be very erotic and he shifted a bit on the couch.

She leaned over to unzip her short riding boots, and Ludlow got a good look at her cleavage. Her breasts were fuller than he had imagined and her skin was pale as moonflower blossoms. She kicked off each boot and set them aside, then unzipped her riding breeches and peeled them off her legs, grimacing in pain as she did so. She pulled her socks off at the same time, carefully folded both, and set them on her shirt.

She stood in front of him in her bra and bikini panties, both of the same lacey blue, with her chin raised slightly and a bit of challenge in her eye. Her legs were muscular and long; her knees a bit knobby. Her belly was flat and she had a small waist, which Ludlow desperately wanted to caress.

"Come help me with these last items, sir. I'm in too much pain to get them off by myself," she said in a husky voice.

"You'll just have to manage on your own," Ludlow said, coughing.

Kate pulled the bra off over her head, slipped out of the panties, then set them on the bundle. She turned back to Ludlow and stood unmoving in the firelight, watching him.

Ludlow sat silently for a long moment. He started to speak, but choked a bit and had to start again. "Just lie down here. I'll be right back," he said.

Kate did as he said. She was in a lot of pain now, her lower back, buttocks and upper thighs were nothing but one long, deep painful throb. She hoped he did have something that would help.

Ludlow pulled a little jar of salve out of his saddlebag and set it on the counter. Then he kicked off his boots and took off his shirt and socks. The jeans he would have to leave for later if he was going to be able to get this particular task completed. It was going to be pretty dicey as it was.

He padded back to the fireplace and saw Kate lying stretched out on the floor. The firelight made a sweet, pale gold teardrop of her naked waist and hips, and Ludlow gritted his teeth and refocused on the task at hand.

He knelt down beside her. She turned to look at him, rising up on one arm, but he gently pressed her back to the floor. She folded her arms under her head and took a deep breath.

He gazed at her for a moment, mesmerized by the shadows on her body that danced ethereal in the firelight. On either side of the base of her spine, where her back flowed into her hips, were two perfectly round dimples. Intrigued, he leaned over and kissed one gently, then traced its outside with the tip of his tongue. Her skin was like creamy satin. Kate gasped and gave a soft moan. She started to turn towards him, but Ludlow laid a hand on her shoulder and gently pressed her back to the floor.

"Be still, honey, and let me do this for you," he said, his voice a bit husky.

Ludlow put a small bit of the salve on his fingers and began massaging it into areas that he knew must be tender. He worked slowly, sometimes earning an 'ouch' when he rubbed a little too hard, but he knew that for the salve to work it had to be well rubbed in. Her skin was so soft he worried a bit that he might damage it with his calloused hands, so he tried to be as gentle as possible.

He massaged from her lower back, down over her buttocks and upper thighs. He knew he probably spent too much time enjoying the curving softness of her lower hips, but he was only human. After about 20 minutes, he was finished, and the salve had all been absorbed. When he was done, he set it aside, and stretched out next to her and kissed her shoulder.

"Is that better?" he asked.

"God, yes. In more ways than you can imagine. When I first lay down here, I was really in a lot of pain. Now, it's only just a little twinge here and there," she said.

"Old Native remedy."

Kate rolled slowly over to face him, and gazed at him, her gray-green eyes languid as a purring cat's. He reached to caress one of her breasts, and she pressed into his touch, her lips parting in a soft sigh. She ran her hand over his chest and ribs, then down his back to his hips. She then pressed herself against him, smiled, and moved her hand to the front of his jeans and felt of him.

"Well, I think I have a remedy for an Old Native with a pretty stiff ailment," she said, grinning wickedly.

Ludlow chuckled and kissed her deeply, then slipped out of his jeans.

Their lovemaking began very slowly as they explored each other. Kate took delight in the velvety, elegant arch of Ludlow's hipbones, and the enticing contrast of soft skin over hard bicep on the inside of his upper arm. He had little body hair, and his muscles were long and lean; his skin had a fine smoothness to it that drove Kate to sublime madness.

Ludlow marveled at the lacy aureoles of her nipples and the soft curve of her neck into her shoulder. He lingered over the tender skin of her wrists, finding a subtle ecstasy in the beat of her pulse against his lips when he kissed her there.

If one discovered a particularly sensitive point of pleasure, it was mercilessly exploited until the other moaned like a person being tortured. They were like two starving people given wholesome food for the first time in their lives, and they reveled in it.

When Ludlow finally entered her, she released his hair from its rawhide thong. It fell down her arms like a black satin curtain, whisper soft, caressing her with each of his movements. It blocked out the night, and the world, for both of them.

Some time later they both fell asleep in front of the dying fire, Kate's head pillowed on Ludlow's shoulder. As they slept, the storm began moving in violently, with bright flashes of lightening and driving rain. Kate woke to find Ludlow carefully sliding his arm out from under her head. He stood up, and began slipping on his jeans.

"What is it?" she asked, looking around sleepily.

"Something's spooking the horses; I'm going to go out and check."

She couldn't hear anything but thunder and the driving rain. She watched as he went to the kitchen and pulled on his boots, then walked shirtless over to the window. He picked up the rifle easily in one hand and looked into the night for a moment. Kate found she had a strange sense of dislocation as she looked at him.

Ludlow stood slightly on the balls of his feet like a cat, his long hair spilling down his naked back and shoulders, which gleamed smoothly golden in the waning firelight. A flash of lightning outlined his face briefly; he gazed into the night with his eyes narrowed and intent. While Ludlow had told her that he didn't have the 'warrior' gene of his family, Kate found herself disagreeing. At that moment, he looked deadly, and she wondered how many of Ludlow's warrior ancestors had stood like this over the centuries, ready to face down whatever threatened that which they held dear. She shivered a bit.

"Do you see anything? What do you think it could be in a storm like this?" she asked.

"I'm not sure," he said, setting the rifle against a wall and pulling on a slicker. "I'll just have a quick look."

"Be careful," she said, suddenly anxious. "Do you want me to come with you?"

He grinned at her and shook his head. "Don't worry. I'll be back in a few minutes. You just keep the covers warm for me. It's probably just a raccoon or possum in the shed, trying to get out of the rain."

Ludlow picked the rifle up and stepped out into the night. It was pitch black and the rain was falling in thick sheets. He was glad he had the cover of the porch roof to walk down to the shed where Dozer and Jerry were stabled. When he got there, Jerry snorted at him in alarm and shied a bit. Ludlow soothed him with a quiet word. He stepped into the stall and stroked the big gelding's neck. Jerry and Dozer both were staring out into the night, heads up and ears pricked forward. Jerry snorted again and took a step backwards.

"What is it, fella?" Ludlow asked, looking out to see what had upset the animal. It was like looking into a black hole.

Finally he stepped out into the rain, covering the rifle with the slicker. He walked out from the shed a few feet and tried not to worry about the lightning.

A sudden flash split the night lighting it like bright day. And then Ludlow saw what had spooked the horses. He raised his rifle quickly and aimed, but lowered it when another flash revealed a tall gray horse standing about 20 feet away. It was looking at Ludlow, calm and unafraid, then he heard hoof beats as the horse trotted off into the night. Ludlow stood for a moment, puzzled, then turned and went back to the shed. He threw Jerry and Dozer some more hay, which they began munching, only occasionally glancing out into the night. He then went back into the cabin. Kate was sitting up with her back against the sofa, watching the door tensely.

"It's all right, sweetheart," he said. "Nothing to worry about."

She sighed in relief, relaxing her shoulders.

Ludlow hung the dripping slicker back up on the rack, kicked off his boots, then walked to the kitchen and pulled a large dishtowel out from under the sink. He dried off the rifle, set it back by the door, then used the towel to dry his hair a bit. It was dripping.

"Here, let me do that," Kate said. She got up and padded over to him, took the towel and began drying his hair as well as his arms and chest.

"You're freezing," she said. "Come over by the fire."

Ludlow smiled and followed her as she walked over to the fireplace. She threw some more wood on, then turned back to him.

"Those pants are wet. Take them off and get under the covers."

He did as she ordered, amused at her bossy fussing. Kate stirred up the fire, laid his jeans carefully on the hearthstone so they could dry, then crawled in beside him, curling against him tightly in the crook of his arm. She pulled the sleeping bags up around both of them. He pulled her close and she stroked his chest.

"Did you see anything?" she asked.

"It was the strangest thing," he said, resting his head against hers. "There was another horse out there. A big gray. He didn't look to be afraid of me at all and just trotted off after he saw me."

He felt Kate stiffen and she looked up at him. He was surprised to see fear in her eyes.

"A silvery horse with a white mane and tail?" she asked.

"Well, his mane and tail were pretty wet, so I couldn't tell about the color really. Looked to be a blue roan or a dappled gray. I only got a couple of glimpses of him in the lightning. I almost shot him before I saw it was a horse. They have cougars up here, sometimes, although they usually have more sense than to come out in a storm like this. I'd have hated to have to shoot one, but didn't want to risk the horses getting hurt, or worse."

Kate hugged him tightly and he was surprised to find she was trembling a bit.

"What is it, honey? You're as spooked as Jerry and Dozer," he asked.

"I've been dreaming of a horse like that," she said quietly.

"What?"

"I started dreaming about him the day Manny died. I've been dreaming about him ever since," she said.

"What are you talking about?"

Kate told him about the dreams she had had about the silvery horse, starting with the night Manny died and ending with the dream she had had the night before.

Ludlow sat in silence for a while, considering. He kissed the top of her head then pulled the sleeping bag up over her shoulder.

"Katie, in Indian Country, there is an old legend about a horse called the Wind Horse. It originally came from the Choctaw, I think, and the myth itself varies from Tribe to Tribe, but this is what my grandfather told me when I was a boy.

"Once, long ago, there was a great horse that was a friend to all the Native people. He was an immortal horse, and was seen throughout the world at various times. When a Native warrior was hurt or wounded, the Wind Horse would come to carry him to safety. If one of the people was sick, the Wind Horse would carry her to a medicine man. One of the many things that made the Wind Horse special was his ability to feel the feelings of the rider.

"There was a lame boy who stumbled and got his foot caught in a bear trap. The trap cut off the boy's foot and he couldn't move. The Wind Horse came for the boy and lay down next to him so the boy could climb on his back.

"When the Wind Horse began carrying the boy, he felt the boy's feelings. He felt great sadness in the boy, because the boy had been a poor outcast of the tribe, and had been teased and ridiculed by the people because of his lameness. Now, the Wind Horse could tell that the boy would not be returning to his people, but would have to go to the Hunting Grounds because he was dying. He carried him through the many lands that lead to the Hunting Grounds and as they traveled the boy began to love the Wind Horse more than anything. The Wind Horse felt the boy's feelings and he too began to love the boy in return. This had not happened before and the Wind Horse found that when he got to the borders of the Hunting Grounds, he did not want to leave the boy. They had bonded and would not be separated. The Wind Horse passed into the Hunting Grounds with the boy, who had been made whole, as are all who pass over. When the Wind Horse departed, all the Native people cried out in grief because they knew he had passed from this world into the next, never to be seen again.

"The Wind Horse heard their grief and said a prayer to the Great Spirit to send the Native people a reminder, so they would never forget the great Wind Horse and his long friendship with them. And, the Great Spirit gave them the Horse in remembrance.

"Some say that the Wind Horse will return one day, when there is great need among The People," Ludlow continued after a pause.

"So, do you think the horse in my dreams is the Wind Horse?" Kate asked, looking up at him, as wondering and wide-eyed as a child. "Or the horse you saw outside tonight?"

"No, Katie. I think your dreams and this horse are just a coincidence," Ludlow said, looking at her and smiling. "But, I do know that I love you like the Wind Horse loved the boy, and would not be parted from you, not even by death."

Kate turned her face to his chest and he realized she was crying. He kissed her hair.

"Darling, is the thought of me loving you so terrifying? Please tell me what's wrong," he said.

She looked up at him. He was smiling at her kindly with a bit of amusement in his eyes.

"I just don't have the right words," she said, lowering her eyes.

"Kate, do you love me?"

"More than my life," she said fiercely.

He lifted her face to his and kissed her wet cheeks gently. "See, you do have the right words."

Ludlow laid her down in front of the fire again and began making love to her, slowly and gently. As he did he tried not to think of what some of The People said of the Wind Horse.

Some said the Wind Horse was the harbinger of Death.

Chapter 14

The next morning, when Kate woke up, she was alone. An uncertainty gripped her when she didn't see Ludlow in the room. She could smell coffee, so she knew Ludlow was somewhere nearby. It was still raining outside, but not as hard as the night before. She had no idea what time it was. She snuggled back down into the sleeping bag, reluctant to leave its soft warmth.

In a few minutes, Ludlow came in and hung his slicker up by the door. He was fully dressed and wearing his hat, which now had a plastic covering on it. He pulled it off and hung it by the door also.

He looked at her and smiled. "Good morning," he said.

"Hi," she said, sitting up. She felt a little guilty, lying about while Ludlow was up doing all the work.

He went over and got two blue enameled coffee mugs out of the cabinet and poured coffee, then came over and sat beside her on the floor. He handed her a cup of coffee. She took the mug from him, tucking the sleeping bag under her arms. The fire had died and it was cool in the cabin.

"Be careful, lazybones," Ludlow said, grinning at her. "It's hot."

Kate took a deep sniff of the aroma coming from the mug, then blew on it to cool it. She took a tentative sip; it was very hot. She set it aside and held out her arms to him, the sleeping bag slid down around her waist.

"Give me a kiss," she said.

Ludlow took her in his arms and kissed her, his fingers tracing the delicate bones of her spine.

"Your fingers are cold," she said, shivering a bit.

"That's the price you pay for sleeping in," he said, smiling.

She rested against him for a moment, then reached for her coffee and took a sip.

"I've about got us packed, there are just a few things left in here, and then we'll be ready to go. It's going to be a bit of a muddy ride. It's not raining nearly as hard as last night, but it's still damp," Ludlow said.

Kate traced the rim of the coffee mug with her finger. "I wish we could stay here," she said sadly.

Ludlow tipped her face up to look at him. "We can always

turn back, Katie."

"No. I want to finish what we started," she said. She sighed and rested her forehead against his chest.

"It's just a couple of hour's ride to the canyon, maybe a little longer in the rain," Ludlow said, rubbing her shoulder. "Are you up to it? Do you feel like you can ride today in the rain? Depending on what happens, maybe we can come back here tonight."

Kate nodded. She'd ridden in rainy weather many times when she was Eventing. She only had a few twinges of pain as she moved. Ludlow's salve was truly miraculous. She almost wished it hadn't worked and she had an excuse for them to stay in the cabin another day. She had a strong feeling they wouldn't come back to this place again.

"I have some warm water over on the stove, and some castile soap in the kitchen. And I pulled a washtub in. I thought you might want a bit of a bath before we go. There's time. I even found some clean towels," he said.

Kate stroked Ludlow's face and kissed his cheek. Not since JQ had anyone been so kind and thoughtful about her needs. "God, how I love you," she said.

He smiled and stood up, then pulled her up after him. She reached down and grabbed the coffee and walked into the kitchen. She took a drink and looked at the washtub.

"Sure you won't join me?" she asked, turning to face him and placing her hand on her naked belly. "I could use someone to wash my back."

Ludlow looked at her hungrily, then gave her a crooked grin and shook his head. "We have plenty of warm baths together in our future, I think," he said, "but I want to see this thing through also. Let's be done with it. If I come over there, we won't get out of this cabin all day and you know it."

Kate sighed and nodded. Ludlow went back outside, deliberately removing himself from temptation.

Kate poured the warm water in the washtub, and took a sponge bath standing up, using a washcloth Ludlow had thoughtfully placed on the side of the tub. She was depressed at the thought of leaving, but Ludlow was right. Best to be done with this. Then they could start making some decisions about what were the next steps in their lives. The castile soap had a minty smell to it that actually cheered her somewhat. Maybe today they would finally discover what had happened to Lindy and Julia and this long search would finally be ended.

Kate made quick work of the bath, now that she was up and around. She dried herself, set the towel on the side of the counter where it could dry, and put the washcloth in the sink. She dressed quickly, pulling clean underwear and socks out of her saddlebags; then she pulled on her riding breeches, the shirt from yesterday, and her boots. She noticed that there were still dishes from the night before to be washed, so she washed them and stacked them neatly in the sink. She checked the fireplace; there were just a few coals there now, nothing to worry about. She set the lantern back where she had originally found it, and rolled up the backpacking mattresses and put them back against the wall. She took a moment to brush her teeth, then put the toothpaste and brush back in its little carrying case she always took with her in the field, and packed it back into the saddlebags. She went and poured herself some more coffee and looked around to see what else needed to be done. About that time, Ludlow came back in. He looked around and nodded.

"I see you've tidied up," he said

"I didn't know what to do with the towel and washcloth, so I just set them aside. I'll need some help to dump the washtub," she said.

"Don't worry about that. When we get home, I'll call the boys and tell them we spent the night here. They won't mind. We're good friends."

"You have lots of good friends here don't you?" she asked.

"It's my home," he said. "I grew up here."

"Well, I hope that I can make good friends here too one day," she said quietly, turning away from him towards the sink. Now that she had broached the subject of the future, she was afraid to see at his reaction.

She needn't have worried. He came up behind her and wrapped his arms around her waist and pulled her against him. He kissed her neck.

"You don't have to worry about that. My family already loves you, and everyone else will too. You'll see."

She turned to look at him uncertainly. He smiled and folded her in his arms.

"Katie, do you remember the first night you came here and you had supper with us?"

"Of course. I was so nervous. I haven't had that much experience with happy family meals, and to tell you the truth I just didn't quite know what to do with myself."

"Do you remember my mother saying something in Shoshone, and everyone getting embarrassed?"

Kate looked up at him, puzzled. "I remember her saying something about the 'woman who became a horse.' Some Native legend about a woman who loved her horse so much she left her husband. Or something like that?"

"Actually, she said a little more than that," Ludlow said. "What she said was that you clearly had the spirit of the 'woman who became a horse', and it was a very lucky thing that I was half horse myself. Otherwise, I might have trouble keeping you at home, with the 'at home' meaning in my bed. It can be interpreted a couple of ways, and she used the term 'home' in front of Missy. But the adults and Dove knew exactly what she meant."

Kate looked up at him, eyes wide. "Oh my God, I would have died if I had known that. How could she know? I mean, how would she know that something was going to happen between us? Or does she always say this type of shocking thing at the dinner table? I noticed she doesn't let things get too boring."

"Mother does like her jokes. But Annie Ludlow has always had an odd sense of things. I guess, in the old days, she would have been considered to be a bit of a witch, or sacred woman. When she said it, I thought she was just teasing me, which she loves to do. But now, I'm not so sure. I think that's why she was so insistent on you wearing Kimmy's dress to the pow-wow. She sensed somehow that there was just a 'rightness' between the two of us, and she wanted to help it along a bit.

"She likes you very much, Katie. And that's saying something. I can't remember my mother giving two hoots for Madeleine or any other woman I've been involved with," he said, caressing her cheek.

"Legions of them, no doubt," Kate said pinching him and scowling.

"Owwww," he said, catching her hand and kissing her palm, "we're going to have to do something about this violent nature of yours. I guess I'll have to beat you, to teach you better manners."

Kate snorted. "Right. Good plan. I'm sure that worked well with all those Amazons in your family," she said, glaring at him. "Don't think I'm going to be any different."

Ludlow laughed then looked at her seriously. "So, are you ready?" he asked.

"Yes. Let's finish what we set out to do," she said.

They packed up the last of their things in the cabin. Ludlow got the down vest he had packed in Kate's saddlebag out and handed it to her. "Cooler today, but not as cold as I thought it would be luckily. You better wear this though, honey," he said.

Ludlow rolled the sleeping bags into two waterproof pouches, then handed Kate her slicker. When they stepped outside she saw the rain had lessened to more of a fine mist, and she was glad. She didn't like the idea of riding in a pouring rainstorm all day.

They walked out to the shed where both horses were saddled but not bridled. They were quietly eating hay and barely turned to Kate and Ludlow when they walked in. Ludlow tied on the bedrolls and saddlebags, as Kate didn't trust herself to tie a competent enough knot in the leather saddle strings to hold up in the wet.

Ludlow handed her medium sized bag made of thick plastic. "Better stick those phones in this, just in case," he said. "We may need them before the day's out."

Kate nodded and did as he asked.

"I put studs in these boots for traction in the mud," he said, lifting Dozer's booted foot and showing her the dull metal nubs sticking out. "I know you probably used something similar when you were Eventing, and know what to look out for."

Kate nodded. All serious Eventers used studs at various times during competition and training, especially in wet weather. She had used them for many years on Manny.

Ludlow then handed her hat to her, which now sported a plastic covering to protect it from the rain.

She looked at it a moment, then put it on. "Well, I guess it's time," she said. "Anything else we need to do?"

"Just one thing." Ludlow caught her by the waist and kissed her so long and deep it made her toes curl. When they parted she was a bit stunned and breathless. "OK. Now I'm ready," he said, taking a deep breath and nodding. He put his own hat on, then turned and grabbed Jerry's bridle off a nearby nail. He put the bridle on the horse and led him out into the yard. He then swung up in the saddle and looked at Kate expectantly.

She stared at him a moment with her mouth slightly agape, then shook her head. He was truly crazy. She slipped the bridle on Dozer, led him out into the yard and mounted.

"We're going to travel up this side of the river for a bit, then make our way down to a crossing upstream, then we'll angle off to the southwest, and hit a creek I know that'll be an easy ride up into the canyon lands. It shouldn't have too much water in it by the time we get there," Ludlow said.

"Well, let's go," she said.

Ludlow nodded and started off to the north following the little road that led to the cabin for a while then angling off back to the west. There wasn't much rain at all now, only a misty drizzle that was more like riding through a low cloud; visibility was very poor and Kate made sure she stuck close to Ludlow.

The land here dropped off gradually and Ludlow followed what looked to be some kind of game trail that wound its way down to the river. They came up on the low crossing that Ludlow had mentioned; the river was very wide here, running over a shallow rocky area. Ludlow rode Jerry into it and Kate followed on Dozer. The river was only fetlock deep on the horses and they splashed through with no problem. The wet weather didn't concern them at all that Kate could tell.

Soon they were across. Ludlow rode Jerry up a gently sloping hill to another mesa. When he got to the top of the hill, he stopped, looking off into the mist. Kate stopped beside him.

"I'll be damned," Ludlow said under his breath.

Kate noticed that the horses were also looking off into the mist, their heads up and their ears pricked forward.

She peered into the mist, trying to see what the horses and Ludlow were looking at. At first she couldn't see anything but the drizzle, but then, about 50 yards away, she began to make out the form of a large gray horse. He was standing on a little rise, looking at them calmly.

"Jesus," she whispered, "that's him. That's the horse from my dream."

Jim looked at her sharply. "That's the same horse I saw last night too. He's probably just a bachelor stallion from one of the wild herds."

"No, Jim. He's not."

Kate pushed Dozer into a trot heading towards the horse. She heard Ludlow cursing, then he was quickly beside her, having pushed Jerry into a lope.

"Kate stop!" Ludlow said. She stopped Dozer and looked at him. She had a slightly dreamy look in her eyes that he did not like at all.

"You can't just ride up on a strange stallion like that; they can be unpredictable," he said.

"He's not strange. This is the horse from my dream."

"Katie," Ludlow said, sidestepping Jerry over towards her so he could take her hand, "how could a dream horse be standing here in front of us right now?"

"I don't know. But that's him."

Ludlow shook his head. The horse was still standing there, watching them. He was relaxed, one rear leg cocked forward with the toe resting on the ground like a ballet dancer en pointe. No wild horse would stand there so relaxed with riders present. And there were no ranches up this way, so it seemed unlikely that he was a ranch horse that had just wandered off.

Plus, he didn't look like a ranch horse. He looked more like the ancient Baroque horses of Austria and the Iberian Peninsula, heavy neck and hindquarters, with a short back and Roman nose. Very much like da Vinci's famous horse sculpture. He had an odd, silvery mist-colored coat, a color that Ludlow had never seen before in a horse.

"He won't hurt us, Jim," Kate said confidently. She and Dozer began moving towards the horse.

"Well, at least let me go first. I'm the one that knows the way, remember?" he said, trotting up beside her. Kate shrugged and let Ludlow take the lead.

When Ludlow got within about 20 feet of the horse, it turned away and started walking at a relaxed pace, in the exact direction they needed to go. Since there was really no other choice and the horse was causing no problems (Jerry and Dozer were both unconcerned about the horse now), Ludlow followed him. As a test, Ludlow sped up into a trot. When he did, the gray horse also moved into a trot, always keeping the 20-foot barrier between them.

"I think he's along for the trip," Kate called out from behind him.

It seemed she was right. They rode another hour or so, the gray horse always staying just a little ahead of them.

When they got to the little creek Ludlow was looking for, the gray horse trotted up the creek a bit, then turned and looked at them expectantly.

Kate rode up beside Ludlow, who had stopped and was watching the horse with a dumbfounded expression on his face.

"Come on, Jim," she said. "He wants us to follow him. It'll be OK."

Kate turned Dozer up into the creek bed, which was a few inches deep in water. So far, they had had to deal with very little mud, and Kate was grateful for that. She heard Ludlow and Jerry trotting up behind her.

"Will you at least let me go first?" Ludlow said grumpily.

"You weren't going, you were sitting and gawking and wasting time," she replied in an exasperated tone. "If you want to fiddle-fart around, that's your own business. I want to see what this guy has to show us."

"Damnedest woman," Ludlow muttered under his breath, pushing Jerry into a trot up the creek.

Kate giggled a bit, then trotted along after Ludlow.

They followed the gray horse up the creek bed as it wound through the hills. In the mist, the shimmery color of his coat made him nearly invisible and ghostly at times. Eventually, they came over a little rise, and the gray horse trotted down into a canyon that was about 70 feet wide and straight as a road in both directions. He turned off to the left, trotted a hundred feet and looked back at them expectantly.

Ludlow studied the canyon floor carefully as he came over the rise. There were a few inches of water, but not enough to be troublesome. "So I guess we keep following him?" Ludlow asked as Kate rode up beside him.

She just watched him with raised eyebrows as she rode past, Dozer splashing along steadily though the water.

Ludlow shook his head in exasperation.

He let Kate take the lead. The strange horse apparently meant them no harm, and he did seem to have some destination in mind, which was more than Ludlow could say for himself. They were in *Deheya'* Canyon, but the canyon ran 30 miles from end to end, and he had no clear idea where Bobby Nardo had driven the wild horses. He thought it was probably down further to the south, closer to the gold mine where the canyon widened to more than 200 feet, but he couldn't be sure. As that was the direction they were heading, it did make some sense to continue following their curious guide. He still had serious doubts of the wisdom of following this strange horse, who didn't act like any horse he had ever seen before. However, he couldn't come up with an alternative plan or at least one Kate would comply with. He found he worried about her safety constantly.

He rode off to Kate's right a bit and made sure the rifle was loose in its scabbard. That way he could see trouble and maybe deal with it before it got to her. She rode along calmly, trusting the horse to lead them where they needed to go. Usually there were echoes in the canyon when Ludlow had passed through it in the past, but the heavy air muffled noise in an odd manner that he found eerie and unnerving.

As if the gray horse weren't eerie and unnerving enough.

After they had ridden for about an hour, the floor of the canyon began rising a bit, and Ludlow noticed that the water was shallower and the way was becoming muddier. The mud was also a strange color and texture, not the white alkali powder that usually stained the canyon floor, but a light brown loam, like it had washed down from the hillsides. Ludlow looked closely at the canyon walls, which were sheer grey rock. Mudslides weren't totally unheard of in the canyon lands, but it wasn't something he wanted to deal with today, or any day. Ludlow began to feel even more uneasy.

Kate had stopped a little ahead of him and was looking down at the ground. She turned to him with a worried look. "Jim, look at this, down here in the mud."

She backed Dozer up a few steps so he could see what she was talking about. He rode up to look.

There in the mud lay the leg bones of a horse; it was only one leg, it even had the delicate bones of the hoof still articulated with cartilage and a few shreds of tattered skin clinging to it. Jerry leaned down to sniff it, snorted, and backed up a few steps.

They turned to look at the gray horse ahead of them. He had stopped and was facing them again. He looked down at the bottom of the canyon and pawed at it deliberately, then he turned and continued walking.

"Stay behind me, Kate, and no arguing," Ludlow said.

They made their way up the canyon, following the horse. The further they rode, the more bones they saw. Soon, the canyon floor was strewn with bones from all the body parts of a horse; all the way from the skulls to the slowly collapsing ribcages to the articulated tailbones with the long tail hairs streaming sadly in the brown mud. It seemed they were walking on a wide road of horse bones. They even began seeing the rotted remnants of horse carcasses that had apparently washed up against the canyon walls; they were old, but there were still whiffs of a carrion smell riding on the thick mist. Ludlow, horrified and sick at the sight, heard a noise and turned to see Kate weeping openly. Jerry and Dozer snorted some and were nervous, but much calmer than Ludlow would ever have expected. Somehow he felt the gray horse was helping to soothe them in this nightmare.

Kate rode beside him and reached out for his hand. He took it wordlessly.

"What happened do you think?" she asked, choking.

"I have no idea, Katie," he said quietly.

The gray horse had trotted ahead and stopped beside something in the canyon about 200 feet ahead of them. In the mist, it looked like a large boulder that had washed down and blocked part of the canyon floor.

"I think he has something else he wants us to look at," Kate said dully.

"I guess we better go see what it is. I hope it's not worse than this. Just stay behind me, Katie."

He wished that he could somehow shield her from all of this, but she was a journalist and this was a story that needed to be told.

"Have you got a camera with you?" he asked.

"Yes. In my Smartphone. I'll take pictures after we see whatever it is our friend wants us to look at."

As they got closer to where the gray horse had stopped, both Kate and Ludlow realized that what they were seeing was not a boulder, but a vehicle.

Ludlow stopped and Kate rode up beside him.

"That's Lindy Abraham's vehicle," she said. The car was sitting on what was left of its tires. Something big had struck it on the driver's side, and it was caved in. On the other side the passenger's door had popped open slightly. Kate could see the dull red paint and the Jeep logo where the mud had been washed away on what was left of the front quarter panel.

Ludlow rode closer then swung down off Jerry into the mud. He looked inside the Jeep.

There, in the back seat, lay the sad decayed and skeletal remains of two people. Ludlow had no doubt who they were. He looked closer and saw they had both been shot in the head. Executed.

Kate started to get down also, but Ludlow stopped her.

"Don't get down, Katie, please," he said. "I don't want you to see this."

"The hell you say," she replied. She got off Dozer and walked over to stand beside him, slipping in the mud a bit. She didn't shrink in horror or cry out. She leaned forward and started to place her hand on the Jeep to look closer, but Ludlow took her hand and gently pulled it away. Ludlow saw the cold anger in her. He understood. He felt that way himself.

"Crime scene, Kate, don't touch anything."

She nodded and went over to her saddlebags and pulled out the Sat phone. She turned it on, but was disappointed to see there was no signal.

"We'll have to get out of the canyon to call Sharon. I can't get a signal here," she said.

"Where's the horse?" Ludlow asked, looking around.

They didn't see him anywhere. He had vanished.

Ludlow shook his head. One thing at a time. He would deal with his thoughts about the strange gray horse later.

"I guess he did what he needed to do," Kate said matter-of-factly. "I'll get some pictures now," she continued, looking at Ludlow.

"Don't take too long," Ludlow told her. "I don't want to spend any more time here than we have to. We need to get out of here quickly and let Sharon know about this so she can call the Nevada State Police."

Ludlow scanned the top of the canyon carefully. He didn't have a good feeling about this at all.

Kate got out her Smartphone and took pictures of the Jeep, and the remains in the back as well as some of the worst of the bone trail.

"Come on," Ludlow said urgently, "that's enough."

Kate nodded and put the Smartphone back in her saddlebag then swung up on Dozer as Ludlow did on Jerry.

"Just a little farther up is another creek bed that goes off to the left. We can hit that and get out of the canyon, then we can see if that phone works. Then it's about a 40-mile ride straight east across the desert to Antelope Valley. I want to get out of here. I've got an alarm going off in my head. We do not need to be here."

"Let's go then," Kate said.

They rode Jerry and Dozer around the Jeep in single file and started to take off at a trot down to the creek bed when they suddenly heard a loud clanging.

"What the hell?" Ludlow said, pulling the rifle quickly.

They turned to see that the gray horse had come back and was pawing at the passenger door on the side of the Jeep. Kate started to ride back and the horse stopped pawing. But when she turned away, he started pawing again.

"This is all we need!" Ludlow said angrily. "He's making enough racket that they will hear him all the way down to the Mine headquarters."

"There's something else he wants us to see. I'll go back. You just stay here," Kate said.

"No way in hell. I'm coming with you," Ludlow said.

So they both rode back. This time, the horse didn't retreat or stop pawing when they approached, but just kept pawing at the passenger door. Finally, the door, already battered, fell off its hinges into the mud and the horse hopped nimbly out of the way then backed up a few steps. He looked at Kate steadily. Kate swung down from the saddle, walked up to the Jeep, and looked in on the crushed passenger's compartment. The gray horse turned and trotted back up the canyon, quickly disappearing into the gloom.

Kate peered into the Jeep. There, lying on the floorboard, was an undamaged, perfectly clean Smartphone in a protective case. She reached for it; it was identical to her own.

"Kate, no. It's a crime scene. Don't contaminate evidence," Ludlow said.

"I think this is evidence we need to carry out with us," she replied, picking up the phone and holding it up to him.

Kate tried to power on the phone, but of course the battery was dead. She quickly went to her own phone, pulled out the battery, and swapped it out with the phone from the Jeep.

"Kate, please!" Ludlow said urgently.

"One moment, honey," she replied distractedly.

The phone powered on and Kate felt a brief sense of triumph. It was fully functional in just a few minutes and she quickly flicked through the applications with her fingers until she found the video gallery. Hoping her instincts were right, she went to the most current video and hit the 'play' button. She knew this was the last video that Julia Evans had made, and she hoped it would give her clues on what had happened here.

As the video played, she saw a nightmare scene with dozens of dead and dying horses. She heard Lindy and Julia talking, but she couldn't make out the words on the small speaker of the Smartphone. She did hear one of the women vomit once. Suddenly, she realized what she was seeing and she was struck with a growing fear and horror. Ludlow was right; they needed to get out of that canyon fast. She turned the Smartphone off, tucked it into her vest, and secured it with a snap, then she swung up on Dozer. She looked at Ludlow.

"You're right. We've got to get out of here," she said.

They took off at a trot down the canyon, glad of the studs on the horses' boots because the footing was uncertain.

"So, what was it you saw?" Ludlow asked, riding beside her.

"These horses were poisoned, Jim. I saw something like this in Africa once; some Maasai tribes people watered their cattle in a gold mining area – the water had been contaminated with heavy metals from the mining operation: cyanide, arsenic, cadmium, and who knows what else. The water was supposed to be contained and cordoned off, but it wasn't."

She looked at him, her face white with fear. "Those cattle of the Maasai had the same symptoms of the horses in that video, Jim. And Lindy and Julia found them before St. Martjin could bury the evidence."

"I'm willing to bet that St. Martjin has had a leakage here of some sort, either from a tailings dam, or from a leach pad itself, somewhere in the operation. If so many horses were poisoned, it could even mean a groundwater contamination. Somewhere on your Reservation, Jim. Your home. OUR home," she amended fiercely.

"And the Mine killed the advocates because they found out," Ludlow said. It was not a question.

"You know they did. Something like this would cost St. Martjin millions, if not billions of dollars in fines and reparations if it were discovered. It could conceivably shut the company down entirely, depending on the amount of damage to the environment."

"They must have run the horses into that box canyon and sealed them off in there. Then buried them with some of their heavy equipment, pushing dirt in from the hillside, along with Evans and Abraham, after they'd executed them," Ludlow said, his voice sick.

"They didn't realize that they buried them in a big wash though. We've had some unusually heavy storms the past couple of months, and it washed all this out into the canyon," he continued, after a moment.

"They'll kill us too if they catch us. You realize that, right?" Kate asked.

Ludlow looked at her grimly and nodded.

"How much farther is that creek bed?" Kate asked

"It's just up ahead. Can you get a signal on that phone yet?"

"I don't dare try while I'm riding, but I'm pretty sure not. We'll have to get completely out and away from this canyon. Plus, the weather is working against us. This fog will kill the signal."

"Let's get out of here then," Ludlow said. He put Jerry into a lope and Kate followed. The horses threw up a spray of mud and water as they ran. Soon, there was a break in the canyon wall to the left and Ludlow swung Jerry through the break, Kate following closely behind him. Ludlow held the Jerry back so Dozer could keep up.

They had been riding down the creek bed for just a short time, when Ludlow heard the sound he had been dreading.

"Hey, you there, stop!" someone yelled loudly.

He looked up and saw two Mine Security guards at the top of the one of the hills that the creek bed bisected. They were standing beside two ATV's and both had what looked to be automatic rifles. What made it worse was they must have heard them coming, so the horses didn't surprise them, but seeing two riders did. He had a few seconds to take some action.

Years of hunting as a boy had made Ludlow a good shot with

a rifle, and he had tried to keep up his edge. He quickly wrapped the tail of the reins securely around the saddle horn and pulled the rifle from the scabbard. Steering Jerry with his knees, he moved the big horse out a little from the wall, aimed, and then fired. He missed, but he expected that. He at least made them duck, which bought him and Kate more time. He aimed again when he saw one of the guards quickly stand up ready to return fire. This time, he hit the man in the shoulder and he went down. The other guard was not so foolish; he shot from behind the ATV and Ludlow heard the zipping noise of bullets flying past them. Kate looked back over at him, her eyes wide. He wished desperately that she had a faster horse. He heard the ATV start up, and immediately felt discouraged. Up ahead, where the creek bed met the plain, he knew there was a perfect place for the guard to ambush them if he got there first. Jerry could outrun an ATV, but Dozer, though sturdy, was not fast. He had to make a quick decision.

"Kate!" he called to her, "stop for a second."

She reined in Dozer and turned towards him. He could tell she was terrified, but she looked at him alertly and without panic.

"Listen, honey, that guy up there is heading for a place he and I both know is good for an ambush. Jerry can outrun that ATV of his, but Dozer can't. I want you to hang back here a minute and let me deal with him."

"Jim, please..."

"No arguments, I've got to go quickly. Just hang back for a bit. Once you hear the gunfire stop, ease on up on this side of the creek bed and see what the situation is. I should be there waiting for you. If not, if something happens, you just head due east and you'll hit Antelope Valley. That's the best plan I've got right now, and I've got to go."

With that, he put Jerry into a gallop and took off down the creek bed.

Kate watched him go and tried to keep from crying. She had no choice but to do as he asked, but it made her sick to think about it. She put Dozer into a slow walk and said a silent prayer for Ludlow's safety.

*

Ludlow put Jerry into the fastest gallop he could manage on the rocky creek bed, again being thankful for the boots and the extra traction they provided. He kept an ear out for the ATV, and heard it just behind him up on the hill. As Jerry ran, Ludlow began making some preparations. He looped the reins over the saddlehorn, then shucked off the bright yellow slicker and let it slide off Jerry's rump. No sense in giving the guy a bigger target. He had eight rounds left in the rifle, and six in his grandfather's old .38 Colt. He had always been a lousy shot with the Colt, so he hoped he could get the job done with the rifle. He paused for a split second at the thought of killing a man, but the memory of the rotted remains of two women in the Jeep quickly dissolved that hesitation. The very thought of Kate having a similar fate put him into a cold, killing rage.

He listened again for the ATV. It was still just behind him, but seemed closer. He knew the guy would be racing to get down the hill and catch him when he came out of the draw. He pushed Jerry a little harder, and the big horse lengthened his stride. He could hear the ATV dropping back behind him slightly.

He saw the opening onto the broad plain up ahead and put the rifle up and aimed it in his mind, where he thought the guard would come down the hill on the ATV. He heard the guard rev the ATV to catch up with him. When Ludlow burst out onto the plain, he squeezed his knees and sat back to put Jerry into a controlled sliding stop, giving him a stable shooting platform. At the same time, he carefully aimed the rifle, turning 90 degrees to his left. The guard came flying off the hill on the ATV at full speed. Ludlow shot once and hit one of the wheels on the ATV, causing it to veer a bit. He aimed again and hit the ground just under the ATV. The guard raised his own weapon and Ludlow fired again, this time hitting the man in the chest. The guard fell off the ATV and rolled in the dirt; the ATV flipped and the engine soon died when the deadman switch under the seat was disengaged.

Ludlow, breathing heavily now, turned forward again to go over and make sure the man was no longer a threat. He took a bit too long, however. As he was turning Jerry towards the man, the guard managed to haul himself up on one arm, aim, and fire.

Ludlow felt as if he had been hit with a sledgehammer on the left side of his ribcage. He managed to get off another round at the man, which did take care of him permanently.

Ludlow sat motionless on Jerry, wondering how bad he had been hit. He reached around with his right hand and touched his side, and it came away a bloody. So far, it was strange; he didn't really feel any pain, but it was very hard to breathe. He just couldn't seem to get enough air. Then, he started feeling a bit weak. He knew that when the adrenalin wore off, he would be in some trouble.

When Kate had heard Ludlow fire the rifle the first time, she had been shocked. In the movies, it was always the bad guys that shot first, and she found herself wrestling with this absurd thought for a few seconds. She was also shocked by the ease he seemed to have in firing a weapon from a running horse. Then, when the bullets came zipping down the creek bed, that had been yet another shock, that those little harmless-seeming *pfffts* could wound and kill. In Africa, she had been near war zones a few times, but never had had anyone shoot at her, a fact of which she was profoundly grateful.

She did as Ludlow asked and rode slowly down the creek bed, sticking as closely to the left as possible. When she came up on his slicker, she had a moment of panic, but then realized that Ludlow had taken off the coat deliberately. She stopped Dozer and picked up the slicker and laid it across her saddle. Ludlow might need it, and there was no sense leaving a trail if they didn't have to.

When she heard the gunfire, she stopped Dozer for a moment; then, when it stopped, she moved him into a trot, then a lope. She couldn't stand this uncertainty any longer. If the Mine Security guard turned out to be the last man standing, she would just have to deal with it. Although she knew it was foolish, she felt she would tear the man to pieces with her bare hands if he had hurt Ludlow.

When she came out from the draw, her breath caught as she saw Ludlow sitting in the saddle with blood running from his left side. So, he had been hit; it was just a matter how badly. He was still in the saddle, which was a good thing. She also noticed that Jerry apparently hadn't been hit, which was also encouraging. Kate quickly came up beside Ludlow and tried to get an idea of how badly he was wounded.

"God, Jim," she said, looking at the wound and feeling a bit sick.

Ludlow looked at her and smiled weakly. Her face was pale, but again, not panicked and that was something he was hoping for.

"The gentleman over there has ceased to be a problem," Ludlow said, trying to sound gallant and offhand but failing miserably, "but I wasn't quick enough to make sure of him, and he inconveniently managed to get a round off. As you can see."

Ludlow swayed in the saddle a moment, then shook his head.

"Kate, we need to get someplace where we can do something about this wound. I don't know how much longer I can stay on this horse."

"Just tell me what to do," she said, looking at him evenly.

"If we go south about a quarter mile there's a little cave up against the hill, more of a ledge really, but it's about the best we're going to do out here right now. It'll at least provide some cover."

Kate nodded, and dismounted. She dug around in her saddlebag and found the quilted riding vest she had worn the day before. She took it over to Ludlow and tucked it into the top of his chaps to make a rudimentary bandage. She took Ludlow's slicker and wrapped it around him the best she could, picked up the rifle he had dropped and put it in the scabbard. Then she unhooked the reins from Jerry's saddlehorn, and passed them over Jerry's head.

"Jim, I'll lead Jerry down to this cave, and we'll see what we can do. You just concentrate on staying in the saddle and keeping that vest up against that wound the best you can."

"Good thinking," he said, smiling weakly. "The way I'm bleeding, anywhere I go, I'm doing nothing but leaving a nice trail so they can come finish off the job."

"Just hang onto the saddlehorn and let me do the work for a change," Kate said, trying to sound cheerful and positive. It was not easy.

She turned Dozer to the right and rode slowly along the side of the hill, frequently looking back to check on Ludlow. She saw that the hill gave way to a cliff that rose steeply from the desert plain where they had been riding. Then she saw the shallow cave. It was small, no more than ten by ten feet, but it would have to do. She rode Dozer up as close as she could get to it then got down to help Ludlow get off Jerry. She walked around to the right of the big gelding and reached up for Ludlow.

"Put your hand on my shoulder, sweetheart, and slide off," she said.

Ludlow put his hand on her shoulder and she grabbed him around the waist. He grimaced in pain and cried out when his left leg slid over the saddle, but was able to stand with her help and they hobbled over into the little cave, which was just tall enough for them to stand up in. Kate helped Ludlow sit on the ground.

"Do you have a first aid kit in your saddlebag?" she asked.

Ludlow looked at her and smiled weakly. "Just a small one. Better than nothing I guess," he replied.

Kate smiled at him encouragingly and kissed him on the cheek, then went to find the first aid kit.

Kate was not totally unfamiliar with gunshot wounds. A few years before, when she was on assignment in Tanzania, Meyers had called and asked her to fly over to the Congo to get a story on a Doctors Without Borders field hospital that had been set up to deal with one of the numerous blood diamond conflicts that occurred in that country. Meyers wanted her there because she spoke passable French and would be able to communicate with the staff of the French humanitarian agency. While she was there, the war spilled over into several large villages and there were numerous civilian casualties. She had wound up being an impromptu field nurse for two weeks and had worked harder than she had ever worked in her life. It was during this crisis that she had her experience with the U.S. Security Services that now were contracting with St. Martjin Mining. They had been hired to provide security for one of the diamond mines in the conflict and had had no compunction about coming into the hospital to look for 'saboteurs' as they called them. Kate still remembered the terrified look on one patient's face when they had hauled him bodily out of the hospital for 'questioning' despite a bad gunshot wound in the shoulder and the outrage of the hospital staff. Kate never saw the man again.

Instead of digging through the saddlebags to search for the first aid kit, she just pulled off both sets and put them in the cave, then went back and grabbed the bedrolls, her vest, and Ludlow's slicker.

She stretched one of the slickers out on the rocky cave floor, unpacked a sleeping bag, and laid it on the slicker.

"Jim, darling, let's get your jacket and shirt off, then we'll move you over here on this and I'll have a look at that wound," she said, smiling calmly. One thing she had learned in the field hospital was that shock was worsened if the patient got excessively frightened and upset, and a calm, positive manner could sometimes go a long way to lessening it.

He cried out weakly as she helped him remove his jacket and shirt, then she helped to move him over to the rudimentary pallet she had made, and turned him on his right side.

"How bad is it?" he asked through clenched teeth.

Kate looked at the wound with disquiet. The bullet looked to have entered just inside the curve of his ribcage, shattered at least one if not two ribs. There were bone fragments in the wound, and she had a feeling that the bullet may have nicked the lung, as she could hear a slight sucking noise when he breathed. She also was concerned that either the bullet or some rib fragments had penetrated the large intestine, as she had a faint whiff of bowel as she leaned over to look. It was still bleeding, but not as badly as before. Bright arterial blood. She lifted one of Ludlow's hands and looked at the nail beds of his fingers. They were slightly pale, but not horribly so. She decided if he were going to bleed out and die he already would have done so. The thought made tears come to her eyes, both in fear and relief.

It was not a pretty situation though. He needed medical attention and he needed it soon.

"Let me get this bandaged and then we'll talk about it," she said quietly.

She pulled off her slicker and laid it face up on the cave floor, then dumped all the contents of both saddlebags on it. She found the first aid kit. It was small, as Ludlow said, but there were some useful items in it. She sorted through everything quickly. She found a knife that she used to cut up an extra cotton shirt of hers into long strips for bandages. She moved the items over next to Ludlow. First, she used all the sterile gauze in the kit to gently pack the wound, then she cut up the vest into thick squares and put them on top of the gauze as padding. She held it with her left hand, and placed her right hand on Ludlow's right shoulder.

"Sit up a bit, darling," she said, smiling gently at him. "I need to secure this dressing."

She helped him to sit up and he groaned and grimaced in pain. She quickly wrapped the strips of shirt around him, and tied them off one by one. It would have to do.

"So what's the verdict, doc?" he asked, smiling weakly.

"Well," she said, stroking his face. "The good news is you're still alive and should be able to hold out for while if you stay still. But I'm not going to lie to you, it's a bad wound, and you need to get to a hospital as soon as possible. If you try to ride, well, you can't ride."

Ludlow looked at her steadily and started to speak.

"Jim, just let me think this through, would you? You said Antelope Valley is 40 miles due east?" she asked.

"That's right."

Ludlow watched her carefully as she stood looking out towards the horses. He was feeling a little better now that the wound had been bandaged. She didn't look particularly frightened, just intent on working through their problems. She had the same look on her face as she did the day before when she and Dozer had nearly plunged 50 feet down the trail. He felt a swift surge of pride in her; she was an amazing woman. If they got through this he planned on spending the rest of his life telling her so.

She seemed to make up her mind about something. She quickly walked out to the horses, pulled the rifle out of its scabbard, then came in and set it next to Ludlow. Then she pulled off Ludlow's heavy western saddle and saddle blanket. She hauled them in and set the saddle behind Ludlow, positioning it so he could rest the right side of his back against it. Then she covered it with the blanket, and helped him position himself on the saddle. She went over to the items on the slicker she had taken out of the saddlebags and got out the Sat phone and another item that was in a small hard case. She opened it and pulled out a small dish antenna, then carried it and the Sat phone out to the mouth of the cave, setting it a good ways outside. She looked up at the sky, then came back in and got a small compass that Ludlow always carried with him. She looked at it, oriented the antenna, and plugged the phone in. She turned it on, watched it tensely for a moment, then he heard her cursing. She moved the antenna around, carefully looking at the compass. Then she turned and brought the phone back in and set it beside Ludlow.

"All right, darling, this is what I have in mind," she said.

Ludlow watched her face carefully.

"I've got a very small signal on this Sat phone that seems to be going up and down slightly. Being close to these hills is interfering with the signal, but the satellite should be coming into line of sight relatively soon and the phone will be operational. I want to leave it here with you and once you get a good enough signal, I want you to call Sharon and tell her what's going on, and ask if they can send an air ambulance out here to pick you up.

They can get a lat/long reading off the Sat phone if you can't tell them how to find you for some reason."

She seemed to choke a bit at that, but took a deep breath and continued.

"And I'm going to take Jerry and hightail it back to Antelope Valley with this video. When I get close enough to Antelope Valley, I should be able to get a signal on my own cell phone and I'll try to call her also. If I can get this video back to Sharon and she can contact the authorities, then St. Martjin should realize that any further actions they take will only make the situation worse for them. Because they are coming after us, right?" she finished, looking at him.

"I'm afraid so," he said weakly. "I only winged that first guy. I'm sure he got on the radio as soon as he was able."

Kate nodded and began gathering up some things she felt she would need. She took off her slicker and changed the battery from Julia's Smartphone to her own. Then she put both the canteens over beside Ludlow; she knew he would probably get thirsty because of the blood loss. She put Sharon's cell phone number on speed dial for both phones, and made sure Ludlow knew what button to push on the Sat phone to call her.

"When you get two bars of signal, the call should go through, honey," she said. There was only one now, and it was flickering.

"I don't like this plan, but I can't think of a better one," Ludlow said, closing his eyes in pain.

She leaned over and kissed him gently. "I love you so much," she said then she went back to her preparations for leaving.

"I think you should take this satellite phone with you though," Ludlow said.

Kate shook her head and smiled at him. "I'm not leaving you here without a way to communicate. Just in case I don't get through. That topic is not open to discussion. When I get close to Antelope Valley, my own phone should work. It won't take me that much time to get there on that speed demon gelding of yours."

She got the other sleeping bag and her own slicker and covered him with them. It was not particularly cold, but she still didn't want him to get hypothermic.

He saw that she was nearly ready to go. "Kate, come over here, please," he said. The thought of her doing this completely on her own made him sick inside, but there was nothing for it. She had to. He knew she was right about the wound. He was feeling very weak.

She came and sat beside him and took his hand.

"One thing you need to watch out for – there's a canyon that cuts across your path that you won't see until you're right on top of it. It's pretty deep, so take care. It's about halfway to Antelope Valley. Jerry can jump it in most places, but he might not see it soon enough, and if you hit it at a bad spot it will be too wide for him. Just remember to watch," Ludlow said, stroking her face.

"I'll watch," she said.

"And take their boots off. It will help with your speed and Dozer won't need them."

Kate nodded.

They sat for a few moments then Kate kissed him gently and stood up to leave.

"I'm leaving Dozer behind. I have no idea if he'll follow us or not."

"Don't worry about Dozer."

She stood for a moment, then turned to him. "Just remember something, Jim Ludlow. I will come to you and bring you home if you can't get there on your own. Now that I've found you, I don't intend on letting you go. I love you too damn much. The only thing I ask is, please don't go where I can't follow."

Ludlow coughed a bit; there were tears in his eyes and he couldn't speak. Then she turned and walked out of the cave without another word. He watched as she pulled the boots off both horses and cast them aside, and transferred the lightweight endurance saddle from Dozer to Jerry. She pulled off Dozer's bridle and set it aside also. She swung up on Jerry, and urged him into a trot; then she was gone. She didn't look back.

Ludlow sat for a while, tears running down his cheeks. She had left so quickly. Now he wished he had told her how much he loved her before she had departed. He felt he would never see her again.

Chapter 15

As soon as Kate got away from the hills, she urged Jerry into a full out gallop and was surprised at the speed the big gelding had in him. She had carefully checked the small hand compass for due east and she would continue to check it to make sure she didn't get off course. The sun was finally starting to come out and she was both glad and worried; glad because it gave her better visibility over the wide plain, but she also knew that if SHE could see better, so could others, and that was not a pleasant thought. The wide plain of the desert was wet, but the damp sandy soil gave good footing, and Kate said a silent prayer of thanks for that. Slippery footing would have been a nightmare.

She checked her watch. It was just past noon. She made plans to rest Jerry at a trot from time to time, even though she was frustrated at the thought. She was terrified for Ludlow and worried about him constantly. Right now, one of her greatest fears was that the Mine Security people would track him back to the cave. Every time she thought of it, she became nearly overwhelmed with fear and rage, but she forced herself to put those fears aside. The best thing she could do for Ludlow right now was to burn up the desert to get to Antelope Valley and help.

She knew that she and Manny could have done 40 miles in about six hours when he had been in absolute peak condition and that was with frequent rest breaks. She hoped that Jerry could beat that time.

After she had been riding an hour, she stopped and let Jerry rest for a moment, then she checked the compass. She had veered off, but not by much. She also checked her Smartphone. No signal. Ludlow said that the canyon was halfway, so it wouldn't be a problem yet. However, it wouldn't do to be complacent about watching for it.

She pushed Jerry into a trot again, then a slow lope, then a trot, then a lope. The big gelding was sweating, but didn't seem particularly tired as of yet. He seemed as anxious to get back to Antelope Valley as she did, as if he knew there was something wrong.

After they had been riding about three hours, Kate heard a noise behind her. She looked back over her shoulder and saw a 4-wheel drive SUV heading straight for her. She gave Jerry a kick to urge him into a fast gallop and he surged forward with a speed she had no idea that he had.

She heard someone shouting over a PA system on the SUV, but couldn't make out what he was saying. She ignored him and concentrated on riding.

When the bullets started zipping through the grass, she tried to urge Jerry on faster, but the big gelding was giving her everything he had. She could hear the SUV coming closer behind her. She briefly wished she had the rifle with her, but knew it would have done her no good. She was a lousy shot just standing still; trying to shoot from a moving horse as Ludlow had done would have been a waste of time and energy.

Now she could hear the PA clearly, they were calling her name, telling her to stop, threatening her. She began to consider stopping and just letting them take her; maybe if she gave them the video and promised to keep quiet, they would get Ludlow the help he so desperately needed.

She knew this was folly however. Lindy Abraham and Julia Evans were proof of that.

She caught a glimpse of something out of the corner of her eye and suddenly she saw the great gray horse that had led them up the bone trail, racing towards her at breakneck speed from the north. In the sunlight, his outline was a bit blurred, and his coat had an odd shine to it, like his coat was made of microscopic prisms. She had no idea what he was up to, but she hoped he had a better plan than she did.

Then she saw the canyon.

It snaked off across the desert, a zigzag maw that stretched as far as she could see in either direction. Not only that, she had had the bad luck to come up on it at a wide spot, it looked to be 60 feet at least. There was no way Jerry could make this, strong as he was. He was running his heart out for her, but she could tell he was tiring. She heard more gunfire and was again relieved to discover that they had escaped being hit.

The gray horse was coming closer at a speed that seemed impossible. When the first inkling of the thought of drawing the rein and giving herself over to Mine Security began to dawn, she realized that the gray horse was right beside them, matching Jerry stride for stride.

Kate felt a chilling cold in her legs, and she realized that the grey horse was actually merging to become one with Jerry, like an overlaid photographic image. Jerry glistened for a moment with the odd prismatic color, then he erupted with a burst of speed so fast Kate had to grab his mane to keep from being left behind. She saw the canyon looming up ahead, coming too fast to be believed. Then, suddenly, she felt Jerry collect himself and he jumped, no FLEW, across the wide gap. She looked down briefly and saw a tiny stream that looked to be miles below; even though she knew it was only a few hundred feet at the most.

She had moved into a forward seat by instinct when Jerry jumped, and as they landed on the other side, with five feet left to spare, she never even looked back at the SUV, but just galloped on. She heard a few more gunshots, but then they were well out of range. They wouldn't bother her again.

When Kate released her hand from Jerry's mane, she saw that it was glowing faintly like the gray horse had earlier, but it faded in a few moments. She didn't stop to consider it, but just kept riding.

Jerry swerved a little to the north, pulling on the rein a bit. She was surprised; this was the first time he had done this. She tried to slow him, so she could check the compass, but he ignored that too and began galloping at a speed that left Kate dumbstruck. The desert sand below seemed to be just a blur.

They ran at that speed for longer than Kate thought was possible. No vehicle could catch them. They had a chance. Jerry wasn't even breathing hard, even though he was running at this amazing speed. She began to have hopes that they were going to make it.

Then, Kate heard a noise she had been dreading, the thump-thump-thump of a helicopter. She nearly cried in frustration. This was something not even a Wind Horse could save her from.

*

Bobby Nardo saw the girl on the horse far sooner than Sam Conner did, but he didn't say anything. The horse was running at a speed that seemed near impossible, and to Bobby's eye he had an odd look about him, a shimmer to his coat that seemed almost ghostlike. They had heard on the radio that the SUV with had been left on the other side of the canyon. Bobby knew the woman must be some kind of rider, to jump the canyon like that. It was something he never had the nerve to do, although when he and Ludlow were boys, Ludlow jumped it frequently.

"There she is," Sam said to Bobby over the microphone in his headset.

"I don't see Ludlow," Bobby said.

"She probably left him behind. Typical," Conner said. He reached behind the seat and got out his rifle, adjusting the scope. He undid his seat harness and swung one booted foot out onto the landing gear.

"What are you doing?" Bobby asked.

"You know goddamn well what I'm doing. You knew it when you saw me put the rifle in. You knew it when I asked you take the door off on this side. Just remember what side you're bread's buttered on, Bobby. And don't think you can get out of trouble by pretending you don't know what's going on. That girl down there has what she needs to put both of us away for life or worse. You're in it just as deep as I am, Bobby, and remember, there ain't no liquor in prison. Just ease over there and keep pace with her and I'll cool her off," Conner said. "I'll aim for the horse if that'll make you less squeamish."

Bobby Nardo did as Sam Conner told him. Conner was right, he had known what was going on at the Mine and had said nothing. What did the girl mean to him anyway? If it were Ludlow, it might be a different story, but it was just the girl. She wasn't worth going to prison over. Besides, Conner was a very good shot. If he said he was going to shoot the horse, he could do so without hitting the girl. Although whether she would survive a fall at that speed, who could say.

He moved the helicopter up to the point they were pacing her, about 100 feet up. Conner put a round in the rifle chamber and took careful aim.

"Just hold it steady, this will be over in just a minute," Conner said.

But suddenly the horse that the girl was riding looked up at them, and Bobby Nardo felt the horse looking right at him, looking INTO him, that he somehow KNEW him, saw right through him, saw everything he had ever been and done, all the awful things, from the things he had done in Afghanistan to the shame he had brought on himself since he came back to Nevada. The shame he had brought to his family. The shame of what he had done to the wild ones.

And Bobby felt such a sense of love, understanding, and

forgiveness that he gasped and tears came to his eyes.

Conner was aiming; Bobby clearly saw his finger increasing the pressure of the trigger with a slow pull.

Bobby Nardo quickly moved the joystick to the right, and the helicopter tipped sharply to the right. Conner was pitched from the cabin and fell the 100 feet to the desert floor.

"Ooops," Bobby said.

Bobby didn't know if the fall would kill Conner or not. He didn't pause to worry about it. He quickly turned the helicopter and headed back towards the mountains.

When Kate had seen the man with the rifle in the helicopter, she had fully expected to be struck down at any moment. However, when she saw him fall, and the helicopter fly off to the west, she was stunned but didn't think much more about it. It was just one more weird thing in the weirdest day of her life.

In about an hour, she was shocked to see Antelope Valley looming in the distance. Jerry had made the journey in incredible time. She noticed that he was slowing though, and his coat was losing that odd sheen that it had had since the canyon. She hoped that he would survive this wild ride.

They were entering Antelope Valley from the west, and she wasn't quite sure where she was. Then she looked and saw the high school up on a hill to her right. She felt a great sense of relief. Soon she would be safe.

She thought about using her cell phone to call, but immediately dismissed the idea. Too great a chance of dropping it, and she was almost there anyway. Just another 10 or 15 minutes and she would finally be to safety. She nearly cried. She wondered if Ludlow had gotten through on the satellite phone; was he on the way to the hospital? Was he even still alive? She wanted so badly to hear his voice, stroke his face, and hold him.

Her relief soon turned to a mingling of exasperation, disgust, and fear, though, when she saw a large SUV parked on a side street facing west. Its pearly color was plainly visible from her position. She had no doubt who it was.

"Jesus, don't these guys EVER give up?" she asked Jerry.

She immediately angled off to the south, heading for the high school.

*

Sharon was sitting in her office with one Victor Shelton, Chief

Security Officer at St. Martjin Mining, and the discussion they were having was giving her a headache. He was telling her a rather bizarre and disjointed story (to her mind) that involved her brother shooting one Mine Security guard in the shoulder and murdering another one in cold blood in some sort of sabotage attempt up near the Mine. The story made no sense, and yet, Jim HAD sneaked off with Kate Wyndham just the day before and headed up that way. She had been furious when Annie had shown her Jim's note, but there had been nothing she could do about it. She had her hands full with all the activities on the Reservation, and it wasn't the first time her brother had just decided to go off for a few days up in the canyonlands. It was the first time since he had come home from Washington that he had taken a woman with him, but Sharon actually found that to be encouraging. The entire family was becoming a bit concerned about the monk-like existence Ludlow had led over the past few years. One thing Sharon knew about her little brother: he was no monk.

"Anyway, Chief White Owl," Shelton was saying in a pleasant, reasonable tone that put Sharon's teeth on edge. "I'm sure you can appreciate the delicacy of the situation and wouldn't want to put your brother at further risk. If you arrest him yourself, then there are going to be the inevitable tiresome questions about conflict of interest, etc. If you just turn him over to us, then we can hand him directly over to the Domestic Terrorism unit of the FBI. Along with that journalist, of course. You have my word that they will both be well treated."

He must think I am the stupidest cop on the face of the earth, Sharon thought disgustedly, *that I would ever consider turning over any prisoner to a private security force.* But she gave him a cool professional smile

"I appreciate your concern, Victor, but I think making decisions along those lines are really premature. I only have your report on what has happened, and it is just, well, we both know it is just hearsay so far. I think it would be prudent to alert the Nevada Department of Public Safety and have them come to manage any investigations that might occur. That is proper protocol, after all."

Shelton watched her carefully for a moment, then nodded.

"You have a very good point as far as not hearing both sides of the story. My people are out looking for Mr. Ludlow and Ms. Wyndham right now. I've given them strict instructions to return them here to Antelope Valley for questioning as soon as they are picked up. But I must caution you, although my men are professional and very well trained, they are understandably emotional about the death and injury of two of their colleagues, and emotional people can be rather...unpredictable at times," he said.

"Victor, pardon my bluntness, but I am confused by your logic. First you say if you keep my brother and Ms. Wyndham in custody, they will be well treated and turned over to the FBI Domestic Terrorism Unit. However, if they are brought back here you have concerns over the 'unpredictability' of your staff?"

Sharon looked at the man steadily with a thin smile on her face.

"Let me just spell out our position here, Victor. It wouldn't be in St. Martjin's best interest for my brother and Kate Wyndham to be brought back to Antelope Valley dead," Sharon said, tiring of the ridiculous conversation. "And, just so you know, I have no intention of my brother becoming another Leonard Peltier. If any harm comes to my brother or Ms. Wyndham, there will be hell to pay, I guarantee it."

He smiled thinly at her and got up to leave.

"Of course. And you are in such an excellent position of strength to deliver that lesson," he said.

He walked out the door and Sharon cursed under her breath.

He was right. He had come into town with at least 20 professional killers and she had a total staff of about 10 police officers, most of whom had the day off after the long weekend. Currently, she had about four that were on duty and none of them was a match for these mercenaries. It would take the State Police hours to get up here in sufficient strength to defuse the situation. Then there was the question of how the investigation might be driven from a political standpoint, as St. Martjin had a huge amount of clout in Carson City. Her cousin Tony had warned her about this repeatedly.

Basically, her situation sucked and she was worried to death about Jim and Kate. But she sat back for a few moments thinking, then made a couple of phone calls.

*

Kate figured that she had been spotted by the Mine Security, but she hoped she had gotten out of sight soon enough to buy her at least a little time. She rode quickly to the high school, worked her way up the far side of the 'U', then turned Jerry loose in the green where she and Ludlow had eaten by the fountain, a lifetime ago it seemed. Jerry seemed tired, but in relatively good shape, all things considered. She hoped he would stay there and not stray into the streets. At least he had plenty of grass and water. She didn't like doing it, but she couldn't come up with a better plan.

She remembered that Semilla had told her the Tribe had an Internet television station at the other end of City Hall. It was not quite 6 p.m. yet, prime time. Surely someone would be in the station. She thought about calling Sharon, but she knew her cell phone was being monitored and her location would be uploaded if she made a call. Mine Security would be on her like a duck on a June bug if she tried it. However, if she could get to the television station, then she had a chance of getting the video uploaded so the public could see it. At that point, any action that St. Martjin took against her or Ludlow would only make the situation worse for them.

She ran down the stairs and across the parking lot, trying to stick to the shadows as much as possible. She hoped that Mine Security was concentrating on monitoring her cell phone and watching the police station, and not paying attention to the communications center.

She saw a glass door that had 'Tribal Communications' written on it and she dashed towards it. Thankfully, it was not locked and opened when she pulled the handle. Once inside, she took off at a trot, trying to find the studio. She saw a young Native woman walking ahead of her in the hallway, carrying a laptop. Kate ran up and grabbed her arm. The girl turned and looked at her, startled.

"I'm Kate Wyndham of the Washington Gazette," she said, hoping a big name newspaper would cut through any residual shock of being seized so rudely. "Where's the studio?"

"Just up that way," the girl replied pointing up the hall. "And to the right. I saw you at the pow-wow the other night."

Kate breathed a sigh of relief, a smart girl.

"I need you to do something for me. It's critical. I need you to get a message to Sharon White Owl and tell her that Kate is doing a broadcast here at the station. I don't care how you do it…"

"Stay away from the Mine Security guys, right?" the girl said intently.

Kate nodded and grinned. "That's right. What's your name?"

"Pamela. You just go up through those double doors and to the right is the control room. There's a reception area right in front of it. The door locks when the 'On Air' sign is lit, but the code is 6994. There's a keypad to the right," the girl said.

"I got it, Pamela. Do you think you can get to Sharon?"

"No problem. I'll find a way. Those guys are all over town tonight and it's got everyone on edge. They've got no fucking right," she said bitterly.

"No, they don't. So let's do something about it. Another thing, Pam, I need you to tell Sharon her brother has been severely wounded and is in a cave 40 miles due west of here," Kate said.

"Jim's hurt?" Pamela asked, her eyes widening with concern.

Kate gave an inward sigh. "Yes, and the longer we talk the greater the danger."

Pam started off down the hall opposite of her original direction at a trot, her laptop swinging alarmingly from side to side.

"Calmly, Pam, don't draw attention to yourself," Kate said. The girl nodded at her and began walking at a fast, but not panicked pace down the hall.

Kate headed towards the double doors that were just up ahead. The 'On Air' sign was lit. She saw the keypad and quickly punched in the numbers and went into the control room. A youngish Native man was sitting at a desk full of computers and other technical equipment. He looked up at surprise when she came in.

"Are you Semilla's husband?" she asked peremptorily.

"That's right, I'm Jack. And you're Kate Wyndham, that journalist…"

"Jack," Kate interrupted, "listen to me. I need you to do something and it's extremely important."

She reached in the pocket of her vest and pulled out Julia Evans' Smartphone.

"Have you got an SD micro card loader in here so you can upload a video to the Internet from the card on this phone?" she asked.

"Of course," he said, looking at her oddly.

"I need you to get the card out of this phone and upload the most current video to Youtube. It's from June 19th. I don't care what Youtube account you use, but just get it out there as quickly as possible. It's HD and about 30 minutes long, so it might take a while," Kate said urgently.

"Ten-fifteen minutes max right now with our connection here...what...?"

"Don't ask questions please. Just do it." Kate looked back at the door. "There may be some Mine Security guys banging on that door in a few minutes, but don't you open it no matter what. I'm going to try to buy you some time..."

"But..."

"No buts, Jack. Just get that video uploaded."

Jack nodded, and she took heart to see him immediately pull the tiny card out of the Smartphone and load it directly into an impressive looking computer that was sitting directly to his right.

"It is absolutely vital to the Tribe that you get that video uploaded, so don't open that fucking door," Kate said emphatically. She didn't hold out much hope that he would mind her if things got too noisy outside in the reception area, but at least she had made the attempt. She only needed to buy him a few minutes.

She walked back out to the reception area and quickly rifled through the drawers looking for a USB cable. She plugged it into the computer then turned the computer on. It asked for a user name and password, and she put in the one from her own laptop, hoping that Semilla had her on the main network with enough privileges to at least pull up a basic screen. It worked, and she blessed Semilla for her competence. She plugged the USB cable into her Smartphone and waited. Within minutes, she heard noises and then she saw several Mine Security personnel coming down the hall at a trot.

She theatrically yanked the Smartphone off its connector and took off at a run down a hallway that angled to the right of the reception area, with no clear idea of where it led. She was relatively confident that they had seen her and fallen for her ruse. She thought that only a couple of them may have stopped to try to get into the control room where Jack was uploading the video or to try to see what she had done on the computer, but most seemed to be following her. She had gotten a good enough lead on them that she was feeling pleased with her cleverness, then, at the end of the hallway, she saw a glass door that opened up onto Main Street in downtown Antelope Valley. She was breathing hard, but she picked up the pace again. If she could get to a busy street, she would probably be safe.

The next thing she knew, she was down on the floor. Her feet had been kicked out from under her as if by magic. And then she felt the cold metal of a gun barrel at her temple.

"Ms. Wyndham," came an icy but pleasant voice; an educated voice. "Finally. I've been anxious to make your acquaintance for some time now. Come in here and sit, please, you must be exhausted. And that will give us time to have a nice, pleasant little chat."

Hard fingers grasped her forearm and pulled her to her feet. Several Mine Security guards came trotting up behind her. They all had guns and looked to be of the size and dimension of wall lockers. But the man that held her arm, who was shrouded in gloom, stopped them with a word.

"Good work, gentlemen. Please take proper precautions to ensure that Ms. Wyndham and I are not interrupted in our business conference. We shouldn't be too long," he said.

She was ushered into a very dim room. The hard fingers moved her upper arm in an odd way and the next thing she knew her hands were cuffed behind her back and she was thrown into a chair. The Smartphone was expertly plucked from her hand during the process. Then, the lights came on in the little room.

It was a small mechanical room with no windows, only brightly painted pipes and tubes and walls and walls of computer equipment. Across from her was her captor, who was casually leaning against a large pipe assembly and looking at her with interest. It was the same man she and Ludlow had seen at the St. Martjin roadblock two days before. Ludlow had mentioned he was Chief Security Officer at the mine.

"Ms Wyndham, please don't do anything foolish like trying to scream. You will not be heard and a woman's screams are so shrill I would find myself quite unnerved. I still have the advantage, as you can see." He held up his handgun. "Shrillness in a room as small as this would move me to violence unnecessarily I'm afraid," he said.

Kate studied the man intently, looking for a weakness, looking for anything she could use against him, a bargaining chip. His empty black eyes unnerved her a bit. Cobras had eyes like that, she knew from experience, but she also knew that cobras generally left you alone if you let them alone. That wasn't the case with this man. However, she did know that to show fear would only increase his sense of dominance and weaken her position. She remembered how Ludlow had dealt with the man before and she decided to try the same tactic. So she just sat and watched him evenly, without saying a word.

The man, she remembered Ludlow had called him Shelton, looked at her with wry amusement.

"Ah. Does the cat have your tongue?" he asked.

Kate still didn't react, but watched the man with as calm as an expression as she could maintain.

"Looks like you've been taking lessons from Mr. Ludlow. Very well. That's where we'll start. Where is Mr. Ludlow?"

"Dead," Kate said, looking at the floor and making sniffling noises that weren't that hard to fake. Every time she thought of Ludlow she wanted to cry.

"That second guard shot him and he died out there in the desert. I left him and rode back here."

"I see. And what did you and Mr. Ludlow find on your little excursion into mine territory."

"You know Goddamned well what we found," she snapped then cursed herself for losing her calm. She took a deep breath and found that centered place inside herself that she always went to before she and Manny used to take a terribly frightening cross-country jump.

"No, I'm afraid I don't," he said. But she felt a tiny shift in his energy, a sense of unease if not fear.

"Well, I guess it wouldn't be the first time that the general didn't know what the troops were doing," she said, shrugging in an offhand manner, trying to achieve a worldly and understanding tone. She must make the attempt to charm this cobra.

He studied her for a moment, as if she were an interesting bug he might place on a pin in his collection.

"Mr. Ludlow told me that you were Chief Security Officer at St. Martjin Mining. Was I informed correctly, sir?" she asked, trying to match his formal tone and meeting his eyes.

"You were," he said, still studying her.

Kate smiled a thin smile at him. "Then I'm sure you

understand the term plausible deniability?" she asked.

Shelton stared at her a moment, amused. "Of course Ms. Wyndham, I am not a child, after all."

"And no doubt an experienced operative," she said, hoping she was hitting the mood and terminology just right. The important thing was to keep him talking. To make him believe she was sympathetic, make him see her as a person. This is what they had taught her in the hostage classes, although she had never expected to be taken like this in her own country. But she was and she had to deal with it.

One thing she did know; the more time she bought, the better off she was.

"I've had a successful and busy career. Ms. Wyndham, is there a point to this?"

"Absolutely, Mr. ?"

"Shelton. Victor Shelton."

"Victor, I have a business proposition for you."

His flat eyes sharpened for a minute. "Really? Please do go on, Ms. Wyndham."

Kate looked at him and smiled prettily. "Call me Kate, please."

Shelton watched her, his head cocked a bit to the side. His eyes narrowed.

"You know I'm a journalist," she said, in a soft voice, "and I came here looking for a story." She looked at him and smiled again, this time in what she hoped was a sultry smile. "People are going to go to jail over this unfortunate incident that has happened at the mine, if not worse. However, if someone who was in a position of authority came forward and told their side of the story, all the warnings given, how management wouldn't pay attention to their cautions etc., a good journalist could paint them very sympathetically as the brave whistleblower whose warnings fell on deaf ears. And it's just a small step after that to make people believe that this person simply wasn't told about some of the foolish decisions that upper management had made without their knowledge or input," she said.

Shelton looked at her with even more interest, then stood up and paced for a few steps. "It's an interesting proposition. And you think you're the person to write such a story?"

"I could be. With the right source."

"I thought journalists were supposed to have integrity and provide fair and balanced reporting," Shelton said in a baiting tone, but he was closely watching her reaction.

"Balance rarely sells copy. Drama does."

Shelton stared at her for a long moment. He placed his pistol back in the holster on his belt. Then he surprised her by laughing out loud. "You are a very fascinating woman," he said, his focus becoming more intense. Uncomfortably so, Kate felt.

She heard a beeping noise and Shelton took a small cell phone from his pocket. He answered, listened for a few moments, then hung up. When he looked at her his face had changed. Now there was a rage that she could sense under his coldness.

"Well, Ms. Wyndham, or Kate, as you prefer. It seems that you are a bit too clever for your own good. My associates have informed me that a video is being aired on the Internet even as we speak; one that is highly incriminating for St. Martjin Mining and, in turn, their security division. A video we never even knew existed. We thought you might just have a few photos, or short films of some of the evidence in the canyon that could be easily erased. Not one that was in *corpus delicti*, as it were.

"So, I'm guessing that somehow you passed off this video to someone else to upload before we intercepted you. Very unfortunate," he continued, shaking his head.

"A minor issue, the way I see it," Kate said, keeping her tone calm and reasonable. "We might even be able to work this to our advantage if we put the right spin on it. The deal still stands," she urged. "We play this right and we can both be rich. You might have to spend a little time in prison, but not much. Juries can be very sympathetic to whistleblowers."

The man approached her with a calm smile on his face, then he exploded and struck her across the face with the back of his hand. She never even saw the blow coming and her head snapped to the right so hard she was surprised her neck didn't break. Kate Wyndham had suffered blows at an early age though. She turned and looked back at him calmly and without tears. She felt blood running out of her mouth, but she still had her teeth. There were some small favors at least.

"It figures that a snoop would try to make a snitch out of me," he hissed. He walked around behind her slowly. She felt his hands grasp her on either side of her head. He had long, strong fingers that dug into her scalp painfully.

She fully expected to be strangled or have her neck broken and she said a silent prayer that Ludlow would be found and saved. Her thoughts were so tightly focused on that one hope that it came as a sharp surprise when Shelton plunged a hand down her shirt and squeezed one of her breasts so hard she cried out. Then he came around in front and sat down on her, straddling her lap, pressing his hardness against her belly. He was heavy and she thought her legs would break. He licked the blood off the corner of her mouth and kissed her, shoving his tongue into her mouth and probing obscenely. Then, he stood up abruptly.

"My dear, it seems like I may be going to prison, or worse. I'd like a little female companionship prior. It's been a while, and will probably be an even longer while before I have such an opportunity again, if ever. This will only be one more felony on a pile of others, and you do have it coming, you know. Might as well be hung for a sheep as a lamb. Oh, and I am hung my dear," he said, giggling.

Kate closed her eyes, sick. The man was a raving lunatic; she had been a fool to direct him down this path.

"I think it only fair to warn you," he said in a playful and lover-like tone, caressing her ear, then running his hand down her shirt again to squeeze her breast, "that I am a man of...exotic tastes. Not too worry though; when we're done, I think you should be mostly intact. Maybe not as pretty as you are now, but vanity is one of the deadly sins, you know."

He jerked her up so hard she thought he would wrench her arm out of its socket, took her over, and shoved her face down onto one of the waist high pipes. He began pushing himself against her hips and grunting loudly. She felt his hands reach around her waist to roughly fumble at the catch on her breeches.

Kate thought she heard some noises out in the hall. But they didn't have anything to do with her. For her there was only Shelton and what he was going to do to her.

Then the door flew open and within moments there were three rapid gunshots. Shelton fell up against her and didn't move. She stood up, shoving him off to the side with her hips. Without looking at the door, she gave the man, who was clearly dead, a savage kick in the groin. Then she turned to see who had fired.

There, outlined in the light of the hall, stood Sharon and a smallish middle aged woman with dark hair streaked with gray. She was an average looking woman, dressed in a nicely cut brown pantsuit. Someone you would pass in the street and never look twice at. She was holding a pistol. She handed the pistol to Sharon, who quickly put it in her belt holster.

"*Toda*, Miriam," Sharon said.

"*Al-Lo-Davar*, Sharon," Miriam said, then she looked at Kate.

"I don't like rapists," she said in heavily accented English.

Sharon came over and searched Shelton's belt and found the handcuff keys. She freed Kate's hands quickly.

"Sharon, Jim's out in the desert, he needs medical help..." Kate said quickly.

Sharon looked at her and smiled. "Bobby Nardo flew Jim in a half hour ago. He's in the hospital right now in surgery."

Kate burst into tears.

Part VI
The River

Chapter 16

Kate sat in the hospital waiting room with the family. She was drinking some hot coffee that Hank had brought her. The family was split in two directions this night, as Kimmy had gone into labor just a few hours earlier. She wasn't having an easy time of it, and Sharon was shuttling back and forth between her daughter and her brother.

Annie was sitting beside Kate and holding her hand. Kate held onto the old woman's brittle fingers like a lifeline.

She couldn't cry anymore, she didn't have any tears left in her. The surgeon had come out a few hours earlier and told them that Ludlow's condition was critical. He had developed peritonitis from the bowel wound and had other serious damage to his left lung. He didn't give odds on Ludlow's survival, but he didn't sound hopeful. Ludlow was breathing on his own, which was a good thing, but the doctor didn't know how much longer that would continue. Ludlow had a Living Will at the hospital that said Do Not Resuscitate, so if, and when, he stopped breathing on his own, the family would have to make some decisions.

Martin Levi had come and was sitting with the family and praying quietly in Shoshone for both Kimmy and Ludlow.

Annie had been dozing for a couple of hours now, although her thin hand never left Kate's. Kate was startled when Annie's eyes flew open and she suddenly sat up. She quickly stood and pulled Kate up after her.

"Come!" Annie said, urging Kate to follow. Annie walked hurriedly to Ludlow's room in the Intensive Care Unit, opened the door and went in.

A nurse barged into the room after them, but Annie turned and spoke to her harshly and angrily in Shoshone. The nurse didn't understand, so she went and got Martin Levi. Annie spoke to Levi in an imperious tone. His eyes widened and he nodded and looked at the nurse.

"Mrs. Ludlow is practicing her religious beliefs; she wants this lady to be with her son," he said.

"But…"

Annie glared at the woman and she retreated, as did Martin when she glared at him.

"I could have told her in English, but they seem to pay more attention when a person speaks in a language they don't understand. Makes no sense to me," Annie said.

Annie pulled up the one chair that was in the small room and placed it beside the bed. Then she gently pushed Kate down on it. She reached for Ludlow's hand, the only one that didn't seem to have something hanging from it and then took Kate's hand and laid Ludlow's hand in hers, then placed Kate's hand gently on the bed.

"He's crossed. But there's still time if you're strong enough," Annie said. Then her eyes filled with tears.

"Bring my boy back to us," she said, and she walked out of the room.

Kate watched her go, confused. Then she looked at Ludlow and wished she could cry. He looked so pale and still, his chest was the only thing moving, and its movement seemed weak, as if each breath was a struggle that he would give up on soon.

His hand seemed hot as a stove to her. She looked at the instrument panel. His fever was lower than it had been earlier, but still high at 101F. She looked at his elegant hand, hands that she loved so much. She laid her forehead on it.

"Jim, darling, please don't go where I can't find you."

Then the exhaustion of the day caught up with her and Kate slipped off into uneasy sleep, her head resting against Ludlow's hand.

*

Ludlow stood in a strange country of golden woodland, azure skies and wide green fields where a large herd of buffalo grazed. Behind him stretched a long river. For some reason, he felt he had crossed the river, but he couldn't remember doing so. He looked down at himself; he was dressed traditionally, as a Shoshone warrior. He couldn't remember dressing in this manner, but it seemed perfectly natural, so he didn't question it. He saw someone coming towards him. As the person approached, he saw it was another young Shoshone warrior riding a great gray horse. Ludlow hoped the other warrior did not want to fight or wrestle, as this place was so peaceful he did not want to have a conflict. However, when the warrior came closer, he smiled and greeted Ludlow in a friendly manner. He looked familiar to Ludlow, but the memory wouldn't come of whom the man was.

"Do I know you?" Ludlow asked the warrior.

The warrior only smiled and shook his head. The man looked

across the river towards the other shore, which was shrouded in mist. He was watching the other side intently and Ludlow turned to look also, thinking that the man may have seen an antelope or an elk.

As he stared into the far mist he was able to make out a figure standing on the edge of the river. The person seemed to be calling to someone and there was such grief and sadness in the voice it made Ludlow sad also. He then saw it was a woman. She was weeping.

"Who is this woman who weeps?" asked the other warrior.

"My love," Ludlow said, knowing suddenly that it was true. "The great love of my spirit," he amended, although he did not know why he said it.

"Would you return to this love of yours?" the other warrior asked, "even if it cost you great pain?"

"I would. I would not be parted from her. She is my beloved. I would not bring her to grief or sorrow."

The other warrior sat silent on the great gray horse for a moment, considering.

"Take my horse," the warrior said, sliding down from the gray horse. "He can take you most of the way across the river, but he cannot travel between worlds now. Once you cross into the threshold, it will become very difficult; it will take all your strength, and hers, for you to return to her. If you are caught in the current, you will be swept into the Void. Are you sure you wish to do this for this woman, the one who weeps?"

"I do."

The other warrior gestured in a courteous manner for Ludlow to take his horse.

Ludlow nodded his thanks to the man then hopped up on the gray horse. "You are very kind to loan me this fine horse. Why would you do such a thing for a stranger?" Ludlow asked.

The young warrior looked at Ludlow and smiled. Ludlow noticed for the first time that the man had an amulet of some sort hanging on a rawhide thong around his neck. He looked closely and saw a silver star inside another star.

"Grandfather," he said, finally recognizing the warrior.

The other man smiled again then turned and walked away.

Ludlow watched for a moment then turned back to the river. He touched his heels to the horse's sides and the horse walked straight into the water.

Ludlow found it to be an odd experience. He was underwater with the horse, he could see broken sunlight streaming through the water, but he could breathe and had no fear of drowning. The river was not deep, but soon he began to see a darkness up ahead that frightened him, although he didn't know why. The horse kept walking until it came right to the dark barrier, and then he stopped. This was the barrier that the horse could not cross. Ludlow looked at the darkness and didn't want to go into it, then, far away, he heard the woman sob. Without looking back, he plunged into the barrier, only to be met with blinding pain. He felt he was drowning. He wanted to call out to the woman, but he couldn't speak. He could dimly see her shadow on the water, but she couldn't see him. Ludlow kept trying to move, but it seemed he was caught in some strange current that wouldn't let him go. The pain was becoming unbearable, and he almost decided to turn back, to see if the horse could take him back to his grandfather. But the horse was no longer there. He turned back towards the woman, and pushed towards her with all his strength.

*

Kate was lost in a land of mist, stumbling and frightened. She knew she was looking desperately for something but couldn't remember what it was. She came to the shore of a river and stopped.

Across the river there lay another mist filled land. Someone was standing there; then she saw two people. One was on a great gray horse that she recognized. Then she remembered why she had come. She began to weep. Her love had gone; he had crossed over without her. She looked up and saw one of the people was riding the great horse into the river. He completely disappeared under the water, which she found curious. She was still weeping and her eyes stung with tears. She leaned into the water to wash the tears from her face and then she saw him.

A man was down there, under the water. She saw his hands reaching up for her, but he was too far away for her to see him clearly. She reached into the water for him, but it was like reaching into icy shards that cut like knives. She cried out in agony but didn't stop reaching for the man. She stretched every muscle and sinew in her body to stretch down to him; the cold sank down to the marrow of her bones. It was torture. She kept her

341

body firmly on the river shore. She knew that she must not fall in or they would both be lost.

She felt the faint brush of his finger and she stretched harder. She would not fail in this. Then she had him. With a great cry she used all her strength to pull him free of the river and up onto the shore beside her. He opened his eyes, looked at her, and smiled.

*

Kate woke up to hear Ludlow coughing weakly, then the room seemed to be filled with nurses, moving around quickly and doing things with the equipment she didn't understand. She looked at Ludlow and saw he was awake and staring at her, though he was still coughing. They were in his hospital room. She smiled at him and he squeezed her hand. She looked at one of the machines; his temperature was 98.6F, back to normal. Then, one of the nurses took her by her shoulders and ushered her out of the room and into the hall. She looked back over her shoulder and saw Ludlow watching her. She smiled at him. She stood outside the hall and they gazed at each other as the nurses did their strange work.

She heard a dripping noise and looked down for a moment at the floor. Her hand and arm was soaking wet and icy; cold water was dripping from them. Why, she didn't know.

She only knew that she'd brought him home.

Epilogue

18 months later

The shadows were getting long in the day and Kate knew Ludlow would be home soon. She had been working on her laptop at a table near Kimmy's windows. She was doing a freelance piece for Meyers and she had promised would be completed by the end of the week. She heard Ludlow's light, quick step as he came across the hayloft, and she came to greet him at the door as she always did. When he came in, he kissed her long and deeply, as he always did. They hated being apart, even for a short period of time, and when they were reunited it was always a joyful occasion.

Ludlow went over to the chair in front of the window, tossing his briefcase down on the floor. He loosened his tie and stared out into the desert. Then he sat down. She came and sank down onto his lap and he wrapped his arms around her waist.

"I don't know why I ever let Marty talk me into this," he said grumpily, "and I hate wearing this suit."

"You look very GQ in it," she replied. "Reminds me of my days in the city, lusting after at all those *duibichi'* lawyers."

"Is that right?" Ludlow asked archly, tickling her a bit on the ribs. Kate giggled and buried her head in his neck.

"You let Marty talk you into it because you are the only one with enough of a legal background to keep those St. Martjin shysters from squirming out of their agreements," she said.

"I know. But don't have to like it. Hopefully we can wind this up soon, or at least cut down on the amount of time I'm spending on it. We've got those new colts to start."

"That's right. By the way, Kimmy came by today with the baby. He is a wild child. She's threatening to put him in some kind of cage."

Ludlow looked at her, concern on his face.

"I still don't think I'm ready for a baby yet," she said, playing with his tie a bit.

"Up to you, honey. I don't care if we have a baby or not. I have you, and that's more than I ever thought I would have in one lifetime. But if you want to have children, I'll step up to the plate and be the best dad I can be," Ludlow said, smiling.

They were silent for a moment.

"Mother and I finally have a settlement worked out on JQ's money," Kate said. "I talked to her today."

"How'd that go?"

"Better than I expected. I think we may actually wind up being on friendly terms one day. But you and I won't have to worry about money now; not that we ever did really, but it's nice to have a cushion."

"How much of a cushion are we talking about?" Ludlow asked. He had never asked Kate about her inheritance.

"Two million, give or take."

Ludlow nearly dropped her on the floor in shock.

"What are we going to do with two million dollars?" he asked incredulously.

"Well, I want to build a house. I love it here in Kimmy's loft, but it is getting a little crowded."

"A two million dollar house?"

"No, silly. Anyway, I don't want to talk about money right now," she continued to play with his tie.

"Oh, Katie, Bobby's getting out of prison on work release. He's coming to the Center. He's going into the equine program."

Kate smiled. "I'm so glad. I'm glad he didn't have to do hard time like so many of the others did. If it hadn't been for him, you wouldn't be here."

"I know," Ludlow said. He pulled Kate closer to him.

*

It had taken some doing for Sharon to tie up the 'loose ends' as far as what happened the night that Mine Security came to town. She had severely downplayed the activities of the casino security people, saying in her reports that they had only provided 'ancillary assistance' during the crisis. However, the reality was they had driven over in force, completely surprised the Mine Security guards and easily disarmed most of them. The Mine Security staff was too professional to try to make a stand against others they quickly recognized as being as deadly and ruthless as themselves. It didn't take long for them to realize that they had been outsmarted and were completely outgunned, so they surrendered easily. Victor Shelton had been the only fatality.

It had been determined that Sharon had shot Victor Shelton in self-defense although no one really dug around in the ballistics evidence too much to confirm it. Sam Conner had been killed in a tragic helicopter accident caused by his own carelessness. Only his mother and two men from a liquor store he frequented attended his funeral.

Jim Ludlow had had to go to a court inquiry in regard to his use of deadly force with the Mine Security guards, but that too had been dismissed as self-defense. Once the video of the dead horses and advocates had gone viral on the Internet, no court had really wanted to dig too deeply into the details of how that video got to the Internet and neither did the Nevada or Federal authorities. Too many had dirty hands as far as St. Martjin Mining was concerned and most were busy scuttling for cover rather than casting blame on people the general public considered to be heroes.

As far as the environmental damage, investigators from the Environmental Protection Agency found that, as Kate had suspected, a wall from a tailings dam had collapsed and caused a huge spill of contaminated water into an area on the west side of the Antelope Valley Reservation. The contaminated liquid wound up in several watering holes used by wild horses. Once symptoms of poisoning began to occur in the animals, the Mine had contacted Sam Conner and they had quickly developed a plan to drive the dying horses into the canyon lands to trap and bury them. St. Martjin had been working quickly and quietly to contain the spill, but didn't want to risk the wild horses' poisoning being discovered and made public.

Conner had made arrangements with Bobby Nardo and another helicopter pilot to drive the horses into the canyon lands then he had worked on the ground with Mine Security to force the sick and dying horses into the blind canyon. The stress of the roundup had significantly increased the effect of the poison on the horses and by the time they made it into the trap, most were near death. Those that weren't were simply shot out of hand. No one knew how Lindy Abraham and Julia Evans had stumbled on the cover-up. According to witnesses, Victor Shelton had executed them.

The EPA was still trying to determine how much of the area had been contaminated by the toxic spill; so far it seemed to be only on the sparsely populated west side of the Reservation, but they were monitoring all water supplies closely. It had not yet been determined how much the BLM managers in Nevada actually knew about the details of the disaster prior to its discovery.

Because of the massive public outrage, Congress finally ordered that the BLM's Wild Horse and Burro program be thoroughly evaluated for mismanagement. The Wild Horse Squad and other wild horse advocate groups were asked to step in and help the BLM come up with workable solutions for managing the wild horses and burros. Harlan Finney was spending most of his time in Washington these days.

Bobby Nardo had found Jim Ludlow simply because Dozer was too big to be missed. The big gelding had stood outside the little cave where Jim had laid wounded, eating everything in sight. When Bobby had discovered Ludlow, he had been feverish and semi-conscious, holding the satellite phone in his hand. Bobby had quickly loaded him into the helicopter and flown him back to Antelope Valley.

Dozer and Jerry had been no worse for wear for their little adventure up in the canyon lands. A couple of Tribe members had ridden out the morning after the incident and retrieved Dozer from the desert.

John Ridley had tried to fight Kate on the property settlement in Washington, but once her lawyer began producing evidence of his numerous peccadilloes, he backed off. Kate was allowed to keep her small farm and John kept the townhouse. Kate was leasing the farm to a friend now; she still wasn't ready to sell, because Manny was buried there and she wasn't ready to let him go just yet.

She had resigned from her job at the Gazette and was having to turn away many job offers. The St. Martjin Mining disaster story was an incredible coup for any journalist. There had been rumors of Kate winning a Pulitzer for the story she had written about it. She didn't care about a Pulitzer or the jobs; the only thing she cared about was waking up every morning in Jim Ludlow's arms.

Kimmy had been shocked when Cactus' first foal had turned out to be a gray, despite being bred to the ranch's Medicine Hat stallion. She had pored over her genetics books to try to figure out how such a thing could have happened. Kate and Ludlow both knew, of course, but never bothered to try to explain it to her.

*

Kate continued to play with Ludlow's tie until she finally got it undone. Then she began unbuttoning his crisp white shirt and stroking the skin underneath. Ludlow had pretty much made a complete recovery from his injuries, although he was plagued with cramping in the muscles over his ribs occasionally. When that happened, Kate rubbed his scarred back with his salve.

She kept slowly unbuttoning the shirt and ran her hand underneath it. Then she nuzzled her way under one of his braids and began stroking the rim of Ludlow's ear with her tongue.

"Mrs. Ludlow, you are acting quite the hussy today," he said.

"That's Ms. Wyndham-Ludlow, thank you very much."

"And an insolent hussy at that. You'll never be a proper Shoshone wife with this behavior."

"Mmmmmmmmmmm," she said. "And what are you going to do about it?"

"I guess it's time for another training session," Ludlow said, laughing and pulling her face to his.

THE END

7366400R0

Made in the USA
Charleston, SC
23 February 2011